MAGGIE SHAYNE

DARKER THAN MIDNIGHT

ISBN 0-7783-2229-7

DARKER THAN MIDNIGHT

www.MIRABooks.com

Printed in U.S.A.

This book is dedicated to my mom, with all my love. All the very best parts of me come from you.

Prologue

Fourteen Years Ago...

Cassandra Marie Jackson clutched her mother's hand as the man who'd raped and murdered her sister rose to his feet to hear the verdict. Time seemed to stretch, and to slow. She could hear the clock in the back of the courtroom, and it seemed there was an unnaturally long pause between every tick. She closed her eyes and tried to block the past, but it came rushing at her, anyway—the memory of that moment when her life had been turned upside down.

The knock at the door came at ten o'clock. She'd been on the sofa, doing homework. Dad was going over some notes—he had to perform surgery early the next morning, and as always, he spent time double-checking everything. Mom was watching a movie and crocheting. The afghan she was working on was almost done. Purple and white. Cassie remembered it perfectly.

She'd looked up briefly when her mother went to answer the door, then frowned when she saw the policeman on the other side. Before the officer said a word, her mother turned, her face pale. Almost as if she knew. "Ben," she called. "Ben, come here."

Dad came in from his study, pausing halfway across the liv-

ing room with a file folder in one hand. He took off his reading glasses, tucked them into his shirt pocket and went to the door.

"Dr. Benjamin Jackson?" the officer asked.

"Yes?"

"Do you have a daughter named Carrie?"

Cassie was off the sofa by then. Something clenched in her stomach when she heard her older sister's name, and she automatically looked at the clock on the wall. It was only ten. Carrie's curfew wasn't until eleven. In some warped way that meant nothing could be wrong.

Her mother was clutching her father's hand as he said, "Yes." But there was something different about his voice that time. It was lifeless, flat.

"I'm very sorry to have to tell you this, Dr. Jackson, Mrs. Jackson, but your daughter…"

Cassie didn't know what else he'd said, but she knew what it meant. Maybe she'd forgotten the words because of what had followed them. Her father dropped the precious notes, white sheets fluttering everywhere, like the feathers of a murdered dove. Her mother screamed; first it was the word "no" over and over again, but then it became a hoarse, choked cry that wasn't a word at all, because there was no word that could express the pain. And with every sound she emitted, it seemed more of her life left her body, until she backed away from the door and dropped gracelessly onto the carpet, empty. Then Cassie's father and the policeman were hovering over her, trying to help her up, to calm her. But there was no calming Mariah Jackson. Not until Dad managed to get a hypodermic from his bag and inject her with something.

Cassie knelt beside her mother on the floor, holding her as tightly as she could, and thinking how wrong it was that she was hugging her weeping mother. She'd never seen her mom like this. Not like this. It was like the end of the world. It was like everything that had ever been was gone.

Torn apart, turned inside out. But she held her mother, because she couldn't think of anything else to do, until, still sobbing, Mariah fell asleep in Cassie's arms, right there on the floor.

Dad had been standing nearby, watching, helpless, and speaking in low tones to the police. There were two of them. Cassie had only seen one at first.

Bending, Dad scooped her mother up and carried her to the sofa.

Cassie had to let her go, but for some reason she couldn't get far from her. She felt as if she might fall into some bottomless pit if she did. Nothing was real, things seemed like a dream—a nightmare. Her sister couldn't be dead. She couldn't be.

And even then she hadn't known the true horror that had visited her family. She thought it must have been a car accident, and wondered which of Carrie's friends had been involved and whether they were hurt, too.

"Will you be all right?" her father asked. "I have to go with the officer…."

To identify the body, Cassie thought, the phrase floating into her mind from countless TV cop shows.

"Officer Crowley can stay with them," the policeman said. And Cassie looked up to see that the second cop was a woman in uniform, standing just inside the doorway, battling tears. She wasn't very old, Cassie thought. Not more than a few years older than Carrie.

Cassie met her father's eyes, nodded to tell him it was all right for him to go. He hugged her hard. Told her he loved her.

She spent the next hour in a state of shock, mostly staring at Carrie's senior-class picture in its frame on the wall. She kept thinking she should be crying. But she couldn't, because it wasn't real. She still expected Carrie to come walking through the front door, asking what all the fuss was about.

Cassie remembered the lady cop telling her that they would catch the man who did it. She made it a promise, a vow, and there was fire in her eyes when she said it.

It was only in that moment that Cassie realized her sister hadn't died in some senseless car accident. Someone had killed her.

Killed her.

Somehow, Cassie got through that night. She would always think that lady cop had a lot to do with it. Her promise that they would get the man had given Cassie a focus—a dark, faceless *him* to hate and wish dead. The man who'd killed her sister. A target for her rage. She hoped the cops wouldn't arrest him—surely they would just shoot him instead. How could they not? He'd killed Carrie.

They hadn't, of course. They'd arrested him.

Jeffrey Allen Dunkirk had been their neighbor for more than a year. A seemingly harmless, always friendly, forty-five-year-old divorced father, who used to pay Cassie and Carrie to watch his twin sons from time to time. He only had the boys every other weekend. The cops said he'd spotted Carrie walking home from her best friend's house, three blocks away, and had stopped and offered her a ride. Then he'd driven her to a park five miles out of town, raped her, strangled her and left her lying in a ditch, with her clothes and her purse tossed in beside her broken eighteen-year-old body. There was no question. His semen was inside her. Her hairs and fingerprints were all over his car. He had no alibi.

In the courtroom, the man standing there, waiting for the verdict to be read, was not the man Cassie knew. He was jittery, jerky, fidgety. Throughout the trial he'd alternated between sitting in a zoned-out stupor, and fidgeting as if he were going to jump out of his chair, while occasionally talking to himself in urgent whispers.

All an act designed to support his claim of insanity, be-

cause it was the only defense his lawyers could come up with. It made Cassie angry enough to claw out his eyes. And maybe that was good, because the anger took the edge off the grief.

A slip of paper was passed from the jury foreman to the bailiff, to the judge, who unfolded and read it, then handed it back to the bailiff, who carried it back to the juror. And finally, the foreman cleared his throat and read.

"In the case of New York State versus Jeffrey Allen Dunkirk, on the charge of murder in the first degree, we the jury find the defendant..."

Cassie's mom squeezed her hand even tighter. Her father just sat there, as if he'd turned to stone.

"Not guilty by reason of mental defect or impairment."

There was a collective gasp in the courtroom, followed by noisy murmurs, even as Cassie's mother slumped in her chair. Cassie turned to her father, seeking his strength, his comfort, but he was on his feet, reaching into his suit jacket while the judge banged his gavel and shouted for silence. Cassie watched, paralyzed with shock, as her father's hand emerged again, with a gun. The weapon bucked hard when it exploded in his hand, three times in quick succession, before men were hurling themselves at him. Cassie's chair was knocked over in the rush, and she landed awkwardly on the floor, her eyes searching for her father beneath the pile of bodies on top of him.

She couldn't see him, and her gaze was drawn to the crowd gathered across the aisle. In the midst of that crowd she could see Jeffrey Allen Dunkirk lying on the floor, a thick red puddle forming around him. Someone said, "He's dead!"

Cassie got to her feet and stumbled to her mother, who was standing, sobbing, her entire body quaking. She put her arms around her mom as men hauled her father to his feet. An officer pulled the esteemed surgeon's hands behind his back and snapped handcuffs around his wrists as he said, "Dr. Benja-

min Jackson, I'm placing you under arrest." Then he put a
hand on her father's shoulder and said, "I'm sorry," before
continuing on, reciting the familiar Miranda rights.

1

Present Day...

River sat on the floor in the room's deepest corner, his back to the wall, his arms wrapped around his waist. He couldn't move them. The straitjacket held them too tightly for that. The room was white, its walls padded like the ones in the old Blackberry High School gymnasium. It didn't smell like the gym, though. No mingling of hardwood floor polish and B.O. Here, the smell was a sickening combination of urine and bleach. Aside from that minor distraction, though, his mind was clouded in an almost pleasant fog, and yet turbulence kept surfacing from its depths. Specific analysis was impossible at this point. He only knew he was in trouble. Terrible trouble. And that he had to do something or he was going to die. So he sat there, rocking and struggling to capture coherence, because he couldn't do anything unless he could remember what it was he had to do.

Sounds brought his head up; the locks on his door were turning. He strained his eyes as the door swung open, and slowly managed to bring the man who entered into focus. Ethan. Thank God.

Ethan crossed the room, a gentle smile on his face. He hun-

kered down in front of River, his white coat spotless and almost too bright, his name tag pinned neatly to a pocket. Dr. E. Melrose, M.D. Chief of Psychiatry. He put a hand on River's shoulder.

"How you doing, pal? Better?"

River shook his head slowly. "Worse," he said. "Getting worse, Ethan."

Ethan frowned, studying River's face, stared into his eyes. It made River think of when they were kids and they would stare at each other until one of them blinked. And then Ethan blinked and River laughed. "I win."

"I'll order more medication," Ethan said.

"No!"

Ethan's reaction—the way he jerked away from River—made its way through the fog in River's mind enough to hurt. Enough to tell him that even his best friend was afraid of him. He licked his dry lips and tried again, though forming sentences was a challenge at best.

"No more drugs."

"I know you don't like taking the meds, Riv, but right now they're the only thing keeping you—"

"You said...I'd get...better." He knew his speech was slurred; he lisped his *s*'s and dulled his *r*'s. He couldn't help it. "I'm getting worse."

"I know. I'm doing all I can for you." Ethan moved to one side, reaching behind River to unfasten the straitjacket. When the sleeves came loose, River lowered his arms, sighing in relief at finally being able to change their position. Then he sat forward and let his friend pull the jacket off him. "Do you feel like talking?"

River nodded. "Try."

"I know. I know it's hard to talk. That's due to the drugs, but...I'm sorry, Riv."

River nodded. "Before Steph died..." His tongue felt thick

and clumsy, and the words he formed in his mind didn't make it all the way to his lips. He felt much like he had on prom night a hundred years ago when he and the jocks from the team had spiked the punch and he'd drunk way more than his share. Ethan had saved his ass that night. Practically carried him home, poured him into bed and then covered for him.

"Wasn't this bad—jus' the blackouts. And not rememememe-mem…"

"Remembering," Ethan finished. "I know."

"Now…I can…barely…funchin…funchin…fun—"

"Function," Ethan said.

Nodding, River lifted a hand to his lips, wiped and felt moisture. "Jesus. Ethan…I'm drooling."

"I know. I know. I didn't expect this, either."

"It's meds. Gotta be. Meds."

Ethan nodded. "It's possible. But River, you've got to stop getting violent with the staff here. It's only making things worse. They're here to help you. The way you've been acting the past few days, I'm afraid that without the medication, you might hurt someone."

River narrowed his eyes on his friend. "Someone… tried…kill me."

"*What?*"

"Pillow…on my face. Couldn't see who. Came up sing—sing—"

"Swinging?"

"And…and they came in. I kep' fighting. I din't know…who—"

"All right, all right. Calm down. Don't get agitated again."

River took a few breaths, wiped the sweat from his forehead with his sleeve. "Not a violent…man. Din't…kill Steph. You know that."

"I know," Ethan said, lowering his eyes.

"S'posed to get better…here."

Ethan sighed. "River, I'm going to review your meds, see where we can start lightening up the doses, and gradually bring you off them. Then we can get an idea where you are without chemical help. And I'll speak to the staff, make sure you're safe. I'll have them keep your room locked while you sleep, have them keep a closer eye on you. All right?"

"Can't jus' stop…meds? Jus' stop them?"

Ethan shook his head slowly. "Not all at once, no. You'd be a mess if we did that. I'll start lowering the doses today. I promise."

River sighed. "Okay. Okay."

"Okay." Ethan clasped his shoulders one last time, then got up and went through the door.

River struggled to his feet, though he had to press his palms to the wall to do it. Then he clung to that wall, pushing himself along it, around a corner and to the door. Exhausted, he leaned against it, his head resting on its smooth, cool surface, his ear pressed tight, because he thought someone might be out there waiting to come in when Ethan left. He had to be careful. Be aware.

"…must be so hard for you, seeing him like this," a woman was saying. "He's not the same man he was when he came here. But I suppose it's eating away at him. He killed his pregnant wife, for heaven's sake."

"Doctor, he's drooling a bit," a second female voice said. "Did you notice it?"

"Yes. I'm afraid he's getting worse," Ethan said. "Showing signs of increased paranoia. Brand-new set of delusions. We're going to need to increase his meds."

"But, Doctor, he's exhibiting extrapyramidal side effects," the second voice said. "Doesn't that indicate he should be taken off the Haldol altogether?"

"Excuse me, who are you exactly?" Ethan asked.

The first woman spoke. "She's new here, Doctor. Forgive

her. Nurse Jensen, Dr. Melrose is an excellent psychiatrist. He knows his job."

"I know mine, too," the nurse said, but softly.

River heard footsteps, then the first nurse again. "I apologize, Doctor. I'll see to it she learns her place."

"Oh, don't be too hard on her. You know how overzealous new nurses can be. Uh, maybe it would be a good idea to keep her away from this particular patient, though. All right? I don't want anything interfering with his treatment."

"You're a good friend. He's lucky to have you," she said. "I'll see to it immediately."

"Thanks, Judy." River heard scraping sounds, knew Ethan was taking his chart from the plastic holder there, probably writing in it. "Meanwhile, let's increase the Haldol. See if it doesn't help."

River groaned softly and gave up his hold on the door, letting himself sink to the floor. Ethan didn't believe him. His best friend didn't believe him. His head spun and he fought, fought hard to latch onto a thought. A single thought, anything, to save himself from the madness that was trying so hard to swallow him up.

He wasn't insane. It was the meds. The meds were killing him. Good. Good. What then? What could help him? He struggled; fog closed in but he pushed it back.

Nurse Jensen...she knew. But no, she couldn't help him. No one could help him. He was on his own. Okay. So he was on his own. And on his own, he had to get out of this place. There. That was it, that was the answer he'd been seeking through the fog. He had to get out of this place.

Cassandra Jackson—Jax to her friends—sat in the front seat of Chief Frankie Parker's SUV as the countryside of Blackberry, Vermont, unwound before her. She'd been here before, but she would never get over the beauty of a Vermont

winter. The entire place looked like a Christmas card—sugar-coated pine trees, leafless maples and poplars glittering with icicles, blankets of snow covering every gentle slope and level field. Frankie drove, smiling and talking nonstop about the benefits of being police chief of a small town. Jax's parents, Ben and Mariah, rode in the back, agreeing with every word Frankie said.

"You were so right about this place, honey," Mariah said. "When you told us a year ago that we'd love it here, I thought you were crazy, but it's wonderful. Truly."

Jax shrugged. "Perfect for you doesn't necessarily mean perfect for me." Which was a lie and she knew it. She'd hit a glass ceiling in the Syracuse Police Department. Maybe because she was a woman, but more likely because her father was a convicted murderer who'd only been out of prison for two years. Either way, she'd gone as far as she could go there.

So when Frankie Parker phoned her with the job offer, she'd been quick to take some vacation time and come up here to check things out. It made a nice excuse to visit her parents.

She'd fallen in love with the town of Blackberry when she'd been up here a year ago, helping a friend and hunting a killer. Her friends were still here—the killer long dead. And now her parents had settled in nearby to boot, adding to the little town's attraction.

"It would be so nice to have you close by, right in the next town," her father said, speaking slow and softly. "After all, we've got a lot of lost time to make up for."

"That *would* be nice," Jax agreed. God knew she hadn't had enough time with her father—a lifetime wouldn't be enough. He'd served twelve hard years in prison, and lost his brilliant medical career because of it. He would never be able to practice medicine again—at least not on human beings. But he hadn't become despondent. He'd written every day, as had she. And he'd begun studying veterinary medicine while still

in prison, and completed his work during the two years since his release. Only six months ago, the AVMA board had voted to grant him a license to practice. He had joined an aging veterinarian at the Blackberry-Pinedale Animal Hospital, and he seemed fulfilled and content.

He'd aged thirty years in prison. He was skinny as a rail, his hair pure white and thinning, and he was quiet—far more quiet than he'd ever been before. Almost as if he was always far too deep in thought to be bothered with conversation.

"It would be nice for me, too," Frankie said. "I've been wanting to retire for months, but reluctant to leave the department in less than capable hands. When I thought of you, Jax, it was like a load off my shoulders. I'm convinced you're the one for the job."

"Yeah, yeah, flattery will probably work. Keep it coming," Jax told her.

Frankie grinned at her, adding wrinkles to her wrinkles. Jax still wasn't used to thinking of a sixty-plus-year-old with kinky silver curls as chief of police, but she knew from experience Frankie Parker was a good cop. Her looks just tended to lull you into thinking she was harmless. That probably worked to her advantage.

"The town board will approve you on my say-so," she said. "No problem there. It's really up to you."

Again Jax nodded. "Why aren't you promoting one of the officers from your department, Frankie?"

"Neither Matthews nor Campanelli are interested," she said. "Too much paperwork, too much pressure. Though, compared to a big department like Syracuse has, you'll find it a piece of cake," she added quickly. "I've got one other, Kurt Parker, but frankly, he hasn't got the temperament for it. Hell, he probably wouldn't be working for me at all if he wasn't my nephew."

Jax nodded, mulling that over. She hadn't met Officer Par-

ker. He'd been away on vacation when she'd been here last. Then she thought of someone else who could fill the position. "What about Josh Kendall? He was DEA. Surely he could fill the spot."

"Kendall?" Frankie shook her head. "I like that we think alike, Jax. Josh was on top of my list. Fact is, I offered him the job and he turned me down flat. I think he and Beth have had enough excitement to last them several lifetimes. They're both content to make their way as the humble keepers of the Blackberry Inn. Can't say as I blame them." She slowed the car, glanced at Jax with a smile. "Here's the house that comes with the job."

Jax looked, then looked again. "You're shitting me."

"Nope."

She'd expected the house, a perk that came along with the job as police chief, to be a functional cracker box at the edge of the village. Instead, Frankie was pulling into the driveway of a flat-roofed, white Victorian that took her breath away. Tall narrow windows were flanked by forest-green shutters, with elaborate scrollwork trim in that same green, as well as mauve. The paint was new. The place looked perfect.

"Town claimed it for back taxes and other money owed a while back. They did some initial repairs, and kept it in tip-top shape since. Were thinking about selling it, but we had a budget surplus this year. I convinced them to offer it to the new police chief, make up for the pay being lower than you could make elsewhere. Told 'em we'd have to do something special to get someone good enough to fill my shoes."

"Must be some damn big shoes," Jax muttered. "What are you, a twelve extra-wide?"

"Ahh, it's not so much. Used to be twice this size," Frankie said. "But an entire wing had to be torn down. Wait till you see inside." She shut the motor off and got out, making footprints in the snow. She tugged her furry collar up to her ears

and trudged forward, taking a set of keys from her black, leatherlike cop-jacket's pocket.

Jax got out, too, waiting for her parents to join her before hurrying toward the front door. She was nearly there when a large black-and-brown dog lunged out from underneath the front porch, barked twice with its pointy ears laid back, then turned and ran away. It vanished into the woods across the street. Jax just stood there, staring after it and swearing under her breath.

"That was a police dog, wasn't it?" Mariah asked. "I think it's a sign!"

Jax pursed her lips and refrained from correcting her mother. She'd always referred to German shepherds as "police dogs" and always would. "That was one sad-looking case," Jax said. "Seemed as if it's been living on tree bark and swamp water."

"Oh, don't worry about *that* dog." Frankie shook her head so that her tight silver curls bounced. "He's a menace. We've been trying to collar him for a year without any luck. He's cagey enough to get by on his own."

Jax tipped her head to one side. "That's odd, isn't it?"

"How so?" Frankie asked.

Jax shrugged. "He's no mongrel, looked like a purebred. He must have belonged to someone once."

"I didn't know you were a dog lover, Jax," Frankie said.

"I could care less about dogs." It was a lie and she knew it, but she didn't want to go blowing her anti-girlie image by painting herself as a bleeding-heart puppy cuddler. "You have a father who's a vet, you pick up a few things, that's all."

"Well, that mutt may be a purebred, but I can tell you he's one hundred percent pure pain in my backside now. Don't worry, Jax, we won't let him pester you. Come on, come see the house."

Jax nodded and followed Chief Frankie inside, trying un-

successfully to put the dog out of her mind. It wasn't easy. His brown eyes had met hers for just a moment, and managed to beam right past her hard-shell exterior to the soft, mushy parts she didn't let anyone see.

She didn't like those parts, kept them concealed and confined. Mostly because she lived and worked in a man's world and she'd learned to act the part. But she knew, too, it was partly because her sister had been soft. She'd been friendly, open and utterly trusting. Jax had learned at sixteen where those soft parts could get you. In her line of work, and in life in general, a woman just couldn't afford to indulge them.

Still, the whole time Frankie showed her around the house, which was just as gorgeous on the inside, she kept thinking about the dog. And before the tour was finished, she'd decided to pick up a bag of dog food and leave some out for him. Of course, she wouldn't tell anyone. But she'd always had a soft spot for strays.

"Now, the fireplace has been checked over thoroughly. It's ready to use, but there's also a new furnace in the basement that heats the place just fine," Frankie said.

Jax nodded, and couldn't help imagining the redbrick fireplace aglow with a big fire, even as she walked around the living room. When she got to the far wall, she hugged her arms. "Chilly on this side of the room." When she spoke she could see her breath. "Whoa, real chilly."

"Must be the side the wind's blowing on," Mariah said, smiling. Her mother, Jax realized, wasn't going to find any fault with the house that might become her daughter's new home. No matter what.

"It's always chilly on the east side of the house. I suspect it could use another layer of insulation," Frankie said. "Upstairs there are three bedrooms and a bathroom. One bathroom down here, as well."

"More than one cop needs," Jax said.

"Sure wouldn't be as cramped as your apartment in Syracuse, would it, Cassie?" Mariah asked.

It wasn't really a question.

"Come on, let me show you the kitchen," Frankie said.

As they trooped through the place, Jax looked back to see her father standing on the far side of the living room, studying the clouds of steam his breath made, a frown etched on his brow.

"Dad?"

He glanced her way, softened his face so the frown vanished.

"You okay?" Jax asked.

He nodded and joined her in the dining room. Mariah and Frankie were already in the kitchen, chattering. Benjamin slipped an arm around his daughter's shoulders. "The place seems lonely," he said. "Almost…sad. I think it needs you."

"Yeah?"

"And it would make your mother awfully happy."

"I know, Dad. I'm considering it, I really am."

"That's all we can ask."

She could have told him she was thinking this whole thing a little too good to be true, and trying to figure out a way to find the catch in the entire offer without hurting Frankie's feelings. Hell, they were just going to hand her a house? Something had to be off. If there wasn't, she'd be an idiot not to take the job. Still, as she took the grand tour, liking the place more with every room she saw, she knew there had to be a downside.

Later, as they drove away from the house, Jax noticed a shape peering out from beneath the snow right beside the place. "Is that a foundation?" she asked.

Frankie glanced where she was looking and nodded. "That was the wing that had to be torn down. It was never part of the original structure, anyway. It was added on in the seventies—seventy-five, I think. Two-car garage and a game room on the ground floor, extra bedrooms up above."

"So what happened to it? Why'd it have to go? Shoddy construction work?"

Frankie shook her head. "There was a fire couple of years back. Sad story, really. A woman was killed." She narrowed her eyes on Jax's face. "That's not gonna spook you now, is it?"

"I don't believe in ghosts, if that's what you mean." Right, so what was that little shiver up her spine just now? she wondered. And deep down in her brain an irritating voice said, "Hey, kid, maybe you just found your downside."

Frankie brightened. "Good. Because I'd like you to spend your two-week vacation at the house," she said. "You can shadow me on the job, get a real feeling for what it will be like to live and work here in Blackberry. After that, if you decide to take the job, the house is yours, rent free. If you stay five years, you get the deed, as well."

"That's an incredibly generous offer, Frankie. Almost too generous." Jax faced the woman, reminded herself Frankie was something of a kindred spirit, and decided to stop pulling punches. "So what's the catch?"

Frankie held her eyes, probably to make it clear she had nothing to hide. "No catch. It's meant to be an offer that's too good to turn down," she said. "Of course, the pay isn't the greatest, but it's nothing to sneeze at, either. Best of all, Blackberry's a safe place to be a cop. Nothing bad ever happens here."

Jax crooked one brow. "Aren't you forgetting your run-in with Mordecai Young last year? I was here for that, Frankie. Remember?"

Frankie's smile died. "Not likely to forget. He murdered my best friend." She sighed, shaking her head. "God rest your soul, Maudie Bickham." Then she focused on Jax again. "That was a once in a lifetime event. Honestly, Jax, I mean it. Bad things don't happen in Blackberry."

Jax nodded, but she thought about the foundation, the fire that had burned a wing of the house. A woman had been killed, Frankie said. Surely that qualified as a "bad thing." Jax wondered briefly if the pristine purity of Blackberry, Vermont was anything more than a convincing and beautiful illusion.

A nurse brought River back to his room, speaking softly to him all the way. He checked her name tag, but she was neither a "Judy" nor a "Jensen." He wasn't really sure why he was checking. When she got him to his room, he looked around—everything here was becoming familiar. The bed. The mesh-lined glass of the single window. The door to the tiny bathroom. He needed to remember what he had to do. That was all he struggled for. To remember what he had to do. Get away. Get out.

"There now, I'm so glad to see you're feeling better this afternoon," the nurse said, leading him to the easy chair, expecting him to sit down, he realized, when she paused there, just looking at him. So he did. Then she brought out the pills, as he had known she would. She poured water from a pitcher and handed him the tiny medicine cup that held the tablets.

Remember, he told himself. *Remember what to do.*

He took the pills, drank the water, swallowed them.

"Let's see," she chirped, as if she were speaking to a four-year-old.

River obediently opened his mouth, lifted his tongue, let her assure herself he'd swallowed the pills.

"Good, good for you, Michael."

He could have told her to call him River. He'd started out correcting everyone here. No one had called him Michael since he was thirteen years old. Ethan's dad had started it that summer after the rapids had gobbled up his canoe and spit him out onto the shore. But River didn't care what anyone called

him anymore. He wasn't sure who the hell he was, anyway, so what difference did it make?

"Now if you put in a good night, you'll get your privileges back tomorrow. You want to go to the community room, don't you?"

He nodded, tried to force a smile, and just wished she would leave so he could try to make himself cough up the pills before he forgot.

"That's good," she said. "You just take it easy for tonight. You've had a hard day. Do you need anything before I go?"

"No."

"All right then. Good night, Michael."

"'Night."

He waited until she had closed the door behind her. He heard the lock snap into place.

Focus. The meds—have to get rid of them.

He got to his feet and went into the bathroom, angry that hurrying wasn't much of an option. He shuffled when he walked. Opening the toilet lid, he leaned over the bowl, stuck a finger down his throat, started to gag.

"Oh, now, Michael. That's no way to behave yourself, is it?"

He straightened fast, but it made him dizzy, and when he spun around he fell, landing on the seat. Which turned out to be a lucky thing, because the orderly standing over him was swinging a knife at him. River's clumsiness caused him to duck the blow that would have slit his throat.

He reacted with the instinct of a veteran cop, not a mental patient. It was almost as if he were standing aside, observing, silently amazed that his years of training hadn't been entirely erased, even by the drugs. His body remembered. It didn't need his mind's coherent instructions to move; it just reacted. He drove his head into the man's belly, shot to his feet as the guy doubled over, clasped his fists together and brought them down as one, hammering the back of the orderly's head.

The man went down hard, his forehead cracking against the toilet seat on the way. And then he just lay there, not moving.

River stared down at him, shocked. His heart was pounding as hard as the drugs would allow.

The drugs! Dammit.

He grabbed up the knife the downed orderly had been wielding, long instinct refusing to let it lie there beside the man. Then he shoved the limp body out from in front of the toilet, and tried again to vomit. He managed to bring up a little. Enough, he hoped. Prayed. Let it be enough.

The orderly still hadn't moved. The toilet seat was cracked, River realized, and so was the bowl underneath it. Water was seeping onto the floor.

River started to shake as he knelt beside the man, checking for a pulse. He wasn't sure he'd be able to find it in his condition even if there had been one. So many drugs floating through his bloodstream—even if he had brought up the most recent batch. Still, he tried to find a pulse. But he didn't think the man was alive.

He sank onto the floor, rocking back and forth, trying to organize his thoughts. He had to get out of here. He had to. But God, it was so hard to think. Maybe if he'd managed to avoid swallowing his meds for a few days. Maybe then he could have—

Not then. Now. You have to get out of here now.

Somehow, he latched onto a thought, a goal. And slowly, clumsily, he began to remove the fallen man's clothes. All of them, even the lanyard around his neck with the magnetically stripped key card. The front of the card bore a photo of the orderly. His name had been Kyle. Kyle W. Maples.

It took forever, the better part of an hour, River thought, or maybe longer. But eventually, he was dressed in the orderly's white uniform, with the hunting knife hidden in a deep pocket and the lanyard around his own neck. The orderly was wear-

ing River's own powder-blue patient pajamas. They were on him crookedly, the top inside out, but it didn't matter. He'd done the best he could.

River lifted the dead man's head by its hair, and grimacing, smashed his face on the toilet seat three times, hard enough to obliterate his features.

When he finished, he managed to empty the remaining contents of his stomach without any trouble at all.

Sighing, breathless, he turned to the sink, washed his face and rinsed his mouth. Then he wet his hands, smoothed down his hair as best he could, wiped the spittle from his chin.

Have to get out. But how? The door's locked from the outside.

Get a nurse to open it. Get a nurse to come in.

Nodding, River hit the bathroom's emergency call button. After a moment, a nurse's voice came on. "What is it, Mr. Corbett?"

He drew a breath, swallowed hard. He was forgetting something, more than likely. He wasn't in any condition to plan an escape that would work. But he had to try. "I...I fell. I'm...hurt."

He released the button and went back into the room, standing against the wall, beside the door. He could hear the nurse's voice coming over the speaker, asking if he were all right, then telling him she would be there promptly. When the lock on the door clicked, he pressed his back to the wall, so that when the door swung open, it hid him.

The nurse paused in the doorway at the sight of the legs sticking out from the open bathroom door. Then she rushed into the bathroom, and he heard her whisper, "Oh, my God," as he slipped out of his room and down the hall.

Within seconds, staff members were rushing toward his room, barely noticing one lone orderly in the corridor, moving in the opposite direction. He found the stair door, used the

key card that hung from the orderly's lanyard to unlock it, and took the stairs rather than the elevators. All the way down, all the way to the basement garage, where his footsteps echoed in the cool, exhaust-scented air.

God, it was getting harder and harder to walk. To focus. Maybe some of the meds had dissolved before he threw them up. Or maybe he was just tired. He didn't know what to do next, and he groped in the orderly's pockets as if for an answer. His hands closed around a set of keys, and he pulled them out and stared at them.

Car keys? They had a remote device on them. The kind with the button you could press to start your car from a distance, another to unlock the doors and yet another that had an emblem of a horn on it. Frowning, River pressed that button and heard, in the distance, two short beeps.

Blinking, trying to focus, he followed the sound, thanking his lucky stars. After a while, he hit the button again, and again the car's horn sounded, guiding him in. It was a small Toyota. Yellow. He hit the unlock button and got behind the wheel. And he knew damn well he shouldn't be driving, but he had no choice.

It was a strain to steer the vehicle. Had another car come along he would have surely hit it, or hit one of the parked cars trying to avoid it. But no other car came, and finally, he was at the gate, where a striped bar blocked his exit, and a little box with a blinking yellow light stood beside him.

He nearly panicked. There was a man inside the small booth, smiling at him and shaking his head, then he pointed at the box and held up a little card.

Right. Put the card in the slot in the box. That's all. He took the lanyard off his neck, turned to thrust the key card into the box and banged his hand against the closed window. Swallowing his panic, he put the window down, tried again. He put the card into the slot. Pulled it back out. The gate rose. The

man in the booth waved at him. River waved back, tried to smile, and struggled to steer the car out of the garage and onto the long strip of pavement that wound away from the Vermont State Mental Hospital.

He pressed the accelerator a little harder and left the place behind.

When he made it to the highway, he hesitated for one brief moment, wondering where on earth he was going to go where they wouldn't find him. Because eventually, they were going to realize the dead man in his room was not Michael "River" Corbett. Hell, they'd probably call what he'd done back there murder.

That would be two on the list. Three, he reminded himself. He mustn't forget—couldn't forget—the baby. Three murders.

It didn't matter if he was found, if he was caught, if he ended up dead—nothing mattered except learning the truth. He had to know what had happened the night of the fire. He couldn't have murdered his wife and his child.

For a moment, as he sat there, turn signal blinking incessantly, he closed his eyes, and it came rushing back to him as if it were happening all over again.

He found himself lying on the lawn in the cool green grass, surrounded by searing heat and light and a stench that burned his lungs. Rex was there, licking his face, whining plaintively. And even as he slowly fought to grasp what was happening, he realized he'd had another damn blackout. Yet another episode when he lost minutes, sometimes hours of his life, only to return to himself with no idea of what he'd done during that time. He patted the dog's head. "Okay, boy, okay. I'm back."

But this time was different. He'd felt it even before he struggled to sit up, and then leaped to his feet at the sight of his beautiful home going up in flames.

He screamed his wife's name, lunged forward, only to be

clasped by a pair of strong hands that held him back. "Easy, Mr. Corbett. Easy. We're doing all we can."

He blinked up at the face of the firefighter, a young man, one he didn't recognize, though he'd met most of the men in Blackberry by then. Rex was barking at the man, and he told the dog it was all right, to quiet down.

Rex sat obediently, but still whined every now and then.

"Thanks," the firefighter said, and then the young man's face changed. It turned ugly as he sniffed. Then he looked at the ground beside River's feet and his eyes widened.

River looked, too. A gasoline can lay there, toppled onto its side, no cap in place. A high-heeled shoe lay beside it, bright orange in the flashing lights.

It might be Steph's shoe. He didn't recognize it, but God knew she had so many—maybe she got out already.

"Just why is it you've got gas on you, pal?" the firefighter asked.

River frowned, and then he smelled the gas, as well. Not just from the fumes that open can emitted. The smell of gas was coming from him. From his hands. From his clothes.

"I think you'd better come with me, Mr. Corbett," the firefighter said. And then he took River by the arm and walked him toward the flashing lights of Frankie Parker's police car, a black-and-white SUV.

A horn blew, jerking River from his muddled thoughts and gap-riddled memories. He looked into the rearview mirror and saw a car behind him, the driver waiting impatiently to get on the highway. Sighing, he flicked his own signal light off again, opting instead to take back roads. Less chance of killing someone. God knew he didn't need any more blood on his hands. And he knew the way. He knew the back roads of Vermont so well he could find his way even from within the thick chemical clouds in his brain.

If he'd murdered Stephanie, he deserved whatever he got.

But dammit, he had to know. He had to know the truth. And there was only one place where he would find it.

He had to go back home to Blackberry.

That was where all the secrets were buried.

2

"Stop!"

Dawn shouted the word and Bryan hit the brakes of her Jeep. It skidded a little on the road, then came to a stop right in front of the empty, beautifully painted Victorian house that sat alone a few yards away.

"What?" Bryan asked. "What's wrong?"

He knew something was. Something had been wrong for months now, and she was running out of ways to deny it, or avoid it, or block it out.

She swallowed hard, tried not to notice the worry in his dark eyes, or the way his hair had fallen over his forehead, making her want to smooth it away. He hadn't cut it since they'd started college. She liked it this way.

"Dawn?"

"There was something in the road...." She watched his face, knowing immediately there had been nothing there. Nothing *he* had been able to see, anyway. Certainly not a woman in a white nightgown, holding a baby in her arms. Certainly not that.

Closing her eyes, she shook her head. "Sorry, Bry. I—it was just a squirrel. I didn't mean to scare you."

He sighed in relief, seemed to relax visibly. "You're wound awfully tight lately, Dawn. I'm really glad you're gonna spend

Thanksgiving break at the inn with Beth and my dad." He smiled. "And me."

She shrugged and chose to ignore the final part of his comment. He knew she needed to cool things off between them. He didn't know why—pretended to accept her decision and be fine with it. But he wasn't fine. She'd hurt him and she knew that. If there were any other way—

"You sure you're okay?" he asked.

"Yeah. I get a little torn. It's tough, trying to find time to spend with both families—breaks from college are few and far between."

He nodded. "At least your adoptive mom is cool with you spending time with your birth mom," he put in. "That helps."

It also helped that her birth mother, Beth, was married to Bryan's dad, Joshua. Or it would have helped, if she weren't trying so hard to put some distance between herself and Bry—for his sake, mostly.

"Let's get going. Beth and Josh are waiting for us," she said.

Bryan set the Jeep into motion. But as they drove away, Dawn couldn't stop her gaze from straying back to that dark, lonely house. And as she did, she saw the woman again, a filmy, nearly transparent shape in the night. Not real, Dawn knew. She wasn't real at all. None of them were.

It's not going to work, you know, she thought. *You're never going to make it work, Father. Never.*

The best restaurant in Blackberry, the Sugar Tree, was a two-story log cabin with picture windows that looked out on to a rolling, snow-covered lawn. In the summer, the hostess told Jax, there were glorious flowers and blossoming trees, a tiny pond with a fountain in the center, and outdoor tables. But this time of year, all the fun was indoors. The second floor was loft-style on all four sides, leaving the center of the place open clear to the rafters. It was a hell of a place.

The hostess seated them at a table near the huge stone fireplace with a window nearby, leaned closer and said, "Welcome back to Blackberry, Lieutenant Jackson. We sure hope you like it enough to stay." She sent her a wink. "Your waitress will be right over to take your drink orders. Enjoy your dinner."

Jax lifted her brows and sent a look at the three coconspirators who sat around the circular table. "So, does the whole town know what I'm doing here?"

"Honey," Frankie said, "this is Blackberry. The whole town probably knows what time you arrived and what your mother made you for breakfast."

"Small towns," Jax said with a shake of her head.

"It's not all bad," her mom told her. "People may know a lot of your business, but not all of it. It's nice that they care enough to want to know what you're willing to share, but also enough to know when to leave it alone."

Jax shot a look at her father.

"She means they don't pry here," her father interjected. "I've confided in Frankie about my past. But I've seen no sign that it's gone any further."

"It hasn't," Frankie assured him. "Nor will it."

He nodded. "I don't deserve your loyalty, Frankie, but I do appreciate it."

"Of course you deserve it." Frankie patted his hand across the table. "We've all done things we wish we could undo."

"Few as much as I," he said softly.

"Dad, you paid for what you did."

He met Jax's eyes, and for a moment they were so dark, so sullen, she didn't even recognize them. But then he looked away. Her father was a haunted man. Sometimes she wondered if he knew the truth—but no. He couldn't possibly. It would kill him if he knew.

Mariah said, "You've had all day to think it over, Cassie.

Don't keep us in suspense any longer than you have to. Have you made a decision yet?"

Jax tore her worried gaze from her father, sent her mother a nod and a smile, then focused on the chief of police. "I've decided to take you up on your offer to stay in the house and shadow you on the job for the next two weeks. And—hell, there's not much point playing cutesy, is there? Unless something really troubling crops up, or you decide to withdraw the offer, I imagine I'll be accepting the job when the two weeks are up."

"Hot damn!" Frankie said with a smile. "Well, this calls for a celebration!" Even as she said it, a pretty young waitress arrived, dressed in black pants with a knife-sharp crease, spotless white blouse, red ribbon tied in a bow at her collar, and carrying an order pad in her hand.

"Champagne?" Frankie asked the others.

"I prefer a nice cold beer," Jax said. "In the bottle."

"Ahh, me, too," Frankie said. "But make mine an N.A., in a frosted mug."

"Mariah and I will have wine. A nice merlot. You choose," Ben told the waitress.

The girl smiled brightly and trotted off to get the drinks. Jax said, "I'm kind of looking forward to spending the night at the house tonight."

"Tonight?" her mother asked.

"Sure. Why not?"

"Well, the power's not turned on. There's no phone yet, no heat...."

"I can have the utilities turned on fast," Frankie said. "But not that fast. By tomorrow, for sure." She shrugged. "On the other hand, I've already got a bed set up in the master bedroom. Even took over some fresh sheets and blankets for you, got it all made up and ready. No other furniture in the place yet—I planned to do that tomorrow, as well."

"You don't need to furnish the house, Frankie. That's asking too much," Jax said.

"Oh, I won't be. Not all by myself. Your parents have some things in storage, and several others around town have items they want to contribute. I mean, you'll want your own things once you decide to make it your permanent home, but these will do for your two-week trial period," Frankie said with a smile, as if she knew damn well Jax would be staying.

"You should stay with us tonight, hon," Mariah said. "It's not safe to be in that house all alone."

Jax put a hand over her mother's on the table. "It'll be an adventure. Like camping out when we were kids."

"Carrie always hated it," Mariah said softly.

"Only because I always managed to find something slimy to put in her sleeping bag before sunup. Frogs, lizards—"

"You were such a brat." Her mother turned her hand over, closing it around Jax's.

"I'll have the fireplace for heat. Dad, you can loan me a couple of your lanterns. It'll be fun."

Mariah looked to her husband as if for backup. But Benjamin was studying his daughter and nodding in reluctant approval. "She's a grown woman, a police officer, Mariah. She'll be fine."

"Thanks, Dad."

He nodded, smiling slightly.

The waitress arrived with their drinks and handed them around. Jax twisted the cap off her longneck bottle. Frankie lifted her mug. "Here's to the newest resident of Blackberry," she said. "Welcome home, Jax."

"Welcome home," her parents echoed.

They clanked their drinks together as the waitress hovered, ready to take their orders.

* * *

Driving the dead orderly's car had become more and more difficult, and finally impossible. The third time River veered off the road, and went skidding through the slush on the shoulder, he'd taken out two mailboxes. At first, he thought he'd hit two human beings. It shook him too much to continue. He didn't want to kill anyone else. He didn't want to end up dead himself—not until he found the answers he needed to find, at least.

Besides, he was pretty sure he'd been seen. Another car had passed, heading in the opposite direction, just as he'd lost control that last time. The driver probably called the cops. Probably reported him as a drunk driver. Maybe not.

Didn't matter. He couldn't drive anymore.

He steered the car up a side road, where the only other tracks in the snow had been made by a logging truck, by the looks of them. And then he drove until the tires spun in the snow.

After that, he got out and took a look around. His mind kept wandering, but he managed to keep tugging it back on track. He knew where he was. In a tall pine forest outside Blackberry. Five miles to town, on foot, but less if he cut through the woods. It had been a while since he'd spent any time in the woods.

He used to, though. All the time. Him and Ethan. When they were kids. The trips with Ethan's dad. Camping and hiking. As adults, they'd bought a hunting cabin together, the two of them. It wasn't far from here—too far to walk, though. An hour by car. It had been their getaway. Stephanie called it their "He-Man Woman Haters Club." God, they'd had some good times there.

River stopped walking, vaguely aware he'd let his mind wander again. He wasn't sure which way he'd gone, had to check his tracks in the snow to tell which direction the road was. "Have to stay focused," he muttered. He managed to get his bearings. The fire trail was off to his left. He headed for

it, knowing it cut kitty-corner through the southeastern edge of Blackberry and ended at the pond across the street from his house.

He was weak, he realized as he set off again. Every step in the packed snow was an effort, and every steamy breath came harder. It was probably no wonder. He'd done nothing but sit in a hospital for a year. The meds had killed his appetite months ago, to the point where only the threat of a feeding tube forced him to down a few bites of the meals that were brought to him, and even that small amount made his stomach buck in rebellion. Four miles. Surely he could manage that much.

He did, but by the time he emerged from the woods across the street from his long-lost home, he was so cold he'd stopped shivering. No coat. He should have taken that into account. The orderly's shoes were a size too small, and designed for padding softly through hospital corridors, not for trudging through snow. River's feet had long since gone numb, so his stumbling gait had more than just a chemical cause.

It was night; he couldn't guess how late, but it wasn't dark. The full moon hung low, spilling its milky light over the snow, over his house. Or what remained of it. He noted the absence of the entire wing, but also noted that the place looked to be in excellent condition, given what had happened.

The square, main part of the house remained, pristine white with those green shutters and purplish trim, colors Steph had chosen. The big oak door. It had an arched, stained-glass panel above that matched the slender ones to either side. He looked up higher, at the tall, narrow bedroom windows on the second floor. One of those bedrooms had been his and Stephanie's. Another was going to be the nursery. The wing had held a two-car garage and a huge family room, with guest rooms upstairs. One of those guest rooms was the room where Stephanie had died.

Gone now, except for bits of the foundation showing

through the snow. Vanished, like his life. And any possible reason he might have had for living it.

He sank to his knees in the snow, braced his hands in its frigid depths to keep from falling facedown. God, he was cold. And dizzy. And so very tired. The walk had drained him. He hadn't walked more than a few yards at a stretch during his time in the hospital. From his room to the community room. More often just within the confines of his room, where he'd preferred to stay alone. He never had to walk to the isolation room, the proverbial "rubber room," where they took him when they decided he had become agitated or violent. He had found himself there a number of times, confined in a straitjacket. Ethan would tell him the things he'd done, but he wouldn't remember them. It was sheer hell to finally realize he was capable of violence during his blackouts. He would never have believed it if Ethan hadn't told him himself, witnessed it himself.

Maybe River *had* killed Stephanie.

His hands were going numb. The wind burned his face and ears. He sat up slowly, his fogged mind telling him he had to find shelter. A warm place to sleep. If he stayed where he was, he'd likely be dead by morning.

With what felt like superhuman effort, he got to his feet again and turned in a slow circle, studying the intact part of his house. Well, not *his* house. Not anymore.

It stood there, dark and silent. Not a light on in the place, no car in the driveway. The house exuded emptiness. As he moved closer he realized there were no curtains in the windows. So maybe his house was still empty. Hell, he didn't wonder at that. Who would want to live in a place with so much horror in its past?

No one. Certainly not him. When it had gone to the town in lieu of taxes he hadn't even cared. He never intended to set foot there again.

And now he was doing just that.

He walked up onto the porch and tried the door. It was locked, naturally. Sighing, he lowered his head and left the porch. He walked around the place, tracking through the snow, until he reached the back door. And by then he was barely holding his eyes open. There was no time for subtlety here. He wasn't going to be able to stay on his feet much longer. He tapped a windowpane with his knuckles, then tapped it a little harder. The third time, he hit it hard enough to break the glass, then he reached through, scratching his arm on the way. He found the doorknob, the lock, flipped it free, opened the door, and stepped into the kitchen.

He stood, none too steadily for a moment, looking around the place. It felt so familiar he almost collapsed from the force of the memories rushing at him. And he could only be grateful it was too dark to see much, or it might have been even worse.

"Just get on with it, already."

There was no kitchen table. No chairs. No place where he could sit to remove his shoes, so he sank onto the floor and wrestled the frozen, snow-coated things off his feet. He'd have killed for a pair of warm, dry socks. His feet were heavy stumps with hardly any feeling left in them, and he sat there for a moment, rubbing them until he felt the intense sensation of needles pricking them all over as the feeling slowly returned.

His feet burned when he managed to get back up on them, and the blood rushed into them. He found a light switch and snapped it on, but nothing happened. Frowning, he limped to the refrigerator, but found it empty, spotless and unplugged. Its door was propped slightly open by a foam block sitting in the bottom.

Clearly, no one had lived in the house for a while. Maybe not since the fire, though someone had made repairs. Maybe

the Fates had finally decided to cut him a break. He stumbled through the kitchen, found the stairway and limped up it. It was even darker in the upstairs hallway, but moonlight flooded through the windows of the first bedroom he reached. It spilled onto a neatly made bed as if angels were pointing the way for him. He almost laughed at the absurdity of the notion, even as he moved forward, clasping the comforter in his eager hands, tugging it back, seeing the thick pillows awaiting his tired head.

He wanted to collapse into the bed right that instant, but managed to hold off long enough to struggle free of his wet, frozen clothes. Then, at last, he crawled into the bed, pulling the covers tight around him, tucking them in on all sides and around the bottoms of his feet. He lay on his side, wrapped in a soft cocoon, and he was still waiting for warmth to seep into his bones when he fell into a deep sleep.

Jax stopped off at her parents' house to pick up the lanterns her father had promised to loan her, but she did so largely to soothe her mother's constant worry. She couldn't blame her mom for worrying about her. She'd lost one daughter, so it was natural she would become overprotective of the other. Even though Jax was on the fast track to thirty, and a decorated police officer, her mother hadn't managed to make the leap. She still worried, still fussed.

Probably always would.

Carrie had been the one who'd needed fussing over—the one who'd thrived on it. She'd been very much a girlie-girl, while Cassie had been the tomboy. It chafed when her mother fussed, but not so much that she would ever complain.

Jax wasn't worried in the least. She could handle herself. She'd kicked the asses of countless perps who thought they could outdo her on the streets. And probably an even greater number of male colleagues in the gym, when they underesti-

mated her abilities. A few responded by developing a grudging respect. Most just got their boxers in a twist over having their ultrafragile male egos bruised, and became more hostile than ever.

Assholes.

It was a fine line she'd learned to walk. Frankly, it was a damn tightrope, and she resented *having* to walk it. Moreover, she was tired of it. Here, it would be different. Instead of an entire city PD full of men to whom she had to prove herself even while tiptoeing over their machismo, she would have three fellow officers. She could make this work. She knew she could. Without tiptoeing, bowing, scraping *or* leaping tall buildings in a single bound.

It was going to be great.

As she pulled her dependable red Ford Taurus into the driveway of the pitch-dark house, she didn't feel a single hint of apprehension about going inside, spending the night there alone. She had her flashlight—always carried one in the car—and her personal handgun strapped to her side, not that she expected to need it. She had a spare gun in the glove compartment for emergencies. There wouldn't be any, of course. After all, nothing bad ever happened in Blackberry.

Right.

The driveway was freshly plowed. Frankie must have made a phone call or her father had sent someone over. There wasn't a lot of snow on the ground, not yet. Six inches of packy, rapidly melting white stuff, with hardly any base to it. Stones and dirt showed through where the plow blade had scraped. She pulled her car to a stop close to the porch, left the headlights on, hit the trunk release button, then got out and went around to the back.

She took the megasize dog dishes from their blue plastic Wal-Mart bag. She'd made a stop on the way back from her parents' at a store they had assured her was almost always

open. She'd purchased some bottled water, a giant bag of dog food, a windup alarm clock, the dog dishes and, most essential of all, a small coffeemaker with filters, a pound of ground roast and a travel mug. She was good to go. The humongous, thick, cushy dog bed had been an afterthought. Another chink in her armor.

She filled the dish with food and left the big bag of dog food there in the trunk for the night. No point bringing it inside and leaving it out where it would attract any curious mice or chipmunks that might have taken up residence in the vacant house.

She took the other purchases out, threading her arm through the plastic handles of the overloaded bag, wedging the dog bed between her inner arm and her body, and, dog dish in one hand, flashlight in the other, she closed the trunk. Then Cassie walked over the nicely plowed driveway toward the porch, seeing that whoever had scraped away the snow had taken a shovel to the sidewalk, too, and even cleaned off the front steps. Nice.

She set the items down, taking only her flashlight and the dog bed with her as she trudged through the snow to the spot where the dog had emerged from underneath the porch today. A couple of boards were missing, giving the shepherd a handy entrance. She shone the light inside, but there was no sign of the dog right now. Still, she shoved the dog bed through the opening, pushing it back as far as she could reach. The cover could be unzipped, removed and washed. The inner part was waterproof and cedar filled. You could empty it out and refill it with fresh stuffing if you wanted. Not that she would. Only a real sucker would go to that much trouble for a stray.

She backed out of the opening once she was satisfied the bed was back far enough to stay dry and be sheltered from the wind. Then she got the bowl of food and tucked it inside the opening, as well.

She decided against filling the water dish just now. It would only freeze overnight, and she had no idea if the dog would be back. He'd probably become accustomed to eating snow or drinking from an icy stream somewhere. Water could wait until tomorrow. She paused a moment, to turn and look around in the darkness, seeing plenty of tracks in the snow around the house, some made by her dad as he'd checked the place out from one end to the other earlier today. Others no doubt made by the big dog snooping around. He'd be back. She was sure of it.

She returned to the car for her duffel bag, in which she'd packed what she hoped were enough clothes for a two-week stay. Slinging it over her shoulder, she returned to the porch, picked up her shopping bag, got out the keys Frankie had given her, and let herself in through the front door.

Damn, but she liked this house. Bathed in moonlight, the cozy living room spread out before her like an old friend opening its arms. The walls were a deep forest-green, the woodwork trim and floorboards, knotty pine. She crossed the room and set her shopping bag on the stone hearth, then knelt to remove the screen. A fire lay ready; a handful of logs were stacked nearby. Another thoughtful surprise from Frankie, or more likely, one of her boys in blue.

She dropped her duffel and dug in her shopping bag for the long-snouted lighter she'd picked up, then flicked it and touched it to the waiting papers. They caught, curling and blazing up. She sat there and watched the fire take off, its flames feeding on the newspapers, then the kindling and then licking hungrily at the larger logs cleverly stacked in a tee-pee shape overtop. She replaced the screen and sat a while longer, holding out her hands to feel the warmth seeping into them, into her body. It felt good. As the room grew warmer she took off her coat and hung it from a doorknob.

When she could safely add more logs without risk of put-

ting out the burgeoning flames, she added several all at once, hoping to create enough heat to warm her even in the upstairs bedroom, and ensure there would be warm, glowing coals when she woke up in the morning.

The far side of the living room was still just as cold, though. She walked along the wall, one hand out, feeling for a draft or some other source for the unnatural chill. But she couldn't find one. That was the side of the house that used to extend farther, she recalled. The one that had burned.

Shivers danced up her spine as she paused near the window. Something caught her eye, and she held her breath, leaned closer to the glass and peered outside. For just an instant she'd glimpsed something—a shape, a vague sense of flowing white fabric. But of course, there was nothing there. Probably a trick of the firelight on the glass.

Sighing, she reached for her new alarm clock, set it by her watch, wound it tight and put the alarm on 6:00 a.m. She wanted to arrive at the Blackberry PD bright and early, and she had to leave time to stop by her parents' place for a shower and one of her mother's high-calorie breakfasts on the way.

Jax was smiling as she hoisted her duffel and flashlight, and walked up the stairs, into the first bedroom. The moon was high now, but a corner could still be seen from the very top of one of the bedroom windows, spilling a small amount of light into the room. It touched the bottom of a bed, and the blue-and-green-patterned comforter Frankie had contributed to the cause.

Jax set her flashlight on the floor and peeled her sweatshirt over her head. Cool air touched her skin—too cold to take off much more, she thought. She'd keep the T-shirt on, maybe her socks, too. But the shoulder holster and sidearm, jeans and suede Columbia boots had to go. She took off the holster first, setting it on the nearby dresser, then bent to untie the first boot. She paused there, because she heard a sound in the room.

A sound she should have noted when she'd first come in, but she supposed she'd been moving around, making noise of her own. In a break between motions, as she reached for her shoelace, she heard it.

Breathing.

A long, slow, relaxed exhale.

A broken, unsteady inhale.

An unnatural pause.

A long, slow exhale.

A soft moan.

Shit.

Jax's hand snapped around the cool metallic grip of her Maglite flashlight. She yanked it up even as she straightened, and aimed its eye at the bed, where the breathing was coming from, training her own eyes that way as well, while reaching to the dresser with her free hand.

There was a man sound asleep in her bed. Her fingers closed on the gun, sliding it smoothly from its holster. Her heart pounding in her chest, she inched closer to the bed.

"Hey! Hey you, wake up!"

There was another low moan, and the man moved a little, then snuggled deeper into the covers with a sigh. He had a face carved of granite. Bones that were unnaturally prominent, but would be sharply delineated even under a normal layer of flesh.

She used her foot to nudge his shoulder, pushing him from his side onto his back, and she saw his collarbones and winced. He had to be a homeless person, though he would be the first one she'd encountered here in Blackberry. She had begun to think they didn't have any.

"Wake up, dammit!"

Eyes flew open, stark and surprised, first confused and then intense in the glow of her flashlight. There was something riveting about them. Something familiar. And then she real-

ized what it was. They held that same wary, mistrusting look she'd seen in the stray dog's eyes. And they were just as brown.

"What the hell are you doing in my house?"

It seemed the eyes widened after an unnatural time, as if it took extra beats for her words to make their way through his mind. Then he leaped out of the bed, stark naked.

God, he was thin. Beautiful, and painfully thin. He'd been muscled once; she could still see the remnants, the lines sculpted in his flesh, just rapidly losing definition. Shrinking.

He glanced down at himself, then at his clothes on the floor near his feet.

"Go ahead, get dressed. But don't try anything."

He reached for the pants. They looked to be part of some sort of uniform—white pants, as if he worked in an ice cream parlor or a hospital or something. Not warm, that was for sure. He pulled them on, did them up. His feet were bare. He pulled on a T-shirt, then a white uniform shirt over it.

"I…umm…I'm sorry. I'll go."

His words were slurred, as if he'd been drinking, but she didn't smell alcohol on his breath. His hair was messy. Dark, too long, as if it hadn't been trimmed in a long time. And his face had the dark shadow of beard coming in, as if he hadn't shaved today or maybe yesterday, either. She lowered the gun, tucked it into the back of her pants while he finished dressing, knowing she could handle him fine without it. He was in no shape to fight her and win.

He took a step toward the bedroom door.

"No, just a minute," she said, shining her light on him. "You're not going anywhere—not until you tell me who you are and what you're doing here."

She saw the hint of panic in his eyes just before he lunged for the door. She stepped into his path, the heel of her hand slamming him square in the chest. The impact put him flat on

his back and sent her flashlight crashing to the floor. It rolled to the fallen man, came to rest with its beam in his eyes.

"I'll ask you again," she said, standing over him. She was a little breathless, but it was from excitement, not exertion. She loved her work—especially this part of it: the rush of adrenaline, the certainty of a win. "Who the hell are you? What are you doing here?"

He got to his feet, picking up her flashlight on the way. She took a step backward, and let him, even while reaching behind her to snug a hand around her handgun, just in case.

He lifted the light, held it high and shone it on her face, so that she had to shield her eyes. "This was a mistake," he said, and it seemed to Jax he had to focus intently on each syllable. He was trying hard not to slur his speech. She thought he might be on something. "I'm going now. Y-you'll n-n-never shee me again."

Then he turned the flashlight off, flipped it over and handed it to her. She could see him in the moonlight, standing there, holding her light out to her. It trembled in his hand. He was shaking. She released her grip on the handgun, reached out to take the light, lowered her guard.

He moved closer, one step, and even as he shoved her chest with the flat of his hand, his foot hooked behind one of hers, ensuring she would go down, and she did. And dammit, she landed on the handgun and bruised her tailbone to hell and gone, which resulted in her barking a stream of cuss words as the man fled. His feet pounded down the stairs.

She surged to her feet, pulling the gun and rubbing her ass with her free hand. Then she grabbed the light and limped into the hall after him as she flicked it on.

The sounds of his retreat were clumsy. He didn't go out the front door, but through the back, through the kitchen, where she thought he might have fallen down once. She raced

through the house, but by the time she reached the kitchen, he was gone.

The back door stood wide open, and as she swung her light around the room, she noticed the broken pane of glass, its sharp fingers pointing inward, while other bits of glass lay on the floor. His point of entry. There were a pair of socks there, too, and puddles where shoes must have been standing.

He'd run out into the Vermont winter night with thin pants, no socks, and no coat that she knew of. And he'd held that flashlight on her in a very telling way. Overhead, above eye level. And in his left hand. He held that flashlight like a cop held a flashlight.

She still had her boots on, no coat, but she'd survive. She had to see where he had gone. So she stepped outside, gun in one hand, flashlight in the other, and studied the footprints in the snow.

He'd headed around the house, and she followed the tracks. She had no intention of chasing this guy down, just wanted to see where he went, whether he had a vehicle or not, and if so, get the stats on it. Make, model, plates.

But she didn't see a car. The tracks vanished at the neatly plowed driveway. She walked around a bit more, and when she heard a sound, she crossed the street and moved off the road a bit, trudging past trees to the large, flat, snow-covered meadow that lay just behind them.

She shone her light around that meadow, looking for footprints, but there were none. She was sure he had come this way. She took a few more steps, shining her light this way and that.

"Why are you running away?" she called. "What is it you have to hide?"

She took a few more steps, then stood still, just listening. The night wind blew softly, whispering and even whining now and then as it blew past the naked limbs of wintry trees. And then there was another sound, a sharp creaking, cracking,

snapping sound that seemed to grow louder. She swung her head left and right, because the sound seemed to be coming from everywhere at once.

And then she felt the icy rush of water over her boots, and snapped her head down. The snowy meadow on which she stood wasn't a meadow at all. It was a pond. A frozen pond. She'd wandered almost to its center, and the ice was giving way beneath her feet.

3

"Oh, hell," she muttered, and then the ice gave way completely, and her body plunged into the freezing water. The shock of the cold engulfed her, made her go rigid, drove the breath from her lungs as the water closed over her head. And then she forced herself to move, to struggle for the surface. She kicked with her legs, reaching above her head with her arms, flailing in search of a handhold. Once, she felt the edges of the ice above her, and tried to grab on, but the ice broke away in her grip.

She tried again, her lungs nearly bursting with need. And this time, something gripped *her*. Some*one* gripped her, a slick hold on one wrist, then the other, and then she was being pulled steadily upward. Her head broke the surface and she sucked in greedy gulps of air even as she blinked her eyes.

The man lay on his belly on the ice beside the hole her body had made. His eyes met hers and held them, clearer than they had been before, but still…off somehow. "Try not to move. I'll get you out."

She nodded, the motion jerky. God, she was so cold her entire body was shaking with it. He crept backward on his belly, drawing her with him. Her upper body slid up onto the ice. But then the ice crumbled and she went into the water again. Still the man didn't let go. He held on to her and kept mov-

ing backward, steadily, constantly, until he'd pulled her onto the ice again. This time, she made it farther, but when the ice gave yet again, it gave utterly, and she realized as she went under for the third time that he was in the water, too. Beside her in the hellish cold. God, they were both going to die.

He put his hands on her waist, thrusting them both up to the surface again. With a solid boost, he shoved her up and out of the water. From the waist up, she was on the surface of the ice. He gripped her backside and pushed her up higher, and she helped, pressing her palms to the ice to pull herself along. She drew her legs up beside her, shivering so hard she could hear her teeth chattering as she looked back at him. He was still in the water, hands on the ice, trying to pull himself up, but he was having no luck. He seemed exhausted.

She reached for him.

He shook his head. "C-c-crawl on your belly b-back to shore. Go on."

"No!" She was panting, breathless. The cold burned through her. "N-not without you." She moved closer, locking her frozen, nearly numb hands underneath his arms. "Come on."

She pulled; he pushed as best he could. And finally, finally, they both lay on the ice, soaked, frozen. And even then she knew it wasn't safe to linger. She struggled to her knees, shook his shoulder. "Let's go."

He lifted his head, nodded once, weakly, and began crawling. When they were nearly to shore, they got to their feet, arms around each other because it was the only way either of them could stand, and trudged off the pond and onto the land, through the line of trees to the road. There, he stopped walking, took his arm from around her shoulders, turned away and started off on his own.

Jax gripped his arm. "C-come inside. Just—to g-g-get warm."

"Can't."

"Have to. You'll d-die out here."

He held her eyes for a moment, finally gave a single nod and walked with her to the house. She wanted to run the rest of the way, but could barely move at all, much less quickly. They mounted the steps and stumbled over the porch and through the door. She closed it, turned the lock and, gripping his arm, led him straight to the fireplace.

"Get the wet things off," she told him, stammering, shivering. "I'll—f-find something."

He nodded, heeled off his shoes and started to undress. Jax struggled out of her boots and then went to work on her soaked, frozen jeans, her numb fingers barely managing the button. As she struggled out of them and felt his eyes on her, she turned to look at him, and saw him focusing on her legs, from her feet to the hem of her T-shirt. The gun that had been tucked in back clattered to the floor, and she stared down at it, then caught him doing the same.

"G-guess that'll be no good to me until I've had a ch-chance to dry it out." She picked the weapon up, kicked the jeans aside and stumbled upstairs to the bedroom, setting the gun in a drawer, removing the clip and tucking it underneath her mattress. Then she peeled off her T-shirt and bra, heading for the bathroom, where, thank goodness, she found a stack of towels. No hot water—not yet. She'd have killed for a hot bath. But towels would do. She wiped her skin dry, wrapped her body in one towel, her hair in another, then opened her duffel bag and shook out its contents. She dragged on a pair of sweat pants, a sweatshirt and thick socks. Then she located another pair of socks, big bulky ones, the most oversize pair of sweatpants she owned, a nightshirt big enough to serve as a T-shirt for him, and a big hooded sweatshirt with the Syracuse University logo in bright orange on the front. She yanked the blanket, pillows and comforter from the bed and still shivering, moved back down the stairs, trailing fabric behind her.

He sat on the floor, naked, knees drawn up, arms locked around them, head resting against them. He was close to the fire, apparently soaking up the heat. For a moment, she hesitated, just looking at him. Sitting there like that, in the firelight, he looked like a sculpture. *Man in Hell,* she thought. Who *was* this stranger who'd just saved her life? And how smart was she to let him into her house?

She sighed, left the bedding on the bottom step, then moved toward him, deciding it wasn't smart at all, but it *was* necessary. She didn't have a choice.

He lifted his head, and those eyes pinned her to the spot.

"Here," she said, handing him a dry towel. "Wipe down and then put these on."

He took the towel from her, seeming wary. She set the clothes on the mantel, then turned her back to him, removing the towel from her head and using it to wipe up the spots of water they'd left on the floor.

When the floor was dry, she took the comforter and spread it there, tossed the pillows on top and set the blanket nearby. Then she moved the fireplace screen aside and added more logs to the fire.

By the time she had replaced the screen, he was dressed. The sweatpants were comically short on his long legs, but the hooded sweatshirt was roomy enough. He'd pulled on the thick socks and rubbed his wet, dark hair with a towel so that it stuck up like the feathers of a wet hen, and he stood there, looking uncomfortable.

She picked up her wet jeans, hung them over the fireplace screen, then reached for his discarded clothes to do the same. But as she began hanging them, he took them from her rather hastily.

She stood there, blinking at him as he clutched the wet garments in his hands. "What are you afraid of?" she asked softly.

He averted his eyes, draping the items over the screen himself, with great care. "I'll go as soon as they're dry."

"You're on the run," she said. "You're in hiding."

He said nothing, just bent to pick up the shoes, and placed them on the hearthstone, nearer the heat.

"Listen, you just saved my life, okay? Stay here until morning. If you don't want me to ask any questions, I won't. I owe you that much."

He stared at her for a long moment. "I...can't...no one can know I've been here."

"No? Why not?"

He lowered his head tiredly.

"I'm sorry. I said I wouldn't ask questions, didn't I?"

He drew a breath, shivered a little.

Jax lay down on the comforter and pulled the blanket over her shoulders. "It's up to you," she said. "Stay or go."

He stared at her for a long moment. Finally, he said, "If you tell anyone...I'm here...I'm as good as dead."

She opened her eyes, met his. She thought he might be a cop. She knew he was in trouble, on the run, from what she didn't know. But he had saved her life, risked his own to do so. And she wasn't the least bit afraid of him. "I sure as hell won't be telling anyone tonight," she said. "No phones hooked up yet. Cell doesn't get reception in this spot, either. You have to drive up the road a mile."

He hesitated a moment longer, then he crawled into her makeshift nest on the floor, curling under the covers beside her.

"Maybe tomorrow," she said, "you'll feel more like talking. Maybe I can help you with...with whatever it is that's wrong."

"No one can help me," he said. And his voice sounded utterly hopeless. It clutched at her heart. Then he went on. "Why do you carry a gun?"

Something told her not to tell him she was a cop. Hell, he'd

find out soon enough if he was in this town long. Everyone here knew she was a cop. But she had a feeling if she told him tonight, he would bolt. Not that she was sure he was a criminal, exactly. But he was definitely running from something.

"Protection," she told him. "A woman, living all alone."

"You're not afraid of living alone."

She lifted her brows and rolled onto her side to face him. "And how do you know that?"

"You're not afraid of me," he told her.

"Should I be?"

He closed his eyes as if the question brought great pain. They didn't open again.

"Should I be afraid of you?" she asked again.

"I don't know." His lashes were wet. Not from the water, but from tears squeezing out from his deep brown eyes. "Maybe. Probably."

Her heart contracted in her chest. His words might be a warning, or a sign of the confusion she'd sensed in him when she'd found him sleeping in her bed. "Maybe I should sleep upstairs," she whispered.

He said nothing, so she started to sit up. And then she gasped as the man's arms came around her. His head lay against her chest, and she thought he might be crying. "Please stay," he said.

Frowning hard, utterly confused and wishing the hell she'd kept her gun with her, she found herself touching his still-damp hair, gently moving her fingers through it. "All right," she said. "All right."

She relaxed against the pillows and held the troubled man, soothing his quaking shoulders, until he went still, and she knew he was deeply asleep.

And then, even though the warmth of the fire was seeping into her, chasing the chill from deep in her bones, soothing her muscles, making her feel sleepy, and even though she hadn't

had a hot-looking man—even a skinny one like this—in her arms in what seemed like an eternity, she eased herself away from him, out from under the covers, and got up to her feet. She stood there a moment, staring down at him as he slept.

A fellow cop, in deep trouble, either real or imagined, had just saved her life. She owed the man. Owed him enough to let him stay the night, let him get warm. Maybe even enough not to turn him in for breaking and entering, or mention his presence here until she had figured out who he was and what was going on with him. She did not, however, owe him so much that she needed to become a naive idiot in order to repay him. She went up to her bedroom and spent the next half hour patiently cleaning and drying her weapon. When she put it back together, she loaded it with a fresh, dry clip. She took the bullets out of the other clip, dried it thoroughly and set it aside. She'd toss the bullets. They might fire, but they might not, and she didn't ever want to be in a predicament where she couldn't be sure her gun would work. She'd buy some more ammo tomorrow.

She went back downstairs, took her pillow from the comforter and her coat from the hook by the door. She wrapped the coat around herself, rested the pillow against the wall and leaned against it, near the fire, in a spot where she could have a full view of her houseguest.

It wasn't a very exciting show. He slept like the dead.

Ethan had turned off his pager after work at his wife's request. They were having dinner with her parents that evening. It was important, she said, and that thing going off in the middle of a conversation was just rude.

He'd indulged her. He always indulged Victoria. And there wasn't much he wouldn't do for her parents. They thought the world of him.

So he'd spent the evening at the Richardsons' endless and

elegant dining room table beneath a crystal chandelier. Their newest pretty maid, Lorraine, served them in her crisp black-and-white uniform. It was nice, the life Randall and Jennifer Richardson shared. A life into which they'd welcomed him with open arms.

They treated him far better than his own father ever had.

So the least he could do was turn off the damn pager.

Of course, it turned out to be the one night he shouldn't have done so.

By the time he and Victoria returned home, the hospital had left six messages on his voice mail. He saw the light blinking even as he helped Victoria out of her coat, the fur soft against his palms. It was rabbit. She'd wanted mink. Maybe next year.

"Oh, honey, must you?" she asked, pursing her lips when she saw his eyes on the telephone. "It's been such a beautiful evening. I was hoping we could end it together."

He slid his hand around her nape, his fingers tickled by the touch of her short brown hair, and kissed her forehead. "There's nothing I'd like more," he told her. "But I'd better at least check, okay?"

Sighing, she nodded, hugged him close, then turned and hurried through the house, lifting her shapely calves in between steps to tug off her stiletto heels. "I'm going to run a bath, love."

"I'll be right up." He watched her go toward the stairs as he punched the button for messages.

Their contents stunned him. He closed his eyes, lowered his head. "Oh, God," he muttered.

Victoria paused halfway up the stairs. He heard her steps cease, heard her whisper, "Darling? I couldn't hear. What is it?"

He lifted his head, met her eyes. "It's River."

Her hand flew to her lips.

"He's...he's dead, baby."

"Oh, Ethan!" Victoria ran back down the stairs and flung

herself into her husband's arms, wrapping her own tight around his neck. He let the phone fall to the floor and held her, felt her body jerking softly with her sobs. "How? Why?"

"Looks like an accident. Apparently, he fell in the bathroom. Hit his skull."

She shook her head where it rested against his shoulder. He felt her tears soaking through the fabric of his shirt. "Poor River. God, poor River."

Ethan nodded. "At least…at least he's not suffering anymore," he told her.

She sniffled. "Maybe…maybe he and Steph can both rest in peace now. Maybe…maybe they'll find each other again—somewhere."

"God, I hope so," he said.

She lifted her head from his shoulder. "Do you have to go in?"

He shook his head. "In the morning. There will be an inquest, an autopsy. But in the morning." He turned her to the side, put his arm around her shoulders and held her close beside him as he started up the stairs.

"I miss them," she said. "The four of us, we used to be so close. We haven't had friends like them since—since Stephanie…"

"I know. I miss them, too."

She lowered her head to his shoulder. "Why do you suppose such terrible things happen to such wonderful people?" she asked softly.

"I don't know, baby. I wish I did."

Jax had no intention of closing her eyes, but at some point she must have, because when she opened them again, the sun was beaming in through the living room windows and the steady, if distant, call of the alarm clock was chirping away in the upstairs bedroom. The fire had died down, though the mound of glowing hot coals still threw off a lot of heat. The

makeshift bed on the floor was empty, and the blanket that had been over the stranger was tucked snugly around her instead. The shoes he'd left on the hearthstone to dry were gone. So, she realized, were his clothes.

Her sweatpants, and the nightshirt she'd loaned him, were folded and stacked atop the bedding. He'd kept the socks and the hooded sweatshirt. She was glad of it. He'd freeze his ass off outside without so much as a jacket.

She searched the house, just for the hell of it, even though she knew the man was long gone. He hadn't even told her his name.

Jax wanted to know who he was, and what he was running from. She really ought to report his presence to Frankie when she saw her this morning, she thought. But she hadn't made up her mind to do so. Having her own private mystery to solve was invigorating, and something deep inside her was telling her to hold off, to learn a little more before blowing the stranger's cover. The memory of the way he'd held her, of the sight of him nude by firelight, may have contributed to that notion, but not a lot. She wasn't a *guy,* after all.

She gathered up the blankets and pillows, and the still-damp towels, and carried the pile upstairs, hanging the towels on the racks in the bathroom, and making up the bed. Then she grabbed some clean clothes, clothes suitable for work in a small-town police department, or at least clothes she hoped were suitable. She wasn't on duty, so she couldn't really show up in her uniform. So she picked out a pair of navy trousers with a neat crease, a white cotton button-down blouse and a navy blazer. She tucked the clothes into a bag, along with fresh undergarments, her shoulder holster and her .45, then was ready to head over to her parents' place for breakfast and a shower.

As she stepped out onto the porch, a noise made her jump a little, but a quick look under the porch told her it was only the big dog, downing the entire bowl of dog food she'd left

for him. "You're a noisy eater," she quipped, and glanced at his backside. "Figures. You're a male."

He stopped eating when she spoke, looking at her as warily as—as the stranger had last night, she thought.

"Hey there, fella," Jax said softly. "You don't have to be afraid. It's all right." She held out a hand, figuring it might be more appealing if there was a steak clutched in her grip, but tried anyway. "Come on. Come say hello."

The dog stared at her, even took a single step forward. But then he lunged past her and loped away, out of sight.

Jax shrugged, put her things in the car and popped the trunk. Then she went back to get the dish—the dog had eaten every last crumb—and refilled it with fresh dog food.

"At least he's getting fed," she muttered, and thought briefly how malnourished her stranger from last night had looked, sitting naked in front of the fire. That "naked in front of the fire" image just wasn't going to quit, was it? she wondered with a smile. What the hell. She was human and straight, and he…he was something. Even though she could see his ribs, his shoulder blades, he was something.

She pushed the thought from her mind and took the dog's bowl back to the porch, only this time, instead of putting it underneath, she set it on the porch itself, hoping to lure the animal closer.

Then she took one last look around, unsure which stray she sought. Seeing no sign of either one of them, she got into her car and drove to her parents' place.

River had awakened groggy, to find himself warm as toast in a bundle of blankets on the floor, in front of a dying fire. As he sat up, searching his memory for clues what he was doing there, his gaze fell on the woman in the corner. She leaned back against the wall, a pillow cushioning her, her head cocked at an angle that would probably result in her having

a stiff neck all day. The red-orange rays of the rising sun painted her face in brushstrokes of light and shadow. Long blond hair framed her face. She had a small nose, round high cheekbones, and the neck of a swan. Deceptive, her fragile looks. She'd knocked him flat on his ass last night. As his gaze slid over her small form, it stopped on the place where her hand rested atop her folded legs, because it held a gun. A .45.

He closed his eyes slowly, and his memory of the night before returned. He examined that memory thoroughly, in search of gaps. He remembered taking refuge here, in his former home. He'd thought it was empty. He remembered waking to find her standing in the bedroom shining a flashlight in his face, demanding to know who he was. And he remembered, vividly, the way she'd taken him out when he'd tried to lunge past her.

He'd escaped into the cold, snowy night, only to hunch in the woods, wondering where the hell he was going to go. And then he'd seen her, creeping out of the house, looking for him, shining that damn light around.

He'd backed off, got out of her range and started to walk away. He still hadn't known where he would go—he only knew he needed to put some distance between himself and the curious woman. But then he'd made the mistake of glancing back, just once more, and he'd seen her walking out across the frozen pond as if she didn't even know what it was. And then he realized she probably didn't.

When she went through the ice, every instinct he'd ever possessed kicked into high gear. He didn't think, he simply reacted, the way any veteran cop would. By the time he stopped to think, he was already on his belly, arms plunging into the icy water in search of the woman.

God, when he thought about how close it had been... He got her out, only to go through himself. And she'd refused to leave him—pulled him out, her tiny body showing its hidden

strength and power. Then she'd insisted he come into the house with her to get warm, even brought him dry clothes to put on.

He'd looked down at himself as he remembered, noting the too-small sweatpants he wore. Then he looked again at the woman, and another memory came. The rush of emotion that had swamped him in his drugged, overwrought state, probably aggravated by nearly freezing to death, and by exhaustion and by hunger, and by being there in that house again. He'd clung to the woman. He might even have wept.

He remembered her hesitation and then slow acceptance. The way her hands had moved through his hair and her voice, deep and comforting somehow, had told him it was okay.

It wasn't, of course. It never would be. But it had been nice to be in a woman's arms. Human contact, physical touch had vanished from his life. It had been limited to being manhandled by orderlies or injected by nurses. No one touched mental patients any more than was absolutely necessary. He hadn't been aware how much he'd missed that, being touched, touching back.

Even now, something in him whispered that he could touch her again. That if he sat there beside her, and wrapped her in his arms, she might not turn away. Amazing, to think she wouldn't—that she hadn't. He was a stranger to her, and she wasn't gullible or naive enough to trust a stranger just because he'd pulled her from the icy jaws of certain death. The gun she held was proof enough of that.

He slid slowly out of the bundle of blankets and took his own clothing from the fireplace screen. It was dry. The knife he'd taken from the orderly was still tucked deep in the pocket of the thin pants. She hadn't found it. His brain was functioning at a better level than it had been last night, and it occurred to him that he ought to stash that blade somewhere, in case it still had the dead orderly's prints on it. It would be the only

proof, beyond his word, that he'd killed the man in self-defense. The longer he carried the blade around, the more likely the prints would get rubbed off.

He left it where it was, for the moment, in the pocket of the pants as he removed his borrowed ones and put them on. He took off the hooded sweatshirt and the nightshirt she'd loaned him. Put on his own T-shirt, then the uniform shirt over it, and after a moment's hesitation, pulled the hood back on over them both. The shoes were dry, so he put them on, as well. He added two blocks of wood to the fire and set the screen in place. Then he took the blanket she'd left wrapped around him, walked across the room to where she lay, and bent low to spread it gently over her.

For a long moment he knelt there, looking at her. She'd given him something last night. A couple of things. A chance to call up the cop that still lived deep inside him—the man he'd believed was long dead. A chance to prove to himself that he *was* still a human being, and maybe not an entirely bad one.

And her touch. Her embrace. Her warmth and her soothing voice.

He wondered if she would ever know how much those things had meant.

Finally, he turned away from her and crept out of the house. He had work to do. A long-buried truth to uncover. And he was damned if he even knew where to begin, but he supposed the first thing was to find a hideaway. A place to live, to sleep, to heal. And food. Damn, he needed food. And clothes to wear. Those would be today's missions, he thought. Today, he would work on covering his basic human needs while the drugs worked their way out of his system.

After that, he'd begin digging into the secrets of his past.

So he walked—walked for hours over back roads, in search of an empty barn or hovel he where he could hole up—but he didn't find anything. Giving that up, he walked to the very

edge of town, thought about lingering in the laundromat until someone left some clothes unattended, and maybe snatching a pair of jeans or an outing shirt that would fit him. But he didn't dare get any closer to town than that. He didn't know if they were looking for him yet. And there was nowhere he'd be able to go where people in this town wouldn't recognize him. His story had been a big one almost two years ago. God, had it really been that long? Retired NYPD cop goes bad. Everyone in town must have been talking about it.

Hell, he didn't have a dime to his name. Nowhere to go. If his bloodstream wasn't so clogged up with a year's worth of psychotropic drugs, he might be able to come up with a way to scam a meal, but as it was, it was useless.

It's not useless, dammit. I can do this. Hell, I have *to* do this.

Swallowing his uncertainty, he pulled the hood up over his head and walked into the town of Blackberry. He would do what he needed to do, make it fast and get back out of town as quickly as possible.

Dawn rose early, and crept through the house while everyone was still asleep. There were no guests at the inn this week. She had the place to herself. Bryan was sound asleep in his room, Beth and Joshua asleep in theirs. She'd been given the guest room of her choice, and she'd deliberately chosen one at the far end of the hall, away from everyone else. Aside from a few raised eyebrows, no one had commented on her pick. She needed privacy. She never knew when they would show up.

Nothing so far today. That was good. A day without them was a good day. As good a day as she got anymore.

She padded downstairs, into the kitchen in her gorilla slippers and plush powder-blue robe, made a pot of coffee and sat at the table to watch it brew. The sun was shining. That couldn't be a bad thing.

When she heard footsteps, she thought someone else was up, and hoped it wasn't Bryan. The two of them alone in the kitchen of the sleepy inn would be too intimate. He didn't understand her withdrawal. How could he?

She stiffened her resolve—it wasn't easy—as she filled a cup with the heavenly smelling brew, and turned to see who was about to join her in the kitchen.

He stood in the doorway, staring at her, and though he didn't look the same way he had the last time she'd seen him, as he'd drawn his last breaths, she knew him. She knew his eyes. He had the most piercing, deep brown eyes she'd ever seen. She couldn't speak, couldn't move. He lifted a hand, took a single step toward her, and the cup fell from her boneless hand. The sound of it shattering seemed to break the paralysis, and her scream broke free of its prison in her chest.

She turned her back, covered her eyes. "No, no, no. I won't see you, I don't want you. Go away, dammit, go away!"

A hand fell on her shoulder, and she lurched away from it so fast she tumbled over a chair, tipping it sideways and landing on the floor beside it.

"Dawn, it's okay. It's okay, babe."

Blinking through her tears, she looked up. It was Bryan, bending over her, looking terrified and sleepy and disheveled. And behind him, Beth and Josh came running into the kitchen, and Josh appeared ready for battle.

"What happened?" Beth asked. "Dawnie, are you okay?"

She blinked, looking past them, her gaze darting from one end of the kitchen to the other. But he wasn't there. Mordecai Young, her father, wasn't there. He was dead. Gone.

"I…I think I was sleepwalking," she managed to say.

She saw them, saw them all looking from the broken cup and spilled coffee on the floor to the nearly full pot on the counter, to the robe and slippers she had put on. They didn't believe her.

She didn't blame them.

4

Jax sipped her coffee and actively resisted the temptation to revisit the platter of sausage links on her mother's perfectly set kitchen table.

"Have some more, hon. You're too thin."

She smiled. Her mother would say she was too thin no matter what her current weight was. Though, in Jax's considered opinion, her mom could use a few pounds of padding. The woman had the body of a thirty-year-old. Only her face showed the signs of her age—or, more likely, the stresses of her past. You didn't see it in her blond hair. She kept it colored, cut and styled to perfection.

"I couldn't eat another bite, Mom. Besides, I have to get into town. Don't want to be late my first day."

"Oh." Mariah frowned. "Oh, well, then, never mind."

Jax slanted a look from her mother to her father, who shook his head. "Don't bother Cassie today, hon. I told you, I can take that stuff over for her and drop the other things off, as well."

Frowning, and curious, Jax said, "What stuff?"

"Your mother has an ice chest packed full of food for you, is all," her father said. "Thinks you might starve to death in a house without groceries, and a whole mile from the nearest store." He pointed to a cooler in the corner of the room. It sat right beside a box of clothing.

Jax smiled, because he'd nailed her mom so well. "I can take it for you."

"No, I won't hear of it," Ben said. "I've got to go into town anyway, take that box of castoffs to the Goodwill."

An idea crept into her brain as she followed his gaze to the huge cardboard box that sat in the corner near the cooler. Piles of folded clothes filled it. She tried to ignore the notion, and couldn't. "What sorts of castoffs?"

"Clothes. Shoes. Your mother didn't throw a thing of mine out the entire time I was…away. Kept everything. Most of those don't even fit me anymore. Came across them in the attic, when we were going through it looking for things you could use for the house."

Mariah shot him a look. "Ben, I asked you a dozen times to sort those things before we ever moved out here. Had you got around to it when you should have, we wouldn't have ended up packing them and moving them with us."

"I told you I didn't need them."

"There were perfectly good things in there!"

Jax held up a hand. Even though their bickering was good-natured, she didn't like it. And she supposed it was silly, after all this time, for her to still be afraid they'd end up splitting like so many couples did after a tragedy. But silly or not, she did worry. Her mother seemed to have recovered, for the most part. But her father—God, there was still something dark and enormous that haunted her father.

Those two had lost a daughter. They'd survived her father's lengthy prison sentence. And yet they'd stayed together. But they were not the same. Neither of them was.

Jax wasn't, either. She'd been the youngest daughter, a tough little hellion, but still… She had become the oldest, abandoned by her big sister, and by her dad, whom she'd thought would always be there for her. She'd become a care-giver to her mother—and there had been no one left to be a

caregiver to her. So she'd grown up and she'd done it fast. Hadn't done her a bit of harm, either, she reminded herself, just in case a hint of self-pity tried to creep in. She didn't believe in that kind of garbage.

Hell, it amazed her how solid her parents' relationship must be to have weathered so much. And yet there was something lurking underneath. Something waiting, ready to pounce and ruin it all. And she thought they both sensed it, even if they didn't know what it was.

"I'll be glad to take those things for you," she said, breaking free of the silence into which she'd fallen. "Really. It's no trouble."

Her father frowned. "Only if you're sure."

"Do you need me to phone Frankie for you, hon?" her mother asked. "I could explain you might be a few minutes late."

Jax laughed. She couldn't help it. She lowered her head and laughed.

"Well…what did I say that's so funny?" Mariah demanded, sounding defensive.

Ben patted her hand. "Honey, our daughter is a grown-up woman. She doesn't need you to write an excuse to her teacher."

Mariah pressed her lips together.

"It'll be fine, Mom. If I leave right now, I can still make it on time. That Taurus knows what to do when I stomp on the gas, and the roads are blessedly bare."

"Don't you even think about breaking any speed limits, Cassie," her mother warned.

Jax got to her feet, gave her mom a hug and a kiss on the cheek. "Thanks for breakfast. It was fabulous."

"You barely touched it."

One egg, two sausage links, a scoop of home fries and a pancake were apparently her mother's idea of barely touching. "I'll see you later, Mom."

Her father grabbed the ice chest and carried it out to her car, sliding it into the back seat. Jax carried the box of clothes, and even as she loaded them in and closed the door, she knew she wasn't going to take them to the Goodwill in town.

She was going to leave them on the porch of her home, right beside the cooler of food. It was stupid. The scrawny hunk was long gone, and she would probably never see him again. Then again, she couldn't very well justify leaving a warm bed and food for a stray dog and not doing as much for a stray human being. Particularly one who'd saved her life.

Dr. Ethan Melrose stood over the slab in the hospital morgue and waited while the attendant pulled a sheet from the dead man's face. They needed to do a postmortem. And since he was both River's doctor and his best friend, he wanted to oversee it personally.

But as soon as he looked at the body, he knew something was wrong.

"How did he do that much damage to his face with a simple fall?"

The attendant flipped open a metal folder, reading from a chart. "Hit the toilet, facefirst."

"No way in hell," Ethan said. "Get this cleaned up. I can't even see him, much less examine him."

He paced the room while the attendant worked, but when he turned again and saw more of the corpse's face, he thought his heart flipped over in his chest. It was pummeled, yes. The nose broken, maybe a cheekbone, too. But he was certain of one thing.

"That man is not Michael Corbett," he said.

"What?"

Lunging forward, Ethan grabbed the dead man's wrist, lifting it. "Jesus, where's his wrist band? Didn't anyone even bother to check his wrist band?"

"Oh, God," the attendant muttered. "He...the patient's room was locked. He was the only one inside. No one even thought to question— Doctor, if this isn't Michael Corbett, then who the hell is it?"

"I don't know. But I think we have a more pressing question to answer right now. If this isn't Michael Corbett, then where the hell is he?"

"Jesus, he escaped."

Ethan nodded. "Better call the state police. And find out the name of every male staff member who was on duty last night. See who's not accounted for."

He walked out of the room, but had to stop halfway down the hall, because his knees were shaking so badly he thought he might fall. He braced his arms against a wall, lowered his head between them. "Dammit, River. Where are you?"

"Welcome to the Blackberry Police Department," Frankie said, beaming a smile at her as Jax walked through the door. The police department took up fully half of a neat brick building with a huge parking lot that rolled out in back of it. The other half held the town post office.

The first room was a reception area, more or less. It held a desk, where a pretty brunette with a nameplate that read Rosie Monroe jumped to her feet as soon as Jax entered the room.

"Hi, Lieutenant Jackson," she said. "I don't think we really met last time you were in town."

"Well, there was a lot going on last time I was in town," Jax said, extending a hand. "Chief Parker tells me you practically run this department."

Rosie shrugged, shaking, her grip entirely too gentle, her hand cool. "I've been here ten years. It's kind of second nature."

Jax released her hand and looked around the room. Besides Rosie's desk, this end held a small sofa and love seat in fake green leather. Between them was a stand with a coffeepot,

creamer and sugar containers, and a large white box that she guessed, from the aroma, contained fresh doughnuts. It had Susy-Q's Bakery stamped on the lid.

The other side of the room opened out wider, held three desks and was lined with file cabinets. Every desk had a type-writer, and there was one computer in the room, which the men apparently had to share.

The officers were coming over now, two of them smiling and vaguely familiar—she'd worked with both of them dur-ing the Mordecai Young incident last year. Good men. She held out a hand. "Campanelli, Matthews, good to see you again."

Bill Campanelli shook her hand warmly, his smile genuine. All of five-six, and nearly as big around, Bill had a thin layer of carrot-red hair remaining on his rapidly balding head, and when he smiled, his whole face lit up. "Same here," he said.

Mike "Icabod" Matthews took his turn, adding a pat to her shoulder. "If anyone can fill Frankie's shoes, we figure it'll be you."

Cassie shook her head. "Either one of you could handle the job," she said.

They exchanged looks and winked. "Neither one of us *wants* it," Campanelli said. "Hell, I retire in five years. And Matthews, he's got so many side projects going he wants to have himself cloned."

"Town couldn't take two of me," the other man joked.

The third man stood off to one side, waiting his turn. His pale blue eyes were cold, his smile forced in his square-jawed face. He was built like a boxer—stocky and solid. Jax knew the type. Big chip on his shoulder and probably had issues working under a woman. It might have been different with Frankie, since she was the man's aunt. But Jax was not only female, but a younger female at that. And stepping into the job he had coveted for himself. She read all of that with her

first look at the guy, pegged him as an asshole, and didn't doubt she'd be proved right, given time.

She extended a hand. "You must be Officer Parker," she said. "It's a pleasure to meet you." It was a lie, but what the hell.

"Lieutenant," he said with a nod.

She almost told him to call her Jax, but decided against it. She'd need every edge she could get with this fellow, and establishing a pattern of respect would be a good start.

"I hear you stayed out at that old empty house last night. How do you like it?"

"Love it," she said.

He lifted his brows, maybe a little surprised. "Really? I'd have thought being way out there like that might make a city girl a little uncomfortable."

"I'm from Syracuse, Officer Parker, not Manhattan."

He shrugged. "Still city, compared to here."

"I *like* the country. It's quiet."

"Not a neighbor within a mile of you," he said. "A lot of the locals claim to have seen things out there, since the fire."

"What kinds of things?" she asked, looking him square in the eye.

"Just things. Things that spooked 'em."

"Guess it's a good thing I don't spook easily. I didn't have power or a phone last night. And even that didn't spook me."

"Those will be on by the time you get home," Frankie told her, coming out of her office to join them. "Power company said by noon today, and the phone guy told me dinnertime at the latest." She smiled. "So did you really like the place?"

"I've never spent a more interesting evening," she said, and it was a perfectly honest answer.

"Well, now you've got me curious. Come on, you can tell me about it while I give you the grand tour."

"Nothing to tell, Frankie. Honest, I love the house."

Frankie led her through the station, showing her the files,

the communal computer, the supply closet, which was packed full. Jax noted a holding cell in what looked like a new part of the station. "Just the one cell?" she asked.

"We didn't have any until this past year," Frankie told her. "It's brand-new."

"What did you do with the criminals before now?"

Overhearing her, Kurt Parker released a bark of laughter. "Hell, honey, this isn't some city police department. We barely *have* any criminals."

She shot him a look, but before she could say a thing, Frankie cut in. "I'm pretty sure I did introduce you, didn't I, Kurt? The woman's name is Lieutenant Jackson. Not 'honey.'"

He looked as if he was about to say something belligerent, but by then the other two officers were chiming in. "You'd think some of us had been raised in a cave," Matthews said.

"Hey, Parker, you want some more coffee? Honey?"

"Yeah, how about it, sweetie pie?"

Parker's face reddened, and he turned to stomp off to his desk as if he had something pressing awaiting him there.

Rolling her eyes, Frankie led Jax into her office and closed the door. There was a smaller desk set up in the corner with a blotter, a cup full of pencils and pens, and a Blackberry Police Department coffee mug with a blue ribbon fastened to the handle.

"Aw, heck. Is that for me?"

"Sure is," Frankie said. "That's your desk. At least, until you move on over to this one." She patted her own desk. "And to answer your earlier question, when we needed to make arrests, we'd call the county boys in. We'd get the paperwork, they'd get to hold the prisoners. It sounds complicated, but we had got it running like clockwork. Still, having a holding cell of our own is nice. And Kurt was right about one thing—we very rarely have to make any arrests."

There was a tap on the door, then it opened and Rosie poked her head through. "Got a call, Chief."

Frankie lifted her brows and waited, and Jax felt herself tense, just as she always did on the job when a call came her way.

"Purdy says someone just snatched some fruit from his produce section, and took off without paying."

Jax blinked. Frankie nodded. "And what did this dangerous felon make off with?"

"An orange and a bunch of grapes, near as he could figure."

Frankie nodded and smiled at Jax. "Welcome to high crime in Blackberry," she said, her eyes twinkling. Then, to Rosie, "Description?"

"Male. Couldn't see his face. He was wearing a blue hooded sweatshirt with some kind of bright orange logo on the front."

Jax felt her own smile freeze in place and slowly die. Damn, she hoped the stranger went back by her place, so he would find the offerings she'd left and not feel compelled to steal. Apparently, he wasn't very good at it. An orange and some grapes? Freaking pathetic.

"Suggestions, Lieutenant Jackson?" Frankie asked.

"Maybe the store's security camera got him on tape?" she said.

"Nope. No security cams around here, except at the bank and post office." She nodded to Rosie. "Why don't you send Kurt over to take a report? He needs something to get his mind off his hurt feelings."

"Sure thing, Chief." Rosie backed out of the office.

Frankie sighed. "May as well get comfortable," she told Jax. "We'll take a look at the notices from the state police, and the county, and then we'll head on over to the coffee shop."

"But there's coffee here," Jax said.

"Ah, but we don't go for coffee. We go for gossip. Best way

to keep your finger on the pulse of this town. The good old grapevine—Blackberry's lifeblood flows through it."

"I can see I've got to get used to a whole new way of working, huh?"

"You'll pick it up in no time, Jax." The telephone on her desk rang, and Frankie reached for it. Her smile faded about three seconds into the phone call. Her face seemed to pale, as she scribbled notes. When she hung up she was already on her feet.

"What have we got?" Jax asked, getting to her feet, as well.

"Trouble. Come with me." She went out of her office. "Rosie, there will be a fax coming through any minute. I'm gonna want a dozen copies, pronto."

"On it," Rosie said, and even as she spoke, the fax machine beside her desk was ringing and churning to life.

Matthews and Campanelli came over from their desks. Kurt Parker had apparently already gone to check out the great produce heist.

"Michael Corbett escaped from the state hospital last night," Frankie said. "Killed an orderly in the process."

"Holy shit," Matthews muttered. "They think he'll head here?"

"He'd be stupid to come here," Frankie said. "But we need to be ready, just in case."

"Wait, someone needs to bring me up to speed," Jax said. "Who is this Corbett? Is he dangerous?"

With a heavy sigh, Frankie turned to her. "Hell, I didn't want to dump all this on you your first night in town and maybe scare you off. But...well, I already told you the house—your house—has a history."

"You said a whole wing was destroyed in a fire, and a woman was killed." A little shiver ran up her spine, but Jax shook it off. She was a cop. Those kinds of shivers had no place in her life. And yet she kept thinking about the odd white shape she'd glimpsed outside, and Kurt Parker's words about

the place spooking people. And the cold spot on one side of the house that never seemed to get warm.

"The house belonged to the Corbetts, and the fire was arson," Frankie said. "Corbett was found on the lawn with a gas can at his feet. His wife died in the fire—was pregnant at the time, too. Corbett claimed he couldn't remember a thing, and he had some history of blackouts to back it up and a top-notch shrink on his side. The D.A. accepted an insanity plea and shipped him off to the state hospital, where everyone expected him to spend the rest of his life."

Jax lifted her brows. "I thought you said nothing bad ever happened here?"

"I may have exaggerated just a tad. Hell, I've only given you the digest version. Rosie, dig out those old files so Jax can get caught up. Got that fax yet?"

"Got it." Rosie handed the faxed sheet to Frankie, who looked at it and shook her head sadly. "That's our man. Shame, crying shame. He was a cop once. A damn good one, as I understand it." She passed the sheet to Jax. "We'll get some posters up around town, keep a keen eye out for him."

Jax barely heard her. Instead, she stared down at the face of the man who had spent the night in her house. The man who had saved her life at the risk of his own, who had wept in her arms and then slipped away before she woke. The man who, even now, might be finding the food and clothing she had provided for him.

Clothing—that belonged to her father, who was an ex-con and couldn't afford to be tied to an escaped killer. God, what the hell had she done?

Her first day on the job, and already she was guilty of aiding and abetting an escaped criminal. That wasn't going to earn her any points. She wouldn't be surprised if Frankie withdrew the job offer when she found out. Jax knew that in her place, that's what she would do.

She couldn't believe she'd done it. She'd helped a murderer—one who'd got off on an insanity plea—much like the man accused of murdering her own sister had nearly done twelve years ago.

And maybe that was why. Not that she believed in fate, or karma or any of that hokey new age garbage. But damn, at the very least, the universe had one sick sense of humor.

He wasn't doing well.

His feet scuffed through the dusting of snow along the winding road's shoulder. He knew he was leaving a distinct trail, but doubted anyone was following it. The cold seemed to knife straight through to his bones. He *ached* with it.

He'd expected to feel better by now. To be starting to feel strong again after a good night's sleep, in a warm, dry place. But he wasn't feeling strong. He was shaky. His head felt heavy and cotton filled, and he was having trouble convincing his feet to pick up off the pavement. His chest hurt, too, ached and burned. And every now and then a full body shiver racked him from head to toe.

Taking the grapes from his pocket, he ate them as he walked. When there was nothing left but the spiny stem, he tossed it, and took out the orange. But he couldn't manage to get a start on peeling it. His fingers were thick and stiff. No dexterity, very little hand-eye coordination.

He closed his eyes, giving up on the orange and dropping it into the pocket of his borrowed hoodie. Then he looked up to gauge how far he'd come, and found himself standing in front of his house—or her house. The place where he'd spent the night.

River lowered his head, shaking it slowly even as the specter of that fireplace rose up to tempt him to come inside. "No," he muttered. "I'm not dragging some stranger into my messed-up life."

He took another step, intending to walk right by the place. But then he saw the ice chest on the porch and hesitated. What the hell?

He moved closer, wondering if the woman could have deliberately left it outside for him to discover, but he found that hard to believe. More likely it was bait of some kind. Surely, by now they'd figured out the dead man in his hospital room wasn't him. Surely, they would have alerted the authorities in this small town, and the word was out. Maybe by now she'd heard about him, and gone to Chief Parker to tell her about the stranger who'd spent the night under her roof. The cooler, left on her porch, could easily be meant to lure him in. They might be waiting, even now. He had no desire to deal with *those* officers again. They were less than gentle, those hometown boys in the Blackberry PD. At least, the one he'd dealt with back then.

His stomach growled and churned. He needed food. His body was at war with his brain. Hell, if he didn't get physically up and running again, this entire mission was no more than one big waste of time.

He crouched in the trees across the street, watched the place for a while. Eventually an electric company truck rolled up. Men went around to the back, messed with the box mounted to the side of the house. They left again. Her power had been turned on.

He waited longer, kept watching the place. No movement. No sign of anyone nearby. Swallowing hard, he came out of his cover, and started moving across the street. He was slow, clumsy and wary. He told himself to turn and run at the first sign of a trap, but doubted he'd be able to outrun anyone. And then he heard a low, deep growl, and froze in his tracks.

The woman had a dog? He didn't remember a dog from last night.

The growling grew louder, and he saw the animal's large

head emerge from underneath the broken boards in the porch. It barked at him once, twice, three times. River went stiff, looking around for people to come running, cops with guns drawn, at the dog's summons, but none came. Maybe it wasn't a trap, after all.

The dog came the rest of the way out; the barking ceased. It looked at him, growling deep, stepping forward, hesitant, wary.

River frowned, eyeing the skinny animal, the way his stomach seemed concave, and the familiar markings on his face. "Rex?" he whispered. Then louder. "Rex, boy? Is it you?"

The dog went still, head tipping to one side. It whined once.

"Rex, it's me. God, boy, you look as bad I must. Come here. Come here, Rex."

Tail wagging slightly, the dog came closer, wary and pausing between steps. River knelt down, right there in the road, and held out a hand. The German shepherd moved nearer, sniffing at him. Then, suddenly, the dog burst into a loud chorus of barks and jumped on him, paws to his chest knocking him flat on his back, tongue licking his face and neck.

River smiled. It hurt, pulling at facial muscles that hadn't been used in months. Burying his hands in Rex's fur, he hugged the dog, and wondered why he was feeling so damn emotional. It was an animal.

But he knew. Rex was a piece of his old life. The life he'd had before everything had been taken from him. The life he'd thought had been entirely obliterated. Rex remained. And if he did, then there was hope.

River pushed the dog off him, and then used his old friend to help pull himself to his feet. Keeping one hand on the animal, he moved across the road and into the driveway, trying to walk in the nicely plowed spots, where he wouldn't leave obvious footprints. He went up onto the porch, then turned, realizing Rex was no longer beside him. The dog sat at the bottom of the steps. Too wary, perhaps, to come closer.

"It's okay, pal. I'm pretty sure there's no one around. Come on." He slapped his hand against his thigh. Rex came up the steps and onto the porch, where he proceeded to explore and sniff the length and breadth, with special attention to the corners and the empty dog food dish that still held a few telltale crumbs.

She'd fed his dog.

River moved to the cooler, lifting the lid up and peering inside. "And now she's feeding me," he muttered.

Tupperware dishes lined the thing. He found one full of homemade rolls, and couldn't stop himself from taking one. He bit into it, then felt Rex's eyes on him, and saw the dog watching intently as he chewed.

"Okay, one for you, too, boy," he said, tossing the dog a roll.

Rex caught it and ate it eagerly, tail wagging, while River examined the other containers. One held a stew, thick with gravy, vegetables and meat. Impossible to eat that, really, without utensils. The next dish he opened held cold fried chicken.

"God, Rex, I think I've died and gone to heaven." He took out two pieces of the chicken and, forgetting his caution, sat right there on the porch to eat them. But before he got more than a bite off the second drumstick, his stomach was protesting. It had been too long. He just couldn't hold food the way he would have liked to. Couldn't do this meal justice.

There were other dishes in the cooler, and bottles of water, as well. He didn't go through them, just peeled the remaining meat off the chicken bone for Rex, then put the bone itself back into the container, because he didn't want the dog eating that, and set the container back in the cooler. He helped himself to a bottle of water, and only as he took his first sip did it occur to him that he hadn't had a drop of water since before leaving the hospital—aside from the icy pond water he'd swallowed last night.

He drained the bottle, too thirsty, suddenly, to take it slow. And then his stomach convulsed and heaved. He ran off the porch, the dog at his heels, and only just made it into the thick brush across the road before he lost his lunch. The heaving left him weak and trembling, his stomach feeling far too queasy for him to even consider trying again to put food into it.

Rex nudged his thigh, whined a little.

He petted the dog's neck and straightened. "It's okay, boy. I'll live. Maybe." Lifting his head, he eyed the house. "You don't suppose I could crawl under that porch with you, rest up for the day, do you?"

The dog barked once, and then the two of them made their way back across the street. River paused long enough to go through the box of clothing. Men's clothing, all of it. There were jeans and flannel shirts, T-shirts and button-down shirts, ties, several pairs of shoes, and best of all, sweaters. Four of them, thick and heavy and warm. And a denim coat with a fleece lining, and even a knit cap.

"Heaven," he said again. He took the jeans, T-shirts, sweaters, socks and the coat. He took only one pair of shoes, a pair of lined, waterproof boots that were more valuable to him right then than a million dollars would have been. He tried to arrange the remaining items—the dress shirts, ties, suit pants and jackets—in such a way that it wasn't utterly obvious things were missing from the box. But it was pretty clear.

He bundled up his treasures, and went, with the dog, to the open spot under the porch, then knelt and crawled in.

And then he let his eyes adjust to the darkness. When they did, he realized that the woman who lived here was a pushover. There was a brand-new dog bed under the porch.

But there was something else even better. Something he had known about, once, but forgotten long ago. There was a hole in the cinder block foundation, made for a casement window. But there was no window in the hole.

He peeked through, into the house's cellar. The furnace was running. The warmth of it touched his face.

He closed his eyes, told himself this woman was too nice to be treated this way. She didn't deserve to have a confessed murderer, much less an escapee from a mental hospital, hiding out in her basement.

And yet he didn't see that he had much of a choice in the matter.

He tossed the clothes into the basement, then went back to the porch to get the bottles of water, the chicken and the rolls from the cooler, and took those back with him. His list of earthly possessions was growing. He had clothes now. He had food and water, and he had shelter. He also had a knife with a six-inch, razor sharp blade and his assailant's fingerprints, he hoped, preserved on the handle. He'd wrapped it in a rag he'd found along the roadside to keep the prints from being smudged. A plastic zipper bag would have been better.

This time, when he crawled underneath the porch, he kept on going, through the missing window, into the cellar.

Turning, he wondered if Rex would try to come in, too. If he did, and she came home, the dog would surely give him away. But Rex was happily curled up on his dog bed, already snoring.

Dawn came out of the laundry room with an overflowing basket of clothes. She tended to let her laundry pile up at the dorm, so she'd brought it all with her to wash during the holiday break. And this was the last of it.

Everyone had been watching her too closely today. It made her want to cut and run, but she kept reminding herself it was only because they cared about her. Still, the searching looks, the leading questions—it was wearing thin.

She walked through the living room with her basket of clothes, and felt the chill as soon as she entered the room. That

chill—it wasn't a normal one. It only came when one of *them* was close, and Dawn's entire body tensed with anticipation.

Beth stood there, talking to a man as a woman stood nearby. The man was tall, slender, dignified looking and soft spoken. He had a worried look about him, and his shoulders nearly slumped from whatever weight they were carrying.

The woman...oh. Her again.

She was semisolid, her white nightgown stained with soot and black spots, as if it had been burned. So was her face, for that matter. One side of it was twisted and scarred. She held a baby in her arms, wrapped in a scorched, sooty blanket, and she stared. Not at Beth, or at the man, but at Dawn.

Dawn's fear turned to anger. It was one thing for them to harass her, entirely another to get within a mile of her family. Screw this. She set the basket down on the floor and marched forward, making her stride aggressive and sending the dead woman a look meant to chase her off.

Beth turned, and Dawn plastered a more pleasant expression on her face, but not before Beth had seen her.

"You feeling all right, Dawn?"

"Fine," she said. And she beamed a smile at the man who was looking her way.

"This is Dr. Melrose, Dawn," Beth said. "He's taking a room for a couple of days."

"It seems silly, my living only an hour from here," he said. "But then again, driving back and forth until my business in town is finished would be even sillier."

"Dawn Jones," she said, taking his hand, which was so icy it nearly made her pull hers away. "Welcome to the Blackberry Inn."

"Thank you."

"So you're a doctor."

"Psychiatrist, actually."

Dawn shot Beth a look, wondering just for a moment if this

was some kind of setup. Had she managed to convince her birth mother that she was losing her mind? Hell, why not? She was half convinced of it herself.

She glanced past the man. The dead woman was gone. For now.

5

When Jax came home from work that afternoon, her father's four-wheel-drive pickup sat in the driveway with the tailgate down. Her front door was unlocked, and when she went inside, she found her house brimming with...stuff. A brown velour sofa stood in her living room, with a glass-topped coffee table in front of it. A television set sat opposite. It wasn't a floor model, so it looked odd there. There were a couple of mismatched, overstuffed chairs, too. A burnt orange one big enough for a linebacker, and a pale blue rocker-recliner. Underneath all of it, a big, braided, oval area rug covered the floor.

Her parents had been busy.

She moved through the dining room, which still held no furniture, and into the kitchen, where her mother was stacking plates in a cupboard and her father was carefully applying caulk to the windowpane in the back door.

"You guys are going to spoil me, aren't you?" Jax asked, leaning in the doorway and folding her arms over her chest.

Her mother looked up, a kerchief over her hair, and beamed a bright smile at her. "Give the independent streak a rest, Cassie. I couldn't have you living here without the barest essentials. Honestly, I don't know how you got by last night—the place was Spartan."

"I didn't need to do anything but sleep, Mom." Jax moved across the room to give her mother a hug, then looked past her into the cupboard, which was stocked with plates, bowls, saucers, coffee cups and glasses. She opened another door to find mixing bowls and measuring cups, and yet another where cookware and bakeware filled the shelves. There was a small kitchen table—metal legs, red Formica top—in the center of the room, with old-fashioned chairs around it—metal frames with padded red vinyl seats and backs. She opened the fridge, found it clean, fresh smelling and stocked with food. The red cooler sat empty on the floor. She wondered briefly if they'd noticed the box of castoffs on her porch as well, but got distracted when she realized the light in the fridge had come on when she'd opened the door.

"Power's on?" she asked, needlessly.

"Phone lines, too," her mother said, pointing to the brand-new cordless telephone resting in its base, which was mounted to the wall. They had to have bought it for her.

"What happened to the window?" her father asked. "You have trouble out here last night?"

Jax sent him a bright smile, one designed to hide the lie. "Trouble? Hell, no. Who in their right mind would give me any trouble? I was clumsy. I, uh, was carrying some wood in, from the pile out back, and I slipped. A log flew out of my hand and smashed right through the window." She shook her head and then moved on to a new subject. "Dad, you didn't see a dog outside when you arrived, did you?"

He shook his head slowly, wiping the caulking knife on a rag and dropping it into his tool belt. The windowpane was repaired and perfect. Her father was just as capable with a hammer and nails as he was with a scalpel and clamps. Just as comfortable in a pair of overalls as he had once been in an expensive suit or surgical scrubs.

"No, I didn't see any. Did see the box of stuff we sent home

with you..." He smiled. "I see you helped yourself to a few things. It was considerably lighter when I took it to the Goodwill. So are you expecting a dog?"

She nodded. "That stray we spotted here the first day. It's been hiding out under the porch sometimes." Her father frowned, and she rushed on. "He's all alone, Dad. Doesn't seem aggressive at all, just wary. I left some food for him and he ate it."

Ben nodded. "I saw the empty bowl. You shouldn't get too close until I've had a look at him. Make sure he's all right."

"I'll be careful. Wait till you get a good look at him, Dad. He's kind of scrawny, a little rough around the edges, but underneath all that, he's gorgeous." She found the fugitive's face, not the dog's, creeping into her mind. "You can tell he's something special. Frankie says he's been making a nuisance of himself for a while, but no one's been able to corner him."

Her dad's lips pulled into a rare smile, not a full one, kind of sad, like all his smiles were. "You thinking of making a pet out of him?"

She was startled by the question, considering where her thoughts had taken her. "I don't even know if I'm staying yet."

"Of course you know," her mother muttered. She picked up the dishpan full of soapy water and poured it down the sink, then wiped her hands on a dish towel. "Well, I know I'll feel better knowing you've at least got the necessities."

"How much did you two spend?"

"Nothing at all," Mariah said. "The dishes have been in my cupboards for years. How many can two people use, after all? Ditto with the extra towels and linens and bedding. Oh, and I didn't get a chance to hang them yet, but we brought you a pile of curtains and rods, too. Just stuff I had in the closets."

"And the food?" Jax opened another cupboard door. "You've stocked the cupboards and the fridge. There's enough here to feed me for six months—if I have half the town in for

snacks every day, that is. And that telephone is new." She looked upward. "You even put lightbulbs in all the fixtures." She sent her mother a suspicious look. "Did you stock the bathroom, as well?"

"It makes your mother happy, being able to do things for you, Cassie. Don't you hurt her feelings by trying to pay us for this stuff." Ben shrugged. "Besides, we do fine at the clinic."

Jax smiled and put a hand on her father's cheek. "I want to spend a morning over there with you one of these days, Dad. I'd love to see you work."

"I enjoy it," he said, and she knew it was nothing short of the truth. There didn't seem to be much in life that gave him pleasure anymore, so that was worth a lot. Jax mourned the loss of his former career—sometimes, she thought, more than he did. "Animals are great," he went on. "They don't argue. They don't judge and they don't hate."

"And they almost never sue," Mariah added, to lighten the weight of Ben's words.

Jax pretended to laugh, but damn, her father's mood worried her. "Do you guys want to stay for dinner? The least I can do is feed you after all this."

"Perfect!" Mariah said, clapping her hands together. "That'll just give me time to hang those curtains."

Her mother, Jax thought, after her parents said good-night, was the Jackson family's answer to Martha Stewart. Sunflower patterned curtains hung in the kitchen windows and there were matching towels and potholders dangling from every cupboard doorknob. The kitchen was fully functional. She'd set a toaster beside Jax's coffeepot on the counter, mounted a paper towel holder to the wall and filled it, set a coffee mug tree on the table and hung clean cups from every branch, filled a sugar bowl and salt and pepper shakers, too.

Even left a pack of sponges and a scrubber near the sink. The place looked as if someone had been living there comfortably for years.

The other rooms were not as complete, but Mariah had made a good start. The dining room was still empty, and begging for furniture. But it had curtains now—Mariah had insisted on hanging them after dinner. The living room was furnished, aside from the lack of a TV stand, and felt cozy. Lacy doilies lay on the arms of the sofa and chairs, a runner on the coffee table, and a stack of coasters sat in the center, next to the TV remote. She'd even placed a framed family photo on the mantel—an old one, from a long time ago, that included the whole family, even Carrie.

Seeing that brought a lump to her throat, but Jax didn't say anything. Her mother didn't like to talk about the past. She remembered—but quietly. It was her way.

Mariah had even hit the bathrooms, filling them with stacks of towels and washcloths, new shower curtains and bath mats, curtains in the windows, toilet paper on the rollers. The woman was a wizard.

By the time her parents left, the house felt much more like a home, and as Jax settled down in the living room with a cup of hot coffee, and the bulging file folder full of photocopies she'd brought home from the Blackberry PD, she couldn't help thinking about how the things from her old apartment back in Syracuse would look here. The wildlife prints on her walls, the entertainment center. Her own TV—wide-screen with surround sound. And her stereo system.

If she decided to stay.

She leaned back in the sofa with a contented sigh, listening to the quiet. Hell, who was she kidding? She was going to stay. She wanted this job.

And that thought brought another: the fact that she may have already blundered herself right out of this job, by giv-

ing refuge to a fugitive. Surely, the best thing she could have done this morning would have been to come clean, immediately. And yet...there was something wrong. Something off about this whole thing. She'd dealt with a lot of criminals, prided herself on her instinct. And that man last night hadn't seemed like a criminal to her. Wounded, wary and probably under the influence of heavy chemicals. Now that she knew he had just escaped from a mental ward, she could understand that a little better. But criminals did not risk their lives to save the lives of strangers. Especially strangers who could turn around and blow the whistle on them the very next day. And he was a cop, on top of all that. A good one, Frankie had said.

If she'd learned nothing more in her life, Jax had learned to give the apparently guilty the benefit of the doubt.

God, how she'd learned that.

So she'd decided to give it one more night. Frankie had let her make copies of the files on the Corbett case, so she could take them home and read them. Get caught up on the facts of the case.

Frankie Parker, Jax discovered as she opened the bulging folder, was one thorough cop.

At the top of the pile were records of Michael Corbett's service with the NYPD. Jax scanned page after page of them, noting several commendations, a nearly spotless record, until a shooting incident in which he had been injured, and which had been investigated by the Internal Affairs Division. Which meant nothing—anytime an officer fired his weapon in the line of duty, it had to be investigated.

She sipped her coffee, flipped a page and found one officer's report on the shooting. She waded through the dry language of the account, knowing from experience she'd find no hint of emotion anywhere within its pages. "Just the facts, ma'am" was more than just a catchphrase. What it came down to was that Corbett and other officers had responded to nu-

merous complaints about a crack house. Suspects in the house opened fire on the police officers almost as soon as they were out of their vehicles, and they returned it. One of the suspects' bullets had hit Corbett in the head before the shooters fled the scene, evading officers who gave chase. Other officers remained with the wounded Corbett until paramedics arrived.

Jax scanned pages until she located the I.A.D.'s final report on the investigation, which cleared Corbett and his fellow officers of any wrongdoing. She frowned, wondering what any of this had to do with the investigation into the murder of Corbett's wife. But then she found her answers. Corbett had been left with a bullet in his brain, and side effects that made it impossible for him to continue in his job. He'd been retired with a clean record and full pension.

Frankie had made her own notes, detailing Corbett's health situation according to information she'd gleaned from interviews with his doctor. She wrote that he was prone to blackouts, periods during which he would lose time, and return to himself with no idea what had transpired. It was during one of those blackouts that his house had been torched, his wife killed.

Neither Frankie nor the state of Vermont were eager to prosecute him for murder, not with the testimony of his doctor likely to get him off on an insanity plea, anyway. The result would have been confinement in a mental hospital. And he'd been willing to take that sentence voluntarily, which saved the state the cost of a trial they might have lost. A hero cop, wounded in the line of duty, didn't make for the easiest defendant.

Jax stared at the pages, but she wasn't seeing the print. Instead, she was recalling the look in the man's eyes last night. The desperate, haunted look about him. No wonder—if he'd killed his wife, and couldn't even remember doing it—hell, that would be enough to haunt anyone. But why would he have risked prison by busting out of the state hospital?

By killing an orderly and then busting out, her inner voice reminded her.

There was more, reams more in the folder, and she turned to a new page and read, and read, until her eyes grew so weary that they drooped slowly closed, and her head fell to one side.

Then there was a sound—a soft sound, like weeping. A woman weeping—and then it changed, and became the gentle coo of a very young baby crying. That snuffly, congested newborn bleat. The smell of smoke touched her nostrils, and a strangled voice whispered....

Help me! Please!

She sat up fast, her eyes flying wide.

The living room was perfectly empty. There were no sounds. No whispers. No babies crying. No smell of smoke. She'd fallen asleep.

No such things as ghosts, she reminded herself, rubbing down the goose bumps that had risen on her arms. Hell, she was letting Kurt Parker's spook stories get to her.

Jax stretched her arms, folded the file and got up from the sofa. She was letting her imagination take hold, and that was totally unlike her. Maybe she'd better call it a night. She turned for the stairs, but stopped in midmotion at a sound—a real one this time. It sounded like something dropping to the floor.

Frowning, she turned her head in the direction from which the sound had come, the kitchen. "Yeah. It's probably a whole troop of ghosts," she taunted herself. "Who you gonna call, Jax?" Sighing, she moved slowly. Because while she didn't believe in spooks, despite her new colleague's tales, she *did* believe in escaped mental patients. Her gun was hanging with her coat in the living room closet—not her choice of a permanent spot to keep it; just where she'd happened to hang it when she came home. Her mother hated seeing it on her. Jax supposed it was a reminder of how dangerous her job could

be, and the thought of her only remaining daughter at risk was a little too much for her to handle.

Mariah was delicate. More so than she let on. There had been far more of her in Carrie than there had ever been in Jax.

Jax took the shoulder holster and pulled it on. She didn't need to check the gun to know it was loaded with a full clip, but there was no bullet in the chamber and the safety was on. She knew her weapon as well as she knew her own body. She kept her hand on the butt as she moved through the house into the kitchen, where she flipped on the light and then stood still, watching, listening.

The room was spotless. The dishes done, leftovers put away, the white ceramic-tiled counters gleaming. The back door was closed and still locked, its new windowpane still in place. Nothing seemed unusual or alarming.

So, then, what was the noise? It didn't make itself.

And I was awake, so I know it wasn't a leftover part of that screwed-up dream.

She moved her gaze slowly to the cellar door, and knew the sound had come from down there. She knew it with the instinct cops developed over time. Exercising any muscle made it stronger, and cops exercised their intuitive muscles constantly. There was something in her basement. She felt it right to her bones.

Drawing a breath, along with her gun, Jax moved to the cellar door, closed her hand on the knob, turned it and pulled the door open. Reaching inside, she flipped the light switch. But there was no response. Her father had replaced every bulb in the house—except this one. Great. She backed off and took her flashlight from the top of the fridge, where she'd left it.

Then she returned to the cellar stairs, putting a round into the chamber of her .45, and keeping her finger close to the safety. She held the flashlight in her left hand, in an overhand grip, and clicked it on.

The staircase was solid. Unfinished boards, not yet dark with age, had been built to replace whatever had been there before. She started down, brushing cobwebs aside with her gun hand when they stuck to her face.

Then she stopped on the third step at another sound. *Breathing,* she thought.

Hell.

She tried to console herself with the idea that if there were anyone at all in her basement, it had to be the man from last night. And then she asked herself why that notion should console her. The man from last night was either a cold-blooded killer or a criminally insane one. Either way spelled danger with a capital *D.* Not that she was worried—she could handle him.

And yet part of her still insisted he was neither of those things. Part of her, that same part that had told her where the noise had come from, believed he was what she had seen last night, before she'd known his history. A cop in trouble. On the run and on the edge. Wounded and alone.

Damn, why did that image make her belly tie up in knots?

She continued down the stairs, shining her light around the cellar's concrete floor. The furnace stood in a corner, water tank and hot water heater in another. There were pipes on the walls ending in unused spigots that would probably hook to a washing machine, should she decide to put one down here. A dryer would fit beside it.

The breathing came again, from behind her this time!

She swung the light, her body and her gun, as her gut tensed. Eyes gleamed back at her. "Hold it right there," she said, lifting the gun and shifting the light.

The dog was peering down at her from outside a missing window high in the basement wall. His tongue hung out as he breathed happily, watching her every move. He wasn't growling, just apparently curious.

She closed her eyes and released her breath in a rush. "Damn, dog, you scared the life out of me." Smiling at her own panic, she realized the missing window looked out on the underside of her front porch, where the dog's bed was stashed.

Okay. So it was probably not the most heat-efficient situation. She wondered if her father would mind installing one more window for her, and knew he wouldn't. Then she took a better look around the basement, and located a bulb in the ceiling, with a chain hanging down. For the hell of it, she pulled the chain and the light came on, filling the basement with a dim glow, just enough to chase the shadows into the farthest corners.

"That's better," she said, turning off her flashlight and sliding it into her belt. She holstered her gun, too, then moved closer to the dog. "So are you thinking about coming inside? Hmm? Is that why you're snooping around the window like that?" She held out a hand.

He sniffed a little, then pulled back abruptly and vanished from the window hole.

Jax sighed. "Well, hell, you'll trust me sooner or later, I guess." Turning, she started back for the stairs, and then paused at the pile of items she saw stacked on a shelf to the left. A stack of clothing, an orange and a Tupperware container.

A chill chased its tail along her spine. She moved closer, picking up the articles of clothing, examining the container, which had chicken inside. Fresh food, not spoiled. "Straight out of Mom's cooler, I'll bet," she muttered. She lifted her light again and shone it on the shelf, the better to see what else might be there. Its beam picked out a long, rag-wrapped shape.

Jax reached for it, and knew what it was as soon as she picked it up, both by its weight and its form. But she unwound the rag, anyway.

The hunting knife had a wooden handle and a four-inch blade, razor sharp on one side, blunt with an inward curve near

the top on its backside. She held it in her palm, the rag still cradling it in her hand.

"Put it down."

Jax spun around, to see the man standing two feet from her. She had the blade in one hand, the light in the other. No free hand to reach for her gun. No problem; she could bean him with the Maglite and put him down for the count.

She stared at him, her heart speeding up. Fight or flight was kicking in, and personally, she preferred fight. Her eyes raked him, head to toe. No weapon; that was the first piece of information she filed away in her mind. No weapon, and he was just standing there, none too steadily, arms at his sides, not making any aggressive moves toward her. His eyes were puffy and unfocused. His face unshaven, hair a mess. He wore jeans, no doubt taken from the box of clothes she'd left out for him, and a sweater over a T-shirt. She could see the white band of the collar at his neck.

"This yours?" she asked, lifting the knife, the handle of which was still wrapped in the rag. "What are you doing, breaking into my house with a knife on you, pal?"

He licked his lips. "Please put it down. Don't smear the prints."

She frowned at that. "Tell me whose prints are on it, and maybe I'll oblige you."

He hesitated, seeming to mull it over, then nodded once, weakly. "A man attacked me with it. Tried to kill me. I ducked, then I hit him and he went down hard. Smashed his head. It killed him. That knife is my only proof it was self-defense."

For a crazed escapee from the looney bin, she thought, he was making a hell of a rational argument. "Okay. I'll be careful not to smear the prints." She wrapped the blade cautiously in its rag, and tucked it between her belt and her jeans, in the back. "I think it's about time you told me who you are, don't you?"

"I can't." His eyes closed slowly, but he forced them open again, even while swaying a little.

"Should I take a stab at it then?" she asked. "No pun intended, of course."

His frown was confused. "My name's River. I..." He swayed again, and this time, he went all the way down, out cold on the floor.

"Hell." Jax left him there and ran up the stairs to tuck her gun belt and the hunting knife both out of reach and out of sight. Then she dashed back down to lean over the fallen man. "You're in sorry shape, you know that?"

He moaned, but didn't respond. Jax knelt down, lifted his upper body, knew she ought to be on the phone right now turning his fugitive ass in. "Hey, wake up, will you?"

His eyes opened, met hers. "Someone's...trying to kill me."

"So you said. You think you can get on your feet? Even as underweight as you are, I prefer not to have to drag you up the stairs."

He gripped her hand. "If you turn me in, they'll find me, and I'll be dead. I need time. That's all. Just time."

"Time to do what?"

He closed his eyes. "To find out the truth."

Jax debated for a long moment, and then decided there was no point hiding what she knew from him. "The truth about what happened to your wife, the night your house burned? Is that the truth you're looking for, Michael?"

He closed his eyes. "How do you know?"

"I'm a cop."

Anguish, that was the emotion that crossed his face. Sheer anguish. But then he met her eyes again. "So was I," he told her.

Dammit, she'd never been so torn. Giving this man shelter went against everything she'd been trained to do. But she couldn't shake the feeling that there was more going on here

than met the eye, more to this man than what she'd read in his file. And a whole lot more to this case.

He'd saved her life. And that was only one of the reasons she wanted to help him. Hell, she didn't believe in the fate and destiny garbage the neo-hippies were spouting these days, but she couldn't help but wonder if this man had been dropped into her life for a reason.

A chance to make it up. To put things right.

She sighed. "And I'm fucking nuttier than he is."

"What?"

"Nothing. Let's just get you upstairs."

"I can't stay here," he muttered, even as she anchored him to her and helped him to his feet. "Just get me to the door. I'll go—"

"You'll be dead by morning if you do."

"If you're going to call—"

"I'm not." She said it before she was even aware she had made the decision. "Not yet, anyway. I need to puzzle this out for myself. And I suppose I owe you a favor, after you pulled me out of that frozen pond. Hell, you're burning up, Michael."

"River," he told her.

She closed her eyes. "Nickname?"

He nodded, then lifted his head. "Yours?"

"Lieutenant Cassandra Jackson, Syracuse Police Department. But you can call me Jax."

"Nickname?" he asked.

She looked at him sharply, saw the barest hint of what might be humor in his eyes. It touched her. "Yeah."

She moved him across the floor, toward the stairs, and they started up them.

"Syracuse?" he asked.

"Yeah, for the moment. I'm off for two weeks."

"Why—" he grunted with effort as they took another step "—Blackberry?"

"Frankie Parker's retiring. I'm up for her job. Unless I get caught aiding and abetting a fugitive, that is."

He closed his eyes. "Sorry."

She shrugged. "Don't be. If I turn you in I plan to claim you broke in, and I found you here, then take credit for the collar."

"Good. I owe you, too. The clothes. The food."

Easing him into the kitchen, Jax helped him into a chair, then she went back to the cellar door and flipped the light switch, nodding in approval when the light downstairs went off. She closed the cellar door. "You manage to eat any of it?"

"Tried," he said. "It…didn't go so well." He leaned back in the chair, head tipping back, eyes falling closed.

He was a mess. Physically, emotionally and probably mentally a mess. A fellow cop in trouble. And if what he said was true, someone was trying to kill him. But if he'd truly killed his wife…his *pregnant* wife…

"I just have to know," he said. "If I did…what they say I did."

It was as if he could read her thoughts. Then again, they probably thought a lot alike. They were both cops. There was a bond there, unwritten, unspoken, but there. And yet…

"Tell me one thing. The insanity plea—was that something you cooked up to get away with the crime, or was it for real?"

He stared into her eyes, his own as clear as she had seen them so far. "I'm not insane," he whispered. "At least, I wasn't."

"But you had blackouts," she said, repeating what she'd read in his file.

He nodded, closing his eyes.

She felt cruel to keep on questioning him when he needed help on so many levels. But she had a decision to make, and she had to make it now. Before this went any further. "And it was during one of those blackouts that your house was set on fire?"

He kept his eyes closed, but she thought moisture was

darkening his lashes. "I don't remember what happened that night. I don't remember."

"When did you decide you had to know the truth? Why now, I mean? You've been holed up at the funny farm for what? A year?"

He shook his head slowly. "A couple of weeks ago. I was sick, threw up my meds a few times, and managed to get lucid just long enough…realized what was happening to me."

"And what was that?"

He opened his eyes then. "Getting worse. Sicker. Losing myself—my mind."

"And did you do anything about it? I mean, busting out wasn't your first move, was it?"

"No. I wrote a letter to my lawyer. Told him I had to know the truth. I wanted…the files sent to me."

She nodded. "And when was the first attempt on your life?"

He met her eyes, frowning. She wondered if she was grasping at straws. Why did she want to believe him?

"The day after I wrote the letter," he said, and she knew from the look in his eyes that he hadn't made the connection himself until just now.

She drew a deep breath, nodding slowly. Okay, okay, so it was possible someone didn't want him to know what had happened that night. Not likely, but possible.

"I won't turn you in tonight," she said. "I'll give you that much. You can rest easy here. I need to…mull things over. I'll figure out what the hell to do in the morning."

He brought his head level. "Even that's too much to ask."

"You didn't ask, River."

6

"Here," Jax said. "Try this."

River opened his eyes, and she was there in front of him, pale angel hair like a silk veil over her face as she bent, placing things on the coffee table. A bowl of steaming soup, a small plate with a handful of crackers on it, a cup of what looked like hot, tinted water and smelled like flowers. Two aspirin tablets.

He'd dozed off on the sofa, he realized. He barely remembered her walking him in here, setting him down. God! Of all places, why did she have to be living in this one? She might look like an angel, but she was a cop. She'd probably already dropped a dime on him, and if she hadn't she would before morning came, despite her promise not to. She was a *cop*.

As she straightened, she turned and caught him looking at her. She wasn't smiling, seemed...pensive. Nervous. Hell, why wouldn't she be?

"It's chicken noodle," she said, nodding at the soup. "Might be easier to keep down than fried chicken."

He nodded and sat up straighter, leaned forward and picked up the spoon. But as he drew it toward his mouth, his hand shook so badly the broth rained onto his lap. By the time he got to taste it, all that remained in the spoon was a single noodle.

He closed his eyes, cursing himself inwardly.

And then he felt warmth—her hand, closing around his as if to take the spoon away. "Let me," she said.

River opened his eyes again, staring at her hand, and he couldn't believe how shaken he was by her touch. It had been a long time. "I'll manage."

She lifted her brows. "They didn't take the pride out of you then, huh? Well, too bad. Lean back, relax. I've got this."

He leaned back against the sofa as she sat down beside him, drawing the bowl of soup with her. Then she spooned a bite into his mouth. It tasted good, warmed and moistened his parched, sore throat and heated his belly when it landed. He accepted another bite, then waited a moment just to see how his stomach was going to react.

"Well?" she asked.

"So far so good." She nodded and spooned up another mouthful. When he'd swallowed it, he said, "I've been pretty heavily drugged."

"Yeah, I knew you were under the influence of something that first night."

"Haldol," he said. "Mostly. I don't know what else they've been giving me."

"You think you need it?" She fed him some more soup.

He decided to stop feeling self-conscious about his helpless state, and knew her matter-of-fact attitude had a lot to do with that. "I never needed anything before.... I was normal. Functional. Except for the occasional blackout."

She nodded. "From the bullet you took on that drug bust."

He blinked. "How do you know so much about my past?"

"First day auditioning for police chief, and in comes a fax featuring the face of the man who saved my life the night before." She shrugged. "I was curious."

"Do they know I was here?"

"No one knows but me, River. Hell, I wasn't even a hundred percent sure you were the same guy in that photo. It was

grainy, black-and-white, and last night it was dark. Besides, you don't look the same now. You're damn scrawny."

"Thanks."

"Oh, hey, it's not a problem." She looked downward at her chest as she said it, and he noticed the print on the front of her T-shirt, read it for the first time. It said "I Dig Scrawny Pale Guys."

River's mouth pulled into a smile, and it felt foreign, unfamiliar. It had been a while since he'd had reason to smile.

"I decided to keep my mouth shut until I could be sure you were the same guy. Decided to read your file first, see if my gut instinct about you was on target."

The bowl was half-empty. He decided to give it a rest, held up a hand to tell her so. She set the spoon down. "Your gut instinct?" he asked.

"Yeah. That you're a good cop having a bad time. That I ought to give you the benefit of the doubt. And that, with a few good meals and some rest, you'd probably be a great lay."

He looked up fast, saw the spark of mischief in her eyes and allowed himself to ignore her teasing. She was trying to lighten the mood, put him at ease. The odd thing was, it was working. "So have you made up your mind?"

She shook her head. "I'll have to let you know on the lay thing. As for the rest…I haven't finished my reading."

His breath caught for a second. "You have the case file here?"

She averted her eyes, and he knew her next words would be a lie. "Not here. You know it wouldn't be allowed out of the station."

He blinked and faced her. He didn't have to ask, because she had to know what he wanted. She pursed her lips. "And even if it were, you're not in any shape to stay up all night reading. Shit, I doubt you'd retain anything even if you could manage it."

"I need to see that file."

"What you need is a hot bath and a good night's sleep. We'll talk about the file in the morning."

He sighed, sensing he'd get nowhere by pushing her. But also sensing she'd be turning him in to the authorities in the morning. If not sooner.

"Try the aspirin. They're coated, and you might have enough in your stomach now to keep you from getting sick. You need to get that fever down."

He took the pills, swallowed them obediently with a sip of the warm tea, wishing to God he had half his old strength back.

"Good. Now, let's try to finish the soup."

Nodding, he let her continue feeding him, and somehow, he managed to down the bowl. Then he drank about half of the tea before his stomach told him enough was enough.

"Come on," she said, taking his arm. Touching him again, as if it was the most normal thing in the world. As if she didn't know he could feel every point of contact like an electric shock. "I ran you a bath while you were passed out on the couch. It ought to be just about cool enough to get your temperature down by now."

He stared at her for a long moment.

"It'll help with the fever," she told him.

But he just kept staring, and then he voiced what was on his mind. "Why are you helping me?"

She held his gaze, didn't look away, but met his eyes dead-on, let him probe and search hers all he wanted. As if she had nothing to hide. She had a frankness to her, a practical, no-nonsense sort of attitude that struck him as genuine.

"You think it's a trick, don't you?" she asked. "Hell, that's what I'd think, in your place. You probably figure I've already turned you in and am now just trying to keep you distracted until someone arrives to cart your sorry ass away to the cracker factory."

He swallowed hard. "It's what I'd do."

"I don't think so." She studied his face for a long moment. "No, not a guy who risks his life to save a stranger who could blow his cover."

"That's why you're helping me, then? Because I pulled you out of that pond?"

Pursing her lips, she looked away from him. "I didn't say I was helping you. But I wouldn't leave a dog out in the cold if it was in the shape you are." She shrugged. "This is just for the night, okay? In the morning…I'm probably going to have to turn you in."

He was surprised she would admit it. Then she met his eyes, and he was even more surprised by what he saw there. She didn't *want* to follow through on that threat. But he thought she'd do it, anyway. "Thanks for the warning."

"I'll feed you breakfast first," she said. "Let you know what I've decided when I've made up my mind. Hell, I'll even give you a head start. And then we're even."

"We're already even," he said. "And then some. If I had a choice—I don't like putting you in this position."

"You didn't put me here. I did. Now let's go. The bath is waiting. And I've got a brand-new spare toothbrush, still in its wrapper, and a pack of disposable razors—so long as you don't mind that they're pink and the shave cream has some kind of prissy floral scent. My mother stocked the bathroom."

He wondered for a moment what kind of razor she used when her mother didn't stock the bathroom. A straightedge? No. Hell, she probably didn't bother to shave at all.

She left him in the bathroom, then took her file folder from her bedroom and tucked it underneath the sofa cushion. Frankie shouldn't have let her remove it from the office, much less make copies to take home. But she saw no harm in it, no risk. Hell, Frankie *trusted* her.

So far Jax hadn't done anything to betray that trust. Not

really. She could cuff this guy and haul him in at any time, so long as he was here. She wouldn't have betrayed anything until and unless she let him walk out of here.

But she didn't intend to do that. Not really. She was going to do some good old-fashioned police work tonight, and by morning, she would have some answers. And then, by God, she was going to personally escort the woebegone suspect directly to Frankie for processing. No matter how much torment she saw in his eyes. She just had to be sure, first—just so she could act with a clear conscience.

She owed him that much.

Moreover, she thought, she owed Jeffrey Allen Dunkirk.

She heard River when he finished in the bath. He pulled the stopper, and the water gurgled down the drain. His footsteps crossed the floor.

Jax hurried back upstairs and met him at the bathroom door. Clean-shaven, wet hair. He wore nothing but a towel slung around his hips, and for a moment her gaze lingered on his chest. He was too thin, but she could see the shadow of the man he must have been. When he filled out again…

She swallowed hard, drew her eyes up to meet his and found them fixed powerfully on her. With a sheepish grin, she shrugged. "Hey, don't act like you mind me looking."

"How do you know I don't?"

"Because you're a guy," she said. "Bedroom's this way." Turning, she led him down the hall, into the only furnished room he'd seen, and snapped on the light.

"I assumed this was your bedroom," he said.

"It is. It's also the only one with a bed at the moment." She moved inside, pulled back the covers for him and turned.

He was standing in the doorway. Hell, this had been his bedroom—his and Stephanie's. The memories that were flooding him threatened to take over.

"Hey." The pretty blond cop snapped her fingers in front of his face. "Earth to River. What's the matter?"

He licked his lips, and she lifted her eyebrows as if she thought she got it.

"Hell, you think I plan for us to sleep together. Again." She rolled her eyes. "I'll be downstairs on the couch, River."

"Oh." He blinked, not bothering to correct her. He wasn't too worried about her sexual teasing. "I can't take your bed and let you sleep on the couch."

"Why? 'Cause you're the big, strong guy?"

River smiled a little. "Yeah. Except for the big, strong part."

It surprised her that he was able to make a joke; he could see it in her eyes. Hell, it surprised him, too.

"You can't sleep on the sofa, River. Anyone who came by would see you. And God forbid that should be my family or Frankie Parker."

"You have family here," he said, nodding slowly.

"My parents. That's part of the reason I'm leaning toward taking the job. To be closer to them." She patted the bed, and he moved slowly closer, sitting down on it. "What about you? You have family, River?"

"Just Ethan."

Lifting her brows, she asked, "Brother?"

"Might as well be. We were best friends growing up. When my parents were killed, his family took me in." He shook his head slowly. "I imagine even he's given up on me now, though, after this latest stunt. Especially if he thinks I murdered that orderly."

She frowned. "Ethan...knows the guy?"

"Probably. He worked at the hospital." When River saw her still frowning, he went on. "Ethan's my shrink. He's the only person who's stood by me through all of this. And I know he's tried his best, but it just wasn't working." He shook his head.

"He didn't believe me, about the attempts on my life at the hospital. He said he did, but…"

She closed her eyes, and he didn't know why. Maybe because she didn't believe him, either. He lay back in the bed and pulled the covers over him. "Whatever you decide in the morning, Cassandra, thank you for tonight. And…for last night."

"Last night you were barely coherent," she said.

"Coherent enough to cling for all I was worth to the one lifeline I'd found in a long time."

He was referring to the way he'd held her, and he could see in her eyes that she knew it. The memory of it made his stomach clench tight, partly with embarrassment at such a show of desperation and emotion. Partly with something else altogether.

"Good night, River," she said.

"Good night, Cassandra."

She made herself leave the room, close the door. Then she went downstairs, grabbed the cordless phone and carried it out onto the porch, where he wouldn't hear her. She hugged her arms as she dialed. It was chilly tonight. Not snowing, no wind. Just a cold breath that told you winter was here to stay.

Beth answered on the first ring. "Maude Bickham's Blackberry Inn," she said cheerfully.

"Beth, it's Jax."

"Well, it's about time!"

Jax frowned in confusion. "What?"

"I have to hear through the Blackberry grapevine that you're in town—maybe for good? And you plant yourself here for a whole day and a half before you even bother to call? What's up with that, Jax?"

Sighing, Jax smiled through her tension. "Mom told me she had let you know I was coming, so I didn't see the need to report the news. And I had every intention of coming over to see you. Give a girl time to unpack, will you?"

"I suppose you can be forgiven—this time," Beth said. "How are you, Jax?"

"Good. I'm…good. And you? How do you like being married? The life of an innkeeper ever get boring?"

"Not on your life. I'm deliriously happy. And Dawn and Bryan are here for Thanksgiving break, so life is good."

"Do I detect a hint of hesitation in your voice?" Jax asked.

Beth sighed. "I'm a little worried about Dawn. She's lost weight. Seems pale, and kind of…I don't know. Off."

Jax frowned, not liking the sounds of that. "Could be just college. Freshman year. It's a major change."

"Yeah. Yeah, that's probably it."

"Listen, Beth, as much as I'm dying to catch up, I'm actually calling because I need a favor—a big one—from your husband. Is he there?"

"Sounds mysterious," Beth said. "Is everything all right?"

"Hell, yes. I'm as self-sufficient as they come."

"Mmm-hmm." Beth sounded doubtful. Or at the very least, speculative. "I'll put Josh on."

A moment later, Joshua Kendall's voice came on the line. Jax didn't waste words. "You still have connections in the cloak-and-dagger community, Kendall?"

"Depends on who's asking. For you—yeah, Jax, I can stir some up."

"Tonight?"

"What's going on?"

She drew a breath, blew it out in a cloud of steam. "Can't tell you that," she said. "But I have an item that might have some prints on it. I need it dusted, and I need the prints run. It has to be discreet, Kendall. And it has to be tonight."

He drew a breath. "It can be done. Tell me, is this important enough for me to lose a night's sleep over?"

"Several," she said. "And besides, I'll owe you big-time."

"I'll make a few calls. Can you bring the item over?"

She looked around, as if in search of the answer, but she knew it without having to find it in the snow. If she left, River would be gone when she got back. He didn't trust her a hell of a lot more than she trusted him right now. "No, I can't leave."

"All right. I'll swing by and pick it up."

She glanced around, spotted her mailbox mounted to a post across the street, and nodded her thanks for the idea. "I'll leave it in the mailbox," she told him.

He paused, and she could almost picture him frowning at the phone. "Is there some reason you don't want me coming to the door?"

"Yeah. There is. So I'll put it in the mailbox. Okay?"

"Jax, are you—"

"Yes, I'm perfectly okay and have been for a number of years without anyone playing hero to my damsel in distress. I hate being worried about, taken care of or looked out for. So really, Josh, don't go there. I'm as capable as you are. Maybe more so."

"Okay," he said. "I didn't mean to offend."

"You didn't."

"I'll call you when I have something. Actually, it shouldn't take more than a few hours."

She lifted her brows. He *was* connected. Even now. "Thanks, Josh."

"Think nothing of it, Jax. You came running when the kids were in trouble. We owe you, anyway."

She smiled. "I got kind of fond of the brats, to be honest."

"They're here for Thanksgiving," he said. "You should join us."

"I imagine my parents will want me with them—but I've been known to pack away two turkey dinners in a single day. What time?"

"You find out what time your parents want you and we'll plan around it."

"You don't have to—"

"We want you here, Jax. I'll talk to you later." Josh hung up the phone.

A whimpering sound drew her gaze, and Jax looked down the porch steps to see the German shepherd standing on the bottom one, looking up at her.

"Hey, there. Just a sec." She ducked into the house, put the phone in its charger stand and opened the fridge to find a few scraps for the dog. Then she headed back outside. She held out a slice of roast beef, part of the offerings her mother had sent home with her.

The dog sniffed, came a little closer, sniffed some more.

"Come on. Come on, now, you can trust me. Take it."

He crept closer still, and finally, snatched the meat and raced away with it.

Jax smiled. "Well, that's progress, I suppose," she muttered, and went back into the house to take the knife from its hiding place. She carried it across the road to where the mailbox stood, and placed it carefully inside.

Before she went in again, she filled the dog's dish with food and moved his bed from underneath the porch, to the porch itself. She was going to get through to him, come hell or high water.

River didn't intend to sleep, but his body didn't give him much of a choice. He was out as soon as he laid his head on the soft pillows. And by the time he opened his eyes again, the sun was already beginning to rise, its pale light filtering in through the bedroom windows. It took him a few moments to get his bearings, to remember where he was and why. Hell, he'd intended to be out of the house before Cassandra woke up this morning. Now he would have to work fast, or find himself behind bars, or worse, right back in the state hospital. And that would end any chance he might have of learning the truth.

He flung back the covers, sat up slowly, waiting for the rush of dizziness to hit him—but it didn't come. His head was clearer today. Maybe the drugs were finally starting to clear from his system.

The clothes he'd pilfered were stacked on the dresser. He dug through the pile for fresh ones, put them on as quickly as he could manage. His shoes were downstairs. Those great ones she'd found for him—given to him.

He closed his eyes briefly, had to forcibly remind himself that he couldn't afford to trust her, no matter how kind she seemed. She couldn't do anything but turn him in. It was her job, the thing she'd been trained to do. He would have liked to believe otherwise, but to do that would be foolish.

He went to the bedroom door, heard the shower running in the bathroom. Damn, she was already up. He was going to have to make this fast. Ducking back into the bedroom, he gathered up the clothes, looking for something in which to carry them, and finally settled for taking the pillowcase from one of the pillows and stuffing the clothes inside. Then he went to the door again, and through it, into the hall.

But he stopped dead when the bathroom door opened, and she stood there, wearing nothing but a towel. Her blond hair was dark with water, straggling over her shoulders, sticking to her face. Droplets beaded on her shoulders and chest. On her face. She was tall, so the towel only came to the tops of her thighs, and he couldn't help but look his fill at her endless legs. Strong and slender, with smooth skin that had gone as pale as the winter. She wasn't into tanning, then.

"Going somewhere?" she asked.

He jerked his eyes up to hers, realized the pillowcase was still in his hands, and licked his lips.

"I haven't called anyone yet, River. Well, one person, but he doesn't count."

A little knot of panic formed in his chest. "Everyone counts."

"Not this guy."

He hesitated, glancing toward the stairs, then back at her.

"God, you really don't trust me, do you?" She pursed her lips. "Look, I've been in the shower for the past fifteen minutes. If I'd called anyone before I got in, they'd have been here by now, wouldn't they?"

He frowned hard, because her answer made sense.

"Stay for breakfast, River. We have to talk. Come with me. I need to get dressed, and you need to be sure I'm not in there dialing up the nearest SWAT team. Come on." She took his hand, and hers was warm, her grip strong and firm for a woman. But he'd already figured out she was no ordinary woman. She drew him with her back into the bedroom where he'd slept. She closed the door behind them, and released his hand, walked to the dresser and opened the top drawer. He watched her pull out a pair of small white panties and a bra of the same color. Opening another drawer, she tugged out a pair of jeans.

She didn't ask him to turn around. She pulled the panties over her feet and drew them up, underneath the towel, not the least bit shy or embarrassed. She repeated the process with the jeans. Then she put her back to him and dropped the towel, naked from the waist up. And even though he couldn't see the front of her, his body began to react. He felt a stirring that told him things were beginning to function the way they once had.

She pulled the bra around her, fastened it in the back and then slipped on a sweater.

He told himself to yank his mind back on track, and accomplished it by reviewing her earlier words. "You said you made one call."

"Yeah. To a friend of mine."

"Cop?"

She looked at him sharply. "He was with the ATF, back

when it was still *called* the ATF. He's retired now, but he still has connections." The way she studied his face, he wondered what she was thinking. But then she went on. "I didn't tell him about you, River. I gave him the knife, asked him to process it for prints and run any he might find."

His brows rose. "And you think he'll do all that without telling anyone?"

"He already did. Now do you want to come downstairs and have some breakfast so I can tell you what he found, or stand there being suspicious of me while having impure thoughts about my bod all day?"

"I wasn't—" he began, then shook his head. "I was, actually."

"Doesn't bother me."

"Doesn't it?"

"Hell, River, I've worked with men my entire adult life. I'd be worried if you didn't look a little. It's not like I haven't done the same to you."

"You reach any verdict?"

She shrugged. "Let's just say I wouldn't toss you out of bed for eating crackers."

There was that disturbing frankness again. "You aren't...an ordinary woman, are you?"

"I'm just an ordinary cop," she said.

He nodded once, set the pillowcase full of his clothes on the bed, and followed her from the room. In the kitchen, she poured coffee from a pot that had been freshly brewed. She must have put it on before her shower, he thought. She set his cup in front of a kitchen chair, then opened the fridge while he sat down. "You think you feel up to eggs?" Then she frowned and looked over her shoulder at him. "No, probably not. We'll go for something that packs more of a nutritional punch. Oatmeal."

"Either way." He took a sip of the coffee, and wondered if it was going to make him ill.

She measured oatmeal and water into a bowl, stuck it into

the microwave and hit a button. "So my friend took the knife to a friend of his, and they lifted some prints off the handle. Then he ran them for us, all off the record. Here." She took a manila envelope from the counter and dropped it on the table in front of him. "This is what came back."

He was stunned, looking from the envelope to her face, but she was already turning away, taking the bowl of oatmeal from the microwave and setting it on the table for him. She set a second bowl in, then went back to the fridge for milk, margarine. "I don't have any syrup. Is brown sugar okay? You want cinnamon?"

"Yeah. Fine." He was opening the envelope, sliding the sheet from it. It was a mug shot, a photo of the orderly who'd attacked him, with the name Edward Ferdinand Martin underneath it.

She was setting brown sugar on the table now, spoons, a plastic container of cinnamon. "Is that the orderly?"

"Yeah. But he wasn't using this name. Wait, I'll show you." He pushed away from the table and headed back upstairs to get the ID badge he'd taken from the dead orderly's shirt. When he brought it back down, she was sitting at the table, stirring her oatmeal and scanning the printout she'd probably already memorized.

River put the ID badge on the table, and she reached for it. "Kyle Maples. Not even very imaginative, is it?"

"Why would he be using a false name?"

She looked up at him, waving the paper in the air. "Man, you *are* rusty, aren't you. Hang in there, pal, you get back in the saddle and it'll all come back to you. The guy had a rap sheet. Violent shit, too. Nothing close to murder, but a couple of robberies where he beat the hell out of the victims. One instance where he broke a guy's legs in exchange for five hundred bucks from a loan shark. He couldn't have got a job at the state mental hospital with a record like this. I'm surprised they didn't run his prints, anyway, find all this and fire his ass."

"Maybe they would have if he'd been there long enough."
She tipped her head to one side. "He was new?"

"I'd never seen him before that day."

Nodding slowly, she took a bite of her oatmeal. "We can check that out today."

He just sat there, still staring at her. "What do you mean, we?"

She set her spoon down, drew a breath. "Look, you told me this guy tried to kill you. His prints are on that knife, he's got a record and he was working under an assumed name. It's pretty clear to me you're telling the truth. You killed him in self-defense—"

"I didn't mean to kill him. I didn't, it just—he went down hard, hit his head."

"Hey, I'm not complaining. Bastard needed killing. Still, it was self-defense. And if someone's trying to kill you in the hospital, you freaking leave. It's common sense."

For a moment he just sat there, staring at her. She believed him. She'd said it, and she meant it. An enormous weight seemed to lift from his shoulders, and that was odd, because up until that moment, he hadn't thought he gave a damn if anyone believed him. Ever.

"Did you know this guy? Did he have any reason in the world to want you dead?"

River shook his head slowly. "I never saw him before that day. Never heard of him—not by either name." He shrugged. "Maybe I busted him—"

"Doubtful. You were NYPD. His records are all out of Michigan. So, he had no motive. We have to consider the possibility that he was working for someone else. Especially since he's hurt people for money in the past."

River blinked slowly as he digested her words. "Someone hired him. Someone who wants me dead."

"Yeah, it looks that way." She nodded at his bowl. "Your oatmeal is getting cold, River."

He looked at it, then back at her. "I…what are you saying, Cassandra?"

She leaned back in her chair, crossed her arms at her waist and stared at him. "I have every reason to believe that turning you in right now would put your life in jeopardy. I can't, in good conscience, do that. I can't."

"It could cost you your job."

"I'm planning to give notice in Syracuse, anyway."

"What about this job? The one here in Blackberry?"

She sighed. "If we get to the truth soon enough, no one ever has to know."

"You can't do this."

"What I can't do is hand you over knowing it's liable to get you dead. How am I supposed to live with something like that?"

"You don't even know me. Why the hell should you care?"

She pursed her lips, lowered her head. "It's not a question of caring. It's a question of doing what's right. Look at you. You don't look to me like you need to be locked up in a rubber room and drugged into oblivion."

He shook his head. "I don't know what I do when I have those blackouts. For all I know, I could be dangerous. I could be dangerous to you."

"Oh, please. I could kick your ass blindfolded."

He looked up fast and saw the twinkle in her eyes. He couldn't resist it, even smiled a little in response. "You probably could at the moment."

"At the moment, hell. I'm talking on your best day, pal."

He liked her. He knew it right then. She had so much life in her it was rubbing off on him, though he'd thought his was pretty much drained and gone.

"Listen," she stated. "You hurting me is the least of my worries. Men don't hurt me. It doesn't happen. It's not even in the realm of possibility. So don't make it an issue."

He tipped his head to one side and thought he'd glimpsed

something in her that he hadn't seen before. She had shadows, secrets inside her. A darkness that wasn't readily apparent.

"I would like you to let me get some help on this. I think Frankie would back me up. I think she'd agree that keeping you here, in my custody, in secret until we get some answers, is the best idea."

He shook his head slowly. "Frankie Parker is a by-the-book cop. She's had to be. It was tough enough for her to be an older female in the position of police chief. If she were a rule bender she never would have lasted a week in the job."

"She's got nothing to lose. She's retiring."

"With a spotless record. And some of her officers haven't got the best opinion of me."

"Really? Which ones?"

He made a face. "I blacked out at the station, while they were questioning me. When I came back, Frankie's nephew was kicking me in the rib cage hard enough to break a couple. Bastard always had it in for me."

"Good."

"Good?" He didn't get it.

"Yeah. I was hoping I'd find an excuse to put a hurting on that putrid little weasel."

He blinked, both at the venom in her tone and the sudden, rigid set of her jaw. She looked as if she meant it. "Let it be. Your job's on the line."

"It figures, he'd hate you on sight," she said. "You were an NYPD cop, a decorated one. He's the type to be threatened by that. Hell, he's threatened by me. I think he wanted Frankie's job for himself."

"All the more reason to keep the local cops in the dark."

"Okay, then," she said. "There's one other person I'd like to let in."

"Your friend the retired ATF agent?"

She shook her head slowly. "No. No, he's got a nice little

life going. I don't want to risk screwing it up. No, I was talking about my father."

"Your father."

She nodded slowly. "Just take the pitch before you decide whether to swing, okay?"

"Okay."

"And eat your oatmeal, for heaven's sake…"

He nodded, and ate a few bites of the oatmeal. It surprised him when he realized he actually felt hungry, and he ate a few more.

"My father is a doctor. Was a doctor."

"Was?"

"A surgeon," she added, not elaborating on her use of the past tense. "He's good, River. Sharp. I'd like to have him take a look at you, see what he thinks about getting this crap out of your system."

He sighed, lowering his head. "I'm fine. I'm feeling better every day."

"Couldn't you just humor me?" She reached across the table to put a hand over one of his, almost as if not quite aware she was doing it.

And again her touch sent rivers of warmth and sensation from the point of contact right up his arm and through his entire body. It didn't make him uncomfortable anymore. He was beginning to look forward to her touches.

"River, he can be trusted. I swear to you, he won't say a word, not even to Mom if I ask him not to.'

He drew a breath. "Let me think about it."

"Okay." She glanced at the clock. "I've got to get in to work." And she squeezed his hand. "Tell me you'll still be here when I get back."

"I…I don't know."

She studied his face for a long moment. "Would a bribe help?" Then she got up, went to the living room and came

back with a thick file folder. "Here." She dropped it on the table. "This is the file on your case. At least it's what Frankie had. She said there were other things she could get later, but this was the gist of it."

He looked up at her.

She said, "Trust me yet?"

"I'm gaining on it." He closed his hand around the file. "Thanks for this, Cassandra."

"You wanna thank me, then don't make me sorry by taking off on me. I've got the bit in my teeth on this one, River. I want to run with it. Nothing gets my blood flowing like a chance to solve a juicy case. Don't deny me having my fun, okay?"

She turned and walked into the living room.

River followed her, thinking he ought to be on his knees in gratitude, even while wondering if she could possibly be for real. She grabbed her coat, pulled it on, then opened the front door. But instead of walking out, she stood still.

"Cassandra?"

She glanced over her shoulder at him and whispered, "Here's my stray. Shh, don't scare him."

He moved up closer to her, looked past her and saw Rex sitting on the porch near an almost empty dog food bowl.

"I've been trying to lure him closer, but he's so wary," she began.

She never finished. Rex gave two sharp barks and lunged through the doorway, launching himself at River. Cassandra just barely ducked the attack. Rex's big paws slammed him in the chest, and River went down on his backside, while the dog licked his face with more enthusiasm than care.

"My God, I thought he was attacking you," Cassandra said, one hand pressing to her chest. "I, uh...take it you two know each other?"

River buried his hands in his friend's fur, rubbed his cheek

against the dog's face and managed to get out from under the brute. "Yeah, you might say that." He sat up, reached up a hand.

Cassandra closed hers around it and tugged him to his feet.

"Cassandra," he said. "Meet Rex. Rex, Cassandra, though she prefers to be called Jax for some unknowable reason."

Cassandra crouched down beside him, stretching a hand tentatively and then letting it hang there while Rex sniffed it. He showed his acceptance by reaching past it to snake his tongue over her face.

She backed away, wiping her cheek with one hand and petting the dog with the other. "I think I liked it better when you were scared of me, pal."

Rex stared at her for a moment, then proceeded to walk through the house, sniffing everything he came to, as if inspecting the place. He found the fireplace in the living room, and flopped to the floor in front of it with a sigh that sounded like an expression of extreme relief.

River swallowed. "That was always his spot," he said. He licked his lips, lowered his eyes and tried not to choke on the lump that came into his throat.

To his surprise, Cassandra's hand clasped his nape. "Now it can be his spot again."

7

Jax walked into the Blackberry Police Department that morning wondering if the secret she was hiding showed on her face. She knew she was doing the right thing—so why did it feel so wrong? God, she felt as if *she* were the criminal.

"Good, you're here," Frankie said as soon as she walked in. "Grab some coffee and come on in here." She walked into the larger part of the main room, where the officers' desks were set up.

Jax filled a cup and followed. The other cops were there. Campanelli sat on the edge of his desk. Matthews leaned against a file cabinet. Kurt Parker sat in his chair. In the middle of the room was another man, sipping coffee from a foam cup. He was tall, rather thin, handsome in a studious way. Narrow face, longish nose, wire-rimmed glasses, nondescript brown hair.

"Cassandra Jackson," Frankie said, "this is Dr. Ethan Melrose."

Jax felt her brows go up even as the man extended his free hand. "Lieutenant Jackson. Chief Parker has told me a lot about you."

"Wish I could say the same," she said, taking his hand, careful not to say too much.

"Dr. Melrose is Michael Corbett's psychiatrist," Frankie explained.

And best friend, Jax thought in silence. No wonder he looked so weary. "I remember from the case file," she said. Then she turned to Frankie. "Has there been a sighting?"

"Not so far," the police chief answered.

"Nonetheless," the doctor interrupted, "I'm certain he'll come here, sooner or later. And probably sooner."

Jax tipped her head to one side. "That doesn't make a lot of sense, does it, Doctor? I mean, he was a cop. He must know this would be the first place people would look for him."

"He's a mental patient, Lieutenant," Melrose said. "And he's not stable. His decisions aren't going to seem rational or logical. He's going to do what comes naturally, and that includes returning to the last place where he was happy and comfortable."

Jax noticed the look Frankie sent her—the one that said the last place this guy had been happy and comfortable had probably been *her* place. Jax crossed the room to Matthews's desk, perched herself on the free corner, deciding to keep quiet and let Melrose do the talking.

"You can bet we'll collar him if we find him," Kurt Parker said. "And if he's in this town, we *will* find him."

Jax sent Parker a glare that was full of warning, and the cocky look on his ugly mug turned into one of confusion.

"I've got no doubt about that," Dr. Melrose said. "The thing is, I don't want him any more traumatized than necessary. If you do locate him, I'd appreciate it if you'd call me. Let me talk to him before you approach him. Give me the chance to try to get him to come in without a struggle. It would be better for everyone."

"You want us to treat him with kid gloves," Kurt interpreted.

"He's a dangerous man in a volatile state, and off his medications to boot," Melrose told him. "He could become violent if approached or confronted. No one wants that."

"Certainly not," Frankie agreed. "Dr. Melrose, I'll do my

best to give you first crack at him. But if it comes down to a choice between letting him slip away, and moving in without your help, we're going to have to move."

"I understand that, Chief," the doctor said. "I'm staying at the Blackberry Inn."

Jax barely restrained a gasp. Had he been there last night, when she'd put in the call to Joshua Kendall?

"You can reach me there, or on my cell phone." He tugged a card from his pocket and handed it to Frankie.

Jax cleared her throat. "Dr. Melrose, it might be helpful if we knew more about this orderly who was killed. Did he have a history of trouble with Corbett?"

Ethan frowned. "I have no idea."

"Well, how long had he been employed at the hospital?"

"I wouldn't know, Lieutenant. And I assure you, it's irrelevant, anyway."

"Probably," she agreed. "Still, I like all the information on a case I'm investigating. And I've found that the more you know about the victim, the more you know about the crime. I mean, when it comes right down to it, we don't have any proof River actually killed that man."

He frowned and tipped his head to one side. "I'm afraid I don't understand." He glanced at Frankie. "Is there suddenly some question as to how the orderly was killed?"

"I think what the lieutenant means," Frankie said, "is that there's always room to question, Dr. Melrose," she explained. "The obvious answer isn't always the right one, and we don't have any eyewitnesses, after all."

He nodded. "Well, I'm sure the Vermont State Police have taken all that into consideration. And…well, I don't mean to tell you your jobs here, but certainly you are aware they are the ones investigating the murder. Your department's only part in this is to find and arrest Michael Corbett if he shows up here in Blackberry."

Frankie lowered her head, a nod of concession. "I am fully aware of that, Doctor. Don't you worry. We'll keep an eye out for Corbett, and we will contact you if we find him."

"Fine. I appreciate that. Before I take my leave, I just have one more question." He turned his sharp gaze on Jax. "How did you know Michael Corbett's nickname was River?"

Jax felt her heart turn a somersault, but kept her face stone-cold expressionless. "Heard someone mention it, I guess."

"Of course you did," Frankie said, lowering a hand to Jax's shoulder. But her grip was firm, rather than friendly. "Don't forget, Doctor, Corbett lived in this town for a year before the incident. Everyone knew him as River."

"I never could stand the guy," Kurt muttered. "Arrogant big-city cops don't belong in Blackberry."

Jax felt the barb, knew it was aimed at her as much as it was at River, though she almost laughed at his referring to Syracuse as a big city. He paced toward her and turned to sit in the nearby chair. She braced a foot on it and gave it a shove, so he landed on his ass on the floor.

Campanelli and Matthews had to turn away to keep from laughing, even as Jax leaned over and extended a hand. "Look before you sit, Kurt. You could have hurt yourself."

He hadn't seen her move the chair, couldn't be sure he hadn't just missed, though he had a pretty damn good idea. He ignored her hand and got up on his own.

"We'll be in touch, Dr. Melrose," Frankie said, completely in the dark and looking irritated with her nephew. "Meanwhile, we do have other work to do, so…"

He nodded. "I'll get out of your hair."

"Good." Frankie stood there, her hand on Jax's shoulder until the man had left the station. Then she said softly, "My office," and turned and walked directly there.

Jax shrugged and followed her, feeling the eyes of the

other cops on her back the entire way. She walked in behind Frankie, who closed the door.

"How did you know he went by 'River'?"

Jax frowned. "I told you, I heard someone say it once. It's no big deal, Frankie."

Frankie studied her for a long moment. Finally, she nodded toward a chair, and Jax sat down. Frankie walked behind her desk. "You know, despite that he's a complete moron, Kurt did make a point out there. Cops from larger departments do tend to come here with something of an attitude. They tend to think we're backwoods, backward and none too sharp. But we're not. We're good cops, just like you are."

"Frankie, I would never think otherwise. Please know that."

She nodded slowly. "You serious about taking on my job?"

"Serious enough that I gave my notice to Syracuse already. But I'm not taking the job yet. I've got two weeks, right?"

Frankie lifted her silvering eyebrows. "Two weeks during which you're…what? Some kind of free agent?"

"Off duty. That's all."

"You break the law, you aren't going to get hired. My recommendation only carries so much weight with the town council, Jax. You dig yourself a hole, and I'm not going to be able to get you out."

"I know that."

Frankie nodded. "Chances are, if River did come back to town, he'd show up at the house. It's where he lived, after all."

"Can't say it hadn't occurred to me."

"We should put surveillance on the place."

"You have a cop *living* in the place. Can't get much better round-the-clock surveillance than that."

"Could be dangerous."

"Oh, come on, Frankie. If I can't hold my own against a scrawny mental patient, I'd better give up and go home right now."

Frankie pursed her lips.

"You've only got three men, Frankie. You send 'em out to my place, you're liable to be left shorthanded. Besides, it wouldn't look good for me."

"How so?"

Jax rolled her eyes. "Kurt's already got a chip on his shoulder where I'm concerned. You tell the men you don't trust me to watch my own place, send them out there to babysit, how am I supposed to step in as their commanding officer later on?"

Frankie sighed, lowered her head. "You have a point. And you're probably right."

Jax had to forcibly restrain herself from sighing in relief.

"You know, Jax, I always had the feeling there was more to this case than met the eye. I did a lot of digging into it. On my own time."

Jax felt the surprise showing on her face. "You did?"

"Mmm. Never could quite wrap my mind around the notion of River Corbett as a killer. Crazy or not. But I didn't find a damn thing that could help him. Seems to me you have the same feeling."

Jax studied her, and finally, she nodded. "Yeah. I do. And I think a background check of the orderly would be a great place to start."

Frankie nodded slowly and picked up the phone. She told Rosie to put her through to Sergeant Christopher Pensky at the Vermont's State Police Investigative Unit, and when she was connected, she said, "Chris? It's Frankie down in Blackberry. Yeah. Yeah, it's been a long time. Oh, getting ready to retire, actually. Coupla' weeks from now if all goes well. Listen, I need a favor. That orderly that was killed at the state hospital. You do any background on him?"

Then she listened, and as she did her eyes met Jax's and widened.

"Well, I'll be. No, I had no reason for asking. Just a routine follow-up question. No big deal. Thanks, Chris."

She hung up the phone and stared into Jax's eyes. "How did you know?"

Jax put on her most innocent expression. "How did I know what? There was something in the guy's background?"

"Just that he was using a false name, had a record and had only been working there a week."

Jax lifted her eyebrows. "So what did his rap sheet look like?"

"Why do I get the feeling you already know?"

"Come on, Frankie, how could I possibly know?"

Frankie narrowed her eyes and began reading from the notes she'd scribbled. "Armed robbery, assault, conspiracy. Seems he sometimes hurt people for money. They're faxing us the information."

Jax nodded. "Makes you wonder, doesn't it?"

"Makes you wonder what?"

She shrugged. "Well, how does a guy like that get hired at a state mental hospital? He had to know they'd run his prints, get the results within a week and fire him on the spot. So why would he want to work there for such a short time?"

"You think he was there to commit some kind of a crime," Frankie said, reading her.

"Probably a crime he'd committed before. I mean, that would be most likely. So, odds are he was either there to rob the place or put a hurting on someone for a fee."

"You're saying he was hired to harm Corbett, making the killing a case of self-defense. And you're reaching, Jax, and I'd like to know just where the hell you're getting all this from."

Jax shrugged. "It's a thought. One of a thousand possibilities that happens to be the one my gut likes the best. That's all."

Frankie swore and snatched her car keys off her desk. "Come with me."

"Where are we—?"

"Just do it!" Frankie stomped out of the office, barking to Rosie that she'd be back in twenty. She made angry foot-prints in the snow all the way to her black-and-white SUV, which was parked in front of the station in its own parking spot. One of the perks of the job, Jax guessed. The chief didn't have to go around back to the parking lot. Frankie opened the door without unlocking it, got in and had the thing in motion before Jax even got her seat belt fastened around her.

"Where are you taking me?" Jax asked her. "Come on, Frankie, I didn't mean to make you angry."

"I'm not angry. I'm frustrated as hell. We're going to my house."

She drove out of the town limits and over a narrow, twist-ing road toward the Blackberry Inn, but pulled into a drive-way a few hundred yards before it. Her house. A ranch-style home that seemed out-of-place amid all the Victorians, but cozy and warm, somehow, with its glass-enclosed front porch filled with enough plants to double as a greenhouse, and a fat black cat snoozing in a pool of sunlight on one sill.

Jax followed Frankie into the house, barely having time to look at it as she rushed to keep up with the woman. Frankie blew past the glass-enclosed porch, through a door that led into a dining room, and through that into what appeared to be a library. The large room's walls were lined with shelves, pa-perback books filling every one of them, and as Frankie moved to the desk at the far end of the room, Jax noticed they were all science fiction novels.

"Wow," she said. "I never would have pegged you as a trek-kie type. Have you read all of—?"

A bang brought her head around. Frankie had dropped a fat manila envelope on her desk, and even now was unwind-ing the string from its tab, flipping it open and taking things out. When she found what she wanted, she handed it to Jax.

"There," she said. "Take a look. A long, thorough look."

Jax did. The woman was gorgeous. A brunette with the bone china features and huge hollow eyes of a runway model. Way too thin. But in a waiflike way that made her beautiful. "Who is she?"

"Stephanie Corbett," Frankie said. "At least she was, before half her house went up in flames and her along with it."

Jax closed her eyes and let that sink in. This was her, River's wife. The one he had allegedly murdered. "She was gorgeous," she said, not knowing what else to say.

"She was young, she was alive and she was pregnant. She didn't deserve to go out that way, Jax. No one does."

"Frankie, I'm the last person in the world to argue with that. You know that."

"I do. I just thought you might need reminding. Every scrap of evidence points to River as the killer. There's nothing to suggest otherwise. Believe me, I tried to find something—anything—but I came up empty. So if you've decided to become this guy's savior for some insane reason, you oughtta know up-front what you're up against."

Jax nodded slowly. "I don't want to be anyone's savior. Believe me, that's the last thing I want. But Frankie, tell me this. What made you try so hard?"

Frankie laid the photo on her desk, sighed heavily. "I didn't think he did it. I didn't want to think he did it. He's a nice guy. Hell, he's a great guy. It was completely out of character. I just… I finally had to let it go. Jax, even he didn't fight it. Didn't argue his innocence."

"Yeah, but couldn't that have been because he couldn't remember what happened?"

Frankie nodded. "It bothered me. It's never stopped bothering me." She closed her eyes. "You're a good cop, Jax. I don't want to see you screw up your career over this."

"It may be a little late for that."

Frankie looked up fast. "You've seen him, haven't you?" Then she held up a hand. "Don't answer that. Hell, if you're bound and determined to dig into this mess, take this." She shoved the photo back into the envelope and handed it to Jax. "It's all the unofficial work I did, everything I learned after the case was supposedly closed. There's a copy of the autopsy report in there. That's on file, too, of course, but it came in after the case was already closed. No trial, no need for it. So there's stuff that was never made public. I don't even know if River knows what's in that report."

"Thank you, Frankie."

"Don't thank me. If you step too far over the line, and this backfires on you, there's not gonna be a damn thing I can do to get you into my office."

"Understood."

"Good." She handed her the SUV's key ring. "You can drive us back. That tank out there comes with the job. You may as well get a feel for it just in case, by some miracle, you don't manage to blow yourself right out of the running."

He pored over the police file throughout the morning, and by noontime, when the chills hit, he'd read it end to end, scrutinized every comma, and was still no closer to knowing the truth. But he'd filled an empty notebook with things to be done. Number one among them should be contacting his lawyer. He'd only barely been aware he'd even had a lawyer. Ethan had taken care of everything. River had been…hell, he'd been in no shape back then.

At any rate, it was around noon that he started feeling cold. He stoked up the fire in the living room and moved his notepad closer to it. But within a few minutes he was shivering. So he made a cup of tea and wrapped a blanket around himself, continuing to jot his plans in his notepad, even as the shivering increased.

* * *

Jax returned home, half-afraid her houseguest wouldn't be there. And it occurred to her that finding him gone should be a relief, but she knew it wouldn't be. There was something about him, something that tugged at her on a level too deep and complicated to analyze right now.

She unlocked the front door and was greeted by Rex, who stood patiently waiting for her to come in, then nudged her hand for a pat on the head.

"Well, you certainly have changed your attitude, haven't you? What, you're my friend now? Huh? Just 'cause I'm shacked up with your favorite guy? Is that it?"

He ignored her, turned and walked through the house into the living room. Jax dropped her car keys and her bundle of papers on the table, and walked in behind him. The heat hit her in the face when she walked in. She thought it must be close to eighty degrees in her drafty old house, and her gaze snapped from the blazing fire in the hearth to the man huddled in a blanket in a chair close to it.

"River?" Alarm surged inside her as she took in his face. It was pale and damp, and he was shivering.

"Ah, hell, River." She hurried to him, pushed his head up and back against the chair so she could press a hand to his forehead. "God, you're burning up."

He opened his eyes. "I like when you touch me."

"I'm calling my father."

He didn't object, or at least not loudly enough to make her take note. In fact, when she let go of him to grab the phone, he just let his head fall back against the chair.

She hit her dad's number at the clinic, with a quick look at her watch as she did. It was only five-twenty. Her father was there most nights until six. She guessed right. The receptionist answered on the second ring. "Pinedale Veterinary Clinic," the woman said.

"I need to speak to Dr. Jackson. This is his daughter. It's important."

"Sure, Miss Jackson. I'll put him right on."

There was a pause, a pause that seemed endless to Jax as she gathered up the police files River had been reading, and tucked them away on a shelf in the coat closet. River slumped in the chair, and she worried that he might fall on the floor. But he didn't quite. She moved closer, put a hand on his shoulder to keep him from tipping any farther.

It hit her that helping River would be a risk for her father. But she didn't see that she had any choice here. They'd just have to be careful. She'd take the full shot if there were any repercussions. She'd protect her dad.

"Hello, honey," he said into her ear.

"Hi, Dad. Listen, um—I need your help and I need you to be extremely discreet about it."

She could almost see him, his narrow face thoughtful as he analyzed her words. After a moment, he said, "What's wrong?"

She bit her lip. "Dad, this is very sensitive. Are we private?"

"Well, of course, Cassie. What's going on?"

She sighed. River slumped in spite of her hand on his shoulder, and she had to quickly tuck the phone between her neck and ear to grip him with both hands. "I have a…a stray here, and no one can know he's here. He's kind of…wanted. And I think he's sick. Really sick, Dad."

Her father hesitated. "This is about that dog?"

"He's got a pretty high fever, shaking with chills, pale."

"The *dog* is *pale*?"

"It's not a dog, Dad. It's a person. I'll explain when you get here. Bring antibiotics and whatever else you think you might need. Please. I really need your help. And…use the back door, okay?" She didn't want her father seeing River until she'd had a chance to prepare him. He was not going to like this.

"Sure, honey. I can be there in a half hour. I was just finishing with a patient here. Border collie—got hit by a car."

"Is it going to be all right?"

"Looks that way. I'll see you soon, hon."

"Thanks, Dad." She let go of River, hit the cutoff and tossed the phone onto the sofa, then turned to lean over her patient.

"Come on, now, River. Come with me." She moved around in front of him, crouched low and pulled his arms around her shoulders. "Come on, help me out here."

He lifted his head a little. She tugged him, and he came off the chair, only to land on it again. Then his arms tightened around her neck and he tried again. "Where we going?"

"Couch." She straightened and he got to his feet with her help. "That's better." She moved him over to the sofa, then crouched slowly so he could sit on its edge. But as soon as he touched down, he fell backward, his arms still locked around her neck, so that he landed on his back, lengthways on the sofa, and she lay atop him, her face inches from his.

His eyes met hers, momentarily clear enough to make her wonder if he'd done the falling bit on purpose, and then his hands threaded in her hair and he drew her head down, closing the distance between his lips and hers. For some illogical reason that had very little to do with his health or her career, she didn't pull away, though she could have. She let him draw her mouth to his, let him kiss her, even relaxed her chest against him, and ran her fingers through his hair as she tipped her head sideways, and kissed him back. His lips against hers were feverish and hot and hungry. His hands on the back of her head pressed and massaged and rubbed, and his chest beneath hers pounded.

She lifted her head, not because she wanted to, but because common sense intervened. The man was burning up with fever, probably didn't even know what he was doing. But damn, he did it well.

He blinked up at her. "I…didn't…mean…"

"You did so." She pulled herself off him, got up on her feet and strode out of the room.

"Cassandra—"

"Stay put, River. I'm getting you some aspirin." She hurried up the stairs and into the second-floor bathroom, then braced her hands on the sink basin and stared at her reflection in the mirror.

"Is that it then?" she asked herself softly. "Is that why you're putting your ass on the line for this guy, because you're hot for him?"

Her reflection didn't answer her. She didn't really think it was possible a physical attraction she'd only just recognized as a full-blown case of the hots could be motivating her to help River. Hell, she hated women who did self-destructive things just because of some male. It was the height of stupidity. And yeah, maybe she realized now that he'd put a match to her loins, that she'd been turned on by him. The flirting she'd told herself was only teasing had been dead-on-balls serious. But she didn't think it was the *only* thing motivating her.

Hell, it was far from the only thing and she knew it.

"Corral the libido, honey. You've got work to do." She cranked on the taps, cupped her hands beneath the flow and splashed cold water on her face. Then she let it drip from her chin while she located a plastic basin and ran it full of cool water. Grabbing a washcloth from the stack and a bottle of aspirin from the cabinet, she carried them and the basin of water back downstairs. She set the aspirin on the coffee table, the basin on the floor, then rushed to the kitchen for a glass of water. When she returned River was sitting up slightly, trying to tug his blanket out from under him to get it around him more thoroughly. He was still shivering.

"Here," she said. "Take these." She handed him three aspirin tablets and the glass of water. He swallowed them down.

"Now sit up a little and I'll get your shirt off. It's soaked."

He sat up, Jax putting her arm around him to help him. And she felt that tingle again. Dammit, she never should have kissed him. Now this heat was going to rear its head every time she got close to the man. What kind of moron cop fell for a suspect? It was the first thing in the book on dumb things a cop could do.

River leaned on her as she tugged the shirt off him, over his head, and then she let him go. He fell backward, and she sat on the edge of the sofa, wet the washcloth and brought it to his chest. His hot, sweaty, magnificent chest. "Damn," she muttered. "You had to throw the switch, didn't you?"

"What?"

"Nothing. You just remember who started it." She wiped his chest with the cool cloth, then wet it again and ran it over his neck, around to his nape. He closed his eyes, sighed, and she knew it felt good to him. One last dunk and then she laid the cloth over his forehead.

By the time she heard her father's car in the driveway, River's fever was coming down, and he was claiming he felt fine. She got up, went to look out, and noticed for the first time that all the curtains in the living room had been drawn shut. Her dad went around the house to the back door. She watched him go.

River was starting to get up.

"No, no, stay there. It's all right, it's just my father."

He blinked at her, his brows bending in confusion.

"I told you I called him," she said. "River, I had to do something—you were burning up with fever. You can trust him. I promise."

She saw his Adam's apple swell and recede as he swallowed, and he nodded once. "Guess I don't have much choice." He let himself fall back again, replacing the cloth on his own forehead.

Jax ran to the kitchen and opened the door before her father even got to it. "Come on in, Dad."

He did, and he hugged her, and then he looked down at Rex and smiled. "My goodness, you're weren't kidding. He is a beauty. Yes, you are." He knelt and gave the German shepherd his due. "So where's this patient?"

"Come on, he's in here."

She took her father's hand. He picked up his bag with the other and let her tug him into the living room.

She watched her father's eyes as he looked at River, lying on the sofa. Then he shifted his gaze to hers again.

"He needs help. And no one can know he's here."

Ben frowned. "So you said on the phone. What I want to know is why?" And when she didn't answer immediately, he added, "Is he some kind of criminal, Cassie?"

She drew a breath. "He saved my life my first night here."

"How?"

"That pond across the street. I thought it was a meadow, and I walked out onto it, went right through the ice. He came out of nowhere, pulled me out and ended up going through, too. He almost drowned, Dad." She closed her eyes briefly. "This could be risky for you—but I'll take the fall if anyone finds out."

Ben's breath escaped him, and though there were still questions in his ever-sad eyes, he didn't need to hear any more than that. "The risk to me isn't an issue, Cassie." He went to the sofa, touched River's face, offered him a slight smile. "I'm Ben Jackson," he said. "Does anything hurt?"

"Throat. Head. Stomach." River seemed to have trouble keeping his eyes open. "What doesn't hurt would make a shorter list."

Ben nodded and turned to Jax. "Have you given him anything?"

"Aspirin, twenty minutes ago. I think his fever's starting to come down some."

"Okay." He took a stethoscope from his bag and spent some time listening to River's chest, before helping him sit up and lean forward so he could listen to his back. Then he laid him down again and used a flashlight to look into his eyes and his throat. "You've probably got pneumonia, son. A little water in your lungs, combined with other factors—the cold, the shock on your body." He turned to Jax. "He should see a doctor, get a prescription for some antibiotics—"

"We can't do that. Can you leave him something?"

Ben frowned, and Jax thought he was really getting worried. But eventually, he nodded. "I can leave you something. Animals take antibiotics, too. Are you taking any medications, Mr....?"

"Not anymore," River said. "But up to a couple of days ago I had as much Haldol in my veins as I did blood, I think."

"Haldol?"

"Dad, it's a long story. He was in mental hospital, under extreme treatment, when an attempt was made on his life. He escaped. He's wanted. And I'm trying to help him."

Ben Jackson didn't react. Her mother would have fired off rounds of objections and questions and concerns. But her father just stayed quiet, considering, taking his time, and when he did reply, it was as if he'd weighed the thousand and one questions that had occurred to him, and picked the most important one.

"What were you being treated for?"

"I took a bullet to the brain in the line of duty. They couldn't remove it without pretty grave risks, so it's still there. It causes blackouts from time to time."

He nodded slowly. "I see." He took a hypodermic from his bag, unwrapped it and filled it with fluid from a vial, then gave River an injection, all the while mulling things over in his mind.

He didn't believe what River had told him. Oh, he was convincing, but Jax knew her father too well. He took a packet

of antibiotics out of his bag and set them on the table. "Take two at a time—they're in dog-size doses. Two in the morning, two at night. This is enough for ten days."

"Thank you," River said. "I…I'll find some way to repay you."

Her father looked him square in the eye. "If you hurt my daughter," he said, his voice gentle and soft, and perfectly calm, "it would be bad. Really bad. Don't doubt that."

Then he turned and took Jax by the arm. "I want a word with you in the kitchen."

She sighed, but went with him, sending a reassuring glance at River over her shoulder. In the kitchen, Ben stopped, turned to face her and said flatly, "That man is lying to you."

8

Jax frowned and moved to the farthest end of the kitchen to make sure River was out of earshot. "What are you talking about?"

Her father gave a hasty glance back toward the doorway. "You don't give Haldol for a brain injury. It's a psychotropic drug, Cassie. It's given for serious mental illness—schizophrenia, for example."

"He's not schizophrenic."

"And you're a psychiatrist now?"

She made a face at her father, vaguely aware he was more animated, more passionate than she'd seen him since he had come out of prison. "Dad, I need you to trust me on this. I'm telling you he has a bullet in his brain. Not a mental illness."

"No. No competent psychiatrist would prescribe Haldol…at least I can't think of a reason…" He lowered his head. "Cassie, is this man staying here with you?"

"Yes. And yes, he's a fugitive. And yes, I know how much it would destroy you and Mom to lose me. Dad, he saved my life. He's not a threat."

"You can't be sure about that. Especially if he's ill and off his meds. Honey, he's entirely unpredictable in this state."

"Or would be," she stated, "if he were schizophrenic. He's not. I've checked into his past and there's nothing even close

to that." She paused, frowning hard. "Tell me, Dad, what would happen to a person who didn't need Haldol and was given it anyway?"

He frowned in turn, his face suddenly even more troubled. "Depends on the dosage. He could become lethargic, extremely docile, weak, unable to focus on specific problems or work through issues in his mind." His eyes narrowed. "Are you telling me you think he was deliberately misprescribed?"

"I don't know," she said slowly. "It's possible. It might be a good way to mess with someone's mind. Would it have an impact on his memory?"

Her father shrugged. "I suppose it could. It's quite likely, in fact."

"I need to get my hands on River's medical records," Jax said, pacing across the kitchen, talking almost to herself. "I need to get the entire case file, both from the state hospital and from his doctor. Am I going to need a court order?"

Her father sighed deeply. "*You* would," he said. "He wouldn't. Those records are his property, he has a right to them." He said it so reluctantly she knew he didn't approve of her helping River. And why would he? Frankly, Jax was surprised her father hadn't thrown him out into the snow. And for just a moment, she wondered why that was. Dad was being awfully calm about all this, for a man who'd lost one daughter to a criminal already.

"So he should, what, just show up and demand them?" she asked.

"Not if he's wanted by the law. He's going to have to work through a lawyer."

"A lawyer would have to turn him in if he knew where River was holing up."

Sighing, Ben said, "A lawyer can't tell what he doesn't know." He put a hand on her shoulder. "Cassie, don't be gullible. Don't make yourself vulnerable just because you feel sorry for the man."

"When have you *ever* known me to be gullible or vulnerable to anyone, Dad?"

He studied her face for a long moment, then nodded. "Never," he said. "I'm not going to tell your mother he's here. It would just worry her. Don't let your guard down, Cassie. Promise me?"

"I promise."

Nodding, he moved back to the doorway and looked through. Jax did, too, and she saw the dog, head on River's chest as River stroked and spoke softly to him. She glanced at her father, saw his brows rise, and knew exactly what he was thinking. He'd always believed dogs to be the best judges of character. If the dog loved the man, he couldn't be all bad.

"You should get him to take a cool bath. I know your instinct is to wrap him up, keep him warm when he's shivering like that, but the fact is, he's too hot and the aspirin you gave him isn't working well enough. You need to cool him down some more."

"Okay."

"Get hold of a thermometer. He wouldn't like the type in my bag." She smiled at that. "If he gets up over a hundred and two, you'd best call me."

"I will."

"Get those antibiotics into him—starting around midnight."

"Not right now?" she asked.

"No. The shot I gave him was penicillin. It should jump-start things. By midnight he should be able to handle the next dose. Then morning and evening thereafter. As close to twelve hours apart as you can manage. And never on an empty stomach. Flood him with liquids, feed him simple, nutritious meals, but nothing too complicated. He needs to build his strength but he may not have much of an appetite for a while. I'll see if I can locate a vial of vitamin K. An injection of that would do him a world of good. If I can I'll bring it over tomorrow."

She nodded. "Thanks, Dad. I don't know what I'd do without you."

"It goes both ways, Cassie. Don't you forget it."

"I won't."

"He shown any symptoms of trouble? Talking to himself? Making up far-fetched stories? Sweating a lot?"

"He didn't sweat at all until that fever hit him. And his only far-fetched story so far is that he left the mental hospital because someone there tried to kill him. I've found physical evidence that makes that story look pretty likely."

He nodded slowly. "Even if it were true, he must have been there for a reason."

"Yeah. And I'm afraid the reason might not have been valid. He might have been set up, Dad, to take the fall for something he didn't do."

Her father went very still, very silent. He lowered his eyes in a way that set Jax's teeth on edge. But no. He didn't know, he couldn't. "Then you have to find out the truth," he said.

It stunned her.

Her father turned for the door, then paused. "When you get hold of those medical records, let me know. I have friends in psychiatry. Some of the best in the business. I could have one of them take a look for you."

"That's on the top of my list. Thanks, Dad."

She went to him, hugged him hard. He kissed her cheek and left the house, though she could tell he hated doing it.

Jax returned to River in the living room. He sat on the sofa, back propped against the corner between its back and its arm, legs bent, blanket pulled tight around his shoulders. He was still pale, but he looked a good deal better than he had before.

"You need a cool bath and a lot of liquids. And I need to go to the grocery store." She put a hand on his forehead. Still damp and hot, but not as hot as before. "Fever's not as bad as it was."

"Your father is worried about you," he said. He said it as if it was the only thing of particular interest to him at the moment. "Really worried."

Jax nodded. "He worries more than most."

"Why is that?"

"Oh, he's got reason, believe me. Tell you what, you take that bath while I run to the store, and then, if you're feeling up to it, I'll tell you about it while we go over some more files. Okay?"

"You got more files?"

She nodded. "Frankie gave me a whole packet full. She was digging into your case on her own time, back when it first went down."

"You're kidding me."

Jax shook her head. "No. But, um…she's on to me, River. I didn't tell her about you," she added quickly at the look of alarm that flashed into his deep brown eyes. "But I slipped a little today when your doctor showed up at the station."

"Ethan is in town?"

She nodded. "Yeah. Said he wanted to be notified if we found you. He seems genuinely concerned."

River closed his eyes. "I hate putting him through this—I just…I don't see that I have any choice."

"Neither do I. I referred to you as River while he was there. He wanted to know how I knew to call you that, and Frankie jumped in and covered for me. I think Ethan was convinced. Frankie wasn't, though."

"Hell." He lowered his head, shaking it slowly.

"She's on your side, River. She never believed you started that fire. That's why she kept on investigating even after you entered your plea. But she couldn't find proof."

He looked surprised by that.

"Still," Jax continued, "I didn't admit anything. And she didn't push."

River shook his head. "I should get the hell out of here. Too many people know. Frankie, your father…"

"Yeah, well…I'm not entirely convinced you're wrong about that. But River, if we need to move you, we have to plan it out first. Find you a safe, logical place to hole up. It would be stupid for you to just walk out the door without a plan. Especially in the shape you're in."

He stared at her, drew a breath, let it out slowly. "I'll manage to run my own bath. Go ahead, run your errands."

She nodded, got to her feet, then turned to him once more. "Will you tell me where you got the nickname?"

He was sitting up by then, looking tired. He pushed a hand through his damp hair, nodding. "When I was a kid, Ethan's dad bought me a canoe. Beautiful thing. Stained wood with a shine so glossy you could see yourself in it. We all went camping together that summer, and Ethan dared me to shoot the rapids with the canoe. Hell, I was never one to resist a dare."

She smiled. "How old were you?"

"Thirteen." He shook his head slowly. "It's a wonder teenage boys survive to adulthood. Anyway, I didn't know there was a freaking waterfall at the end of the rapids. Ethan knew—he'd been camping there before. Thought it was a big joke. He never expected it would damn near kill me."

Jax felt her smile die. "You went over the falls?"

He nodded. "Yeah. The canoe was demolished, and I almost was myself. Broke my wrist and a couple of ribs—damn near drowned." He shook his head. "Poor Ethan. I think his father was madder than I was."

She lifted her brows. "And this was your best friend."

"*Is* my best friend. We were kids." He shrugged. "It's a guy thing. Women don't get it."

"I bet your parents never let you go camping with him again," she said.

He shrugged. "My parents were gone by then. I was part of his family."

"I see."

She didn't, she realized. But there was something niggling at her. Something telling her there was more here than met the eye. And the entire time she was wandering the aisles of Purdy's Grocery, picking out ginger ale, chicken soup, gelatin, vitamins and extra strength pain and fever medication, the new information was processing its way through her brain. River's best friend had nearly got him killed when he was a kid. And had been in charge of his care when someone else had tried to kill him as an adult. Was it coincidence? Or was there more to Ethan Melrose than met the eye?

"Lieutenant Jackson?"

She turned, shopping basket in hand, and came face-to-face with the man himself. He was impressive looking. Expensive suit, not a wrinkle in it, and not the same one he'd been wearing this morning. Nails trimmed and clean, glasses smudge free, hair neat and gelled enough to stay that way. He cared about his appearance. She filed that bit of information away and painted a smile on her face.

"Please," she said, "call me Jax. Everyone does." Not everyone, she thought. River called her Cassandra. No one else called her that. "What's wrong, aren't they feeding you well at the inn?"

"They feed me too well," he said. "If I stay around long, I'll have to spend a week in the gym when I get home."

She smiled, nodding in agreement as she glanced at his purchases. Antacid tablets, bottled water. "I hope you're not sick."

He shook his head. "Nerves. I'm worried about River."

"I'm sorry. I should have realized. Are you...staying in town long?"

"I really don't know what my plans are. My home is only

an hour away. I just—I just feel like I need to be here, you know? If he shows up here, I'll stay. If he surfaces somewhere else I'll go to him immediately."

"You really care about this patient, don't you?"

"River's more than a patient. He's also a friend." He sighed. "There's not much I wouldn't do for him."

Jax put a hand on his forearm. "I wonder if he knows how lucky he is to have you on his side."

"It hasn't done him much good, not that I haven't tried."

"I'm sure you've done your best, Dr. Melrose."

"Ethan," he corrected, and he put his hand over hers on his arm. "Jax…would I be out of line if I asked you to have dinner with me while I'm in town?"

She met his eyes, smiled slowly. "You'd be out of line if you didn't," she said softly. "Tomorrow night?"

"Absolutely. Can I pick you up?"

"Why don't we meet at the restaurant instead? Say seven o'clock?"

He nodded. "I'll be looking forward to it."

"So will I." She wanted to take her hand away from his, but she couldn't do that and still seem flirtatious, so she let it remain there, until he finally lowered his own.

"Good night then," he said.

She nodded, and kept the smile on her face as she paid for her purchases and headed back to her car. When she drove back to the house, she told herself this dinner was an excellent opportunity to get more information about Ethan, and about his diagnosis and treatment of River.

When she got back to the house, River was sitting in a chair at the small kitchen table. His hair was wet from the cool bath. He wore jeans and a T-shirt. He didn't look up when she came in.

She closed and locked the door, set the grocery bag on the

counter and began taking items out of it. "Are you feeling any better?" she asked.

He didn't reply.

She set the tea bags on a cupboard shelf, then several cans of soup and packets of gelatin mix. "Are you hungry? Dad said you should be eating as much as you can manage. You need to get your strength back."

He still didn't reply, and when she took the bottle of ginger ale from the bag and turned to the fridge, she looked at him, wondering why.

He sat still, hands in his lap, gaze seemingly turned inward. He wasn't looking at her. He didn't even appear to be hearing her.

Jax put the bottles in the fridge and then went to him. She knelt beside his chair to put her eyes level with his. "River?"

Nothing. She touched his face, felt no trace of any remaining fever. Then she tried snapping her fingers in front of his eyes. "River? Come on, talk to me." She gripped his shoulders, shook him slightly.

Rex came toward her, growling a warning, so she stopped. "All right. All right, boy, I'm not going to hurt him."

The dog whined and then lay down on River's feet.

Frowning, and completely unsure what to do, Jax put away the remaining groceries, set the pain reliever on the counter, folded the paper bag and tucked it into a drawer under the sink. She kept a close eye on him as she got a glass down and filled it with ginger ale. Returning to the table, she touched his face again. Seemed she couldn't stop herself from touching him.

She was still standing there, one hand on his cheek, when he blinked, sucked in a sharp breath and looked right into her eyes, his own completely confused. "What…?"

"It's okay. I think…you zoned out for a few minutes. That's all."

River's eyes widened and he surged to his feet. "Oh God.

Are you all right?" He gripped her shoulders, searching her face. "Did I hurt you, did I—"

"River, for crying out loud, I'm fine." She clasped his face between her palms to make him stand still. "I'm fine. Okay?"

He sighed, lowering his head slowly. "How long have I been…out?"

"That's what this was, then? One of your blackouts?"

He nodded, not looking at her. "I don't remember anything since I got out of the tub and got dressed."

She nodded. "Well, depending on how long you were in the tub, I'd say this lasted fifteen to twenty minutes, at the most. I just got back from the store."

Slowly, he lifted his head. "Did I do anything? Threaten you or—"

"River, you didn't do anything but sit there and stare at the empty space in front of your nose. I don't think you could have done anything if you'd wanted to."

He frowned and sank into his chair. "I never know. Steph always said it was like I was asleep with my eyes open."

"That's exactly what it was like."

"But it's not *always* like that."

"No?" Jax sighed and pulled out a chair to sit beside him. "River, has anyone ever witnessed you doing anything *besides* sitting still during one of these blackouts?"

He lowered his head. "Yeah. I'm afraid so. That's another reason I shouldn't be staying here, Cassandra. I could hurt you. I get violent sometimes, agitated. I lash out at whatever or whoever is close enough."

She nodded slowly. "Your wife told you that?"

"No. She never saw me like that. At least…not until…" He closed his eyes, shook his head, not able or maybe not willing to complete the sentence.

"So who *has* seen you like that? Who told you that you get violent when you black out?"

He sighed. "Ethan."

"Ethan," she repeated. "And he's the only one?"

"Yeah. Thank God."

She pursed her lips. "Yeah. Thank God for friends like Ethan."

"Don't. Don't sound like you doubt his motives. Ethan's the only person who's stood by me through all of this. God, I'd have fallen apart without him."

"River, I hate to be the one to break it to you, but you pretty much fell apart *with* him."

He gnawed his lip, shook his head. "He did the best he could. No one could have done better."

"Maybe. Maybe not. Listen, I want you to contact your lawyer. The man who brought your plea to the D.A. and negotiated on your behalf. His name was in the file on your case. Derrick Brown. Do you remember him?"

"Yeah. But I already wrote him once and it didn't do any good."

"Are you sure he ever got the letter?"

Clearly he hadn't considered that.

"I want you to tell him to get copies of all your medical records from the state hospital, and swear him to secrecy. Don't tell him where you are. He'll be obligated to pass along any information as to your whereabouts, if he's asked. Maybe even if he's not. Depends on how ethical he is and what he believes about you, I imagine. But he can damn well get your records."

"What's that going to tell us?"

She sighed, and decided against voicing her growing gut feeling that Ethan Melrose might not be as good a friend as he seemed. Yet she couldn't keep the whole truth from River. "My father says you don't treat a brain injury with Haldol."

He frowned, lifting his head. "I thought you said your father is a surgeon, not a psychiatrist."

"He's a veterinarian, actually. Was a surgeon once. And he's going to confirm it with some psychiatrist friends of his, but his initial reaction is that you are either schizophrenic or being treated incorrectly. We need to know which it is."

"Ethan never said I was schizophrenic."

"That's because you're not."

He was quiet, maybe mulling that over in his mind. So she got out the big envelope from Frankie and set it on the table. "I'm gonna make us some dinner. And then we're going to comb through these files, okay?"

He looked at her, and seemingly forgot about the matter at hand as he did. "And you're going to tell me why your dad worries so much about your safety," he reminded her.

"Isn't it normal for a father to worry about his little girl?"

"Not when the little girl is the sharpest and maybe the toughest cop I've met in twenty years, no."

She lifted her brows at the compliment. "You'd be one of very few people to know my secrets, River. But hell, maybe that would make you feel better about being forced to trust me with so many of yours, huh?"

"I do trust you. We're way past the point where you could have been orchestrating all of this just to get a pair of handcuffs on me and take me to the nearest jail cell."

"Hey, don't rule out the handcuffs just yet." She sent him a wink, caught the surprised and interested look he sent in return. But even then she sensed there were things he was holding back. She sensed it right to her core. "I got some ham and cheese, and an excellent loaf of twelve grain bread. Soup and sandwiches sound good?"

"Sounds good to my head. I'll have to let you know about my stomach."

"How is the rest of you feeling?"

He shrugged. "My chest is kind of…heavy. My throat's a

little sore and my head aches. And even with all that I feel better than I have in a year."

She smiled. "You keep doing that well and I might even let you have a potato chip."

"Just one?"

"Not really. I didn't buy any junk food, but it was tempting."

He smiled. "I like you, Cassandra Jackson. I don't know why the hell you're trying to save my worthless ass, but I'm grateful."

She turned to the counter, reached for a can of soup and took out a loaf of bread. "Well, then, maybe I should tell you why." Drawing a breath, she said, "When I was sixteen, I had a sister."

"I saw the photo on the hearth. She's gorgeous. You two look a lot alike."

"She was killed."

She heard him suck in a breath. "When?"

"Shortly after that photo was taken, as a matter of fact."

As she made the sandwiches, warmed the soup and spilled her guts, River listened in what seemed like rapt interest. She found herself telling him more than she'd ever told anyone, talking about her feelings of helplessness, her anger at her father for the act that had robbed her and her mom of him for twelve long years, when they'd already lost Carrie. Her admiration of her parents—the power of their marriage at having survived two such devastating crises. And on and on.

By the time she finished, she had sliced the sandwiches diagonally and put them on plates on the table. She'd poured the soup into two bowls and got herself a Diet Coke from the fridge. He already had the glass of ginger ale she'd poured for him.

She sat down and found him staring at her.

"So that's the story," she said.

He sighed, seemingly amazed. "It explains a lot."

"Does it?"

He nodded. "It's why you're so self-sufficient, so independent. Almost fiercely so."

"And how does it explain that?"

He shrugged. "You were the baby of the family. And then all of the sudden, you were…well, basically, the head of the family. Your big sister was gone. Your dad was in prison and you said yourself your mom was barely functional for years after. You had to step up. Seems to me you never stepped back down."

She tilted her head to one side, studying his eyes, nodded a little. "That makes sense, I guess. Maybe it's true. I know I'm as uncomfortable as hell with the notion of needing anyone. Depending on anyone, for any reason, you know?"

"Sure you are." He shook his head slowly. "Your father's done time. Hard time. I can't quite wrap my mind around that. He doesn't…he doesn't fit the profile of an ex-con."

"He didn't fit the profile of a killer, either."

River's eyes were focused on her face. "I'm even more confused, Cassandra. The man who killed your sister was about to get off on an insanity plea."

"Just like you did?" she said, reading his thoughts.

"Yeah. It would stand to reason you'd be the first person to throw me back in the pit."

"I know. Believe me, I know it looks odd."

He searched her face. "But there's more to the story, isn't there?"

She met his eyes, swallowed hard, wanted to tell him, and told herself that was a stupid thing to want.

"You can trust me, you know. I owe you more than anyone probably ever will. You can tell me, Cassandra."

"I…I've never told anyone."

"Maybe you need to."

Maybe she did. "It's sensitive, River. You can never tell another soul. Promise me. It would kill my father. It would *kill* him, and he doesn't deserve that."

River frowned and studied her face. "I promise. I won't re-
peat it. Not even under torture. And besides, I have a feeling
I already know what you're going to say."

He did. She could see in his eyes that he'd guessed. And
she let herself say the words she had never said to anyone in
her life. "Jeffrey Allen Dunkirk didn't do it. He didn't kill my
sister. My father shot an innocent man."

9

Jax felt panicky the minute the words left her lips. Why the hell was she telling this man her deepest secret? Giving him the power to destroy her family?

She didn't know. Hell, she didn't know.

"I shouldn't have—"

"It's all right." His hand covered hers on the table. "I'll take it to my grave, Cassandra. I promise you that. I'll take it to my grave."

She lifted her head and stared into his eyes. They were intense and honest. And she found herself believing in that honesty, and cursed herself for a sap all at once. She closed her eyes, lowered her head. "Dunkirk had a lousy lawyer. They had my sister's DNA in his car, his semen in her body. He'd had sex with her. I'll never know if it was against her will. She always seemed to like him way more than...than made sense. You know?"

"Young girl, older man. It's been known to happen."

"Yeah. Maybe. But he didn't kill her."

"You know who did?"

Jax nodded slowly. "She had a boyfriend—Jarred—but she was getting ready to break up with him. I knew that—I never knew if she'd told him or was about to. He went to hell after her death, started drinking. Eight years later he hanged

himself. Didn't leave a note, at least not that we knew of at the time."

"But there *was* a note?"

She closed her eyes. "I never saw it. I was a rookie cop at SPD by then. Jarred's mother came to me. Told me she didn't want her son's memory sullied, but couldn't carry the guilt of not telling someone about it. He *had* left a note. She'd concealed it. In it, he confessed to murdering my sister. Apparently, he saw her with Dunkirk, and it sent him into a rage. He waited until she was alone, then told her he needed to talk to her, and convinced her to get into his car. He took her outside of town and strangled her, ditched her body. He took her clothes off after, to make it look like a rape. He knew she'd just had sex with Dunkirk. I guess he figured they'd both be punished that way. And he was right."

River closed his eyes tightly, as if he were in pain.

"His mother told me it was up to me whether my parents should know the truth, but she said she would deny she ever said anything if I took it to the police or the D.A. Her son was dead. She didn't want his memory destroyed, and she didn't think it would do any good, anyway." Jax sighed. "I couldn't argue with her. And I couldn't tell my parents. My father was a healer, you know? It's been hard enough on him living with the fact that he took the life of a killer. It eats away at him, day and night. He'll never forgive himself, even though he feels it was the only way to see justice done. What would it do to him to know he actually murdered an innocent man?"

"Not entirely innocent," River said. "He had sex with a teenage girl. Willing or otherwise, that's pretty low."

"I agree. But it's not worthy of a death sentence." She shook her head. "It would kill Dad. It would *kill* him. And I can't think of a single reason to make him and Mom suffer more than they already have. They lost a daughter. Dad did twelve years hard time. Lost his career, his license to practice medicine, their home, their savings, their reputation. Everything."

"They didn't lose you."

She smiled softly. "More importantly, they didn't lose each other. They're still together, despite it all. They've picked up the pieces and built a life for themselves. I can't rob them of that."

"You're doing the right thing," River said. "I'd do exactly the same."

She drew a breath, looked at her soup, sitting there on the table getting cold.

"Lose your appetite?" he asked her.

"Actually, I feel…good. I've been keeping that secret for a long time. Maybe I needed to tell someone."

"I'm glad it was me."

She wondered if she was, too. But somehow, she didn't believe River would betray her. And maybe that didn't make a lot of sense, but her instincts had never steered her wrong. If she'd been the woman she was now, instead of the girl she'd been at sixteen, those instincts would have told her something was off. In hindsight, she could see the signs. Dunkirk had been faking his mental illness, but not his grief. And not his fear. She'd seen a lot of killers try to show remorse they didn't really feel. His had been real. It had broken his heart that Carrie had been killed. He'd had a shadow of the same haunted, hollow look of loss in his eyes that she had seen in her parents'. Not to the same degree, of course, but still… Hell, maybe he'd really cared for her sister.

It was the same look she saw in River's eyes when he talked about his wife—though he really hadn't talked about her much, so far.

Jax picked up a triangle-shaped half of her sandwich, dipped it into the soup and took a bite. River did likewise. Then he said, "Has it occurred to you, Cassandra, that just because Dunkirk was innocent, it doesn't mean that I am?"

She swallowed her food and met his eyes. "I know that. And I know you don't remember whether you set that fire or

not. I'm not deluding myself about you, River. But I also know there's something not right about all of this. I don't think that orderly just decided to apply for a job under a false name and kill a mental patient for the hell of it. Someone hired him, someone put him up to it."

"That doesn't prove anything."

"It proves someone wants you dead, and if they do, they must have a motive. And maybe that motive is to make sure you never remember what really happened that night."

"I'd like to believe that. But I was a cop, Cassandra. I put a lot of people behind bars. There are a lot of people out there with reason to want me dead. It might not have had anything to do with what happened to Stephanie."

Jax nodded. "So we take this like any other case. We start ruling them out, one by one." She was warming up now, and she wolfed down the rest of her sandwich, then reached for the envelope Frankie had given her. "But let's go through what we have first, huh? And how about that call to your lawyer? We need to get that done, too."

"He's going to have to report it if he hears from me."

"I know. That's why we should phone him from somewhere besides here. We don't want to tip him off to where you are right away. You look a lot better. You up for a drive?"

River could have kicked himself for the urges that kept slipping into his thoughts. The ones that whispered through his mind the entire time she was telling her story. *Touch her. Hug her. Hold her.*

Bad ideas, every last one of them. And not only because he was still feeling like hell. Cassandra Jackson was not the kind of woman who needed comfort. She was the kind who gave it freely, but would probably shun it if offered in return. She seemed to prize her independence too highly to need any emotional support from anyone else. Besides, he was a man

scraping bottom. Hardly in a position to have a damn thing to offer. He'd slipped once, his hand sliding over hers before his brain even knew what it was up to. And once there, he'd had a hell of a time convincing it to let go. The brush of her warm skin against his was the closest thing to ecstasy he'd known since…since he'd kissed her. He'd been in the grips of a fever, not thinking clearly. When her face hovered close to his, instinct had taken over and he'd been in no condition to argue. And he could taste her mouth, still.

He wished he couldn't. The last woman he'd cared about had wound up dead. If he had any freaking honor left in him, he'd get as far away from Cassandra Jackson as he could. She was risking more than just her career by helping him. She might very well be risking her life.

"Come on," she said. "I feel a plan coming on." She took his hand again, drawing him to his feet.

"You can't afford to be seen with me." He said it more as a means to distract his mind from the power of her touch than for any other reason. And he knew, now, that it wasn't just any human touch he craved—it was hers. Every time she touched him he wanted it more.

"It's dark outside," she said. "The car's close to the house. And you can duck down if we meet traffic."

"That'll look even more suspicious."

"Shit, the locals see me with some stranger's head in my lap, they'll just think I got lucky." She smiled at him in a way that sent his pulse racing and put ideas into his head.

There wasn't a shy bone in her body.

He wasn't used to a woman like her. He wasn't used to any woman at all.

She opened the door, stepped out onto the porch. Rex pushed past River and loped out to stand beside her. The way he looked around, River could almost believe he knew what was going on.

"All clear, come on," she said. She reached back and took River's hand again, and he jogged beside her to the car and quickly got in the passenger side.

Cassandra went to the driver's door, but opened the back one first. He was surprised to see Rex jump easily into the car, and sit upright on the back seat. Cassandra got behind the wheel. And she had that envelope in her hands. He hadn't noticed her grabbing it on the way out.

"You're bringing the dog?" he asked.

"He wanted a ride." She shrugged. "Brought this, too. Figured we could read on the way."

He nodded, and she drove. River opened the envelope, began pulling things out, one by one, curious as to what the file contained. But when he got to the file folder marked Autopsy Report, he stopped.

"God," he whispered.

Cassandra glanced at him, then at the folder in his lap. It bore his wife's name. The corner of a photograph was visible inside. Just the white edge, nothing else. His imagination filled in a lot more, but before he could open the file, it had been snatched from his lap.

He looked up at Cassandra. She was tucking the autopsy folder above the visor. "Not that. Not yet, River. That one we need to go over when we're home, sitting down, and ready for it. Okay?"

She was protecting him. He knew that, and it chafed, and yet he couldn't even argue that he didn't need it. If she hadn't stopped him, he'd have immersed himself in that file and probably plunged himself into despair, regret, maybe even another blackout. He needed to be sharp to talk to his lawyer.

He flipped through the other contents of the folder. There were a lot of interviews. With his neighbors, men and women who'd worked with him at NYPD, men he'd arrested.... "Hell," he muttered.

"What?"

"Frankie—she has a list here. It has to include damn near every violent offender I ever had a hand in busting. Notes next to every name."

"What kinds of notes?"

He read a few. "Deceased. Incarcerated. Alibi." He blinked. "A few just have question marks next to their names."

She nodded. "She must have checked them out herself. I bet the question marks are the ones whose whereabouts on the night of the fire can't be verified."

"Damn. The woman is good."

"The woman didn't believe you did it." Jax shook her head. "I don't think she does even now." She nodded and kept driving. "This is great. She's done a lot of the work for us. We can just pick up where she left off."

He shook his own head. It was hard to believe someone had been that convinced of his innocence at a time when he'd thought the entire world believed him guilty.

"Let's make a list of what you're going to say to the lawyer when you get him on the phone. You don't want to stay on too long. It's unlikely they messed with his lines, being that any conversations you have with him are confidential. But your location is not. They might try to run a trace."

"Okay."

He found a pen in the cup holder between the seats, flipped over a sheet of paper from the envelope and took notes on the back as they planned.

"Here we are," she said, pulling her car into a convenience store parking lot twenty miles north of Blackberry. "Pay phone's right here. And the store's closed, so no witnesses. I'll get the home number. Better than leaving a message."

He nodded. "If it's listed. Derrick Brown. Burlington."

She nodded and they both got out of the car, leaving Rex in the back seat. Cassandra dropped a quarter and dialed in-

formation. A moment later, she was punching in the lawyer's home number. Then she handed the phone to River and said, "It's ringing."

He swallowed hard and lifted the cheat sheet. There was a streetlight above the convenience store parking lot, so he could see all right.

A man finally answered. "Hello?"

"I'm calling for Derrick Brown," River said.

"Speaking. What can I do for you?"

"Brown, this is Michael Corbett. I need your help."

"Jesus!" The lawyer lowered his voice, caught his breath. "Listen, do you realize I'm obligated to tell the police I heard from you, and where you're calling from?"

"Yeah. I know that. But you're my attorney. Tell them you're negotiating my surrender, okay? I just need a little time."

"For what, Michael?"

He looked at his list. "I wrote you a letter from the state hospital a few weeks ago. Did you ever receive it?"

"No."

River repeated the word, his eyes on Cassandra's. Her hunch had been right. Someone had intercepted the note and then sent a thug to kill him. Maybe. He shook off the knowledge and forced himself to go on. "I want you to get all my medical records. All of them, everything from the Vermont State Mental Hospital, what they've been giving me, what my diagnosis was. Everything Ethan Melrose has. And everything from before, when I was shot on duty in New York. I want them all delivered to your office. And I want you to have them gone over by the best psychiatrist you can find."

Jax frowned at him, and River covered the mouthpiece. "Let's keep your dad's hands as clean as we can," he explained. And she nodded.

"You think you've been misprescribed?" Brown asked.

"Yeah. And then some."

"Is that why you killed the orderly?"

"He tried to kill me. I hit him in self-defense and he cracked his head on the toilet. I didn't mean to kill him. I have the knife with his prints on it. Since then I've learned he has a record, and was working under a false name."

"*What?*"

"His real name is Edward Ferdinand Martin," he said, reading it from the cheat sheet. "The state police know it. Check with them. It's the truth."

"Damn."

"Do I have any money left?"

"Yeah. Yeah, you gave me power of attorney over your assets when you went in. The only thing I've taken out is the monthly payment to the hospital. The account's still open, Michael."

"I need some cash."

"If I give you any, I could be disbarred."

"It's my money."

"I know." There was a sigh. "Listen, I can send you some. Where are you staying?"

"I thought you were supposed to be on my side?"

"Hang up, River," Cassandra said.

He met her eyes, nodded. "Get those records, get them checked. I'm telling you, someone's trying to kill me. You're my attorney. You have to look into this. I have an unimpeachable witness to this phone call. I end up dead, it's gonna be on your shoulders in a very public way."

"All right. I'll do it. I will."

River nodded. "I'll check in again in a couple of days. If I find anything on my end, I'll send it to you. You have a fax number?"

"Same as the office number, just change the last digit from a five to a four."

River nodded. "Thanks. Don't let me down." He hung up

the phone before the man could reply. Then he looked at Cassandra. "Think he'll do it?"

"He won't dare not do it. If there's a chance you're telling the truth and he fails to act and you end up dead, he could be in deep trouble."

He nodded. "So that's done."

"Yeah. That's done." She nodded at him. "So, you ready to head home?"

He looked up at the sky, at the stars. He'd been imprisoned in a mental hospital for more than a year, out only long enough for the arduous trip to Blackberry, when he'd been too out of his mind to appreciate it, and cooped up inside her house ever since. "There's a park up the road a little ways. Should be deserted this time of night. You feel like taking a walk?"

"If you do."

"I do," he told her. "Let's go."

The park was deserted, and Jax was glad. They followed the winding, paved path—well, she and River did. Rex wanted no part of a paved and shoveled path when there was perfectly good snow on either side. He loped ahead of them, made a giant loop and raced back, only to nip playfully at their hands as he passed them and did it all over again.

"He must be feeling cooped up in the house," Jax said. "He's used to running pretty free."

"I was starting to feel cooped up myself, and I haven't been running free in a long time."

She nodded. "I had a feeling you were getting antsy."

"How could you tell?"

She shrugged. "I would've been. I mean, it was one thing when you were weak and too sick to do much more than wiggle. But you're getting better now. Stronger. At least, since that one setback earlier."

He nodded when she looked him in the eye for confirmation of that.

"So I couldn't see how you could spend all day in the house and not get a little itchy to be out. Hell, I was half-afraid I'd come home tonight and find you gone."

"Were you?"

He was gazing at her a little intently. She narrowed her eyes and looked right back at him. "You doubt it?"

He shrugged. "Seems to me it might be a relief for you to come home and find me gone," he said.

"Now why would you say that?"

"Oh, come on, Cassandra. I'm in your space, in your home, sick and damn near helpless most of the time—"

"That's passed."

"—and my being there is putting your career in jeopardy. Maybe...maybe your life, too."

She stopped walking, turned and looked up at him. "You're not a danger to me. Do you understand? You're not."

He stood still a moment, staring down at her. The wind whispered through the trees around them, and she could taste snow on the air. River's hand rose slowly and came to her cheek. It rested there like a caress, then he pushed her hair off her face and tucked it behind her ear as if that had been his sole purpose in touching her. He started to take it away, but Jax covered it with her own, and held his eyes in turn.

"You're not a danger to me."

He didn't move. Didn't move closer, to kiss her, as she was hoping he would, even while she thought it was probably the dumbest craving she could possibly have at the moment. But he didn't move away, either. He just stood there with his palm cupping her cheek, her hand covering his and his eyes probing hers. He didn't move.

So she did.

She leaned in, tipped her head up and pressed her mouth

to his. His lips were cool and soft, and they grew softer when hers touched them, relaxing and becoming pliable and then parting when he kissed her back. His hand slid from her cheek to her nape, while the other one wrapped around her waist to hold her closer. She twined one arm around his neck and used the other to clutch his shoulder, vaguely aware that her nails were sinking in like a cat's kneading claws.

She stopped feeling the cold wind when his mouth pushed hers open and his tongue traced her lips. Her hips arched against his as her entire body pressed closer, tighter. And he was reacting the same way, holding her more fiercely, kissing her more deeply, until he was bending her backward over his arm and she was holding on for dear life.

Rex barked, loudly and repeatedly, then wedged his head between their bodies in search of attention.

Jax opened her eyes to find River staring at her as if he were seeing her for the first time. He blinked, seemed to shake himself as he got his footing, lifting her upright again, holding her until he was sure she was steady.

"I d-didn't…" he stammered. "We shouldn't…"

She looked at him. "I know where you're going with that and you can just stop. You're not going to hurt me, River. You wouldn't."

"Cassandra, I loved my wife."

The words hit with a little more sting than they probably should have. She averted her eyes quickly to try not to let it show. "Hey, of course you did. Probably still do. That's not what this is about."

"No. No, I'm not saying…" He took her arm. "Cassandra, what I mean is that I loved her and maybe I killed her, anyway."

"You didn't."

"But what if I did?"

"River, even a lunatic needs a motive. Come on, there was nothing. You were getting along, expecting your first baby."

He shook his head. "Things were far from perfect."

"Like how?" She turned, slipped her arm around his waist and started them walking back toward the car.

He sighed. "She hated living out here, for one thing. Just hated it. Too far from everything, too little to do, and then there was dealing with my blackouts and memory loss. It was a lot." He lowered his head, shook it slowly. "She probably would have left me if it hadn't been for Ethan."

Jax looked up quickly. "Ethan again, huh?"

River nodded. "I was already seeing him a couple of times a week. We managed to convince her to go, too. I think being able to open up, do a little venting about her frustration, helped a lot."

Jax was studying his face as they walked. The salt that had been scattered on the paved trail to keep it free of snow crunched under her shoes. "River, why did you feel the need to see a therapist twice a week? You didn't have a mental problem."

"No, but there was the stress. It was a lot to deal with. Enforced retirement, being basically disabled. The lost time I could never really get back. My uncertainty about my marriage. To tell you the truth, I was getting ready to let her go."

"Let her go—you mean divorce her?"

He nodded. "She never would have left me. Too much guilt—abandoning her disabled hero-cop husband wasn't something Steph could have done. Ever. So I figured I'd let her off the hook. The therapy seemed to help her feel better about herself, but she just kept getting more and more distant from me. I really thought it was over. After all that time."

"How long were you married?"

"Only seven years. But we were together a lot longer. Hell, ever since I figured out girls didn't smell bad, really."

She made herself smile. "Childhood sweethearts?"

He shrugged. "Stephanie was every guy's dream girl back

then. She flitted from one of us to another like a little bird too full of energy to alight very long on one branch. Had us all pretty crazy before graduation. But I was the lucky one who ended up marrying her a couple of years later."

Jax nodded. "So then, she knew Ethan, too?"

"Yeah. She knew him as long as I did. That made it easier, you know? Having Ethan and Victoria in Burlington made the transition from living in New York to living out here a little bit more bearable."

"Victoria?" Jax asked.

River nodded. "Ethan's wife. She's a sweetheart."

Blinking, Jax said, "He's still with her, then?"

"Hell, as far as I know. Why?"

"Just curious." She lowered her eyes. "So what happened then? After things were looking so grim for you and Stephanie?"

He gave a sad, wistful smile. "Everything changed. She came to me one night, told me she was pregnant, and that we were starting over, she and I. She said she was determined to make our marriage work, even apologized for letting it get so far off track."

Jax watched the emotions cross his face as he spoke. She saw worry, and then heartbreak, and then joy and relief all chase each other through his eyes. "I thought everything was going to be all right. And then the next thing I know, the damn house is burning, and for some reason she's inside, and I'm out on the lawn with a freaking gasoline can at my feet and gas all over my hands."

Jax nodded slowly. "And matches, right?"

He looked at her.

"You had matches. Or a lighter or something."

"No."

"No? Not even in your pockets?"

"No."

"Or on the ground nearby?"

"Doesn't prove anything, Cassandra. I could have tossed them into the fire after I set it."

"Seems like if you'd done that, you'd have tossed the gas can, too. But you didn't. It doesn't make a lot of sense, does it, River? I mean, you're not a smoker—weren't then, were you?"

"No."

"How did you get outside?" she asked.

He seemed to search his memory. "I couldn't sleep. Went out for a walk. At some point, I must have blacked out."

"Um-hmm. So when you went out for that walk you wouldn't have had matches or a lighter on you. And it was on the walk that you blacked out. So where did you get the gas? Where did you get the matches? And where did they go?"

He blinked slowly. "I don't know."

She nodded, drew a deep breath. "The wing that burned…I understand it was guest rooms, mostly."

"And a big family room, and a two-car garage," he stated.

"So what was your wife doing in that wing? Where was she when you left her for your walk?"

He frowned. "In our bedroom. The one at the top of the stairs."

"So what made her get up and go into the other part of the house?"

"I don't know."

Nodding slowly, Jax said, "I think we need to find out. Let's get home, huh? We still need to go through the rest of Frankie's tome, and it's already late."

He nodded and they got back into her car, Rex making snowy pawprints on the back seat. Once inside, he shook himself, and droplets flew everywhere. In the front, River and Jax both ducked and laughed. They met each other's eyes for just a moment, and both fell silent as their smiles died. Jax pulled her seat belt around her, buckled it up and got the car underway. It was stupid, what she was feeling. She'd never

been one to deny her physical urges out of any sense of guilt or the silly notion that good girls didn't do those things. She enjoyed sex. And every once in a while, she had sex, and she never let it mean a damn thing.

The fact that she barely knew the man didn't bother her so much. She just felt a little guilty. He was still weak, and pretty messed up over all that had happened to him. He was vulnerable. A guy like that was liable to read more into casual sex than she would like. He was liable to get clingy. Needy. Romantic.

The notion made her stomach heave.

She really should just get the idea right out of her head.

But damn, she wanted to jump his bones before this was over.

They pulled into the driveway a half hour later. Jax looked around to be sure no one was in sight—of course no one was. Who would be lurking on a dark country road in the middle of a winter night? No one, that's who. She gave River a nod, and he got out, came around the car to where she stood with Rex, and the three of them walked up onto the porch.

Jax reached for the doorknob, keys in hand, then stopped short at Rex's low, menacing growl.

She looked from the dog to River. "What—?"

"Shh." He put a finger to his lips and reached for the door himself. His hand covered the knob. He whispered, "It's unlocked."

"Don't move a muscle," she told him. Then she tiptoed down the steps, dashed to the car and snagged her spare piece from the glove compartment. It was another .45, identical to the one she carried. She hurried back to the porch and put it into his hand.

He looked surprised, but there was no time to be. Jax drew her handgun from its holster, held it barrel up, her back to the wall beside the door. She met River's eyes, nodded once.

He flung the door open, and the two of them entered, guns leading the way. He went high and to the right, she went low and to the left, both scanning the room, each alert for any threat to the other.

Rex raced past them, hurrying through the house, but not running. Just sniffing everything he came to. His growl had faded, and he wasn't barking.

When it seemed there was no one nearby, River hit the light switch. Jax looked around her house. The cushions were off the sofa, the screen away from the fireplace, ashes scattered as if someone had been digging for buried treasure. The throw rug had been yanked up and lay in a corner, folded over itself. In the kitchen every cupboard had been opened, and items yanked out. They lay all over the counter and floor, flour and rice spilled everywhere. The fridge was much the same.

She looked at the cellar door. Swallowed hard.

"Rex," River said.

The dog bounded to his side instantly. "Let's see how much you remember, huh, pal?" Then he opened the cellar door. "Find the man!"

Rex woofed loudly and bounded down the stairs.

10

Rex was gone only moments, before he returned to the top of the stairs and sat at River's feet. "Good boy," River said, stroking the dog. He lowered the gun. "The house is clear."

"I agree with you, but we probably ought to check upstairs, just to be sure." Jax glanced at the dog. "You think he'd obey me?"

"I don't know. I was kind of surprised he remembered for me. But you can try."

River walked with her into the living room, the dog lumbering between them, looking from one to the other, his entire posture expectant.

"It's like he knows we're going to tell him to do something," Jax said.

River nodded. "It's his favorite game—though he prefers actually finding someone."

"Yeah, well, I hope you don't mind, Rex, but I prefer you don't." She stopped at the foot of the stairs. Rex stopped, too, sat obediently and looked to River.

Jax said, "Rex! Find the man, Rex. Find the man." She pointed up the stairway, and the dog gave a happy yip and ran up the stairs. She followed, and watched him going down the hall, nose to the floor, then in the air. He entered each bedroom, and as he did, she saw the mess the intruder had left, and her heart sank.

"God, whoever it was, they trashed the place."

"Whoever it was, they know you have a man staying with you," River added. He nodded at the pile of clothing strewn about the bedroom floor. "This isn't good, Cassandra."

"I know." She shrugged. "Hey, I can always say I got hard up and brought home some local for a roll in the sheets."

Rex returned and sat at her feet. "That's a good dog, Rex. Good boy." She stroked and petted him, and he seemed to bask in the attention. "We should give him a treat."

"Yeah. And clean up this mess. But I think the most important thing is to figure out who did this." River sighed. "Maybe you should call Frankie."

She shook her head. "Then she'd have the boys out here snooping around. No, I think we'd better keep this to ourselves until we know what's going on."

"You could be in danger," he said. "If whoever was trying to kill me in the hospital has somehow tracked me down here—"

"We're two armed cops, River. Good ones." Rex lifted a paw and pressed it to her thigh, probably because she'd stopped petting him, but it made her smile. "Sorry, Rex. Make that three. No one's gonna mess with us. They try and I'll be happy to rip out their liver."

River sighed. "Hell. That orderly's uniform was in here. And the ID badge. If they found it—"

"They didn't."

He looked at her, frowning. "How do you know?"

"I took it, River. Name badge, shoes, everything you were wearing that night. It's sealed in a plastic bag and stashed off-site. So's the knife by now."

He held her gaze for a moment. "What about the case file?"

"Hell." She ran downstairs and checked in the coat closet. Then lowered her head in defeat. She turned, saw him at the top of the stairs, waiting. "It's gone."

"Dammit."

"Doesn't matter. I'm working the case. My having copies of the file isn't all that shocking."

"You *are* working the case," he said as she moved back up the stairs. "You've been collecting evidence all along. The knife, the orderly's clothes…"

"Still am," she said. "I may get busted for not turning you in immediately, but they won't get me for sloppy police work. Not ever."

"I believe that." He moved into the bedroom, began picking things up.

She joined him, secretly thanking the Fates she'd taken the additional files from Frankie's private investigation with them tonight. She'd hate to drag her friend into the trouble she might be creating for herself. It was bad enough someone knew she'd brought home copies of the official files.

When they'd finished restoring the upstairs to order, they moved below. Jax made sure every curtain was drawn and every door locked, though whoever had come in had made short work of the lock on the front door earlier tonight. She'd need new ones, good ones. She made a mental note.

When they'd finally finished, she brewed a pot of tea, and they sat in front of the fireplace, with Frankie's files spread out on the floor between them. Rex lay close enough to River that the dog's head touched his thigh. The big shepherd didn't like to get too far from his favorite guy. She didn't blame him, Jax thought.

She cleared her throat and averted her eyes when River caught them on his face. "You know, the D.A. didn't even insist on having a second opinion on your case before accepting your insanity plea?"

"I know."

"Don't you find that unusual? In my sister's case the state put on three experts to counter Dunkirk's shrink. The defense put on five in his favor." She shook her head. "Those five all believed his phony mental illness. Quacks."

River sighed. "You don't like psychiatrists."

"Don't trust 'em," she said.

"In my case, I think it helped that Ethan was the chief of psychiatry at the state hospital. And it didn't hurt that he was a friend of the D.A. Not to mention the governor."

She lifted her eyebrows. "He's that connected?"

"Victoria's family is one of the most prominent in the state. She sits on the board of directors at the state hospital."

"Hmm, no wonder he's head shrink there, then."

River nodded. "He married very well."

She set her folder down, leaned back on her hands and stretched her legs out in front of her. "Tell me about you and Ethan. About your friendship. You were always close?"

"No, not always. I was a jock. He was...not."

"Nerd?"

"Genius would be the more accurate term. But yeah, he had that bookish thing going on. Hated sports. I think he might have grown to like athletics in time if his father hadn't pushed so hard."

"His father was a jock?"

"His father was my high school football coach. He was good, too. Played in college, was drafted by New England in his senior year, but he took a bad hit and blew out his knee his first time on the field. He couldn't play again after that."

"That's heartbreaking. So he turned to coaching."

River nodded. "He got himself qualified as a phys ed teacher and coached on the side. That's how I got to know him. I wasn't on his team yet, just played for my middle school team. But he took notice of me. My grades were bad, I was in danger of being ineligible to play. He hooked me up with a tutor. His son, Ethan."

She nodded. "Doesn't sound like the beginning of a great friendship."

"It wasn't at first. Hell, I think Ethan was a little jealous of me for a while."

"Over his father?"

River nodded. "Not for long, though. We got close. Really close. We were like brothers. Even before my parents died and his family took me in."

He pulled out a folder, looked at it briefly, then closed his eyes and set it on the floor. It was the autopsy report. Jax swallowed the dryness in her throat. She didn't want to look at the damn thing, but supposed they would have to sooner or later.

"How did your parents die, River?"

He looked from the folder to her face. "Car wreck. On their way home from celebrating their twentieth anniversary."

"What happened?"

He shook his head. "Skid marks showed another car met them head-on. They went off the road and rolled over. The other car never stopped. They figured it was a drunk driver, but they never got him." He lowered his head. "That's when I decided to become a cop. So I could put people like that away. And I don't know—maybe I thought someday I'd get the bastard who killed them."

"How old were you?"

"I was twelve."

He met her eyes, and she saw in them a perfect reflection of her own childhood grief. Her own tragic loss. The pain that never went away. "At least I still had my parents," she said softly.

He turned his hand in hers, and held it. "No you didn't," he said. "Not really. But I had Ethan. And Ellen and Joe, his parents. But mostly, Ethan. I don't know what the hell I'd have done without him."

She nodded. "So there was no more jealousy, no competition between you, after that?"

A little of the grief faded from his eyes. "There was always that. But it was good-natured, you know? Like him daring me with the canoe in the rapids."

"That was a dare that almost got you killed, River," she said softly.

He nodded. "Yeah, but he couldn't have known that. You should have seen him. He was more scared than I was. No, our rivalry was more like a running joke. We both knew he had it all over me in every way that mattered."

"Did he?"

River nodded. "Oh, hell yes. He won all the awards, got all the scholarships, graduated valedictorian of our class, and went on to Harvard. Married into one of the most prominent families in the Northeast." He smiled. "I was just a cop."

She nodded. "Do you still stay in touch with his family?"

River's grip on her hand tightened. "Not since..." He licked his lips, cleared his throat. "They were as fond of Steph as they were of me. I haven't heard from any of them since her death. I don't blame them. They believe I killed her. It's..."

"I don't believe you killed her," Jax said softly.

"You don't want to believe it. You want me to be your chance to right an old wrong. But you know saving me isn't going to bring Dunkirk back from the dead, or undo what your father did."

"You think that's all this is about? Some kind of third-party act of contrition?"

He took his hand away from hers. "That's all it can be about."

"You don't know me very well if you believe that."

"And you don't know me at all. Cassandra, I can't...there can't be anything between us."

The fire snapped, warming her face. She probed his eyes and saw everything she was feeling reflected back at her from their depths. And instead of acknowledging it, she said, "Oh, come on with the melodramatic bullshit. There already is something between us, River. Physical attraction. Nothing scary. Nothing earth-shattering. Just that."

He closed his eyes. "I can't…"

"Yeah, well. I'm liable to wear you down, you stick around long enough. I can be a real pain in the ass that way."

He smiled, letting her teasing humor break the tension. She was pretty sure he knew she was only half-kidding. Then he looked at the file folder again, and his smile died. "Let's get this over with, huh? We both need some sleep."

"Okay." She moved closer to him on the floor, the better to see inside the folder.

He braced himself visibly and flipped it open. Autopsy photos. White flesh. Closed eyes. Singed hair. Burns in places, but not to any great extent. Not to the extent that the fire had killed her. The smoke probably got to her first, and Jax thought that was fortunate.

River was frozen, staring at the photos. Not blinking. Jax reached for them, gathered them up and took them away. She set them facedown on the floor beside her. "River? You okay?"

He was so still she thought he might have slipped into another blackout. But he drew a sudden breath, nodded once, firmly. "I'm okay."

She nodded, too, and then leaned over the folder. They read together in silence. The pages described the condition of Stephanie Corbett's remains in excruciating detail. Third degree burns to the arms and back and face. A blunt trauma injury to the head, more likely from a blow than a fall. Cause of death had been smoke inhalation, but the means of death was listed as homicide.

Then came the part about the child she'd been carrying. Approximately twelve weeks gestation. Normal weight and size, apparently healthy, and male.

River rocked backward, pressing his hands to his head. "It was a boy. They never told me."

"I'm so sorry," she whispered.

"I couldn't have done this. I couldn't have killed my own baby."

"You didn't."

"We don't know that."

"Yeah," she said softly. "I'm sorry, River, but I'm afraid we do. Look at this."

He lowered his hands from his face, and she glimpsed the unshed tears shimmering in his eyes. Blinking them away, he leaned over the paper and read the lines that began near the tip of her finger.

Then he blinked up at her, looking more confused than she'd ever seen anyone look. "That can't be right."

"I imagine it was double-checked. They wouldn't put something like that in here without being sure. The child your wife was carrying wasn't yours, River."

Something smashed, and they both jumped to their feet. But it was only a coffee mug someone had left on the windowsill on the constantly cold side of the room. It must have fallen to the floor and broken.

"Jesus, that scared me," Jax muttered. Then she patted Rex, because he was snarling and the fur on his back bristled upward as he stared at the wall. "It's all right, boy, there's nothing there."

River blinked. "Whose coffee mug is that?" he asked.

Jax frowned, got to her feet and went to pick it up. It was an Asian patterned, rose-colored mug, broken into three neat chunks, and it was as cold as if it had come from the freezer. "I don't know. Must be one of the hand-me-downs my mother brought over."

He was standing beside her, staring at the pieces she held. "It's just like Stephanie's favorite set. They were the only ones she'd use for her morning coffee."

Jax put a hand on his chest as he stared at the wall. "Don't start seeing bogeymen in the shadows, River. This is nothing. It's a coincidence."

"Do you feel how cold it is here?"

She nodded. "Yeah. It's always cold on this side of the room."

"Didn't used to be," he said. "This used to be where the entry to the other wing was. Here, and off the far end of the hallway upstairs. Is it cold there, too?"

"What, are you seeing ghosts now, River? Come on, don't make me put you back on the damn Haldol."

He looked at her, his eyes unsteady.

"It was nothing. A cup fell off a freaking windowsill. You've got enough real problems without making up imaginary ones."

He lowered his gaze, nodded. "Yeah. You're right. Just…the timing. Just when we read that the baby wasn't mine. God, I can't believe that."

The cop in her knew that the obvious conclusion would be that this was River's true motive for murdering his wife. But she could see him, see his eyes, the shock and the horror. He hadn't known about this. He hadn't had the first clue.

"Stephanie…was with another man," he whispered, as if it had just occurred to him.

"Yeah, it would seem so. I'm sorry, River. You okay?"

He looked at her, nodded distractedly.

"Good, because we need to find out who. Next to you, River, he'd be the obvious suspect in her murder."

"No." He shook his head, even as he got to his feet. "No way, there's no way. It's a mistake. My wife didn't cheat on me. She *didn't*." He crossed the room in angry strides, kicked the folder and sent papers flying like a miniature explosion. The act made Jax jump, and even Rex seemed startled. The dog moved to put himself between Jax and River, almost as if he were…protecting her.

River stood there, looking from the mess he'd made to Jax's face. He held up his hands, started to say something, then just backed slowly away from her. Finally, he turned and went up the stairs.

Jax followed but he flung a hand behind him, palm flat and facing her. "Don't, Cassandra. Just…just don't."

He continued up the stairs, into the bedroom, closing the door behind him.

Cassandra sighed, swallowed and fought with her urge to go after him. It wouldn't do any good, she thought. Not now.

So she turned to the papers strewn everywhere, and slowly picked them up and put them back in order. And when she'd finished, she carried them to the kitchen table, sat down and began reading. She didn't intend to stop until she'd finished, even though she kept feeling as if someone were watching her. Every time she looked up, there was no one there.

Dawn lay in the bed, shivering, and they were standing in the room staring at her. Not saying anything, just staring at her. That woman in scorched white, with the baby. And Mordecai, on the opposite side of her bed. Young again, handsome, with a deep sadness in his brown eyes.

She'd told them to go away, she'd tried to ignore them and fall to sleep, but she couldn't get warm, not with the chill they brought into the room penetrating her very bones.

She couldn't stand this!.

Finally, she flung back the covers, sprang to her feet and ran out of her bedroom with little shivers chasing themselves up and down her spine until she'd put a hundred feet between herself and that room.

God, how she hated them.

She wandered down to the kitchen, thinking a hot cocoa might help relax her, or at least provide a good excuse to keep from going back to bed. But when she stepped into the kitchen, the shrink, Dr. Melrose, was there, sipping a cup of tea and staring pensively out the window.

He turned, sent her a smile that didn't cover up whatever else was going on with him. He had a lot on his mind, that guy.

"You couldn't sleep, either, huh?"

"No." She moved to the stove, set the kettle on the burner.

"Anything you want to talk about?" he asked.

She lowered her head, not turning around. "You'd have me committed by morning."

"No chance of that, Dawn. You're no danger to yourself, or anyone else. You're perfectly functional."

She turned slowly, looked him up and down. "Do you know who my father was?"

"No. Should I?"

She nodded. "Ever hear the name Mordecai Young?"

His brows went up, that look of horrified recognition she'd grown used to seeing, appearing in his eyes.

"I see you have," she said.

"To be honest, I've studied his story to some degree. He's a fascinating case."

"Really," she said, not surprised. She'd heard there were classes in shrink school devoted to the study of her father. "So what do you make of him? Was he gifted, or just insane?" She turned to the stove, half watching him as she went about putting her cup of cocoa together.

"I think he might have been a bit of both, actually." The doctor pulled out a chair and sat down at the table. He was wearing a brown plush robe over blue pajamas, and a pair of corduroy slippers covered his feet. "You know, as a scientist, I'm basically a skeptic. But in your father's case..." He lowered his head, shaking it slowly. "Well, there seems to be a lot of evidence that he really did possess some sort of... of...well, he knew a lot of things he had no way of knowing."

"So you think his gift was genuine?"

"I think it might have been. I also think he was suffering from a serious mental illness."

She tilted her head. "That's kind of what I thought.

But…do you think it was the gift that made him insane? Or the insanity that gave him the gift?"

"I have no idea." He tilted his head to one side and studied her. "This is bothering you on a very deep level, isn't it, Dawn?"

She nodded. "Deeper than you could probably imagine."

His lips pulled into a slight, sympathetic smile. "I don't see many private patients anymore. But I see a few. I'd be willing to make time if you'd like to come to my office."

"Your office?"

He nodded. "Neutral ground. No one likely to walk in and interrupt. If you'd like to talk about this some more, it might be easier there."

She licked her lips and studied him. He seemed sincere. "I'll think about it. Seriously, I will."

"Okay."

She hugged her cocoa cup in her hands and got to her feet. "Thanks, Doc."

"You bet, Dawn."

Sighing, she headed back up the stairs to her room. It was empty when she got there. No more chill. She let the warmth of the cocoa mug heat her hands and whispered, "Please stay away from me tonight. I just want to get some sleep. Okay?"

There was no answer.

River paced. He sat and he thought, and then he paced some more. He battled tears and fought against denial. He knew damn well Steph had loved him. Things had been good between them. She'd told him they were going to start over, that they were going to be all right.

He closed his eyes and sank onto the bed, lowering his head. Yeah, things had been good. At the end. Before that, though, their marriage had been strained. For a while, he'd been sure it was over. That she was on the verge of leaving him.

He'd never once believed it would have been for someone else. Never.

But now…now whispers of memory came crawling out of the depths of his mind. Things he'd seen and ignored. Things he hadn't wanted to see, but could no longer deny. Times when she'd gone out shopping and come home without any bags. Too many times. Occasions when she'd hung up the phone as soon as he'd walked into a room.

The time when she'd gone to visit a friend he'd later learned had been out of town that week. And so many days when she'd simply been away without explanation.

He fisted his hands in his hair. He'd been stupid. Blind. Or had he?

"River?"

He lifted his head when Cassandra's voice came from the other side of his bedroom door.

"Can I come in?"

He got up, blinked to clear his eyes, hoped to Christ his anguish didn't show on his face—and then he wondered why he hoped it. Cassandra wasn't going to buy that this wasn't killing him. She was too insightful, too sharp for that.

He opened the bedroom door and drew a breath. "I'm sorry about…acting like an idiot downstairs."

"Don't be. This is hell on you, River, and it would be on anyone. You're not made of stone."

He shook his head. "No reason to take it out on you. I blew up down there. I lost it, and—"

"Yeah. That was one scary burst of temper. You scattered the hell out of those sheets of paper."

He frowned, searching her face. She was getting at something, but he wasn't sure what.

"Your idea of 'losing it' is kicking a file folder across the room. You didn't break anything. You didn't scream or yell. You didn't knock me over the skull and burn the house down, River."

He lowered his head, getting it now. "That doesn't mean I'm incapable of it."

"Can I come in or not?" she asked.

He sighed. "Not the best idea, Cassandra."

She lifted her hands. He saw the cups in them, smelled the rich chocolate wafting from them. "Yeah, I figured it would take a little bribe. So I brought hot cocoa."

His mouth pulled into a slight smile at the coaxing tone, and the innocent expression she put on to go with it—an expression he knew to be utterly false. "Well, hell, you should have said so." He pulled the door wider, stepped aside.

She walked in, set a mug on the dresser beside the bed, then walked to the other side and placed the second mug on the nightstand. She sat on the bed with her back to the head-board, legs stretching out on the mattress, then turned those eyes his way and patted the spot beside her.

Damn, but this was not a good idea. Still, he crossed the room, sat on the bed, mimicking her position before taking his cup.

She sipped her cocoa. "So have you been asleep yet?"

"Right."

She shrugged. "You were awfully quiet up here. I was hoping you'd caught a nap. You need one."

"So do you," he said. "Have you slept?"

"No, I finished reading the file."

"Find anything else earth-shattering?"

"No. Bits and pieces, nothing that adds up to anything. No clues as to who—" She bit her lip, didn't finish.

"Who my wife was fucking," he said.

She flinched a little when he said it. And he knew damn well it wasn't the language. She'd worked with men her entire career. She was used to the language and threw it around herself when the need arose. He thought it was the fact that it had come from him that caused the involuntary

twitch. "Maybe you were right, and it was a mistake in the lab work."

"No. It was no mistake. I've been sitting up here, thinking." She shot him a look and he said, "Okay, wallowing. I'm a pathetic, self-pitying asshole."

"You're allowed. But only for another half hour."

Again, she drew a smile out of him when he hadn't thought there had been one left. How the hell did she do that? She wouldn't let him get away with pouting, with being morose and feeling sorry for himself. Good for her.

"So you've been thinking…" she prompted.

He had to look away from her face before any thinking could resume. "Yeah," he said, studying his cup of cocoa instead. "There were signs. I just didn't want to see them."

She nodded. "Try being a cop, instead of a grieving husband, if you can, River. Not the easiest thing. But pretend it's not Steph you're talking about. Pretend it's a case. A stranger. What's the evidence?"

He blinked, nodded, knew she was right. Wasn't sure it was possible, but it was the only way he had even a shot of seeing through the fog of emotions to the clarity of truth.

"I'd walk into the room and she'd just hang up the phone. Not say goodbye, nothing. Just hang up."

"You ever go pick it up and hit Redial?"

"No. Should have. I was probably afraid of what I'd find out."

She nodded. "We can really do a number on ourselves when we don't want to know something, can't we? What else?"

"Shopping trips where she didn't buy anything. Visiting friends who weren't even in town at the time. A lot of times she should have been home and wasn't."

"I don't suppose you remember any dates?"

He frowned, shooting her a look. She was digging into his private hell, digging like any good cop trying to solve a case.

Darker than Midnight 189

Part of him resented it, and part of him admired her for it. Most of him was grateful. She was trying to help him. And so what if her reasons were entirely selfish? An effort to ease her conscience of a guilty secret.

That bothered him. Bothered him a lot more than it ought to, given everything else he had to worry about.

"Actually, I remember a couple of dates," he said. "Only because they were important." He couldn't look at her as he went on. "One was Halloween. She never missed Halloween, used to dress up for the trick-or-treaters. Another was my birthday."

He was sorely afraid Cassandra would express sympathy, and he knew he couldn't handle it if she did. He braced himself for it, for her to gasp and ask how any wife could stand her husband up on his birthday. She didn't. Instead she set her cocoa down, opened the drawer of the nightstand and took out a pad and pen. "October thirty-first," she said, jotting it down. "And...?"

"September twenty-fourth."

She wrote down the date. "And this would have been of...what, year before last?"

"Yeah."

"Good. That gives us a couple of dates we can check. If we can figure out where she was we might be closer to learning who was with her."

He nodded. It was a logical, practical approach.

"Do you have any...suspicions, River? Of who it might have been?"

He closed his eyes.

Her hand settled on the back of his neck, rubbed him there like a trainer would massage a boxer between rounds. "I know it's hard," she said.

"No. No suspicions. Hell, she didn't even know anyone out here. Didn't make any friends. She was miserable."

She nodded. "She knew Ethan, though."

He shook his head. "It wasn't Ethan. He wouldn't do that to me. Hell, even if he would, he wouldn't do it to Victoria. He adores his wife."

Cassandra tilted her head to one side. "I saw him in the grocery store earlier. Did I tell you?"

River turned toward her. Her hand was still massaging his nape and it felt damn good. "No. You didn't mention it."

She nodded. "He asked me to go out with him. Dinner tomorrow night. Didn't mention he was married."

River couldn't reply to that, because it was as if she was speaking a foreign language. It didn't make any sense.

"I said I'd go."

"The hell you will."

The words came without warning, without forethought. A knee-jerk reaction that didn't make any more sense than anything else in this messed-up conversation.

She lifted her brows and blinked at him. "Look, what better way can you think of for me to pump him for information? See what he lets slip?"

"You don't need to pump Ethan for information. And you'd better believe if he asked you out, it was for the same damn reason you accepted. He thinks you know something. Bet on it."

She shrugged, drained her cup and set it on the nightstand. "Well, naturally. It's not like there's a chance in hell he could be attracted to me."

"Oh, come on, Cassandra, you know damn well that's not what I meant. A freaking dead man would be attracted to you."

Her smile was slow and knowing. "Dead man, huh? How about an escaped mental patient hopped up on Haldol?"

River held her eyes. "Yeah. Him, too."

She took the cup from his hand and set it beside hers. "So is he going to do anything about it?"

"No." He shook his head firmly.

"Come on, River. Do you really think I came up here to talk about the case?"

"It would be a mistake. I can't... Jesus, with everything else. No. It's just a bad idea, Cassandra."

She shrugged. "It's been a while for me. I'll bet it's been a lot longer for you. I'm not much for romanticism, River. I learned young that you never know for sure when your time is up. So I'm big on living in the moment." She dipped into her pocket, pulled out a handful of cellophane-wrapped packets. "I—uh—picked these up at the store. In case you change your mind." She leaned over him, set the condoms on his dresser.

Before she could lean back again, he caught her shoulders, and she looked up into his eyes, waiting. What the hell was she doing? Was this another attempt at repairing mistakes made in the past? Soothing her conscience over the death of an innocent man?

His eyes fixed on her mouth. She licked her lips, and the thoughts that flooded his mind were damn near overwhelming. But the one thing more powerful in his mind was the knowledge that he might hurt her. He might kill her.

"You should get some sleep," he said at a last.

She pursed her lips. "I'm not sure if you're being noble or stubborn." She sighed and climbed off the bed.

Stupid, he thought in silence. *I'm being freakin' stupid.*

"Good night, River."

"'Night."

She left the room. Closed the door.

He lay there, arguing with himself for all of ten minutes. Then he surged out of the bed and opened the door. He heard the shower running, knew she was in it, suppressed a moan that welled up from his soul.

Silently he moved closer to the bathroom. The door wasn't closed tightly. It hung open just a bit. He could see inside. He

could see the tub, with its sliding glass door. He could see *her* beyond the frosted glass. She stood beneath the spray, a flesh-toned blur. Her hands sliding over her body. Over her belly. Between her thighs.

River spun away, lunged back into his bedroom and closed the door. Head tipped back, eyes closed, he stood there in an agony of self-denial and knew he would never sleep. Or if he did, she was going to haunt his dreams.

He reminded himself sharply that he had damn good reason not to get any closer to this woman than he already was. He didn't know what he was capable of. He didn't know when he might black out again, and God, what if he did? What if he did and came back to himself only to find her lying dead at his feet?

Deep down, he realized the real fear that was eating at him, tormenting him. Because frankly, he didn't see how any grown man could have failed to recognize the signs of his wife's in-fidelity, could remain blind to them for as long as he had.

So what if he hadn't? What if, deep down, he'd known the truth about Stephanie? What if that was the reason he'd killed her?

11

Jax woke to the sound of her alarm clock, and managed to sit up, locate it and silence its irritating bleat all without opening her eyes. She took her time about that, arching her back and stretching her arms thoroughly before finally taking a bleary-eyed look around the living room. "I have *got* to get another bed in this house," she muttered, flinging off her blanket and sliding to her feet.

Rex got up when she did. He'd been asleep in front of the fire. And just like her, he stretched tiredly, before padding to the door and looking back at her.

"Yeah, yeah. Okay." She went to the door and let the dog out. Then, barefoot, she made her way into the kitchen and hit the button on the coffeemaker. She'd filled it the night before so it was ready to brew. Then she returned to the living room to fold up her blanket, pick up her pillow, and carried the two of them upstairs to stash them in a closet. No need alerting any further break-and-enter types that she was sleeping on the sofa.

She slid the blanket and pillow onto their shelf, then turned to look at the closed bedroom door. Poor River. She probably shouldn't have come on to him the way she had last night. Part of her wondered why she'd done it. It was true, she wasn't a prude when it came to sex. But she wasn't prone to sleeping

with strangers or bedding men on the first date, either. She couldn't deny the attraction between them. And she knew men. Hell, she'd been around them all her life. That man needed to get laid. Badly. He was practically climbing the walls with frustration, and his ego had suffered the worst blow the male ego could suffer. It needed shoring up. And since he was clearly as attracted as she was, she'd seen no reason not to indulge.

Still, she didn't suppose he was used to women with a practical approach to sex. She wondered what his wife had been like. Not loyal, that was for sure. Jax might be okay with casual sex when the need arose—both parties willing and all precautions taken, of course—but she didn't think she could ever cheat on the man she loved. If she ever fell in love, that was. An eventuality that seemed pretty doubtful most of the time.

She smiled. She wasn't usually attracted to cops. Interesting.

She wondered if he'd managed to catch any sleep, and crept to the door, opened it just a crack to peer in at him.

A neatly made bed lay in a startlingly neat bedroom. Not an escaped mental patient in sight. Frowning, she pushed the door open wider. "River?"

Nothing. And the cups she'd left on the dresser were gone. Vaguely, she recalled seeing them resting in the dish drainer when she'd gone out to turn on the coffeepot. She shifted her gaze to the other dresser, then began opening drawers. The condoms she'd left on top were inside now. But nothing else was there. No clothes. Nothing.

Hell, she couldn't believe her proposition last night had scared him away. No, it couldn't be that. He was up to something. But where the hell could he go without a...

She ran to the bedroom window, pushed the curtains aside and blinked down at her driveway. Her very empty driveway.

"That son of a—"

A note was propped on the windowsill. Just a page from

the notepad in the dresser, folded in half with her name scrawled on the outside.

Sighing, she picked it up, unfolded it.

"Don't panic," she read. "This has nothing to do with last night. I just have a couple of things I have to do. If all goes well, I'll be back tonight. Do me a favor, though—stay away from Ethan. And just in case I don't see you, thanks. For everything, Cassandra, including the ego-stroking. It did me a world of good."

It was signed "R."

She pursed her lips, crushed the note in her fist, and turned to carry it down the stairs to the living room, where she tossed it into the hearth.

"What's that?"

She spun around and saw Ethan Melrose standing in her front doorway, staring in at her. Hell, she hadn't relocked it when she'd let Rex out.

Rex. Where the hell was…?

A sudden explosion of barking told her that wherever he'd been, the dog was back now, and not happy to see a strange man standing on *his* porch. She lunged forward, grabbed Ethan by the arm and jerked him inside, slamming the door just before Rex could take a chunk out of his ass.

He was clearly startled. "Jesus, what the hell was that?"

"Stray dog," she muttered. And she wondered if he'd recognized Rex. Surely Ethan would be familiar with his best friend's old pet. "He's not usually aggressive. I've been feeding him."

Ethan lifted his brows. "Trying to make friends?"

"He's a great dog," she said. "He needs a home, and I'm all alone, so—"

"You are?" He was looking around the house, past her, almost as if he expected to see someone there. "I could have sworn I heard a man's voice when I was knocking."

Oh, no he didn't, she thought. He hadn't heard a damn thing. Because River hadn't been here. So if he suspected a man *was* around, he had other reasons for it. The guy was on a fishing expedition. She immediately wondered if he'd been the one who'd trashed her place last night, and she bristled inwardly at the notion, but tried to keep it from showing. Bastard.

"No one here but me," she said. "I just made coffee. Do you want to come in and have a cup?"

"Sure. Thanks." She stepped aside, mentally reviewing where she'd put the files and notes on River's case. She'd been shaken enough by the break-in that she'd taken precautions. Stuffed them inside an empty cereal box and slid it, upright, onto the top shelf of a cupboard. She sent a sideways glance at the note she'd crumbled and tossed into the fire. There was nothing left but ash. She smiled a little as she led the way into the kitchen, nodded to a chair and got down a pair of coffee cups.

Filling them, she carried them to the table…and caught him eyeing the two matching cups in the dish drainer. Shit. She set the coffee on the table, then opened the fridge, grabbed the milk and the orange juice. Then she fetched a third cup from the cupboard, set it beside her own and filled it with juice.

Ethan frowned at her.

"It's a habit. Two-fisted drinker," she said with what she hoped was a casual smile. "I never have something as bad for me as caffeine without adding something good for me to cancel it out. O.J.'s the drink of choice this week."

"I see."

"So what brings you by, Dr. Melrose?"

He sipped his coffee. "I thought we were on a first-name basis now."

"Oops. Sorry, I forgot. Have you got more information for me?"

"Maybe," he said. "The hospital administrator was phoned

at home last night. Seems an urgent fax had been sent to the records department."

She lifted her brows. "And?"

"It was from Corbett's lawyer, demanding that copies of all his medical records be sent to his office by the end of business hours today."

Jax frowned as hard as she could. "Are you telling me that your escaped lunatic—"

He grimaced and held up a hand. "Patient. Not lunatic."

She lowered her head. "I'm sorry. That wasn't very sensitive of me. He's your friend, after all." Peering up, she watched his face. There was only genuine worry in his eyes. "So let me try that again. Are you telling me that a mental patient as disturbed as this one managed to escape from the hospital, contact an attorney and…and what? Launch some kind of…malpractice investigation?"

"I don't know. I thought you might have some idea."

"Hell, I didn't even know he had a lawyer." She held up a hand. "Wait, yes I did. It was in the case file—what was the guy's name, Berger?"

"Brown." Ethan was watching her face. Probably thought he was some kind of expert at reading people, being a shrink. Too bad he was dealing with a seasoned cop who knew more about reading faces than he ever would. With him it was a matter of treating patients. With her, it was a matter of life and death.

"His lawyer will have to report it if he has any knowledge of Corbett's whereabouts," she said.

"He says he doesn't."

She sighed. "So why did you think I'd know anything about this, Ethan?"

He shrugged, adding milk to his coffee and stirring slowly. "I don't know. You're living in his house, feeding his dog—"

"His dog?" She blinked and feigned surprise. "You mean that German shepherd outside?"

"Yeah. I never knew what happened to him. Guess he's been fending for himself all this time."

"Well, I'll be damned." She sipped her own coffee, black, and made a point to take a sip of the orange juice afterward. "Hey! Do you know the dog's name?"

He nodded. "Rex."

"Rex. That fits him."

"Yeah, as in T-Rex." He shook his head. "That animal ought to be put down."

"Oh, he's not so bad. I mean, he doesn't seem to like you very much, but he's been a doll to me." She smiled. "So was there anything else, Ethan? I'm not rushing you or anything, but I need to get ready for work."

"No. No, that was all." He slugged half the coffee down in a single gulp and got to his feet. "I'm looking forward to tonight."

"Me, too."

He nodded, set the cup on the sink and then walked with Jax to the door. She said, "Better let me get the dog." Then she opened the door and stepped out onto the porch. Rex was there, waiting. She gripped his collar and held on, tugging him out of Ethan's path.

As soon as he stepped out the door, Rex pulled against her, growling deep and low. She had to drop to her knees and wrap her arms around his neck to keep him still. "Stop it, Rex. Behave."

Ethan came out, and Jax managed to drag and wrestle the dog inside the house, then pulled the door closed while remaining on the outside. "Sorry about that. Have a good day, Ethan."

"You, too, Jax." He started down the steps, then stopped and turned. "By the way, where is your car?"

She blinked, and sought an answer, found one, and only

missed a single beat in the process. "It was making a noise. My father wanted to take a look at it for me."

"So…you need a ride to work?"

"Oh, that's so sweet of you. Thanks, but Frankie's picking me up." She made a face. "Anytime now, to be honest. I'd better hustle."

"Yeah, you'd better. See you at seven, okay?"

"I can hardly wait." She waited until he was safely in his car—a silver Mercedes, no less—to open the door just enough to wedge herself back inside.

Rex sat on the other side, trying to get out, but she spoke a sharp command—one she'd heard the canine handlers use on the job. "Rex. Stand down!"

The dog sat instantly. But the fur on his haunches bristled and his ears were laid back. He did not like his master's best friend.

Jax patted his head. "I'm not overly fond of him myself, boy." Then she hurried to call Frankie for a ride, before Ethan had a chance to call her himself and catch her in a lie.

River had managed to grab a few hours sleep the night before. He'd come wide-awake before dawn, and knew there was no chance of going to sleep again. His dreams had alternated between sheer delight—images of Cassandra wrapped up in his arms, her limbs twisted around his body, not a scrap of clothing in sight—and sheer agony when the faces in his mind changed and became not his and Cassandra's, but the faces of his wife and his best friend. Stephanie and Ethan.

All night he'd told himself it couldn't be true. It wasn't possible. But as much as he searched his mind, he couldn't think of another man who'd been close to Steph. Not that close. Not close enough to…

He shut his thoughts down and got out of bed. He had to know. And he thought he'd come up with a way to find out.

Cassandra had given him the idea when she'd mentioned the value of knowing exact dates when Stephanie might have been meeting with her lover.

River needed to go to Burlington. He needed to get to Ethan's office. And if he left now, he could make it there before anyone else was around. He wrote a note to Cassandra and left it on the windowsill. Then he made his bed quickly, tossed his few belongings into a pillowcase and slung it over his shoulder. As an afterthought, he snatched up the two cups and rinsed them in the bathroom sink. He left them in the dish drainer, then went back into the still-dark living room.

For a moment, he was brought up short, caught by the sight of Cassandra asleep on the sofa, drenched in firelight. She had angel's hair, he thought as he stood there, looking at the way it spread around her on the pillow. But there was a lot more to her than the way she looked. She was solid. Strong, assertive, smart and entirely self-sufficient.

Stephanie hadn't been. She'd been dependent and needy. She'd needed him, whole and strong, and when he'd let her down, she fell apart. Hell, could he blame her for turning to another man? He'd stopped being the man she could rely on. And even then, she'd been sorry. He was certain she'd been sorry, certain she'd meant it when she'd vowed they would work things out.

He sighed, dragged his gaze away from Cassandra and went to the door, quietly lifting her keys from the little rack on which they hung. He took the car key off the ring and put the others back. Then he took one last look at her.

He wondered if she'd been mortally offended when he'd turned down her offer last night. And then he almost smiled, because he knew better. She knew he wanted her. She wouldn't take his rejection personally and she wouldn't become moody and petulant about it. Hell, she probably figured it was his loss, and that it was only a matter of time anyway.

Maybe she was right about that.

Sighing in real regret, he slipped out of the house, all without alerting Rex or waking Cassandra. He put the car in neutral and let it roll backward out of the driveway, before starting the engine and driving away. It was still dark outside. He worried a little about how she would get to work, but knew she'd just catch a ride with someone. She was resourceful enough to find a way to work and come up with a believable lie about why she needed one. She didn't need him worrying about her.

Now, an hour later, he stood outside the small brick building that housed Ethan Melrose's office. He'd been in private practice before landing the job as chief of psychiatry at the state hospital, thanks to his wife's connections. He'd kept his office open, though his private patients were few and far between. His practice was extremely exclusive. He treated the very wealthy who were lucky enough to travel in his social circle and who needed psychiatric help guaranteed to be discreet, not to mention expensive. And he'd treated his two best friends—Stephanie and River.

If he kept an appointment book or a diary, it would be there, in his private office, River thought. He'd parked the car a block away, and around a corner. He'd fed the meter a quarter he found in the cup holder. Then he walked. No point risking anyone seeing it. He didn't want Cassandra's car spotted near the scene of a crime.

He didn't have time to be subtle. And he didn't imagine he had the skills to break in without setting off any alarms even if he did. So he pulled out the gloves he'd found in Ben Jackson's box of castoffs, smashed the glass out of the window in the back door, reached in and unlocked it.

From there on he had to move fast. He headed through the reception area and into Ethan's office, straight to the desk. Its drawers were locked, but the locks were flimsy, and yanking

hard was all it took to drag them open. He made quick work of thumbing through them—was momentarily elated when he found a date book. Then he realized it was for this year. He needed the one from two years ago.

The telephone was ringing by then. Probably the police or Ethan's security company, calling to check whether whoever had opened the door had the right password or something.

He turned to the file cabinets, wrenching them open, flipping through the files. He thought if there were any with his name on them—or Stephanie's—he'd take them. But there were none.

Dammit, he wasn't leaving here without something!

He scanned the bookshelves, but saw nothing of any use to him. Then he returned to the desk, his eyes straining to see something useful on its surface.

Sirens sounded in the distance. Dammit, he had to move.

He snatched the Rolodex—he wasn't even sure why—and ran out of the place, out the back door, kitty-corner through the lot in back, and dived into Cassandra's car. He took off and was already around a corner onto a side street a block away by the time the police vehicles went screaming by.

Breathing a sigh of relief, he kept on driving. He was going to have to try Ethan's home. That was the only answer. But it was getting light outside now. He was going to have to wait until tonight, when darkness covered him again.

In the meantime, there were other things he could do.

He drove into the city, to the office of his attorney, pulled the car around to the back of the building next door. Which gave him a good view of the attorney's parking lot. Then he crouched down and waited.

He didn't have to wait long. He watched the car, a sleek black Lexus, pull into the lawyer's parking spot, and he stayed low, and dialed the man's mobile number on Jax's cell phone.

He watched Brown get out of the car and then stand still to answer his phone.

"Derrick Brown," he said.

"Walk to the coffee shop across the street. Go to the take-out window and order yourself some coffee."

He hung up before Brown could reply, then watched as the man gave a nervous glance around him and finally started across the lot, and then across the street.

River went across as well, stepping up behind him in line. He looked around. There was no one else there, but there was an un-marked police car parked in the office lot. It had been out of sight from his vantage point earlier. Good thing he'd been careful.

"Derrick," he said. "Don't turn around, okay?"

The lawyer stopped in his tracks. He looked left and right from behind his round, wire-rimmed glasses, as if for assistance in case he should need it, but he didn't turn around. He was scared. If he'd had enough hair in that dark horseshoe pattern remaining on his head, River thought it would have stood on end. And no wonder, he told himself. He thinks I'm insane and a killer.

"I'm not here to hurt you. Hell, why would I want to hurt you? You're about the only guy who can help me."

"And I intend to. I—I faxed the hospital last night. I'll have your records by day's end."

River nodded. "Thanks. I appreciate it. That probably explains why the police are watching your office."

"The police—"

"Don't turn around," River reminded him.

The man calmed, faced front. A girl appeared at the window and he ordered coffee. When she went to get it, he said, "Michael, you should turn yourself in. It's dangerous, you being on the run like this. The police are hunting for you—you could get hurt."

"If I go in right now, I'll be worse than hurt. I don't have a choice, Derrick. Besides, do I seem crazy to you?"

The attorney blinked, looking now at River through his re-

flection in the window glass. "Frankly, no. But the last time I saw you in the hospital—"

"The last time you saw me in the hospital I was pumped so full of psychotropic drugs I barely knew my own name. I'm off them. They've had time to clear out of my bloodstream. That's the only difference. I've still got the same head injury I had before."

Brown was frowning, searching his face.

"Don't you get it? It was the drugs. They were making me lose my mind."

The lawyer blinked, then nodded slowly. "I didn't expect to be convinced, Corbett, but…you've got me wondering. What you told me on the phone about that orderly was true. He had a record, was using a false name—" He started to reach into his coat.

River grabbed his arm fast, and the man went still.

"Sorry," River said. "I've been a cop a long time. What are you reaching for?"

Brown licked his lips. "Money. Cash. I took some out of your account on the way in this morning. I kind of expected you'd show up, or send someone." He lowered his hands.

"Take it out and set it there on the counter. Be casual."

Slowly, Brown removed an envelope full of cash from his pocket and set it on the counter where the cream and sugar were located.

River closed his eyes in relief. "Thank you."

Brown nodded. "I'm going to have to tell the police I saw you this morning, if they ask," he said.

"I know. It's okay, they're gonna know I was in town today anyway. And hell, it's only a matter of time before they look for me here. I should go."

"Wait. There's one more thing." The attorney started to reach into another pocket, then stopped, his hand hovering above it as his eyes sought permission in the window glass.

This was an outer pocket. There was no telltale bulge in the fabric of his coat. River nodded to tell him to go ahead, and he did, pulling out a key, setting it on the counter, as well.

"This is to a storage unit, out on the East Ridge Road. Hide-Away Storage. Your belongings, everything that was left in the house, it's all out there. Unit seven. I figured you might need some things."

He nodded. "Do the police have to know you told me about this?"

He licked his lips. "No, I don't have to tell them…not unless you tell me you're going to be there. You're not, are you?"

"Of course not," River said. Then he nodded. "Thank you, Brown. You're not going to regret this. I mean—even if it turns out I really did…what they say I did…that doesn't change the fact that someone tried to kill me in that hospital. Twice."

"You still don't remember…what happened the night of the fire?" Brown asked.

"No. I'm beginning to wonder if I ever will."

"I'll do everything I can for you, Corbett. You have my word on it."

River nodded. He'd wondered whether Brown would be the kind of man he could trust. He'd barely known him before—Ethan had been the one who'd hooked him up with the lawyer. River hadn't been in any state then to take care of such things. Now that he'd talked with him, River thought Derrick Brown was all right—maybe even one of the good guys. "Go on, your coffee's ready."

"Are you…going to be all right?" the lawyer asked.

"It doesn't matter," River told him. "All that matters is finding out the truth. That's all I care about right now."

Brown studied him in the window glass for a long moment, as he paid for his coffee and took his cup. Then he said, "I actually believe you. Take care, Corbett." He turned and went back across the street.

River took the envelope and the key, then went back to Cassandra's car, got in and pulled away.

He passed a police cruiser coming from the other direction on the way out of town. Part of him wanted to go straight to the storage unit to go through his possessions. But another part of him wanted to get back to Blackberry—back to Cassandra. He hadn't known her long, but he thought he knew her well enough to guess she would keep that date with Ethan tonight unless he could come up with some solid reason why she shouldn't.

And as much as he feared *he* might be some kind of a threat to Cassandra, he was starting to wonder if Ethan might be, as well.

12

Jax couldn't focus on work all morning. She couldn't believe she was worrying about a grown man—a cop, for heaven's sake—the way a nervous parent might worry about a child. But she was doing exactly that and it was out of character. She wasn't a caregiver. Wasn't a nurturer. She didn't want anyone depending on her and she didn't intend to ever depend on anyone else.

And besides, she knew damn well River could take care of himself. Even if he was still on the weak side. A little underweight. Probably running on very little sleep and a whole lot of tension.

She closed her eyes. It was almost lunch hour when the phone rang, and Rosie handed it to her as Jax passed the desk with her fifth or sixth cup of coffee.

Her mind hoped it was River. It wasn't.

"Hey, Jax. It's Beth. I'm taking you up on that promise to spend some time catching up. And guess who else is backing me up on this?"

She frowned and couldn't come up with an answer.

"Dawn, of course," Beth chirped, before Jax could have replied. "She wondered if you wanted to slip away for lunch with her and me. She'd love to see you."

"I don't know…I've got a lot going on, Beth."

"I know you do. I'd kill to know what. Listen, we can

make it quick—maybe meet at the diner across from the station? Grab a sandwich and a coffee? Half hour, tops. And you'll be within shouting distance if Blackberry suddenly erupts in a major crime spree. Come on."

From somewhere close to Beth, Dawn's voice called, "Pleeeease?"

Jax smiled. "Tell the kid I'm not buying the girlie voice." She wasn't. Dawn was way older than her birth certificate claimed. She'd been through more than most women three times her age. "All right. I'll come."

"Great. Ten minutes?"

"I'll be there." Jax hung up the phone and smiled her thanks to Rosie. Then she went into the chief's office. "Hey, Frankie. I'm going to take lunch."

"In a minute. Close the door." Frankie looked up, frowning, her graying eyebrows bending together.

Jax closed the door and took a seat.

"You're a nervous wreck today. Any particular reason?"

"Nothing I want to talk about."

"And your folks will confirm what you told me about your car, if I ask them?"

"If you ask them. Though I might resent you checking up on me like that."

Frankie sighed. "I just had a call from Burlington PD. There was a break-in early this morning."

"So why is that our problem?" Jax asked.

Frankie pursed her lips. "It was at the private office of Dr. Ethan Melrose."

Jax brought her head up fast.

"Yeah, I thought that would get your attention."

"Did they catch him?" Jax was almost breathless, until Frankie shook her head slowly.

"No. No witnesses. A little damage. They're not sure yet if anything was taken. The incident was confined to Mel-

rose's office itself—desk was rifled, file cabinets broken into."
She drew a long, deep breath. "Any ideas?"

"Yeah, I have ideas—the same ideas you have, the same
ones any halfway decent cop would have. Our fugitive is trying to find something in his shrink's office. Unless you've got
reason to suspect someone else?"

"No. My question is, what's he using for transportation?"

"I don't know, Frankie. Maybe he sprouted wings and flew
to Burlington." She hoped biting sarcasm would cover her in-
creasing discomfort. She did not like lying to another cop. It
wasn't something she'd had much practice doing. "Why?" she
asked after a moment. "Did anyone get a look at the car?"

Frankie let the question hang there for a long moment, her
eyes probing, before she finally said, "No. No one saw anything."

Jax barely kept herself from releasing a sigh.

"You were saying something about lunch?"

"Yeah." She nodded, glad of the change in subject. Frankie
could have pushed a lot harder than she had. She'd simply
chosen not to, and Jax was grateful. "I'm meeting Beth and
Dawn across the street."

"Dawnie's back in town?" Frankie's eyes lit up, and it
seemed she was finally distracted from the bone she'd been
gnawing. "What about Bryan?"

"Yeah, they're both here. Thanksgiving break."

"Well, go on. And you tell that girl to come by and see me
while she's here. I want to hear all about college."

"I will," Jax said. "If you need me—"

She waved a hand. "I'll know where to find you. Take your
time. Not much we can do here, anyway."

Jax nodded and got to her feet. She grabbed her coat on
the way out, and walked into the brilliant sunshine. It wasn't
officially winter, at least not according to the calendar. But
you couldn't tell it by looking around. The road was still bare,
shiny and wet. The base coat of snow hadn't formed on its sur-

face yet. It would be safer when it did; black ice was a killer this time of year. Still, there were salt pellets scattered around. No giant snowbanks along the sides, as there would be later in the season. Just a little slush, and it was rapidly melting. Bits of snow clung here and there, to rooftops, to trees, in the corners of some of the shop windows. But it was melting rapidly. It must be in the midforties, Jax thought, and would probably hit fifty before the afternoon was out.

She crossed the street and walked under the green-and-white-striped awning into Jeffrey's. The place was small, and included a long gray granite counter always stocked with the latest edition of the *Blackberry Gazette* for the customers to peruse. The booths lining the opposite wall were made of the same material, their seats padded in coffee-shop red vinyl. In between there were a handful of round wrought-iron tables with matching chairs, two apiece.

She chose a booth, slid into the side that faced the door, and ordered a glass of water to counteract the coffee she'd been slugging all morning.

Dawn and Beth came through the door before the water was even delivered to the table, and Dawn stared at her for a moment—no, not at her. Past her. So intently that Jax found herself looking over her shoulder to see who was standing there. But there was no one, and when she looked back again, Dawn jerked her gaze on target, smiled brightly and hurried across the room. Nineteen, and getting more beautiful all the time, Jax thought as she got up for a hug hello.

The kid had eyes that wouldn't quit. Deep blue and thickly fringed with dark lashes, despite her naturally butterscotch-blond hair that hung halfway down to her—

Dawn tugged off her knitted hat, and Jax gaped. "You cut your hair!"

"Yep. You like it?" Dawn finger combed the sleek locks, parted on the side and cut short.

"I love it. But God, you look like a grown-up now."

"I am a grown-up now," she said.

Beth smoothed Dawn's hair herself. "I love it, too," she said. "But it does make me feel kind of old." Dawn made a face at her, and Beth made one right back, then turned to Jax. "So how's your day going?"

"I thought small-town life would be quiet to the point of boredom. It's not proving true."

"So there's some excitement going on. I thought as much. Can you talk about it, Jax?" Dawn asked.

She shook her head, but the look in Beth's eyes told her she, too, suspected something was up. No doubt Josh had filled her in on his late night mission on Jax's behalf. She was probably worrying. Unlike Jax, Beth *was* a nurturer.

"It's no big deal, really."

Dawn frowned, looked troubled.

"What's wrong, Dawn?" Jax asked, not liking the dark look that came and went in her young friend's eyes.

"Nothing." Dawn plastered her bright smile back in place as they all sat down, and turned to the waitress when she came to their booth. "Diet Coke and hot cocoa. And a house salad, dressing on the side."

"Don't tell me you're worried about your weight," Jax said. "You should pig out while you're still young enough to enjoy it."

"I'm actively dodging the freshman ten," Dawn said. "So far, so good. But I won't be dodging too hard tonight. Beth's making fried chicken for dinner." She tipped her head to one side. "You should come."

"I wish I could, but I made plans."

"Really?" Beth leaned over the table. "Sounds juicy."

The waitress cleared her throat, and Beth looked up. "Oh, sorry. Uh—I'll have a burger. No fries or potato chips or anything on the side. And a hot cocoa sounds great."

Jax rolled her eyes. "God, not you, too?" Then she looked at the waitress. "Make it three hot cocoas. I'll have a turkey sandwich with provolone. Extra mayo. And you don't need to hold my potato chips. In fact, I'll eat hers, too."

"Rebel," Beth accused as the waitress hurried away. "So tell me about these other plans. What's up?"

"Nothing big. I'm having dinner with your guest. Ethan Melrose."

Dawn jerked so suddenly that her hand hit Jax's water glass and tipped it over. The water spilled, ice cubes sliding everywhere. They all jumped to their feet at once, grabbed their napkins and started wiping.

"God, I'm such a klutz sometimes," Dawn said.

Jax stopped wiping and looked at the girl's face. "Are you sure you're okay?"

"Yeah. I don't know what that was. A twitch." She grinned. "Maybe it's something new. The freshman twitch."

The waitress came with a towel and finished cleaning up the water. They sat back down. Beth said, "So you're dating the doctor, huh?"

"Hardly. It's business."

"That patient of his who escaped from the mental hospital?" Beth asked.

Dawn gaped at her. "You didn't tell me we had a mental patient on the loose. Is he in town?"

"Who knows?" Beth asked. "I heard he burned his house down with his wife inside. Killed her, and she was pregnant at the time."

Dawn went so utterly white that Jax thought the girl was going to pass out cold.

"Dawn?" Jax asked.

"It was *your* house, wasn't it? The one where you're staying." The way she said it, it wasn't really a question.

"Yeah," Jax told her. "How did you know?"

"I...don't know." She made a visible effort to compose herself, gave her head a shake. "It's just so sad, is all." Dawn averted her eyes as if the subject were closed, and turned her attention to the jukebox mounted to the booth's wall.

Beth focused on Jax again, but she was sending worried looks Dawn's way every few seconds. "I don't know about your plans with the doc, though, Jax. He got a call this morning and said he had to head back to Burlington. Said he didn't know for sure if he'd be back tonight." She lifted a brow. "You know what that was about?"

"Yeah, there was a break-in at his office. No big deal."

"Well, if he cancels your dinner, the invitation is open," Beth said.

The waitress brought their food, and the conversation turned to more comfortable topics. Dawn talked about her classes, her dorm room, her teachers. But she seemed to be forcing it, and Jax got the feeling her mind was on something else. Something to do with the dead woman in Beth's story. And she didn't mention Bryan the entire time.

Jax wondered how things were between them. They'd been getting pretty close last she knew—so much so they'd decided to attend the same college this fall. Jax had thought they were too young to be getting serious, but she had no idea just how far things had gone. Or whether they were still going.

She'd have to ask Beth about it when they were alone. Jax was certain something was bothering Dawn, but she wasn't sure if it was Bryan, or something else.

Then she rolled her eyes. The girl had two mothers watching over her. She didn't need a third. And Jax had enough to worry about without adding imaginary problems to the mix.

She was worried about River. Much as she hated to admit it, she was.

When lunch was over she waved goodbye to Dawn and

Beth, headed back to the department and told Frankie she'd like to go home for the afternoon, if that was all right.

The older woman looked at her oddly, but didn't ask any questions. She just nodded, and quipped, "You're not on the payroll yet, Jax. You can pretty well come and go as you please."

Jax nodded, told Frankie to call if she needed her, and asked Bill to give her a lift home.

When she got there, her car was sitting in the driveway, and she almost went limp in relief. She thanked Bill and went to the door, waited for him to leave before she walked in.

River was there, standing near a window in the living room, his body hidden by a curtain. She was certain he'd watched her get out of the car, ready to duck out of sight if Bill decided to come in with her.

She pursed her lips and blew every bit of air from her lungs. Then she marched straight to River, wrapped her arms around his neck and held on tight. "You are a total ass, you know that?"

He was stiff for a moment, but she didn't let go, and a second later, he muttered, "Hell," and slid his arms around her waist, hugging her back. "A guy could almost think you'd been worried about him."

"I don't worry about anyone."

"Bull."

She rested her head on his chest. "You broke into Ethan's office, didn't you?"

"Yeah. But I didn't get caught, and I made sure your car wasn't spotted."

She backed away and looked up at his face. "That was a stupid thing to do, River."

"It was the only thing to do."

"Why? The lawyer's going to get your medical records. You didn't need to go steal them."

"I didn't."

"Then what—?"

He silenced her by pressing his mouth to hers.

The kiss took her by surprise. She twined her arms more tightly around his neck and returned the kiss more eagerly than was probably polite. It set her on fire, and she opened her mouth, inviting more. He gave her more, his tongue twining with hers until he'd stolen her breath and jump-started her heart rate. When he finally lifted his head, passion clouded his eyes. He swallowed hard and backed away. "You're killing me, you know that?"

She felt cold without his arms around her, wanted to dive right back into them, but restrained herself. "Not my intent, River."

"No, I didn't think it was."

She sighed. It was clear he wasn't ready to go any further, and the kiss had been nothing more than an impulse.

"I like you," he said at length.

"Well, hell, what's not to like?"

"I'm just in no position right now to—to—"

"To jump my bones?" She walked as casually as she could manage to the sofa, plunked herself down onto its cushions and tried to pretend she wasn't itching to rip the clothes off him and take matters into her own hands.

"To start any kind of a relationship."

"Well, that's a relief, because I'm not, either."

He frowned at her, but didn't join her on the sofa. Instead he took a seat a safe distance from her, in the overstuffed chair. The big chicken. She rolled her eyes and drew a throw pillow into her lap. "When did I give you the impression I wanted a relationship?"

"I don't know. I just…"

"Look, I'm not a blushing virgin. And I'm not on the hunt for a life mate. Don't read so much into a passing physical at-

traction. I do not equate sexual gratification with romantic involvement, River. I'm not going to wake up in the morning convinced I'm madly in love."

He looked her square in the eye. "I might."

She blinked, utterly shocked. So much so that she almost jumped to her feet. She managed not to, settled for just saying, "If that's the case, consider the offer withdrawn. I'm not into hearts and flowers." Then she narrowed her eyes on him. "Or are you just trying to scare me off? Hell, River, a simple 'thanks, but no thanks' would suffice."

He shrugged. "It's not that I don't want you."

"Jeez, cut the drama. Forget it. If you get hard up, do what I do and take care of it manually." She did get up then, and walked to the kitchen, needing something to distract her from the odd rush of conflicting emotions his confession had stirred inside her. She went to the coffeepot, changed her mind and poured a glass of V-8 juice instead. "So did you find anything useful at Ethan's office?"

"No." He got up and came into the kitchen. She stood leaning against the counter and sipping her juice. "I was hoping for his old appointment books—personal ones, you know? I thought we could see if anything corresponded with the times when Steph was inexplicably absent. But there was nothing at the office. If he has anything like that, it must be at his house."

She lowered the glass and licked the juice from her lips. "You are *not* thinking about breaking into his house."

"Aren't I?"

"River, can't you just wait for the medical records? We find discrepancies, we get a search warrant, and—"

"And by then he'll have hidden or destroyed anything incriminating. He might have already."

"So you finally believe it might have been him?"

"I think I have to consider the possibility," he said, and he didn't look as if he liked it.

"Breaking into his house isn't the way to find out for sure, River."

"It's the only way I can think of."

She set the glass down hard. "You're being obstinate. And you're going to get yourself thrown right back into that hospital if you don't use your head."

She knew he didn't agree, but didn't say so. "I saw my lawyer today. Met him at a coffee shop so I wouldn't be spotted near the office. He gave me some cash, and the key to the storage unit where all my belongings have been stashed since the town took possession of the house."

She tipped her head to one side. "Did you check it out?"

He shook his own head. "I was hoping you'd come with me for that."

Jax lifted her brows.

"I…it might be tough. It might get dicey. Maybe even enough to induce a blackout."

"They're emotionally induced?"

He shrugged. "I don't know. I honestly don't know what the hell induces them. I also don't trust myself not to miss something important. My head's not working on all eight cylinders yet, you know? Besides, I'm too close to it to be objective."

"You think there might be something there?"

"I don't know. It's worth a look, though. Will you go with me?"

She pursed her lips. "Where is it?"

"About forty minutes from here, fifteen miles this side of Burlington."

She glanced at the clock. "Okay. Let's do it."

"You don't want to wait until nightfall?"

Jax drained her glass and set it down. "I have a date tonight, River. I plan to talk to Ethan…at length."

"I wish you wouldn't. If he is somehow involved in any of this—hell, Cassandra, he could be dangerous."

"Like the shit you've been doing today *wasn't* dangerous?"

"It's my problem. My risk to take. Not yours."

"It's my *job* to take risks. You're a cop, you know that."

"I don't want you to do it."

"Why? Are you really worried about me, River? Or are you just afraid he'll be willing to scratch that itch of mine for me? Don't worry. He's not my type."

"And I am?"

Oh, yeah, she thought. He was. Dark, dangerous, so good-looking it made her mouth water. He was her type, all right, damaged cranium and all. She didn't say it. She just looked at him and let him read whatever he wanted to in her eyes.

"Fuck this," he muttered, and then slid his arms around her and pulled her tightly against him, taking her mouth as if he really meant it this time. He bent her backward over the counter, one hand on her buttocks, tugging her closer. His hips ground against her, and she felt him, hard beneath his jeans.

She wanted him. Despite his earlier warnings, she wanted him bad, and she wanted him now. Jax had always been one for instant gratification. She didn't hold back now. She didn't care what he thought of her—she just gave herself over to the moment and knew she wasn't going to regret it.

His hand moved, sliding up to her waistband and diving inside her jeans, in the back, palm skimming over bare skin, cupping and squeezing her there. She rocked her hips against him to let him know that was good, and she pulled her own hands up and between them, shoved his chest so he backed away just slightly, and then tugged her blouse up over her head and tossed it aside. She yanked off the bra, as well.

He stared at her chest. She had great tits and she knew it. He seemed to agree, because a second later both his hands were on them, and then his mouth. As soon as his warm tongue flicked over her nipple, her body quaked and quivered, and she clutched his head in her hands and arched closer. He

took the cue, sucking the entire nipple, drawing hard on it, tugging and biting.

Oh, he was so good. She moaned a little louder every time his teeth closed on her, to let him know she liked it. His reaction was just what she wanted. He bit her harder, and pinched the other nipple while he did.

He was making her knees weak. She drew her hands between them again, and unfastened her jeans, then undid his and shoved them down over his hips, boxers and all. She wrapped his erection in one hand, which she slid up and down, thumb playing with the tip where there was already a droplet of moisture beading.

He was big.

He stopped suckling and straightened, put his hand over hers and took it away. "It's been too long," he said.

She smiled, knowing he would come in her hand if she didn't give it a rest. So she willingly released him, shoved her jeans off, and stepped out of them. He peeled off his shirt and stood there looking at her, not touching, except with his eyes, and that was plenty. And yet nowhere near enough. She reached for his hand and drew it to her, pressing it between her legs. He watched her face as his fingers parted, explored, entered her. She knew he felt how wet she was, how ready. "Been a long time for me, too," she told him. "Don't make it much longer, okay?"

He slid his fingers in deeper, withdrew them slowly, pinched her clit and made her gasp. Enough already. She twisted her arms around his neck, pulled herself up him, wrapped her legs around his waist and wriggled herself into position over him. And then she slid him home and he tipped his head backward, groaning loud. He filled her, stretched her, driving the breath from her lungs.

He staggered forward, until he pushed her up against a wall, and drove into her, deeper than before. Then he spun her

away from the wall and dropped to his knees on the floor. His hands clasped her hips as he pushed into her, holding her to take him, all of him. She arched backward in pure pleasure, and when she did he took her breast in his mouth again. Driving, biting, sucking, driving again, holding her and giving her everything. All of him.

She clutched him with her entire body when the orgasm broke through her, and she felt him releasing into her, felt him tense and stiffen, and moan as he climaxed. Then he wound his arms around her. He held her so tightly she almost couldn't breathe, and for a long while she didn't want to, because her body was still pulsing with pleasure.

When her brain cells floated back from orbit and settled into place again, she found herself cradled in his arms, her legs wrapped around him, and her head tucked between his neck and shoulder. He was holding her tenderly, still kneeling, rocking a little, kissing her hair now and then.

She licked her lips, found her voice. "If I'd known you were that good, I wouldn't have taken no for an answer the first time."

He looked at the clock. "I lasted a whole ten minutes."

"Best ten minutes I ever spent," she said. "And it was long enough." She lifted her head, looked into his eyes, saw something there and wondered if it was the afterglow of passion, or something else. Then she decided she didn't want to know. Gently, she extricated herself. "If we're going to head to that rental unit…"

"I know," he said. But he was looking at her still. Looking at her in a way that made her want to squirm.

"So I'll duck into the shower. Be out in a flash."

"You want company?"

She forced a smile. "Not this time, River. But you hold that thought."

13

The sprawling rental place sat in the middle of a flat, open field, and consisted of three long buildings, each with large white doors front and back. Every white door had a giant black numeral painted on it, and an 800 number was painted on the sloped metal roof of the building nearest the road. River assumed the office was off-site, since there wasn't anything resembling one there. The driveways were paved, smooth blacktop spreading right up to the doors.

He glanced at Cassandra as she pulled her car in. She hadn't said much on the drive here, and when she had spoken it had been about his case, about his health, about her job or the house. Not once had she brought up what had happened between them this afternoon. He hadn't bought into her claims that sex between them wouldn't mean anything. God knew it had been shattering to him. And not just because it had been mind-blowing in its intensity. There had been more. Just knowing her that way, being inside her, a part of her—it felt intimate. It felt important.

He supposed he'd better keep that to himself. She was trying hard to go with the illusion that it was casual, nothing more than mutual pleasure, a little much-needed release for them both. And maybe for her it was.

But not for him.

"There it is," she said. "You have the key?"

He dipped into his pocket and drew it out. "Got it."

She pulled the car to a stop. "This is good, out of sight from the road."

He nodded. His unit was on the back side of the first building, nearly in the center of it. No one would notice them parked here, not unless they were specifically looking for them. He got a little shiver up his spine at that thought.

Cassandra noticed it and looked at him. "What's wrong?"

River sighed. "Maybe you should drop me off, go for a drive, and then come back later."

Her brows went up. "I thought you wanted me with you for this."

"I did. I do. It just occurred to me that my lawyer probably knows I'll be here today. He could have tipped someone off. And even if he didn't, it's no secret he stored my stuff here. If the cops thought of it, they could be watching this place."

"Hell, River, if he had tipped anyone off, or the cops were watching, we'd be surrounded already." She frowned and tilted her head to one side. "You getting some kind of protective urge toward me now that we've slept together?"

He averted his eyes. "No more than I already had."

"I don't do the helpless female bit, so do us both a favor and fight that urge. Okay?"

"I'll try my best."

She nodded, opened her door and got out. "Let's do this, then."

He got out as well, took a careful look around, listened to the sounds around him. He didn't hear much. A crow scolding another. The breeze whistling around the edges of the buildings. A car way off in the distance. Moving to the overhead door, he used his key to open the lock. Then he pulled the door upward.

There was a light, but he didn't need it to see the past. It

rushed toward him in the flood of sunshine that invaded the long-hidden shadows. He saw his car—a six-year-old Chevy Blazer, red with silver side stripes—and then he was in it, driving through the countryside, with Steph laughing in the passenger seat. A U-Haul trailer tagging behind them, carrying everything they owned to their new home, their new life.

"River?"

Surrounding the car were other ghosts—the furniture. The sofa and chairs they'd picked out together. The dining room set. Their dresser. Oh, God, the crib. They'd bought it the day she'd told him she was pregnant, jumping the gun when they didn't even have a room ready for it yet.

"River?" Cassandra's hand settled on his shoulder. "You okay?" He blinked the ghosts away, gave his head a shake. "Yeah." Stacked amid the rest were boxes. Everything, an entire life, reduced to boxes, each one labeled in black ink. Dishes. Bedding. Clothes. Shoes.

He closed his eyes.

"Maybe you're the one who needs to take a drive, huh?" Cassandra asked. "I can go through this stuff while you—"

"No. We're here, let's just get it over with."

Nodding, she moved away from him, located the light switch and flicked it on. She didn't pause to examine much, but went to the Blazer, peering inside. "Huh," she said. "Keys are in it."

He wasn't surprised. There wasn't much need to take the keys out when the vehicle was locked up tight. "No plates," he said. "Registration, inspection, insurance, all expired."

"Still, it's wheels. You think it still runs?"

"Battery's probably gone dead."

She nodded, moving on past the Blazer to the nearest stack of boxes. She dug in, finding one marked "Personal Items" and pulling it free. She sat on the floor with the box in front of her, opened the lid and began pawing through the contents.

He didn't want to, but he forced himself to move deeper into the past and do the same. But every item he pulled from the box he chose was like a knife in his heart. Photos of him and Steph, together, happy. Her makeup and hairbrushes. Her jewelry.

"Anything?" Cassandra asked. She'd gone through three boxes, rapidly, efficiently. Nothing close to the way he was doing, taking out each item, touching it as if it could somehow erase the past, fighting his way through the pain to the point where he could set it aside and reach for another.

"Here. Let me finish this one. You grab another box, huh? Pick a good one. I'm not bothering with the ones marked clothes or bedding or the like."

He nodded as she sat down, closer to him than before, and pulled the box to her. He watched her as she began sorting the items, her movements crisp, brisk, emotionless. Then he turned to the stacks of boxes and started moving them aside in search of one that might hold items of interest. They'd have to go through them all, eventually. But that would take time. Several visits back here. He wasn't looking forward to it.

He moved another box, then frowned at the white surface that stood behind them. "What the hell is this?"

"What?" Cassandra set her box aside and got up, coming closer, peering through the opening in the boxes. "Is it your fridge?"

He shook his head. "Our fridge is still in the house. Fridge, stove, dishwasher, furnace. Part of the deal I made with the town. They covered my legal expenses, kept the taxes paid up, and paid for my care at the state hospital—up to a max of two hundred K. That ran out in the first six months. They got the house, property and major appliances. Besides, it's not a fridge."

"Okay, freezer, then." She moved aside a few more boxes, and he joined her, until they had exposed the thing completely. "See? It's your freezer."

He blinked, shaking his head. "A freezer is a major appliance, Cassandra. If we'd had one, it would have gone with the house. But that's a moot point because…we didn't have a freezer. That's not mine."

Cassandra drew a breath, lifted her chin and went to the chest-type freezer, gripping the lid and tugging upward, but it didn't budge. "Locked."

"Figures." He looked around. "I used to have tools. A bunch of them…" He rummaged through the piles.

"There should be a tire iron in the Blazer, right?"

He glanced at her, surprised he hadn't thought of it himself, and went to the car, located the tire iron–slash–jack handle, and carried it to the freezer. He was wedging the narrow end under the freezer's door when she put a hand on his shoulder.

"You sure we should do that?"

"How else are we going to know what's inside?"

Cassandra held his eyes. "Maybe we should tip Frankie off about this. Let her check it out."

"We don't know if there's anything to tip her off about."

"River, I can't think of too many reasons to hide a locked freezer inside a locked storage unit. I don't think you can, either."

"We won't know until we look." He hesitated, then added, "If you want to wait outside—"

"Yeah, right. Open the damn thing already."

He nodded once and pushed on the bar for all he was worth. The lid came up slightly, and he jammed the iron in farther, and pushed harder. A second later, Cassandra's hands were bracketing his on the bar, and she was pushing, too.

The lid snapped upward all at once, the end of the bar springing up with it and narrowly missing her face. She jumped back as it clattered onto the cement floor and the lid fell down again.

"You okay?" he asked, checking her for injuries. He didn't see any.

"It missed me. I'm fine." She turned to the freezer, and he saw the way she braced herself, squaring her shoulders, clenching her jaw. "Here goes nothing." She opened the lid, which came easily now that the lock was broken. The stench that filled the place turned his stomach.

They stood side by side, shoulders touching, looking down into the freezer. There was only one item inside. A large, lumpy object entirely encased in black plastic trash bags.

Cassandra reached into a pocket, pulled out a jackknife, flipped it open. Then she leaned over and, with the sharp side up, carefully cut a long slice in the plastic, near the rounded end. She handed the knife to River without looking up. He took it, eyes on the bag as Cassandra took hold of the edges of the plastic and pulled them apart. Then she pulled her hands backward, staring at what she'd revealed.

A face. A human face, partially decomposed, before it had dried to a leathery texture, probably due to the airtight conditions, fixed in an eternal grimace. River knew that face, even in this state.

"It's Arty," he muttered.

She frowned.

"Arty Mullins. He used to mow our lawn in the summer, shoveled the walk in the winter, just to earn a few extra bucks." River closed his eyes, lowered his head, shaking it slowly. "He wouldn't have hurt a fly. Had the mind of a child. Used to spend his days walking the streets, offering to help people. Lived in a halfway house—up until he moved away."

"I don't think he ever moved away," Cassandra said.

"Hell, he didn't deserve this."

"No one deserves this," Cassandra muttered. She reached for the freezer's lid, lowered it slowly. "We have to let someone know about this, River."

"Yeah. One more murder charge to add to the pile against me."

"You don't know that. Hell, did you even have a motive to want this guy dead?"

He lifted his head, met her eyes. "Come on, Cassandra. You're a cop. You tell me. If you were trying to make a case, what would you say?"

She couldn't hold his gaze. "I suppose…he might have been a witness. Maybe he saw what happened that night."

"Exactly."

"Yeah, except for one thing."

"What would that be?" He knew his voice was lifeless, grim. He felt pretty grim right now.

"You didn't kill this man, River. You said this unit was rented for you *after* you went into the hospital. You couldn't have stashed him here."

He narrowed his eyes, searching hers.

"And that means someone else killed him, maybe because that someone knew what Arty saw that night. Knew, maybe, that it would have cleared you, and implicated them."

"You're reaching."

"It's the only thing that makes sense."

"Not the *only* thing." He shook his head slowly. "How can you be so sure it wasn't me, Cassandra? Maybe the freezer was with my other stuff when it was moved here for me. Maybe no one ever bothered to look inside. How the hell is it that you believe in me more than I believe in myself right now?"

She shrugged. "I don't know. You're not a killer. Killers don't run around half drowning themselves in freezing water trying to save the life of a bungling stranger, River. They just don't."

He sighed. "You're biased."

"No I'm not. I believed in you before you jumped my bones. Though I admit that was good enough to sway me."

Shaking his head slowly, he ignored her little joke. "You're trying to atone for what your father did. And I'm your big chance."

"You think I'm that capable of self-delusion? That bad at being a cop?"

"I didn't say you were a bad cop."

"You'd better not. 'Cause it's not something I'd let slip by, River. I'm a good cop. Damn good. I've got instincts like nobody I know and I'm telling you right now, you didn't kill this guy. And you didn't kill your wife, either."

River closed his eyes. "I wish the hell I could be as sure of that as you are."

"You will be, once the facts are out. Until then, why don't you just trust me on this one. Stop questioning yourself. Unload some of that unearned guilt from your brain and maybe it'll make room for your own cop sense to come back, full bore. Okay?"

He nodded slowly. Then he turned back to the box of personal belongings she'd been going through. "You find anything in there?"

"Hell, with Arty, I damn near forgot." She moved to the box, dropped to her knees and took something out—a book, its cover made of purple crushed velvet. A little lock held it closed. "Is this yours?"

He frowned. "No. I've never seen it before."

"Must be hers, then. Stephanie's. Looks like a journal or a diary."

He heard a car on the highway, could have sworn it slowed as it passed. "We'd better get out of here. The police will find anything else, if there's anything else to be found."

"Okay." She dropped the velvet book into her coat pocket. "They'll know that freezer was broken into."

He shrugged. "I'll call in an anonymous tip from a pay phone. Claim I was going to burglarize the place, found the body and got scared off."

"See that?" she asked. "Your cop sense is coming back already. That's a good plan."

"Not really, but it's the best I can think of. It'll blow up in our faces if anyone saw your car here and describes it later."

"That's a chance we'll have to take."

He wished to hell he could match her optimistic attitude, but he was damned if he could. Everything they found just served to make him look more guilty.

For a moment as they locked the storage unit and got back into her car, he stopped to think about how far he would have got on any of this without Cassandra's help. Not very damn far, he thought. He'd have probably frozen to death in a snow-drift somewhere.

He caught her looking at her watch as she drove, and it hit him why. "You're still planning to keep that date with Ethan, aren't you?"

"Yeah, I am," she said. "And you're still planning to break into his house and search for his old date books."

He nodded. "I don't have much choice, the way I see it."

"Well, you picked a good night for it. I phoned his house today."

River frowned at her. "Why did you do that?"

"My friend Beth—she owns the inn where he's staying while he's in town—told me he had to go back to Burlington. Probably because of the break-in at his office. So I phoned his house. My excuse was going to be that I wanted to check whether we were still on for dinner, that I lost the cell phone number he gave me, and looked up his home number in the book. My real reason was that I was hoping to get a word or two with his wife."

"Victoria? Why?"

"Because he never mentioned he was married. I don't know, I thought I could strike up a conversation, maybe something would slip."

"So did you talk to her?"

She shook her head. "No. The message on the machine

says she's unavailable until Monday, and gives another number where she can be reached. I think it's a cell number and I'm betting money she's out of town for the weekend."

He closed his eyes, racked his brain. "What's the date?"

"November fifteenth. Why?"

"Mid-November—hell, it's the annual hospital fund-raiser. She practically runs it. Usually spends the weekend at her parents'."

"For what hospital?"

He frowned. "The same one where I lived, until recently. Her father is its largest benefactor. She's on the board of directors—I told you that, didn't I?"

Cassandra nodded.

"Victoria does a lot of work for the cause, even heads up the volunteer program there."

"So she's out. If he's with me, you'll have a clear shot at the house."

"Jesus, so now you're an accomplice."

"I'm already harboring a fugitive, River. It's not like this is going to make it worse. Besides, once we prove you didn't do any of this, I'll be vindicated."

"The law's the law, Cassandra. Cops aren't allowed to break it, even if they have a damn good reason."

"Your life is in danger. In this case, I'm within the law. Sort of. Just as long as I can prove it in the end."

He nodded. "There's a pay phone up ahead," he said. "Pull in and I'll place a call to Frankie."

"Okay."

She steered the car into the small parking lot of a gas station, which had closed an hour ago. River got out and she did, too. They went to the phone, and he picked up the receiver.

Sirens howled in the distance, getting closer. Frowning, a little bubble of panic rising up in his chest, he froze with the phone in his hand.

Cassandra gripped his arm. "Get out of sight. Go on!"

River slammed the telephone down and ran around the small station, to the back of it. He found a scrubby shrub back there and crouched beneath it, peering out to keep an eye on Cassandra. He'd be damned if he was going to hightail it to safety and leave her to clean up his mess.

A fire truck went screaming past. Two more close behind it. Then a state police cruiser came speeding toward them. Cassandra watched the fire trucks pass, but then flipped open her wallet, flashing her shield. Holding it high and face-out, she stepped onto the shoulder of the road as the cruiser approached.

It slowed, pulled over. The window came down. She said, "I'm off duty, but if you need any help…"

The cop inside shook his head. "We've got it covered."

"So what's up?"

He pointed ahead. "Structure fire, some rental storage place a half hour from here."

Cassandra nodded, patted the side of the cruiser. "Better let you go to it, then. Be safe."

"Thanks."

The car pulled away. She waited until it was out of sight to turn toward where he was lurking and wave a hand. River returned to her there by her car. "Did you hear?" she asked.

"Yeah. And I don't think it was coincidence. Someone knows we were there, and they probably know what we found."

"Think the firefighters will find Arty still there? Or burned to cinders?"

"There hasn't been time for him to burn to cinders. So I think him and his freezer are probably long gone."

She nodded. "If an exam of his body would have implicated you, River, they'd have left it. Which means maybe an exam of his body would have cleared you."

He nodded. "I was thinking the same thing."

"Really? Wow, a positive thought. I can hardly believe it." He smirked at her, but she rushed right on. "We've got to find that body, River."

"That's what you're getting from this, huh?"

"That's what I'm getting."

"So much for your top-of-the-line-cop sense, then."

"What's that supposed to mean?"

He met her eyes. "Someone knows we saw that body. Someone who doesn't want anyone else to know it exists."

"Oh, come on, you don't know that. Maybe they intended to burn the place to the ground before anyone ever found the body. Maybe they didn't get there until after we left."

"That would be one hell of a coincidence, wouldn't it?"

"So? It could have happened."

He shook his head firmly. "We're probably lucky they didn't firebomb the place while we were still inside."

"The fact that they didn't must be a good sign, though," she said. "If they'd wanted to kill us, why wait until we leave?"

"The only thing it's a sign of is that we got out of there before they had the chance or the time or a freakin' lighter. Arty is proof enough they're willing to kill. We're in danger, Cassandra. *You* are in danger, because of me."

14

"I don't like it," River said.

Jax stood in front of the bedroom mirror, smoothed the dressy brown pants and straightened their narrow gold belt. She wore a silk blouse, off white, tucked in, top two buttons undone.

"I think it looks good," she argued, making her voice defensive. Then she met his eyes in the mirror and saw that he was in no mood to joke with her.

"You know damn well that's not what I meant."

"I know. I also know we're out of time. I told Ethan I'd meet him at the restaurant at seven. It's ten of." She turned from the mirror to face River, but he stayed where he was, looking at her.

"What?" she asked.

"I was curious how different dating-Cassandra would look from everyday-Cassandra."

"Not different at all. Hair's down and the clothes are slightly dressier. Disappointed?"

"Yeah. That it's for Ethan instead of me." River reached out and buttoned one of the buttons she'd left undone.

"You just do what you have to do. And be quick. If we finish dinner and he wants to leave, I'm going to have to explain why my car's not in the parking lot."

"I'll need three hours at the outside."

"I can keep him three hours," she promised.

River nodded, looking as if he had more to say but holding back whatever it might have been. "I just hope I can find a diary, a date book—better yet, Stephanie's files there." He looked at the journal they'd taken from the storage unit. "We've got to find out who—"

"I flipped through it, River. I didn't see anything obvious. I wish we had more time—"

"I have to get into Ethan's house while I have the chance," River said. "I can read the journal more thoroughly afterward."

"That's what I thought, too."

"So let's do this thing then."

She nodded and handed him the car keys. He wore black jeans, a jacket and a knit cap. Looked for all the world like a burglar about to ply his trade. "You might as well drive," she said. "Drop me near the Sugar Tree. When you get back, park in the lot and just wait for me. Okay?"

He took the keys from her with a nod, and they walked to the car.

Ethan rose when Jax walked in, smiled a greeting, though the smile looked plastic. She returned it, knowing her own was no more genuine. Beyond the fake smile, she thought as she crossed the restaurant, he looked tired. Worn. His eyes had dark circles under them and she thought the crow's-feet had deepened overnight. Funny, how she could be convinced he was the bad guy one minute, and doubting it the next. It was impossible to look at the man and not believe his worry was genuine.

He pulled out her chair when she reached the table. Every bit the gentleman. "You look great, Jax."

"Thanks, Ethan. It's good to see you." She sat down and he returned to his own seat.

"Good to see you, too. I wasn't sure I was going to be able to make it."

"I know. I heard about the break-in at your office."

He pursed his lips, lowered his head. "It had to be River," he said.

The waiter came by to take her drink order. Ethan was already sipping wine. Jax decided a beer would be okay now, since she would have three hours to process it into porcelain before she'd be behind the wheel. As the waiter went off to get her longneck, she noticed the menu on the table, but didn't bother looking at it. They had all night. She had other things on her to-do list that were more important here. And making the evening last was right on top.

"Ethan, why do you think River would want to break into your office? What could he be looking for?"

He shook his head. "Jesus, I don't know. Especially when he's already had his lawyer demand copies of all his medical records from the hospital."

She frowned hard. "Why do you think he would do that?" she asked, even while trying to remember if this was information she should or shouldn't have.

"I think...I think what you said earlier might be right on target. He might suspect me of some kind of...malpractice. Or worse."

He honest to God looked frazzled, like a man on the edge. Well, hell, of course he was freaking out. He didn't want his reputation ruined. "Do you really think River is in any state to come up with something like that?" she asked. "A theory like that? I mean, I thought he was pretty much... well, you know."

"Insane?" he asked. He pursed his lips, shaking his head slowly. "He's not. Or at least, he wasn't. He's been getting worse and worse, and it's killing me to see it. I can only assume it's the guilt of what he did, eating away at him. There's

not much to do in a mental hospital, besides think. Remember. And now he's out there, somewhere…"

Jax frowned even harder, because the man had moisture gathering in his eyes. What in the hell was this?

He closed them, gave his head a quick shake. "Sorry."

The waiter returned with her beer, set it on the table while she was still trying to puzzle the man out. He said, "Are you ready to order, or do you need more time?"

She blinked at the waiter, then down at the menu. "Uh…yeah. More time."

Nodding, the man hurried away. Jax tipped her head to one side, studying Ethan. "You really are worried about him, aren't you?"

"Yeah. Worried. Guilt racked. I'm the one who put him in that hospital. I'm the one caring for him. You must know by now that orderly he killed was a felon working under a false name."

She nodded and her mind raced. Ethan had nothing to lose by admitting that to her—he must know she would have heard about the orderly's true identity. He could be covering. One big act. If it was, he was good.

"So how does a guy like that get hired at a state hospital? And why?" Ethan asked.

Right, she thought. *I won't ask you the same question, if you manage to convince me you don't know by asking it first. Good move, Doc.* "I don't know."

"River told me someone had tried to kill him. I thought it was just…just another delusion."

"And now?" she asked, watching his face.

He looked her straight in the eye. "Now I'm not so sure."

She nodded slowly. "He'll be all right."

Ethan shook his head. "How? For God's sake, how can he be?"

Jax saw the waiter heading their way, held up a hand to fend him off. "Ethan, I wasn't just repeating a tired cliché. I

think he'll be all right because he's been all right so far. Apparently, that is. He must be managing on his own, and he must be thinking pretty clearly if he's contacted his lawyer and gone looking for clues in your office. Right?"

He narrowed his eyes on her. "He wasn't capable of doing any of those things in the hospital. Someone must be helping him."

She lowered her head, flipped the menu open at last and ran a forefinger along the list of entrées, barely reading them as her eyes skimmed past. "I suppose it's possible."

"Is it you, Jax?"

"Me?" She looked up fast, feigning surprise. "I'm a *cop*, Ethan."

"Yeah. A cop who's living in River's house, taking care of his dog and taking one hell of an interest in his case."

She wondered how he was so sure of her overblown interest in the case. Was he basing it on their conversations, on local gossip? Or was it, perhaps, because the bastard had broken into her house and stolen her copies of the police file?

She rolled her eyes. "Of course I'm taking an interest in the case. Hadn't you heard? I'm Blackberry's next chief of police. And this is the biggest thing to hit town since—well, hell, since Mordecai Young. For a shrink, you have a big imagination, Doc. Me, helping a killer." She shook her head as if the very idea were ludicrous.

The waiter came again, and this time she welcomed the interruption. She didn't even care that she'd barely looked at the menu. She could wing it. "I'll have a steak. T-bone. Rare. Baked potato. Sour cream *and* butter."

He jotted it down and nodded. "Coleslaw, baby carrots or mixed veggies?"

"The slaw."

"And what kind of dressing for your salad?"

She almost told him to skip the salad, but bit her tongue.

Salad meant more courses, and more courses meant more time. She needed to make this meal last as long as possible. Though with Ethan's questions it wasn't going to be a fun-filled evening.

"Ranch," she said.

The waiter turned to Ethan, who rattled off his order just as carelessly as Jax had. "Poached salmon, brown rice, mixed vegetables." He watched the waiter go and then turned to her again, his eyes intense. "I never thought River had it in him to hurt his wife, Jax. But he did. I don't want to see the same thing happen to you."

"Me?" She lifted her brows, released a single bark of laughter and leaned back in her chair, shaking her head. "Hell, Ethan, have you ever got your wires crossed. If I knew where River was, I'd be hauling his ass in and claiming all the credit. Not sitting here having dinner with his head doctor."

He probed her eyes for a long moment, then finally nodded. "All right. Just…be careful."

"I'm always careful."

River drove slowly past the site of the storage units where everything he'd owned had been. God, when he'd got over the shock of seeing his past life all packed in neatly labeled boxes, he'd thought things had been about to get a hell of a lot easier. He would have clothes, shoes, personal things, a coat, for God's sake. He'd even been doing mental acrobatics trying to figure a way he could take the Blazer.

Gone again. All of it. The unit was gutted. And he supposed he was no worse off than he'd been before. But he felt worse off. He'd have been happier never getting close—close enough to feel his old life, to taste it. Freedom. From confinement, from guilt, from constant doubt and unending pursuit and mind-bending questions. Sweet freedom.

So close.

He thought about turning the car around and pulling into the rental place, maybe taking a look around in the debris. But he knew better. The cops probably had it under surveillance, or would at least be going by to check it out periodically. They would expect him to go there. They probably thought he was the one who'd burned it.

He ought to let his lawyer know he hadn't. Not to mention the little fact that there had been a body there. Brown wouldn't like it. He wouldn't like it a bit, as he'd been the one with the key. It would implicate him, wouldn't it?

If Arty's body had been found in the burned-out unit, River thought Cassandra would have heard about it by now. So it must not have been. And there was no point in his going back there to look for it now and getting caught. It was either long gone before the fire started, or in police custody. It wouldn't still be there at the site either way.

So he forced himself to keep on driving, and resisted the almost irresistible urge to go back. He drove until he came to Burlington, and then he parked Cassandra's car a half mile from Ethan's house, in a small pull-off along the edge of a side road.

He didn't leave it running. That would only draw attention. He pocketed the keys and got out. Tugging his collar up over his ears, he trudged through the snow. He had a few tools in his pockets—things he'd scavenged from the house and from Cassandra's car. A tiny screwdriver, needle-nose pliers, long pieces of wire. But he didn't think he'd need them.

He knew his way around Ethan's house as well as he did his own. It rested at the end of a pretty, winding lane. Its driveways were always perfectly plowed, its walkways perfectly shoveled. Out back there was a manmade pond with geese who'd become so fat and lazy they didn't even fly south anymore, but wintered right there, living on handouts from the Melroses.

Victoria would have the place decked out for the holidays

before too long, he thought, as he stood outside the sprawling white Georgian. It was aglow now, its specially placed outdoor lights beaming from the ground level up onto the house to show it off. But for the holidays, oh man, it would just glitter. She had to hire extra men to get her Christmas display ready to go. She used to hire Arty every year, and would drive all the way down to Blackberry to give him a ride in to do the job.

Poor Arty…he wouldn't be helping out this year.

Work on the holiday display would begin soon—the gala light show had to be ready to be turned on after Thanksgiving dinner. As soon as the table was cleared. It was Victoria's tradition.

River sighed, imagining the way the house would look in a couple of weeks when those lights came on, and remembering the last Thanksgiving before Steph had died. They'd had dinner here, with Ethan and Victoria. God, how he missed them.

Sighing, he walked up the driveway, right to the house, staying in the clear, paved driveway and the perfectly spotless sidewalk to avoid leaving any prints. He went to the garage, rather than the house door, wondering if Ethan had fixed the problem he'd discovered summer before last. River tugged on the automatic garage door. It shouldn't have moved at all. But it rose almost a foot before it stopped and refused to go further.

River shook his head. "Such a minor adjustment, pal. You've *got* to get this thing fixed."

He lay down on his back and slid underneath the door and into the garage. Then he got to his feet, closed the garage door and gave his eyes a minute to adjust to the dimness inside.

It took a while, but gradually, things took shape. Neither Ethan's Mercedes nor Victoria's Miata were in their spots, but the Mercedes ML-500 SUV held court, taking up the third slot and then some. River walked to the door that led into the kitchen—a door without any alarm system and one they rarely kept locked. No need when the garage door was supposed to

be secure. He hoped he wouldn't run into a housekeeper working late. But he didn't think he would. Vicki didn't have live-in help, and there were no other vehicles around.

He stepped into the kitchen—the door to the garage was unlocked, as usual. God, for such a smart guy, Ethan was pretty stupid about his home security.

The kitchen gleamed, chrome and black and white. Black range and side-by-side refrigerator-freezer and dishwasher and convection oven. White cupboards. Black-and-white ceramic tiles on the counter, and white marble veined with black on the floor. He'd always loved this kitchen. He could almost smell Victoria's turkey baking in the oven just being here again. Well, Miranda's turkey—the cook did all the work.

He moved into the dining room, trying to walk lightly, making very little noise just in case—and tried, too, to prevent himself from being distracted by memories. He continued through the living room, noticing with a stab of pain that the blown-up photo of him and Ethan, arm in arm, at the age of thirteen, was no longer hanging over the mantel. It hurt that it was gone.

Swallowing the pain, he moved on. There were several parts of the house he meant to check out before he left here tonight. Ethan's den, his home office and his bedroom.

And if he didn't find what he needed there, he'd check out the rest of the house, too. It was big, but it was empty. He could take his time.

"We'd all given up hope by then," Ethan said. "Everyone had stopped searching for the little runt, except for River. Hell, as the night wore on, we were starting to get more worried about him than we were about the pup. But then River comes dragging in, an hour and a half past curfew, mud from one end of him to the other. And Dad starts yelling at him for being late, and being filthy, and all of a sudden I realize that

the mud-covered lump under his arm is wiggling. And these eyes open up and look at me, and Dad just breaks off, right in the middle of one of the best heads of steam he's ever worked up." Ethan shrugged. "Well, for River anyway. He was always pissed at me for one reason or another, and yelling like a lunatic. But hardly ever with River."

Jax studied him, sensing a little bitterness, a little pain in him just then. "Why is that, Ethan?" She wanted to hear the rest of the story, but more, she wanted to know what made this guy tick.

He shrugged. "Ah, River was a jock. So was Dad. He played football in college. Got drafted into the NFL right out of his senior year—they gave him nice money, too. But he was injured during the first game of the season. He never played again—not professionally, anyway."

"That's a shame."

"It is. He wanted a jock for a son—someone to do what he couldn't. I was…well, a nerd. Something of a disappointment."

"I seriously doubt that, Ethan."

"You shouldn't. I think he saw River as the son he would have wanted." He closed his eyes. "I used to be so jealous of that."

"Used to be?"

He lifted his head, nodded. "Dad was furious when River decided to become a cop instead of pursuing a career as an athlete. River insisted he wasn't that good—Dad argued that he could be if he would just give it all he had. River didn't want to do that, and so on and so on." Ethan shrugged. "Once they started fighting over it, I realized it wasn't me who'd disappointed my father. And it wasn't River. Dad wasn't going to be happy with any of us because we couldn't give him back his lost career, or help him reclaim that glory. We never would have been able to, even if we'd tried. He was unhappy with himself."

She smiled slowly. "You are so insightful. You know, you'd make a good psychiatrist."

He smiled back at her, looking slightly more relaxed. "That's a really good idea."

"I distracted you from your story," she said. "River came home late, got yelled at and had a muddy something under his arm. Was it the missing puppy?"

Ethan nodded. "Yeah. It was Oliver. I never thought we'd see him again. He'd dug his way out of his kennel and wandered into a swamp a mile from home. I don't know how the hell River found the runt, but he just wouldn't quit looking. Just wouldn't give up."

She sat there staring at this man, wondering if he honestly loved River as much as he seemed to, or if he was just very good at manipulating people into seeing what he wanted them to see.

"You full?" Ethan asked.

She glanced at her empty plate and then to her watch. She needed to kill more time. "I am stuffed, and was planning to demurely turn down dessert—but I've got to tell you, that chocolate concoction they're having at the next table is giving me second thoughts."

He put a hand over hers. "I would really like to take you somewhere else for dessert," he said. "What do you say?"

"Where did you have in mind?"

"You're gonna have to trust me. I promise, it'll be worth it."

"Well..." She pretended to think it over, then nodded and said, "But only if we can take your car. I'm not in the mood for driving, and frankly, I love the feel of a Mercedes."

"You've got it." He waved to the waiter, who quickly came to take his credit card. Ten minutes later, they were getting into his vehicle.

It was already running. He'd started it from inside the restaurant. Its headlights were on and its heated seats were warm and waiting. "Damn," she muttered, as she ran a hand over the supple leather. "I've *got* to get one of these."

Ethan smiled. "You like it?"

"It's fabulous. Not likely I'll ever afford one on a cop's salary, but hell, a girl can dream."

"My wife has a Miata, but frankly, she drives this whenever she gets the chance. I think she's wishing she'd chosen luxury over sporty good looks."

Jax blinked in shock. She had not been expecting him to mention his wife—thinking he'd been—well hell, coming on to her. Now she didn't know what to think.

More and more the guy was seeming like he really was the nice, decent human being River kept describing to her.

He drove, and it was only a good distance later that she realized they were heading toward Burlington. God, she thought, please don't get the notion of stopping by your house. Don't, don't, don't.

River went through every likely spot in the house, but he didn't find any files on Stephanie. He didn't find much of anything at all, until he went into the den—Ethan's inner sanctum. It was the place where the guys hung out after a meal, where they gathered to have a cigar after dinner, or to catch a baseball game. Ethan wasn't big on sports, but tolerated them as excuses for social gatherings. As long as it wasn't football. River supposed he could understand that.

Victoria had no interest in the den. She never went in there, hated the stench of cigar smoke. River remembered her wrinkling her nose whenever she'd had to stick her head into the room, the pretty face somehow even prettier with that grimace on it.

Stepping into the den brought back memories. And the pictures on the walls brought back more. The blown-up image of him and Ethan, the one that used to hang in the living room, was here. So were shots of River and Steph, and others showing all four of them together.

He got a little dizzy, closed his eyes and pressed his hands to his head to silence the familiar buzzing that was going on inside. "Jesus, not now," he whispered. He did not need a blackout now.

He clutched the back of the chair nearest him, struggled to stay focused, and shot a look across the room at the door on the far side, the one that led into the backyard. Better to get out of here now, he thought, and took two unsteady steps toward the door. And then his vision went. And his will went with it. He sank onto the floor as every thought evaporated, and his legs folded beneath him.

15

"You were right," Jax said, scraping the last of the chocolate syrup from the banana split container. "I can't believe you found banana splits in November."

"You just have to know where to look. Riv and I used to work here, summer before our senior year. I cooked, he waited tables."

"Seems like you got the tougher job. I can say that, having done both myself," she said.

"River was a draw. Girls always flocked to him. It was better for business having him out front with the customers."

"I think you're selling yourself short," she said. She didn't, not really. He was awkward and stiff, which seemed to be his normal state. Still, it didn't hurt to make nice. And then move on to a safer subject. "Where are we going now?"

Ethan gave her a smile. "I just have a quick stop. I'm not up to anything, I promise."

A little chill settled in her belly and Jax tried to squelch it. "I believe you. I just…" She looked at her watch for effect. "I really ought to be getting home."

"I'll get you home before you know it."

She wasn't paying much attention to what he was saying, because he had pulled the car into a curving lane, and the headlights bathed a house that was beyond magnificent. Huge, sprawling, immaculate. Oh, God it couldn't be—

He stopped the car and shut it off. Her throat went dry. "Is this…your house?"

"Yeah. It's even nicer on the inside. I wish Vicki were home so you could meet her, but—no matter. Come on in, I'll just be a minute."

She didn't want to go in. She wanted to lock the car doors and keep him from going in himself, force him, somehow, to leave. But she couldn't come up with a believable reason. God, she hoped River wasn't still there. Please, she thought, let him have found what he needed and got the hell out of there by now.

Ethan climbed out of the car and she followed, moving with deliberate slowness. The wide door was of dark wood, framed in stained glass panels, with a brass knocker that looked antique. He inserted a key, and swung it open, then waited for her to go in before him.

Jax did, almost on tiptoe, holding her breath as she strained to hear a single sound in the house. Ethan came in behind her and punched some buttons on a panel. A security system. Hell, how could River have managed to get inside without setting off its bells and whistles? Maybe he hadn't. Maybe he'd decided it wasn't worth the risk.

Lights came on. She hadn't even heard Ethan hit the switch, and the sudden brightness startled her. And then she watched him watching her, and realized she probably ought to show some interest in her surroundings. She took a quick survey of the room, nodded in approval when she couldn't care less what the place was like. "Nice," she said. "So what was it you needed to pick up?"

"My PalmPilot. I'm lost without the damn thing. Amazing how dependent we get on technology, isn't it? Makes you wonder what we'd do if we suddenly lost it all."

"You thinking Armageddon might come, Ethan?"

He laughed. "God, I hope not. Have a seat. You want a drink or—"

"No, just grab the thingie and let's go."

He frowned at her. "You uncomfortable here for some reason, Jax?"

She shrugged. "Just wondering what your wife would think."

The line, delivered deadpan, seemed to bring him up short. "You're right, she'd probably jump to all the wrong conclusions."

That statement made Jax wonder if the woman had reason not to trust her husband, but she didn't ask.

"Wait here," he said. "I'll be right back."

He started down a hall. She couldn't wait where she was; she had to know what was going on. If he walked in on River—hell, that wasn't going to happen. It couldn't happen. No one's luck was that bad. Either way, she had to be with him. So she followed, and Ethan stopped, turned and frowned at her.

She shrugged. "I just…get to see more of the house this way."

"Suit yourself," he said. "It's in the den, right over here."

He walked through a set of double doors, went to the desk that sat on the far side of the room, not bothering with a light, and opened a drawer. "I could have sworn it was right—"

He reached to the desk lamp as he said it, flicked it on.

At that instant River burst up from behind the desk, knocking Ethan flat on his back. At least she thought it was River. She could barely tell with the knit cap pulled down over his face, a couple of holes torn in it for vision's sake.

He spun around, lunging toward the glass door in the back, but froze as he spotted Jax standing there.

She waved a hand at him, urgently telling him to go. And he did, but by then Ethan was pulling himself up onto his feet again, cussing aloud. River flung the door open and bolted, and Ethan lunged outside after him.

It was only as Jax burst outside behind them both that she

glimpsed the gun in Ethan's hand. He must have had it in the desk. Hell.

"Ethan, wait!"

He didn't even pause, just stopped running and leveled the weapon.

"No, dammit!" She slammed into him even as the gun exploded, spitting fire into the night. He stumbled at her blow, but didn't fall. Jax yanked the gun out of his hand, casting a panicked look toward where River had gone. But she didn't see him.

"What did you do that for?" Ethan demanded, clearly pissed off.

"What did *I*—Jesus, Ethan, you can't shoot an intruder in the back when he's running away. That's way beyond self-defense. You want to do time? Lose your license to practice medicine to boot?"

He pursed his lips. Jax started off in the direction River had been heading, but stopped and turned sharply when Ethan came behind her. "Go on back to the house and wait. I'll check this out."

"I can't let you go after a burglar alone—"

"I'm a cop, Ethan. I do it all the time. Besides," she said, lifting his firearm, "I've got your gun." She also had her own, but she wasn't about to mention it. He might think it meant he could have his back, and there was no way in hell...

He sighed, then brightened. "I'll call 911, get you some backup." He started searching his pockets.

She almost snapped off an order that he shouldn't do that, but bit it back. It would sound pretty damn suspicious for a cop to tell a man not to report a break-in at his home. Not to mention a possible shooting.

"Damn," he said. "Cell phone's in the car."

"Call from the house," she said, latching onto the excuse to get rid of him. She had to get to River, make sure he was all right.

She started off again, hoping Ethan would do the same, and waited until she heard his footsteps crunching over the cold ground back toward the house to glance over her shoulder. He was doing as he'd promised. Going into the house. She walked faster, lurching into a run as soon as she heard the door close.

"River?" she called in a harsh, overloud whisper.

What she wouldn't have given for a flashlight. Hell, was that blood on the ground? She bent closer, checking out the grapefruit-size patch of dark red staining the snow, then rose again, looking around. "River, where are you?"

A deep moan brought her head sharply to the left. She saw a partially frozen pond, with Canadian geese huddled together along the shore. And then the shape in the snow. She hurried toward it. Moments later she was kneeling beside River, peeling off the knitted hat, cradling his face in her palms and gently smacking his cheeks to get him to open his eyes. "Come on, come on, snap out of it. We don't have time for this."

She smacked a little harder. His eyes popped open and took a moment to focus on her face. A heartbeat later recognition kicked in. She said, "Where are you hit?"

"Where's Ethan?" he asked.

She dropped his head, and turned to begin searching his body for signs of injury. "In the house calling the cops. We don't have much time to get you the hell out of here. Now where are you—oh, damn." The blood was seeping steadily from the back of one leg. She gripped his hip and rolled him onto his side, but she could barely see in the darkness. She lowered him again, then reached for his belt, rapidly unbuckling it and sliding it from the loops of his jeans.

"Hell, Jax, this isn't the time."

She slid her gaze upward, met his. "Making bad jokes? Maybe you're not at death's door just yet, then."

"I don't think so."

"Yeah, well, don't be so sure. Was it worth all this, River? Did you at least find something useful in there?"

"No records on Steph, but..." He pulled a black leather-bound booklet from the back of his jeans and held it up. "I got this."

"Yeah. You also got shot. I'd say all in all, you kind of lost this round, pal." She slid the belt around his thigh, then stopped and drew away. "You have to do this, River. I go back there covered in blood, and it's going to look fishy. I mean, I could probably talk my way around it with Ethan, but those cops he's calling—"

He nodded and shoved the book back into his jeans. Then he sat up, took both ends of the belt, pulled it around his thigh, above the spot where the bullet had hit him, and knotted it tight. He gritted his teeth in pain, but tightened the belt mercilessly anyway, and Jax was glad he did.

"There's no exit wound," she said. "The bullet must still be in there."

"Yeah, I was thinking of starting a collection."

"Real funny. You leave the car somewhere?"

He nodded. "That way, first left, about a half mile."

"Let's go. We'll hit the pavement so we don't leave tracks in the snow, and hope you're not laying a blood trail. All right?"

He nodded and let her pull him up. She hauled his arm around her shoulder and got him out of the ditch and onto the blacktop. Then she moved as fast as she could. Clearly, it was hurting him badly to walk on the wounded leg, and it probably wasn't doing the injury any good, either, but they didn't have much choice.

"We have to get off this road before the cops get here," she said. "And they won't be slow. Not when this was Ethan's second break-in of the day, and their hottest fugitive in years is responsible. Hell, they'll probably bring a freaking army."

He glanced up at her, his face contorting with every step, and said, "Glad you still think I'm hot."

"Jesus, River, this is not funny. If they see me helping you—"

"If they see you helping me, Jax, I'll spin around and clock you in the jaw. Gently, of course. And you can go down on your ass and I can run for it. Say you were giving chase, that you had me."

She thought that her footprints back there in the snow where he'd been lying were going to tell an entirely different story, but she didn't say so.

"You're right," he said. "They're going to pull out all the stops to catch me. Hell, they think I killed Stephanie. And that orderly. And Arty, if they found the freezer."

"I think Frankie would have called me by now if there were talk of a body in a freezer, River."

He stumbled, and she pulled his arm around her shoulders a little farther, readjusting her hold on him. She kept one arm around his waist, supporting him as much as he would let her. "You gonna make it?"

"Got to." He moved his head. "There's the side road. It's bare, no snow. We should be all right."

They walked around the corner and down the second road, which was gravel lined and narrow, but fortunately, not snow covered. She picked up the pace, even though she knew it was hurting him. Hell, if he were caught he would be killed. She believed that, and she was damned if she could figure out who was wishing him dead, plotting his demise. She wanted to think it was Ethan. He was the easy suspect. But he was too easy, and her gut wasn't ready to bet their lives on it.

"There's the car," River said.

She nodded, spotting it up ahead, and walking even faster. To his credit, he didn't complain. Didn't grunt in pain or make a single protest. Then again, it was his life that was

hanging by a thread, not hers. They made it to the car. She wrenched open the driver's door and helped him ease inside.

"Damn Ethan and his dumb luck," River muttered. He fished the keys from his pocket and stuck them in the switch. "I don't imagine he's fired a gun more than five times in his whole freaking life, and he manages to hit a moving target."

She fastened his seat belt around him, only realizing what a nurturing thing it was as she heard the click. Giving herself a mental smack upside the head, she took her hands away. "At least he missed the femoral artery or you'd have bled out by now."

"That's reassuring."

"And it's the left leg, so you can drive. Thank God the car's an automatic." She met his eyes. "Think you can make it home?"

"I'll make it."

She nodded. "If the bleeding starts again—"

"I'll cinch it up tighter. Don't worry. We're gonna need to clean the car. If they check—"

"They're not going to have a reason in the world to suspect me, River. No one's going to check my car. Unless you keep talking until the cops get here and spot it."

She started to straighten, but River caught her head in his hands, pulled her close and pressed a kiss to her mouth.

When he let her go again, he said, "Thanks for having my back."

"Yeah. Just get the hell out of here, will you?"

He nodded. She backed out of the car and closed his door, watched as he pulled it into motion and headed down the dirt road, away from the main one. He probably knew a shortcut or alternate route that would avoid the cops.

Hell, the cops.

She turned and ran back the way she had come, scanning the roadside until she spotted a limb she could reach without leaving tracks in the snow, one drooping from a pine tree. She snapped it off, and kept running, back to where she'd found

River lying, and then she took her time, did her best to wipe out the marks her knees had made, and a few of her footprints in the snow, while leaving one set of her own, and all of River's pretty much alone. It was tough, in the dark, but her eyes had adjusted by now. She thought she was seeing everything. She heard sirens, and knew she'd run out of time.

She turned and walked through the snow back to the paved part of the driveway, tossing the branch under the first tree she saw, then hauled out her shield, and kept the gun tucked out of sight. As soon as the cars came howling into the drive, she held up her ID, letting their headlights catch it in their glare.

The cars stopped, officers got out, several coming toward her at once.

"Jackson," she said. "Up from Syracuse, New York."

"Ryder," the cop in the lead said, extending a hand. "What have you got?"

She shook his hand, wondering belatedly whether she had blood on hers. She didn't think so. "Dr. Melrose and I walked in on an intruder at approximately—" she glanced at her watch "—21:45. He was in the den—first floor, rear of the house. He fled, exiting through that door there—" she pointed as she spoke. "Crossed the back lawn. Melrose had a freaking firearm. Took a shot at him as he fled." She shook her head.

"He have a license for it?" Ryder asked.

"I have no doubt. But using it was unnecessary. I disarmed him, sent him to the house to call you all, and headed out here to investigate."

"He hit the prowler?"

She nodded, then led them straight to the bloodstained snow where River had been lying, and pointed. Ryder pulled out a flashlight and aimed its beam at the snow. "He went down, here, for a minute. Maybe two. Then took off again," Jax explained. "I've searched the area. No sign of him. I think he's long gone."

Ryder nodded, turned to his men. "Fan out, search the

area." Then he returned his attention to her again, his light moving with his eyes, until she shielded her own. "You've got a little blood on you."

She followed the light, saw the blood on her blouse, swallowed hard. "I didn't have a light. Had to get pretty close to that spot to see if it was blood. I'm surprised I didn't smear more on me than that."

He nodded. "Okay. You get a look at the perp? See if he had a car somewhere?"

She shook her head. "No. It was too dark and then he was gone. I didn't hear any vehicle, though. My guess is he's still on foot." Better to keep them here, searching the area, and give River plenty of time to get safely away.

"All right."

Ethan was hurrying from the house now, down the driveway to where she stood. "Thank God," he said, taking in the entire situation with a swift glance. "Did you find him?"

"Not yet," Ryder said.

"He's hit, though."

Ethan blinked as if he'd been stunned by Jax's words. He met her eyes and it was clear he knew he had just shot his best friend. "I didn't mean—" he began.

"No one ever does," she snapped. "Listen, I need to get my ass home, and I've got no wheels here."

"I can drive you—" Ethan began.

"We need to get a statement from you, Dr. Melrose."

"Of course." He looked at Jax again. "You can take my car. I have the SUV, anyway."

She nodded. "Walk me back? They can wait five minutes for that statement."

He frowned, but nodded, and she started back toward the house. She remained several steps ahead of him, so that he had to run to catch up, and even then she kept her brisk pace unchanged. "So why'd you do it, Ethan?"

"What?"

"We both know your burglar had to be River." She stopped abruptly, turned and stared him in the eye. "So tell me, why did you shoot the man you keep telling me was the best friend you ever had? The man you were close to tears about earlier? Why did you try to shoot him in the back, Ethan?"

He frowned deeply, and for a moment she thought he would deny that was what he had done, but he didn't. He faced her. "I didn't think," he blurted. "Jesus, you don't know what went through me after I pulled that trigger and realized it might be River running from the house. I just—I just reacted, that's all."

"You shoot at fleeing prowlers so often it's become a reflex action, huh?"

"Don't make it sound like that, Jax. If it had hit me sooner that it might be River I never would have—"

"Might be River? Ethan, you know damn well it was River. You just told me no more than two hours ago you were certain River was the one who'd broken into your office today. So who else would break into your home a few hours later? Who else could it have possibly been?"

"I'm a lousy shot!" he exclaimed. "I probably wouldn't even have hit him if you hadn't slammed into me like that."

"Yeah, or maybe you'd have killed him."

He spun away from her, let his head fall forward as if his neck had turned to water, and pushed his hands through his hair. "Did you see him? Is he all right?"

"If I'd seen him, he'd be on his way to a hospital, and in custody," she said, and she didn't even feel guilty about the bald-faced lie. It was getting easier and easier to lie for River. "But there is a pretty good size patch of bloodstained snow over there," she stated, and when he turned, looking horrified, she nodded toward where River had fallen. "So we know you at least wounded him. Nice job, Ethan. That's the work of a true friend, right there."

"I told you, I wasn't thinking. God, I would never deliberately shoot River."

"Wouldn't you?" she asked. "Because you know, it occurs to me that someone seems to want him dead. Someone hired that goon at the hospital, pulled strings to get him in there despite his record. Maybe even delayed the mandatory background check. River told you he'd been attacked and I'm beginning to think that wasn't a delusion, after all. And now you've shot him for no good reason whatsoever."

Ethan was silent for a long moment, studying her.

"Makes you wonder," she said. "You got the keys or what?"

He nodded, tugged them from a pocket and slapped them into her hand. "I'm not the one trying to kill River, Jax. I swear to you. I'm not. I thought I aimed low and to the left. I really did. I just wanted him to stop running, end this insanity once and for all."

She studied his eyes, watching for signs of deception. It occurred to her that the bullet had been low and to the left, just not far enough. Then again, he wasn't an experienced marksman. And she *had* knocked him off balance.

She pursed her lips, sighed and lowered her head. "I'm sorry if I was rough on you. I just had to be sure."

"And now you are?"

She lifted her head again, put a smile on her face. "More than I was. Thanks for the loaner. I'll take good care of it and get it right back to you, okay?"

He nodded. "Before all this—I mean, it didn't end well, Jax, but I enjoyed having dinner with you." He reached out as he said it, tucking a strand of hair behind her ear.

She covered his hand with hers. "Me, too," she said. "Maybe next time we can invite Victoria along. I'd really like to meet her."

He stiffened just a little at the reminder of his wife. Jax knew he hadn't asked her out with the intent of hitting on her.

It had been about the case, about River. She believed that. But that had changed, just for a moment, just now. Whether he'd intended it or not—she'd felt it.

Dawn woke from a sound sleep to see the woman standing at the foot of her bed, staring at her.

She sat up fast, startled. "What the—" But then the fear faded, because the woman was the same one she'd been seeing for days now. Maybe the shock was wearing off. She didn't look at all menacing. Just rather lost, and maybe frightened. Dawn softened her voice, squared her shoulders. She was tired of ignoring them and demanding they go away. It wasn't working, anyway. Maybe she should try to find out what the hell they wanted from her.

Swallowing her fear, she forced words to her lips, but they came out shaky. "Who are you?"

The woman didn't speak. She just stood there, staring.

God, what was the point of her showing up all the time if she wasn't going to say anything? "You want something from me, right?"

The woman nodded. The movement revealed the scarred and sooty side of her face, and it almost made Dawn change her mind about trying to communicate. Goose bumps rose on her skin and not just from the deathly chill. She was scared.

"Well, if you want something, you're going have to tell me what it is."

The woman opened her mouth and moved her lips, though Dawn couldn't hear a word. She flung back her covers and got out of bed, but didn't move any closer. Something inside was stirring. She wanted to know what the woman was trying so hard to say.

"I'm sorry, I can't hear you." She touched her own ears and shook her head in case the woman couldn't hear her, either. Dawn shivered a little as the woman seemed to grow more ag-

itated. Her eyes widened, the veins in her neck standing out as she moved her mouth more urgently, spewing forth a stream of words that were soundless, and yet emphatic.

Dawn could almost hear them now, whispers reaching her, but nothing more. She stepped closer, forgetting her fear for an instant as she stretched out a hand. "Calm down. Take it easy. It'll be all right, just—"

She stopped speaking then, because she had lowered her hand to the woman's shoulder, a gesture of comfort, and when her eyes shifted to her hand so she could correct her aim, she saw it—she *saw* it—move right through the woman.

Of course it did. It wasn't a surprise, it was just…surreal. And disorienting. It made her stomach heave and her head spin. Her body turned to ice in the instant before the woman simply opened her mouth as wide as she could and screamed. And even though Dawn didn't hear the scream with her ears, she *felt* it. It reverberated through every part of her body. She felt it in her chest and in her teeth, the way you felt the music at a Godsmack concert—would feel it even if you were stone-deaf. It went on and on, until she thought her head would split, and she pressed her hands to her ears and closed her eyes in self-defense.

It stopped. The sensation stopped all at once. She lifted her head, opened her eyes, lowered her hands.

The woman was gone.

Dawn sank onto the bed, blinking her wide eyes and trying to keep her heart from pounding a hole through her chest. "I don't want this," she whispered. "God, I don't want this. If I refuse it, it has to go away, doesn't it? It has to stop. If I just refuse to help them they'll stop coming. So I won't." She lifted her head, looked around the room at the emptiness. "I won't help you, do you hear me? I won't. I *won't!*"

16

Jax pulled the Mercedes into the driveway beside her own car, and even remembered to hit the lock button on the key ring when she got out and hurried around the luxury vehicle. She slowed her pace as she reached her Taurus, leaning over and peering through the driver's side window.

River was there, slumped over the steering wheel. Hell. The feeling of fear that hit her like a tidal wave almost put her on her knees. And maybe that was when she knew that all her talk about casual sex, and him not meaning a thing to her, was bullshit.

She opened the door and gripped him by the nape. "Hey. Come on, wake up. Talk to me, River."

His eyes fluttered, but didn't stay open. He was still alive. Thank God.

"Come on." She smacked his cheek. "Come on, you've got to shove over, at least. Lemme in the damn car."

Again his eyes opened, and he lifted his head this time. She knew he understood her, because he braced his good leg on the floor and pushed himself over the console and into the passenger side. His entire face contorted with pain. Jax leaned in, tried to help him move. He got everything over except his legs. She saw that the belt he'd used as a tourniquet had loos-

ened, and fresh blood gleamed from his jeans, which were already soaked in it.

She helped him ease his good leg over, and then lifted the wounded one and slid herself into the seat. Then she lowered the injured leg onto her lap. "Just leave it," she said, twisting the key, pulling the door closed. "Keeping it elevated is a good idea, don't you think?"

"Mmm." He leaned back on the door. She hit the lock button so he wouldn't fall out. "No hospital," he muttered, eyes closed, lips barely parting enough to let vowels escape between consonants.

"Just one," she said. "But don't worry. You'll be the only human patient in the place."

He frowned, but then his brows relaxed. "You're taking me to the vet."

She felt the car move when something hit it in the side, and she jumped, but it was only Rex standing with his paws on her window. "How did he get out?"

"He was throwing such a fit when he heard me pull in," River said.

She looked at him, realized the house key was on the ring with her car key. "If you got that far, River, why on earth didn't you just wait for me inside?"

He took a breath, as if talking was a real effort. "Didn't want to get blood all over the house."

He hadn't been being neat, but careful. She got out, mindful of River's leg, and opened the back door. Rex leaped inside and sat up on the back seat as if he were a well-raised child. Jax closed the door and returned to her former spot, then backed the car out and headed toward the Blackberry-Pinedale Animal Hospital.

As she drove, she picked up her cell phone and punched in her dad's number. When he answered, she said, "Hi, Dad.

Listen, I'm on my way to the clinic. Can you meet me there? It's an emergency."

"Oh, no," her father said. "Is it Rex or—?"

"No, it's the other stray. Wound to the leg," she said, cutting him off. She didn't think anyone was monitoring her calls, but it paid to be careful. "He's lost a lot of blood. I'll be there in ten minutes, Dad."

"I'll be ready and waiting, hon. Try not to worry. You putting pressure on the wound?"

"Yeah, and I have it elevated."

"Put the heat on in the car. Keep him warm. I'll see you in ten minutes."

She nodded and hit the cutoff button, then cranked up the heat. "Hang in there, River. You're going to be okay."

He didn't answer, and when she looked at him, she realized he'd lost consciousness. Damn. Rex leaned over the seat and licked River's face, whining a little. Jax pressed down harder on the accelerator.

When she pulled up to the door of the clinic and got out, her father came hurrying toward the car. "I'll help you get him in," he said.

"That's good, 'cause I'm gonna need it."

Her father opened the back door and Rex jumped out and bunted him in the thigh, demanding a pat on the head. "I thought you said it wasn't Rex."

She nodded toward River, who lay slumped in the car.

Her father swore. Her father *never* swore.

"He's been shot, Dad. I can't take him to a hospital, or he'll end up in custody, and if that happens he'll be dead."

Her father looked her in the eye. "If I'm caught treating a human being, honey, I—"

"I know, Dad. I know it's asking a lot. But his life depends on it. If not I wouldn't even ask."

He leaned into the car, looked at the blood-soaked jeans, then backed out and nodded. "Let's get him inside."

When River opened his eyes, there was a dog licking his face. He blinked the room into focus. Orange walls, textured paint, white cabinets. He was lying on a table with a sheet over him, and he didn't think he had any pants on.

He felt weak as he lifted the sheet and his head at the same time. No, he definitely didn't have any pants on. Shorts. A T-shirt, and a thick bandage around his thigh.

"Easy, River. You're going to be all right. Dad got the bullet out."

He lifted his brows, turned to see Jax standing on one side of his makeshift bed, her father on the other. "Thank you, Ben. I don't imagine this was without risk for you, was it?"

Ben smiled, shrugged. "Only if I get caught. If anyone asks, it was Rex here who had the surgery. He came home from the woods with a bullet in his leg. Probably a hunter with a lousy aim. Who knows? I fixed him up, and set him up with some prophylactic antibiotics." He picked up a fat brown bottle and shook it. "Stop the others. These are stronger. One every eight hours for ten days. Rex."

River nodded slowly. "I don't know how I'm ever going to manage payback for this one, Doc."

"Your dog's shots are all up-to-date now, too," Dr. Jackson said. "I figured as long as he was here." He looked at the dog, then at his daughter. "Get him licensed, for heaven's sake."

"Rex or River?"

River groaned at the bad joke.

Ben only sighed. "Stay off the leg for a while. I don't have any crutches here, naturally."

"Naturally," River said.

"But you can pick up a pair at any drugstore. You'll need them or at least a cane, just for a few days."

"I'll try."

"Thanks, Dad," Jax said.

Ben nodded, hugged his daughter, then said, "Let's get you home, River."

"I'm all for that." He started to get up, but both Jax and her father hurried to either side of him, each pulling one of his arms around their shoulders. They barely let him support an ounce of his own weight as they helped him to the back door, and through it to where the car waited.

He got into the back seat, leg extended. The dog got to ride in the front, sitting up on the passenger seat, looking as if he thought he'd just been promoted to human.

Cassandra's father hurried back inside. Lights went off one by one as the car rolled away, leaving the clinic.

Later that night, Jax had River installed on the sofa, a cup of tea on the coffee table beside him, a lamp glowing nearby. He was propped up on pillows, with his leg elevated, and his best friend's appointment book open in front of him, and as he perused the entries, he began to see a pattern.

Cassandra walked in with a steaming bowl of soup. The woman seemed to think soup was good for just about everything. Not that he minded. Soup *was* good. Especially hers. She tended to dress it up with sprinkles of grated cheese, extra seasonings and croutons.

"Look at this," he said, as she set the soup on the table. "Most of these are dates when Stephanie had her appointments with Ethan. Some I knew about, some I didn't. This one was on my birthday."

"Does it note the time of day for any of them?" Jax took the book from him, looked at the dates.

"Two. It was always two. That's how I remember. Tuesdays and Thursdays at two was her schedule for her therapy.

But that's not what it says in Ethan's date book. Look at his notations for those same dates—that same time."

"Harrington, 2:00 p.m.," she read. Then she flipped pages, and found the next date. "Same thing here...and here." She looked up from the date book. "What or who is Harrington?"

"I don't know."

"Well, we can start in the phone book. Check that name in all the local towns, see if we find any clues."

He nodded. "Good idea. You have phone books?"

"Are you kidding? My mother thinks of everything." She continued flipping through the date book, stopping at the back cover, pulling out a small card that had been tucked into the flap there. "But we don't need them." She handed him the card.

He read it. "Harrington Inn: Vermont's Most Romantic Hideaway."

It hit him like a sledgehammer. He thought he sucked in a sharp breath, and then he had to try to suck in another, because for a moment he wasn't getting any air.

"We don't know anything for sure," Cassandra said. "Not yet."

But he did. He felt it right down in his gut. Ethan didn't have any file, any medical records on Stephanie, even though he did on every other patient. Which meant she had never *been* a patient. All her appointment dates had been spent at that inn. With him.

River closed his eyes against the rush of pain.

And then Jax touched him and he breathed again.

Jax made herself a bowl of soup, sat beside River to eat it while they watched a little late-night TV, which she'd turned on to distract him from the thoughts that must be torturing him. It was looking more and more as if his wife had betrayed him with his best friend. God, he must be in hell.

"So it's decided then," Jax said. They'd finished eating, and

she'd carried the bowls into the kitchen and rinsed them. When she came back, he'd turned the television off. He needed to sleep. "We visit the Harrington in the morning."

"We?" he asked. "You don't have to go into the station in the morning?"

"It's Saturday. Frankie told me to take weekends off." She smiled, remembering. "As I recall, her exact words were, 'Best take the weekends off for now, girl. You accept this job, they'll probably be the last ones you ever have to yourself.'"

Jax looked at River, still smiling, but he wasn't. His eyes had turned serious. "If they find out you've been helping me, accepting the job might not even be an option anymore."

"Then it was never meant to be," she said, but she kept her eyes averted. She was growing fond of this stupid little town. And that dumb-ass little police department.

"I know you want the job, Cassandra," River said softly. "You don't have to pretend you don't care."

"It's not important. Not in the scheme of things. I can get a job anywhere." She met his eyes, but she wasn't fooling him. They both knew it was a lie. "You've only got one life, River, and we can't blow our shot at saving it just to pad my chances at landing a job."

"Even if it is your dream job?"

She sent him a look. "Stop it."

"I'm really sorry, you know. I never meant to drag you into any of this."

"You didn't drag me anywhere. Except out of a frozen pond."

He sighed and shifted position on the sofa. "I wish I could undo it."

"What? Pulling me out of the pond?" She set a throw pillow on the coffee table. Then she crouched on the floor and slid her hands around his calf, lifted his leg and rested it on the pillow.

"Getting you involved in my mess. It's dangerous, Cassandra, and if anything happens to you—"

"Nothing's going to happen to me."

"I'd leave if I thought it would help."

"I wouldn't let you."

"You wouldn't stop me." He held her eyes. His were so intense they almost made her squirm. She didn't like that kind of intensity in a man's eyes—not when they were looking at her. It wasn't good. She told herself that. But herself wasn't listening. She felt warm all over when he looked at her that way. And she wanted him. Every time she got close to this man, she wanted him.

"But at this point," he added, "I think it's too late. I think whoever burned that storage unit and broke in here the other night knows you're helping me. And that puts you at risk."

She shrugged. "So you're not gonna leave because you want to stick around and play the hero? Look out for me?"

He made a face. "Yeah, I know. You're more likely to do that for me than I am for you, but a guy has to have his delusions."

She nodded. "How's the leg?"

"Hurts like hell. But I'll be all right."

"You're going to have to sleep down here tonight. No way are you going to be able to make the stairs."

He eyed her. "I can handle them."

She shook her head.

"Try me," he said.

"Don't tempt me or I might." It was meant as a joke, a little flirtatious teasing to lighten the mood. But the fire that leaped into his eyes set a matching one in her belly. Damn, she couldn't seem to help herself. Or stop herself from pushing it a little further. "And then my father's going to want to know how those nice stitches he put into your thigh got torn out."

His eyes were intense and deep, and his fingers brushed over her jaw. "You trying to distract me or comfort me? Whichever it is, it's working."

She averted her eyes, not comfortable with the softness in

his tone, or the depth to which his eyes tried to dig into her soul, because it stirred up softness and depth inside her—and she just wasn't ready for that. "I was only kidding, River. I'm not so hard up I have to attack a wounded man…unless he felt completely up to it and was utterly willing."

"You wouldn't be the one doing the attacking—how's that for willing?"

She smiled and decided she was overthinking this thing almost as badly as he was. "Just about perfect."

"It's just…it's not my wounded leg I'm worried about."

"No?"

"No. You know what I'm worried about."

She rolled her eyes and thought, Here we go again. "Yeah. I know what you're worried about. You've got a giant pain-in-the-ass Wolfman complex."

"Wolfman?" He looked utterly perplexed.

"Wolfman," she said. "Didn't you see it? The Universal classic? Lon Chaney Jr.? The Gypsy woman tells him he's destined to kill what he loves. That's the real curse he bears, not that he turns into a wolf by the full moon, but that he can't love anyone without putting their lives in danger."

River lowered his eyes, and she saw the pain in his face.

Jax put her palms to his cheeks and made him look at her. "*His* curse. But it's not yours, River. Because you didn't kill Stephanie."

"We still can't be sure of that. What if I did? God knows every clue we find just adds more motive. More reasons I might have lost it and…" He shook his head slowly. "What if it *is* my curse? What then?"

She shrugged. "Okay, I'll play along. Suppose it is your curse? It still wouldn't apply here."

"Why the hell not?"

"Because you don't love me. And you're not going to. I don't want you to." Just saying it drove the truth home to her.

That it was a lie. An outright lie. God, what was happening to her?

He nodded, but didn't meet her eyes.

"Good. So we're clear on that?"

"Clear as a bell." He didn't sound any too happy about it, though. It made her wonder if he was feeling the same things she was. And that scared her even more.

"Great. I'll get us some blankets, then. And don't worry, River. I'll be gentle."

17

"So who was she?"

Ethan turned sharply at the familiar sound of Victoria's voice coming to him from their bedroom. He'd finally finished explaining himself to the police and escorting them around the property as they conducted a thorough search.

"God, Vicki, you scared me half to death." He tipped his head to one side, studying her face. Beautiful, clear of any hint of makeup and starting to show the touch of time. She sat up in the bed, legs under the covers, a book open on her lap. "I didn't even know you were home. Why didn't you say something?"

She blinked. "You brought a woman here, Ethan. I didn't know what to think."

"Oh, honey." He tugged his tie from his shirt as he moved toward the bed, then sat down beside her, stroking a hand over her cheek, searching her eyes. "Baby, you didn't think—" He shook his head and started over. "That woman is a cop. She's working with Frankie Parker over in Blackberry."

She blinked then, some of the worry easing from her eyes. "She's trying to find River?"

"I don't know. To tell you the truth, I have a feeling she knows more about him than she's letting on. Might even be helping him."

He'd gone so far as to break into her house, to find out just

how much she did know—and found men's clothes in the bedroom, and River's police file. It didn't prove anything. But he didn't like what he was thinking.

"I don't understand," Victoria said, her voice very soft.

"The lady cop, Jax is her name—she's been staying at River's house. You know the town owns it now."

"I didn't realize."

He nodded. "I took her to dinner—solely to talk about the case, see if I could get her to tell me anything. Stopped back here to pick up my PDA. There are some notes on it I need for tomorrow. That's all, Vicki."

"Pick it up? Why? Where were you going?"

God, this wasn't going to sound good, he thought. "I was going back to Blackberry. I've been staying at the inn over there. While you've been at your parents'. Alone, Vicki. Completely alone. I just thought I should be close in case River surfaces."

"Are you that certain he's there?"

He nodded. "I'm sure of it."

Victoria lowered her head, and her breath rushed out of her. "It's not that I don't trust you," she whispered. "I do. It was just—for a moment when I saw you come in with her, I thought—"

"I know. I promise you, Vicki, I will never hurt you like that again. Never. I swear."

"I know. I believe you." She wrapped her hand around his. "I was telling myself how foolish I was being—that I should come out and let you know I was here—but then I heard a gunshot. And everything went crazy after that. You were phoning the police and that woman was outside, running around in the snow. What happened, Ethan?"

He lowered his eyes. "There was an intruder in the house. God, and you were here alone."

She frowned, searching his face. "I came home early be-

cause I wasn't feeling well. Took a sleeping pill. He must have already been here when I came in—but I...I never heard a thing until you and that woman arrived."

He slid onto the bed beside her, wrapped his arms around her and held her close to his chest. "I took a shot at him as he ran away. Jax—Lieutenant Jackson, that is—said I hit him." He pushed a hand through his hair. "I don't know what I was thinking. I thought I aimed low, but it was so stupid to even point the gun in his direction. I don't know how I could have hit him. God, Vicki, I'm pretty sure I shot River tonight."

"You shot at an intruder. You were protecting your home—our home. Protecting *me*, Ethan."

Her hands curled in his hair, and he lowered his head to her chest and fought against the tears that tried to escape.

"He was running away," he whispered. "Jax said I could be charged."

She tugged his head upward, stared down at his face. "Did you tell the police that?"

"No. I told them I was too shaken to remember details. They agreed to take a more thorough statement in the morning." He closed his eyes. "They wouldn't have done that for anyone else."

"You're a respected doctor."

"I'm your father's son-in-law," he said, knowing full well it wasn't his own reputation that was respected and admired enough to earn favorable treatment from the police.

"Either way," she told him. "In the morning, you tell the police he was turning around. Lifting a gun, as if to fire back at you. That's when you shot. I'll say I saw the entire thing from the bedroom window."

He closed his eyes. "Jax was there. She saw what I did."

"It was dark, Ethan. She couldn't have seen too clearly. And what would she have to gain by hurting you? Did they find poor River lying out there somewhere? I didn't see an ambulance."

"No. No, he got away."

"Well, there you have it. How badly could he be hurt if he got away?"

He sighed, nodding slowly. "He could be all right. I guess."

"He's all right. There's no point in you being arrested and investigated and all of that when he's probably fine and you never intended to hurt him. Is there?"

"I...suppose not."

"Then tell them just what I told you when they come back tomorrow. This Jax person—she won't contradict you. I'm sure of it."

River hadn't expected Jax to turn the conversation the way she had, and he still wasn't sure if she was serious or only teasing him when she came back down the stairs, her arms stacked high with blankets and pillows.

He'd limped to the fireplace in the meantime, tossed in a few more logs. She didn't bring the blankets to the sofa. Instead, she dropped them in a pile on the floor in front of the fire. He would have started making them into a bed but he couldn't stop looking at her. And he was damned if he knew why. She wasn't wearing anything particularly sexy. A hockey jersey. Period. But there was something about how big it was around her, about her long legs and bare feet, about the way her hair was down and loose, that made him... Damn.

She ignored his hungry eyes, though he knew damn well she noticed him looking. Instead of making one of her trademark smart-ass comments, she just started unfolding thick blankets on the floor. "You gonna sleep in your clothes, River?"

"Nope."

"Good."

She arranged the pillows, spread more blankets. By the time she finished, she'd created a nest on the floor that looked

more inviting than any bed River thought he'd ever seen. And
the fire had taken off nicely, was throwing enough heat to
make him lazy. Rex lay close to the fireplace, snoring. River
sat on the edge of the couch and managed to work his way
out of the scrubs her father had loaned him. His jeans had been
beyond redemption. Then he tugged the sweater off over his
head. He didn't have a T-shirt on underneath, and he wondered
if he should find one.

But she was already pulling back the covers. She'd stacked
a couple of pillows up for him to use as a prop for his leg. "Here,"
she said. "Dad said to keep it elevated, so this is your side."

River wanted her. He wanted to fold her up in his arms in
that soft nest, and make love to her all night long. He wondered if she had any idea how much he wanted that. But casual sex wasn't easy for him. Never had been. He was a
hopeless romantic, and he was halfway in love with her already. That first night—hell, it had sent him over the edge of
ecstasy, given him a heartful of longing for things that could
never be. Making love to her again would be—it would be a
disaster. She wasn't a hearts-and-flowers kind of woman,
didn't want any part of that sort of thing, especially with a loser
like him—busted up brain, blackouts and declared legally insane by the state of Vermont. And possibly a killer to boot.

Hell, he was surprised she was even willing to let a man
like him touch her.

He sighed and limped to the bedding, crawled inside. She
crawled right in beside him, almost before he got settled
down, and then she was leaning over, fluffing the pillows underneath his thigh, positioning his leg more comfortably.

He put a hand over hers on his leg. "It's fine."

"It could have killed you," she said. "If he'd aimed
higher—"

"Don't."

She lay down beside him, one hand on his chest, her head

tucked near his shoulder. "I was kidding, before," she told him. "You can relax, River, I'm not going to jump your bones tonight."

He looked down at her. "Then maybe you could turn your head just a little?"

She frowned, lifted her head and sent him a questioning look.

"Your breath is wafting over my neck. And you smell too damn good to resist." Her face changed, but before she could say another word, much less move away, he muttered, "Damn. Too late." He cupped her nape, drew her close and kissed her. And he kept on kissing her, kept on holding her, and wondered why he'd thought even for a minute that he would be able to sleep with her and do otherwise.

She responded to his kiss, parted her lips and twisted her arms around his neck to hold on tight. He felt her body heat, and the way she arched against him. But he pulled back slightly, breaking the kiss and staring at her in the firelight. "Not so fast, hmm?"

"Why not?"

He didn't say anything. Instead he sat up and reached down to the bottom of the hockey jersey she wore. Half expecting her to slap his hands away, he lifted it slowly and pulled it over her head. She wasn't wearing anything underneath, and he almost smiled, knowing she'd been hoping for another round.

He looked at her for a long moment. Let his eyes roam the length of her, from her thighs to her waist to her breasts. And he saw the way she squirmed and started to get impatient. Before she got around to barking at him, he touched her. He put one hand on her foot. Caressed it slowly, lifted it in his hand and bent to press his lips to it. He kissed the top, and then the ankle, and the sole, and then each toe, one by one.

She shivered, but pretended not to. "Into feet, are you?" she whispered.

"Only yours."

She jerked her foot away from him so fast it startled him. And then he looked into her eyes and knew why. She didn't want him to care. She wanted it fast, sexual but not personal. She wanted it meaningless but good. He didn't think he could give her that. He didn't freaking want to.

He clasped her foot and lifted it to his mouth again, this time caressing her ankle and kissing his way along her calf, all the way to the hollow behind her knee, where he licked, tasting her salt, her skin.

She sat up a little, one hand on the back of his head. "Hell, River, what are you…"

"Just relax," he whispered. "Relax. Lay back. Close your eyes."

"But I don't—"

He turned his head so that his mouth touched her hand, and then he kissed her fingers, her knuckles. He used his free hand to caress her other arm, and then her waist, and her rib cage. He turned her palm up and tickled its center with his tongue, before moving to her wrists, up her inner arms.

Her breath whispered out of her. A little of her tension eased, and by the time he reached her neck, she was tipping her head to one side to give him access. He used it, catching the skin of her throat in his lips, suckling and even nipping a little, while feathering his fingers on her nape.

And then he kissed her collarbones, and moved lower, making his way toward the rising mound of her breast, and all around it, kissing and tasting, darting his tongue over every part except where she wanted him to. He watched her nipple harden and lengthen as if reaching out for his touch, for his kiss. He worked slowly, lazily, loving the looks that crossed her face and the way her body was beginning to quiver as her breaths grew shorter, more shallow.

With his hand on her other breast, he flicked his fingertips over the nipple, keeping his eyes turned upward to watch her

face. She caught her lower lip between her teeth. He kept watching her as he lifted his head slightly, just enough to let him slide his tongue over her nipple, in a long, slow lap. And then again. And then he flicked it back and forth rapidly.

She whispered a cuss word and clasped a handful of his hair in her fist. His arms were wrapped around her waist, helping her arch toward him, thrusting her breasts upward for easy access. He finally sucked her nipple into his mouth, drew on it hard and deeply, then he bit just a little, and then a little more until she whimpered and told him to take her, hard and deep and *now*.

"In a minute," he promised as he slid his arms from around her waist, found her hands with his and guided one of them to each of her breasts. He covered her fingers with his own, guiding them to her nipples, and squeezing them hard, so she pinched herself. Then he let go of her hands, pleased when she didn't move them away, and he mouthed her belly, and her navel, and lower, lower. He pushed her thighs wide and ran his hands up and down the insides of them, and then he pressed his face to her mound, her center, kissing, teasing, waiting, feeling her responses and listening to the sounds coming from her lips. He kissed her hard, and her knees bent, rose and fell wide, her lips opened to him.

"Beautiful," he whispered. And he kissed her again, open and exposed and vulnerable. He kissed her again, and then again, and then he licked her the way he had licked her breasts. Long, slow strokes, then short hard ones that flicked and punished. He used his hands to spread her wide, so he could delve deep into her, taste and take the depths of her. He wanted to drink her. He wanted to devour her, and he did. He drove his tongue into her, flushing her inside—ravaging her. He had to have her, all of her. He had to make her come.

He lifted his eyes to her face, but couldn't see it. Only her hands on her breasts, the tips of her nipples swelling from the

pressure of her own fingers pinching and rolling and tugging on them.

He ate her deeply, and when his teeth scraped over her clit, which was bulging as if it would pop, he devoted his attention to that little nub. He flicked his tongue over it, and then he sucked it into his mouth and gnawed it with his teeth.

She screamed. He loved it. He reached up with his hands, closed his fingers over hers on her nipples and pressed, making her pinch herself harder while his mouth worked to ravage her center. And then he left her to keep his unspoken command, and he moved his hands between her legs again. He slid his fingers into her, invading her and licking and sucking her. He felt it when she started to come. He felt her muscles tighten around his fingers.

She screamed again as she came. Screamed and tried to push his head away from her, but he wasn't finished, and by the time he was, she was quivering. Just lying there in spasms, shivering and shaking and crying. He crawled up her body. He stopped to lick and nibble her breasts as he settled himself in the cradle of her thighs, and slid inside her.

She groaned as he moved, drawing back and sinking into her again and again. He slid his hands underneath her buttocks so he could tip it up and hold her to him, and then he drove into her again. She lifted her legs and wrapped them around his waist.

She was his. His. Maybe not forever, but right then, at that moment. She gave herself to him, and he wished he would never have to let her go.

Cassandra didn't complain, didn't seek escape. If anything, she pushed harder, took him deeper by arching her body to meet his. He sat up, pulling her legs around his waist, his hands at her backside. Her breasts were within reach of his mouth in this position and he took one of them. They moved together as if they were fused somehow, and he could

almost believe he felt the sensations rushing through her as well as his own.

She moaned his name as her body exploded around him. She went tight, so tight he thought she might break, and she clung to him, quaking and shaking until he joined her in the heights of pleasure.

They clung that way until the aftershocks began to fade. He held her so close he could feel her heartbeat as their bodies slowly unclenched. Eventually, he lowered her to the nest on the floor, and lay down with her, pulling her into his arms, cradling her against him, holding her and rocking her and loving her....

Yes. Loving her.

Damn, he was in serious trouble here.

Jax lay there, wrapped up in River's arms, for a solid hour before her brain cells returned to their proper alignment and she realized exactly what she was doing. She was *snuggling* with him.

Her eyes widened a little and she sat up fast, so startled by her behavior and his that she almost shot all the way to her feet. But instead, she managed to stay seated.

"What's wrong?"

He sat up, too, but slowly, with an expression on his face that looked for all the world like utter satisfaction. Like a man who'd just finished packing away a feast and wanted nothing more than to lie around and digest it.

She, on the other hand, felt more like throwing up.

"I...I need a shower."

She started to rise, but he caught her hand and held on. "Wait. Wait. I'm sorry. I didn't mean... I mean, I thought you wanted... Jax, tell me this wasn't a mistake."

She shook her head. "River, I don't—"

"You don't want love," he said softly.

That wasn't what she was going to say. She was going to say she didn't have any regrets, or that she didn't know what the hell she wanted anymore.

He stroked her hair before she could figure out how to reply, and he said, "Don't worry, Cassandra. I don't, either."

He didn't? Well, that should be a relief, shouldn't it? Why did it feel so horrible then? She faked a smile and got to her feet. "Then I guess we understand each other."

"Yeah." He licked his lips and looked away from her. She got the distinct feeling he had a lot more to say, but didn't.

"So...I guess I'll go take my shower."

"All right."

He let go of her wrist, and Jax hurried away as fast as she could without breaking into a run. She felt pursued. She felt panicky. She closed the bathroom door, leaned back against it and tried to catch her breath, analyze the feelings and thoughts chasing through her mind. But she couldn't. She couldn't even catch hold of one, much less explore and examine it.

She felt just the way she had felt the handful of times when she had been under fire on the job. When bullets were flying at her, doing their best to hit her, to kill her, her entire body would become tense and hyperaware. She'd be half expecting the blow of one of those hot pieces of lead, and half focused on avoiding it while shooting back, the fight-or-flight response. Her adrenal glands were pumping and she wanted to do something. Scream at River and throw him out of the house. Sneak out the back door and run away, never looking back. Or run back down the stairs and wrap herself up in him as completely as she could.

"Jesus, what's wrong with me?"

She went to the shower, turned on the faucets and adjusted the temperature a little hotter than she usually liked it. Then she stepped into the spray and let it pound her.

By the time she got out the sun was only a few hours away from rising. She went to the bedroom, rather than back downstairs, and collapsed on the bed, wrapping herself up in the covers, hiding beneath them, wondering why her belly was still queasy and her skin still tingled and her heart was still misfiring. God, she couldn't be falling in love…could she?

Hours later, she woke slowly, sitting up and blinking away the sleep as she realized the sun was high, and there was a sound disrupting her rest. She glanced at the clock through bleary eyes: 9:15. Hell, she never slept this late. Not even on Sundays. It was totally unlike her. She woke at six every morning, with or without the aid of an alarm clock, and being up most of the night before seldom had any impact on that.

She realized she would probably still be sleeping if not for that sound….

That sound. The soft steady purr of a motor running. And footsteps…on the front porch? Rex growled from somewhere far away.

She got to her feet and hurried to the closet for a robe, pulled it on as fast as possible, and ran to the window to look outside just in time to see Ethan Melrose's Mercedes pulling away.

"Hell." She turned and raced down the stairs. Then came up short at the sight of River lying there in the blankets on the floor. The fire had burned hot during the night, and he'd thrown the covers off of his chest. He lay on his back, arms splayed, head flung to one side, eyes closed as his chest rose and fell with the steady rhythm of his breathing. Rex had apparently decided to take the spot Jax had left vacant. The dog was curled close beside River, head resting on one arm. Apparently he hadn't been disturbed enough by the noise to get up and investigate. Only enough to lift his head and growl a little before snuggling down again. "Some police dog," she muttered, deliberately using her mother's term.

River was gorgeous. He was filling out the way he ought to, and she loved to look at him. And to touch him. And...

She pursed her lips and remembered her mission, dragged her gaze away from him and focused on the front door. Its lock was still turned, but the curtain gaped. Anyone looking inside...

She stepped to the door, opened it, very careful not to let the movement change the curtain's position. She wanted to see what their morning visitor might have seen, had he peeked inside. Stepping outside, barefoot on the cold wood of the porch, she pulled the door closed again, and bent her head to peer through.

River lay in plain sight, still bathed in the glow of coals and the dying flames from the fireplace. His face was perfectly visible.

Sighing, she straightened again, glancing at the porch itself, but there was no snow to hold any footprints, and the path from the driveway to the porch steps was also clear.

"Damn."

She opened the door and went back inside, rubbing her arms against the cold. She headed to the fireplace, removed the screen as quietly as she could, and tossed the last two logs from the pile onto the coals. Then she tiptoed to the kitchen to put on a pot of coffee.

It was as she was pouring water into the pot that she felt soft hands close on her shoulders, soft lips nuzzle her neck and sleepy whispers reach her ear. "You didn't come back last night."

Man, this had to stop. It *had* to stop. It was too intimate, this early-morning, pre-coffee nuzzling. So why did it feel so good? So...right? She moved slightly, just enough to escape his touch. "Yeah. I, uh—I got to thinking it probably would be better if we cooled it for a while. With the sex, I mean."

She glanced up at him. He looked so hurt that she had to avert her eyes from the pain in his. She felt like an assassin.

And it hurt her so badly to say it that she knew she was right. It was the only possible thing she could do. She needed to sort out the foreign feelings swirling around inside her. She needed clarity. Objectivity. Distance.

"Oh," was all he said. Then, "Are you worried about—we didn't use protection either time. Do you think—"

She shook her head. "I'm pretty sure I'm at the wrong part of my cycle for that to be a problem," she said.

"I think someone may have seen you here, River." Amazing, she thought, that she was saying it more to change the subject than due to the urgency of the fact. Even though it *was* urgent. "Whoever it was left in Ethan's car, so I'm guessing it must have been him. Had to have been someone with a set of keys. The set he gave me are still hanging on the rack by the front door."

"So…?" He knew there had to be more.

"I heard footsteps on the porch just before the car left. And I'm telling you, if he peered through the window, he saw you. You were in plain sight."

"Hell." River lowered his head quickly. "That clinches it, then. I have to leave."

"No you don't." Wait a minute, hadn't she just decided she needed distance? *Not that much distance. Two feet is more than I want. I'm pathetic.*

"Yeah, I do," he said. "If Ethan knows I'm here, he's going to have to try to find me. To see me. He might even turn me in. And that would ruin your career, Cassandra."

She shrugged. "It's going to *make* my career when we find proof you were set up, River."

"If we do." He swallowed. "If I was."

She shook her head, refusing to consider the alternative. "We'll talk about where you're going to stay later. This morning we've got some errands to run." She looked at him more thor-

oughly, in search of signs of pain or trouble with the leg. "You're not supposed to be on that leg without a cane or a crutch."

"It's a lot better this morning. A little sore. I'll be fine. I think I can even manage the stairs now."

She nodded, deciding to take his word for it rather than fussing over him. It was so unlike her to fuss. And yet she was having trouble keeping herself from doing it. "Go on and get ready then, River. I'm going to fill a couple of travel mugs with coffee, and give Rex his morning meal and a quick run outside. He's going to be cooped up all day in the car with us again."

Rex barked, and she knelt and rubbed his head. "What you need is a doggy door and the backyard fenced in, don't you, boy? Then you could come and go as you pleased. Yes, you could."

"I always intended to do that for him," River said.

She shrugged, and realized Rex was River's dog, not hers. If they did find proof of his innocence he would probably want his dog back. Hell, he'd probably want his house back, as well.

"I'll be quick," he told her. "In case Ethan tips off the authorities. Search party could show up any minute."

"I have a feeling Frankie would give me a heads-up before raiding the place," Jax said.

"Yeah, and if that's true, Ethan has probably already thought of it. He can read people."

"Like he read you?" she asked. "As insane, as a killer?"

He closed his eyes. "We don't know he was wrong about me. Not for sure."

"I know," she said. And it sounded a little too...breathy and romantic, and she rolled her eyes. "Go take your shower, will you? We don't have all day."

He nodded, a slight smile appearing on his face, and limped away.

18

River had showered and dressed, and Jax had downed two cups of coffee, started the car and filled their travel mugs a half hour later. They were on their way out when the telephone rang.

Sighing, Jax snatched up the receiver. "Hello?"

"Hello, Jax. How's your weekend off going?"

She smiled at the familiar voice. "Fine, Frankie. How about yours?"

"Very funny. You know perfectly well I'm on call twenty-four-seven."

"Why do I get the feeling I'm on call right now?" Jax asked her. She sent a look at River, who was standing by the door. He held her gaze, his eyes like a physical touch that made her warm and cold at the same time. The car was running in the driveway, exhaust making clouds in the wintry air. "What do you need, Frankie?"

"I had a call from Mrs. Ethan Melrose this morning."

"You're kidding me. What did she want?"

"You, I'm afraid. She wants to talk to you, alone."

"About?"

"The Corbett case."

Jax blinked slowly. River was coming closer now, his eyes curious, probing. "Why would Victoria Melrose want to talk to me about River Corbett?" As she said it, Jax leaned closer

to River, putting her ear and the phone close to his, and tipping the receiver so he could listen in.

"I wish I knew," Frankie said. "If you'd rather not do this, I can forward the request to the state police. She'll just have to understand that, technically, it's their case."

"She didn't call the state police, Frankie. She called me. I just wish I knew why."

"Well, I guess there's only one way to find out. She wants you to meet her, to talk. Forty-five East Main, Burlington."

"What's there?" Jax asked.

"It's a coffee house. Perfectly safe. Still, you can take one of the boys with you if you—"

"No, that's all right. I'll go alone, like she wants. See what she has to say. What time?"

"Eleven."

Jax glanced at the clock and knew she'd have to leave right then to make the appointment. "All right. I'll go now."

"Thanks, Jax. I don't have any reason to think this is high risk, but you watch your back, just in case. From what I understand, Victoria Melrose was Stephanie Corbett's best friend. Could still be some emotions running pretty high, there."

"Will do."

"And I'll be expecting to hear what you find out later on."

"You've got it. Bye for now, Frankie."

Jax hung up the phone and turned to River. "Change of plans. You go to that inn without me. It's not like you'll be recognized there. It's in Burlington not Blackberry. Your face hasn't gone out over the airwaves or anything like that. I'll have a nice chat with Victoria and see what she has to say. All right?"

"I don't like it." He was frowning hard, and she knew he was trying to think of any reason Victoria Melrose might want to talk to her, but seemed to be drawing a blank, just as she had.

"Do you have some reason not to trust her?" Jax asked.

River met her eyes. "No. I've always adored the woman. I just...I don't know what she wants. I don't understand why she would want to talk to you."

"Maybe she knows something, River. If Ethan *was* involved in any of this, maybe she's ready to talk. We have to find out."

"I could go."

"She didn't ask for you. Listen, you can drop me there, and take the car on to the inn. We'll scope this coffee house out first, and pick a spot a couple of blocks away to meet up when you get back—say around noon?"

"You think you're gonna need a whole hour?"

"What can she do to me in an hour?" Jax lifted her brows. "She's not a body builder or anything, is she?"

"She's a pixie stick," he said.

"Good. I used to *eat* pixie sticks." Jax winked. "Besides, you'll need an hour to get to that inn, ask the questions that need asking, and get back to me. Come on, River. Don't go all overprotective on me, it'll only piss me off."

He sighed but nodded. "Take your sidearm," he told her.

"I'm never without it," she promised. "You'd better take the spare. And don't forget our backup," she said with a look at Rex, who was standing by the door, ready for another ride in the car.

"So you still haven't told your family that you were planning to see me here in the office today?" Dr. Melrose asked.

Dawn sighed and lowered her head. "It's not that I'm ashamed of it. It's just—I really prefer to get things straight in my head before I try to explain to anyone else, you know?"

"Even Bryan?"

She nodded. "Especially Bryan."

"Why is that?" He leaned back in his chair, twisting his

pen slowly in one hand. He had made a special effort for her, opening his office to see her on a weekend. She knew weekend appointments were not the norm. But he was good at his job—Beth said he was the top shrink at the state hospital. And Dawn was scared. She was tired of keeping all this to herself.

"I don't know. I think Bryan would be angry with me for doubting my own sanity."

"You don't think he'd understand?"

She shook her head. "How could he understand? God, how could anyone understand this? My father was completely insane, and now it seems like I'm heading in the same direction."

The doctor nodded. He had a way about him that let Dawn know he was really listening, really absorbing everything she said. It helped.

"You know, Dawn, when we first talked, I told you I had done quite a bit of reading about your father. Tell me how it is you feel his gift is manifesting in you."

"Gift? God, it's no gift. It's more like a curse."

"That depends, I suppose. Are you…hearing voices the way he did?"

"No. No. Mostly it's just…like a heightened intuition. Like I know things I shouldn't know." She watched him to gauge his reaction to that. She still hadn't decided just how much more she was going to tell him.

He nodded slowly. "Like—when the phone is going to ring."

"And who it's going to be. And sometimes, what they're going to say."

"I see."

"It started out with simple things. Really small stuff, like a stray thought that turned out to be true later on. I thought it was coincidence, at first."

He watched as he listened, seemed completely involved in what she had to say. "It happens to all of us. You think of a

song and turn on the radio and it's playing. Or you wonder about an old friend and then run into them later in the day."

"Yeah. Yeah, that's it exactly. But then it started getting bigger. I would know more complex things, more details."

He was nodding enthusiastically. "It's important, Dawn, that you know this doesn't mean you're insane. A lot of people have—or believe themselves to have—extra sensory perception. And most of them are perfectly sane."

She blinked and searched his face. "But you don't think it's real."

"What I think isn't important."

"But I want to know."

He shrugged. "I really haven't seen anything to convince me one way or the other. I have…an open mind on the subject."

She sighed softly, bowing her head. "It's…it's changing now. I've started…seeing things."

"What sorts of things?" he asked, unruffled, unalarmed by her revelation.

She'd expected him to react, and she wondered if he had, deep down. If he was just very good and very practiced at hiding it. "People. I think…I think they're people who have died."

"I see. Is there any one person in particular that you see more often than others?"

She thought a moment before answering. "You mean, besides my father?"

"You see your father?"

She nodded. "Yeah. But I don't want to talk about him. There's someone else. A woman."

"A woman."

"I saw her out near my friend Jax's house one day. And at the inn that day when you first arrived. I saw her again in the diner when we met Jax for lunch—Beth and I, that is. The other night she was standing at the foot of my bed."

He made a note, his brows drawn close. "Did she say anything?"

"She was trying to. I couldn't hear anything. And then she got so frustrated she screamed—it was like a banshee's wail or something. Just all-encompassing."

"You *heard* her when she screamed?"

"No. I *felt* her."

He nodded, wrote some more. "Interesting. Tell me, Dawn, do you find it odd that the one thing you *can't* do is hear this woman? When, according to all I've read, that was the part your father talked about more than anything else—hearing voices?"

She shrugged. "I guess…I hadn't thought about that."

"What do you think this woman wants?" he asked.

"I don't know. If I could have heard what she was trying so hard to say, I might, but as it is, I just don't know."

"I think you do."

She tipped her head sideways, frowning at him. "How could I?"

"Just trust yourself for a moment, Dawn. Pretend everything you need to know is already inside your mind. Just take a total shot in the dark. If you had to guess, what would you think she was trying to say to you? What is it you think she might say when you finally get to where you can hear her? If you ever do."

"That would just be guessing."

"So guess. Just try it—what harm can it do?"

She heaved a deep sigh and nodded slowly, but she knew this game wasn't going to give her any answers. Guessing wasn't the same as knowing. "I suppose—I'd think it was some kind of a warning. I imagine she might be trying to tell me someone is in danger." Dawn blinked as she mulled that over. "Yeah, because it *couldn't* be anything good she's trying to tell me. And she's so frustrated it's like she expects me

to *do* something to…I don't know. Prevent it, maybe. And I think it's something to do with Jax, because she showed up twice around her. Near the house, you know, and then the diner. She was standing right behind her."

He nodded. "That's very good. Now what's going on with your friend Jax that makes you think she might be in danger?"

She shot him a look. "*I'm* not the one who thinks she's in danger. This woman is." But she was thinking even as she said it. Thinking that Jax was a cop, in search of an escaped mental patient and living in his former home. That *had* to be it. It had to be that she was at risk from the fugitive. And it made sense, too, given that Dawn had begun to wonder if the dead woman haunting her mind was the same one who'd died in that house, in the fire.

Hell, she should warn Jax. She should have warned her long before now, but she was too damn busy worrying about her own mental health.

And she still was. But that didn't mean she could let Jax walk into danger.

She looked up at the doctor. And then she gasped and jumped to her feet.

The woman was standing on the far side of the office. Just standing there, staring at her, holding her baby in her arms. Her dress was burned, her face was scarred. She was so beautiful and so horrible all at once.

"What is it? What is it, Dawn? Are you seeing something now?" Dr. Melrose asked. He got to his feet slowly and turned his head to look where Dawn was staring.

"Listen, Dr. Melrose, I don't want you carting me off to a rubber room somewhere, okay?"

"I've got no reason to do that, Dawn."

Dawn nodded. "She's standing there." She pointed. And then she narrowed her eyes, because the woman faded and

vanished, and there was nothing left but the framed photograph on the wall. She'd been standing right in front of it.

Dawn's eyes widened. "Oh, my God," she whispered. "That's her."

"It's all right. Try asking her what she wants, Dawn."

"No, no. She's gone. She's gone, but *that* is her. That woman in the photo." She pointed.

Dr. Melrose looked at the photograph. It showed four people, two couples. Clearly the stylish woman in the incredible orange pumps standing in the circle of Dr. Melrose's arm was his wife. Beside them stood another couple.

And then Dawn knew. She knew that what she had been sensing was absolute fact. And she couldn't doubt it anymore, because there was a photograph to prove it. "That woman in the photo—she's the woman who died in the fire, isn't she? The one whose husband escaped from the mental hospital? Corbett—that was their name."

The doctor nodded slowly. She expected him to comfort her, to tell her it wasn't a mental illness and to suggest a dozen ways she might have glimpsed the woman's face in the past, or heard the name, or somehow had her image implanted into her own subconscious. But he didn't say anything. He sank back into his chair as if the wind had been knocked out of him. And she wondered why he was reacting so strongly when he'd been utterly unflappable up to now.

Dawn swallowed hard. "I've got to go."

"Wait," he said quickly. "Dawn, what did she say to you?"

"Nothing." Dawn gathered up her jacket, her purse. "I told you, I can't hear her."

"But you *know* something. Something has occurred to you that hadn't before. Hasn't it?"

She frowned and realized that something had. The clear knowledge that she should not be talking to this man about any of this. The dead woman had appeared near him, too.

Twice now. She should be talking to one person about this, and one person only. Jax.

And there was something else in her mind, something about a river.

She schooled her face into a mask of calm. "No. There's nothing. It's like she just popped up to startle me." She frowned and looked again at the photo, squinting her eyes, making a show of it. "You know, that isn't her at all. Not even close, actually. I just—I guess I panicked. I'm sorry, Dr. Melrose, I really want to stop now. This is upsetting. I just want to forget about all of it and hope it goes away."

"If you really want to be rid of it, Dawn, we could try some medication."

She blinked and looked at him. Medication? After one visit? Wasn't that odd? Aloud, she said, "Yeah. Let's try that."

"I'll phone you in a prescription," he said. "Blackberry Pharmacy, if that's all right. We'll start easy, see how it works. Okay?"

"Thank you, Doctor. I honestly don't know how I would have got through all this without you."

He nodded, and she hurried toward the door. The doctor stood up and moved behind her, grabbing his own coat on the way. "I'll walk you to your car," he said.

She felt a cold chill down her nape as she started for the door. And the woman appeared there, blocking her way, shaking her head slowly, side to side.

What? Dawn thought desperately. *Are you telling me this guy is dangerous? Jesus, did you wait long enough, do you think?*

The woman looked down at Dawn's coat pocket, and even as she did, Dawn heard the familiar bleat of her cell phone.

She snatched it up as if grabbing a life jacket. "Hello?"

"Hey, Dawn. It's Bry. Where are you?"

The woman nodded. She nodded insistently.

"I'm with Dr. Ethan Melrose, Bry. I'm at his office, in Burlington, and I'm just heading out. He offered to walk me

to my car. And then I'm coming straight home, no stops along the way. No one else I plan to see. There's no one else here."

"What the hell is going on, Dawn?"

"I'm leaving now. Oh, you're that close? Good, I'll see you in five minutes then. Tell you what? Why don't you stay on the line with me the entire time?" She turned. "Bye, Dr. Melrose. Thanks for everything."

He looked deflated, and maybe curious. But the woman in the doorway appeared relieved. She didn't vanish, but moved aside, as if to tell Dawn it was okay for her to leave now.

Bryan was shooting questions at her. "Do you want me to call a cop or something? Are you in trouble?"

"Not yet. I'm walking to my car now." She got out of the building and glanced back. The doctor hadn't followed. She grabbed for her keys with her free hand, and fought not to break into a run. "He's not following me. But I think he wanted to. I'm on to something here, Bry. Something to do with the escapee Jax is after. And the doc knows something, too, and he knows I know something, though I don't know what it is. Yet."

"You're not making any sense, Dawn."

"I know." She got to the Jeep, hit the button to pop the locks, jumped in fast and hit the button again, locking it down. She glanced back, and the doc was standing in the open doorway. "Dammit, he's coming."

"Who? Melrose? Jesus—Dad! Dad, come here. I think Dawn's in trouble."

She jammed the key into the switch, twisted it and started the engine, then slammed the car into Reverse and swung around in a wide arc even as the doctor came toward the car, holding up a hand as if asking her to wait up a sec.

"You still okay?"

"I am. *He* won't be if he doesn't get the hell out of my way." She jammed the car into Drive and gunned it. Tires spun.

Squealing assaulted her ears and hot rubber her nostrils, and then it caught and lurched, and the good doctor ducked aside. The car exploded into the road, forcing another onto the shoulder to avoid hitting her, and then she ran the red light and turned toward home.

It was only as the little clinic vanished behind her that Dawn slowed down a little, and dared to breathe again.

She glanced to the side. The woman was sitting there in the passenger seat, and Dawn shrieked and almost went off the road.

"Jesus, Dawn, what is it?" Bryan cried into the phone. "Dawn!"

"I'm okay. I'm okay. He's not following. I just—I was startled."

"I'm coming down there."

"No need. I'm on my way home." The woman shook her head, side to side. "No? Okay. No, I'm not on my way home."

"Where are you going?"

Dawn looked at the woman. She was so sad. There were tears welling in her pretty eyes, spilling over her blackened, charred cheek. She pointed, and sighing, Dawn took the corner she indicated. "I don't know where I'm going yet, Bryan. But it looks like I'm headed downtown. Why don't you start for Burlington? Keep the phone on and I'll keep you posted as to where I end up."

"I'll be there. Be safe, Dawn. I need you to be okay."

She smiled slowly. "I'm about the furthest thing from okay you've ever seen, Bry. And the furthest thing from what you need, too. But I need your help."

"I'm on my way."

Jax had River drop her off a block from the designated meeting place in Burlington, then watched him drive out of sight, and turned to walk along the sidewalk to the coffee

house. It was a sunny day, and there was no snow sticking to anything the way there was out in Blackberry. It was always warmer in the city—even a tiny, small-town city like this one. The sun warmed the sidewalk and glared in her eyes, and Jax lowered her sunglasses from her head to her nose. She felt a little shiver of unease as she wondered what Victoria Melrose could want from her, but she knew from River that the two couples had been close. Maybe she wanted to help. Maybe she thought she knew something.

Maybe she was about to implicate her husband. That possibility was the most enticing of all. Despite River's denials, Jax couldn't help but suspect Ethan's involvement in all of this. At the very least, she thought he was guilty of malpractice in treating his best friend. River was *perfectly* sane. She'd lived with the man for almost a week now, and he was fine. Functional, rational and fine. Clearly, he had not needed the vat of chemicals Ethan had been pumping into his bloodstream.

She looked ahead of her at the brick buildings and pretty storefronts, the benches on the sidewalk here and there with no other purpose than to give pedestrians a place to rest their feet. She decided she liked Vermont. It had a fresh, clean feeling—a healthy energy to it. She drew a deep lungful of the crisp air, spotted the coffee house across the street, looked both ways and stepped onto the crosswalk.

The car came out of nowhere.

Jax caught movement in her peripheral vision, and in the time it took her to jerk her head around fully, the vehicle was on her. A speeding glimpse of shining silver, and then the hood of the thing slammed her, launched her. She was airborne— then the impact. Her body crashing to the pavement. An explosion of pain rocked through her, with darkness close on its heels. She fought it, knew she was in trouble, had to stay awake.

Footsteps. Pain. Hands gripping her wrists. Pulling. Dragging her body over the blacktop. Oh, God, that hurt. She

moaned, tried to speak, to shout, to pull free, but she was barely making any movements at all. She couldn't see—there was hot blood stinging her eyes. And then there was more pain as her upper body was lifted, crammed and shoved inside. A door slammed. She couldn't move. And finally, she lost her battle to cling to the light.

Dawn rounded a corner, and then stopped the car in the middle of a downtown Burlington street, staring straight ahead and not sure what she was seeing.

A block ahead of her was a car—a Silver Mercedes. Its back door was open, and Dawn swore she saw a pair of feet dangling from it. But then the person who stood at the car door, swathed in a parka with the hood up, bent down to shove the feet into the car, slammed the back door and got behind the wheel. Then the car spun around in the street and sped away.

Dawn stomped on the gas, and her car lurched ahead to where the other one had been. Items littered the road, and she stopped and got out, racing from one to the other. There was a cell phone. And a handgun.

"Jeez, what is this?" She picked up the phone and looked at its display, quickly hit a button. The screen read, "Your number is 315-555-8738."

"Jax," she whispered. "That's Jax's phone!"

A pedestrian shouted to another, "Did you see that? That car just ran some woman down like a dog!"

Dawn looked ahead, in the direction the Mercedes had gone, and knew that the dead woman had led her there. To help Jax. Dawn dived into her car again, tossing the cell phone and handgun onto the seat, jammed the Jeep into gear and took off after the Mercedes, hoping to God she could catch up to it again, and having no clue what she would do when she did.

As she drove, she grabbed her own cell phone and hit the button. "Bryan," she told the phone.

It did the rest, and within a few seconds, Bryan was picking up.

"Dawn? What happened? We got cut off."

"Yeah. Listen, something's happened to Jax. I'm pretty sure I just saw her being stuffed into the back of a Mercedes. I'm following."

"Wait a sec. Wait just a— Dawnie, are you okay?"

"Fine. Wait, I think I see them." She pressed harder on the accelerator, got a little closer. "Yeah. Okay, I've got them in sight. I'm going to hang back so they don't spot me."

"Tell me exactly what happened," Bryan said.

"God, there's no time for all that now. Listen, I'm pretty sure someone in a Mercedes ran Jax down in the street, Bryan, then shoved her into their car and took off with her."

"Where are you?"

"Just turned off East Main onto the highway—heading south."

"I'm calling Frankie Parker. And I'm coming to back you up. Don't get too close, Dawn. Don't put yourself at risk."

"I won't." The phone beeped, and she glanced at its screen. "I'm losing the signal, Bry."

"Stay on as long as you can. Don't hang—"

The rest didn't come through. The phone's digital panel told her there was no signal, and she flicked it off and dropped it onto the seat of the car. She sped past a man standing on the side of the highway, staring at her, and caught her breath as she realized it was Mordecai.

"You stay away from me!" she shouted. And when she looked in her rearview mirror, he was gone.

"Hold on, Jax," she whispered. She owed the lady cop a lot. And this was her chance to pay a little bit of it back.

River showed a photo of his wife to the desk clerk at the Harrington Inn. It was a gorgeous little place. A huge log

cabin, ten miles from the Burlington city limits, set on a piece of property that could pass for paradise. It had a pond, a little waterfall, a footbridge that spanned it and a water wheel in the stream that bisected the rolling green lawn. There were patches of snow here and there, few and far between, and a blotch or two of white on the shingled brown roof.

The inside was just as impressive, a double-decker dining room off the cathedral-ceilinged lobby. Wide curving staircase that wound up to the guest rooms, of which there couldn't be more than a couple of dozen at most. An intimate hideaway.

His stomach knotted.

The manager smiled at him and shook his head. "I'm sorry, sir. I don't know her. Is she missing?"

He held up a hand then, delaying River's reply as he caught the eye of a woman in a maid's uniform who'd been coming down the stairs. "Fresh linens in room six, Sylvie."

"*Sí, señor.* Right away." She moved behind the desk, glancing at the photo on the counter as she did, and doing a double take. She looked up at the manager, who met her eyes with a dismissive stare, and then turned back to River.

"You were saying?"

"The woman in the photo is dead," River said. "Murdered." His voice sounded just as lifeless. "More than a year ago. But it seems as if the wrong man was blamed for the crime. I'm looking into it."

The manager appeared alarmed. "I assure you this has no connection to us, whatsoever."

River shook his head slowly. "She was never here?"

"Never. I would remember her if she had been. I've been the manager here for seven years, and I assure you, I've never seen this woman."

River blinked slowly, letting that settle in. It was a relief. Was it possible he'd been wrong, that his wife had not been having an affair with his best friend?

"Would you mind if I questioned some of your staff? Maybe someone else might remember—"

"I'm afraid I really can't let you do that. Bad for business, you understand."

Screw business, River thought, but he agreed. He'd find a way to question the employees here before the day was out. Whether this guy liked it or not.

He thanked the manager, took the photo and left the inn. Limping with the help of the wooden cane he'd picked up on the way there, he followed the winding stone path lined with holly bushes to the parking lot where he'd left Cassandra's car.

"*Señor! Señor,* wait."

He turned and saw a woman tugging a huge down-filled jacket around her even as she hurried toward him. It was, he realized, the housekeeper he'd glimpsed inside. She must have come out a different exit and cut around in front of him.

He moved toward her, and even before he reached her his stomach was sinking.

"That woman—the one in the photo—I saw her on the news after she died. It was tragic. Tragic. Miss Stephanie was kind to everyone. Always."

He blinked, and tried not to let his throat close up. It was tough. "You knew her then?"

"*Sí.* She came here all the time. With a man who was not her husband."

He closed his eyes slowly. "She was having an affair."

"That's why her husband murdered her. At least that's what I always thought. He must have found out about her and the doctor."

River's head came up fast. "The doctor?"

"*Sí.* Dr. Melrose. He's a regular here. She wasn't the first woman he brought. But he pays well, very well, for our discretion. And he's a friend of Mr. Monteray—the manager."

"Why did the manager lie?"

"This inn caters to the wealthy, *señor.* They count on us to keep their visits to ourselves."

River thought that required a response, but he couldn't get words to form, couldn't make a sound. He lowered his head and tried to squeeze the tears back, not to let them show. They burned. His chest burned, his throat, too. The knowledge burned.

Stephanie and Ethan. God, his wife and his best friend. No question. Not anymore.

"I'm sorry," the housekeeper said. "I just thought—telling the truth was the right thing to do. What Jesus would do."

River glanced at the way she fingered the tiny gold cross she wore on a chain around her neck and he nodded. "Thank you. It *was* the right thing to do. I'm grateful." He was choked and hoarse, but at least he managed to speak.

"*Dios,*" she whispered, pressing one hand to her chest as she stared at his face. "Are you the husband?"

"No." He shook his head slowly. "No, just a friend of the family." He turned and moved past her to the parking lot, got into Jax's car, where Rex sat waiting, and took off. But a mile down the road, he had to pull off to the side, because his chest was heaving and he didn't know how to deal with the overwhelming emotions that were flooding him right now. All he could think of was Cassandra. If he could only get to her, talk to her....

God, she had tried so hard to warn him off, to slow him down. And he was letting himself fall, anyway. It was way more than physical attraction—he knew that, and thought she did, as well. He'd tried not to feel anything. But he'd failed. And right now, the betrayal, the shock of learning what the last woman he had loved had done to him, was coloring everything. It was just as well Cassandra didn't want any involvement. He sure as hell didn't want it, either.

And yet he needed to talk to her. To hear her voice.

He didn't have a cell phone. She did, but it was only twenty minutes until he had to meet her, anyway. He thought he could probably stand it that long. He put the car into gear and drove into Burlington, to the parking lot two blocks from the coffee house where he and Cassandra were supposed to meet.

But she wasn't there—the police were. His heart jumped into his throat, and he sat in the middle of the road, staring.

The street was cordoned off at the intersection near the coffee house. Yellow tape crisscrossed it, and cops were walking around, taking pictures.

A pedestrian walked past along the sidewalk, and River put the window down and called out, "What happened over there?"

"Man, they don't even know. Weird shit. Someone said a woman was hit by a car, but I didn't see anyone hurt. No ambulance or anything." He shrugged.

River swallowed his fear and nosed the car into the parking lot, then turned it around and drove back out. He headed the opposite way, then right and right again, until he found a vacant parking space and pulled over. Leaving the car running, and the cane inside, he got out, put a quarter in the meter and limped through the alley, emerging right in front of the coffee house.

He turned up the collar of his coat, tugged down the knit hat and wished to hell he had a pair of sunglasses to better hide his face as he walked up to the rawest rookie. Easy to tell which one he was, too, by that kind of lost look in his eyes, as he wondered if there were anything he was supposed to be doing and wasn't.

"What's going on?" River asked.

The rookie said, "I'm sorry, sir, you'll have to—"

"I'm a cop. Sergeant Samuels, NYPD," River said, giving his long-ago partner's name. "Here on vacation. Anything I can do to help?"

The kid looked relieved not to have to do crowd control. "It was a hit-and-run. I think we've got it covered."

"Hit-and-run?" River asked. As he did, his eyes scanned

the pavement, and he saw blood—a tiny puddle, and then a smeared trail. His own blood turned to ice.

"With a twist," the rookie said. "Witness says the driver dragged the victim into the back seat and took off with her."

River tried to keep the look of horror from his face. "Do we know who the victim is?"

The rookie nodded. "That's why the place is crawling with uniforms. Word is, she was a cop."

"Jesus," River whispered. "They have a line on her yet?"

"Some teenager witnessed it and followed her a ways, was on the cell phone with her boyfriend till the signal ran out. All we have is her last known location."

"South of town?" River asked, guessing as much, because that was the direction in which several police vehicles had just sped off.

"Yeah, off exit ten. That's all we know." He lifted his head. "You wanna meet the chief? He could tell you if you could do something to help."

River pretended to look at his watch—though he wasn't wearing one. "I gotta go, but I'll check back in with you later. Thanks for the info."

Another cop glanced his way, frowned and started coming toward him. River saw recognition in the man's eyes, or thought he did. Hell. He turned around and headed back through the alley, and he could feel the hairs on his nape standing up—that sense of pursuit. Once out of sight, he moved faster into a run, limped out the other side, dived into the car and took off. And even as he did, he saw the cop coming through the alley, glimpsing the car and speaking into a radio.

They were on to him. And if they realized he was driving Cassandra Jackson's car, they would be pursuing him in short order.

Didn't matter. He had to find her. He had to find Cassandra.

_19_

Jax had no idea where she was when she opened her eyes. The room was blurry—but it was that: a room. And it felt as if it had been a long time since anyone had used it. A chill, and a sort of musty dampness, permeated the air.

She blinked and tried to bring things into focus. There wasn't much light. What came through the windows was filtered by slatted shutters pulled tight, and grime-coated glass in between. Instinctively, she kept quiet, knowing she was in trouble, but not clear on why. So she remained still, moving little, and waiting for the dust in her mind to settle.

She'd been in Burlington. Yes. Heading to the coffee house to meet with Victoria Melrose. She remembered walking down the sidewalk, recalled the sunshine, the cool air, the benches. Crossing the road.

Oh, God. The car speeding toward her, crashing into her, her body being pounded by the hood and then by the pavement. Hell, no wonder she was hurting so much.

She didn't see or sense anyone in the room, so she dragged herself up into a sitting position, wincing at the pain in her side that the movement brought. Dizziness rose like a wave, then subsided, leaving her weak, but clear enough to take stock.

She was in a room with four walls, a window in the two on either side of her, a door in the wall that faced her, and a

wood-burning stove at her back. The place was paneled in what looked like real wood. The floor beneath her was covered in a braided round rug that left the four corners bare, where she saw hardwood. No other doors or doorways. It looked like a one-room shack. A deer head was mounted on one wall, its marble eyes glinting at her. There was a tiny, cot-size set of bunk beds in one corner, and a wooden table with a couple of chairs stood in the center of the room. A few easy chairs occupied other corners, and a magazine rack full to bursting sat beside one of them. There were cupboards on one of the walls, above a counter made of polished pine boards. The potbellied wood stove was trimmed in silver metal that included the words Round Oak. It was pretty, and not cheap, probably an antique. A blue metal coffeepot with white speckles sat atop it, but the stove was stone cold and the pot, she suspected, empty.

"It's a hunting cabin," she whispered. And again she eyed the windows, the door, seeing nothing to stop her from getting up and walking out.

Except, of course, for pain. She drew a breath and tried to take stock of her body, now that she had a handle on her bearings. There was a lot of pain in a lot of places, and it took her a moment to focus in on any one specific complaint. She closed her eyes and put her attention on her feet, which felt all right, except that one was shoeless. And that ankle throbbed. She moved her foot a little, left then right, ran her hand over the ankle, feeling for protrusions or lumps. It was swollen, but she didn't think broken. Sprained, then. And damn, it hurt.

She continued moving her attention up her body—shins and calves felt all right. Her knees were scraped, but that was minor. Thighs were good. One hip must be bruised, but it wasn't serious. Pelvis felt okay. Belly wasn't hurting and it wasn't distended, either, which she took as a good sign. Lower

back—she ran her fingertips up and down her spine from the middle to the tailbone, relieved that she could feel her own touch, and there wasn't any pain. Then she lifted her arm, to try to touch her spine from the nape down as far as she could reach, but stopped at a sharp stab in her side.

"Ow!"

She lowered her arm again, slowly, and ran her other hand over her side and waist. "Damn." She could feel the broken ribs. More than one, she thought, but how many in all she had no idea. It hurt like hell. She drew a breath, noting when the pain kicked in harder. Had she punctured a lung? She tried to focus on her breathing, on what exactly hurt, but she couldn't be sure. She felt her own pulse, and it was good and strong. She wasn't dizzy or feeling cold. She didn't think there was internal bleeding. If there was she would feel more than just pain, right?

Okay, so her spine seemed all right, but her ribs were in sorry shape. She continued her exploration. Chest, neck, collarbones—okay. Arms, elbows, shoulders—a little stiff in one shoulder. Sore and achy, especially when she moved the left arm a lot. Jaw, nose, cheeks. One cheek was tender to the touch, and she imagined she'd smacked it into the pavement on impact. Probably bruised it. No big deal. She could hear okay. She thought her eyesight was normal, though it was hard to be sure in this dimly lit room. And her head didn't seem to be split, though there was one hell of a goose egg forming on one side, just above the temple. She didn't feel sick to her stomach. Probably not a concussion, then.

Okay. She wasn't going to be able to run too fast. The ankle and the ribs were her biggest problems, as far as fighting or escaping. Good to know where she stood. She reached to her waist for her gun, but it wasn't there. She didn't know if it had been knocked to the pavement with her shoe, or if whoever brought her here had taken it from her.

No cell phone, either. Great.

She gripped the cold metal of the woodstove behind her, and tugged herself to her feet, wincing when she put weight on the sprained ankle. Damn, that was going to be sheer hell. Best not walk on it until she had to. She hopped to the nearest window, peering between the slats to see outside. Woods. That was all she saw. Just woods. Trees devoid of leaves. Stiff brown weeds sprouting from the patchy snow. She hopped to the other window and saw a similar view. A quick look at her watch told her two hours had passed since she'd been assaulted by a speeding Mercedes.

A speeding *silver* Mercedes. "If I live through this, Ethan Melrose, I am going to kick your ass," she muttered. And then she moved toward the door, shoved against it, but it wouldn't open. She tried harder, but it was solidly blocked. She didn't think she could bust through it even at full strength.

Fine. She turned to the windows, went to the first one and tried to open it. But the sash was sealed. "Not a problem," she said, turning to look around the room for something useful.

Her eyes were adjusting to the darkness by now. She saw the fire poker hanging from a nail in the wall behind the wood stove, took it down and went back to the window, using it to smash the glass out of the frame. Then she shoved at the shutters.

Blocked. Just like the door. And a closer inspection of the tiny crevice of light that ran vertically along each side told her why. There was something over them, holding them. Like a board nailed on from the outside.

Spinning around, she went to the other window, unwilling to give up even though she fully expected to find this window's shutters sealed, as well. This one had a stand underneath it, covered in a dusty old sheet. She decided to get up onto it, and maybe kick the shutters open from there.

The sheet had to go. No use falling and doing even more damage to her body. She yanked it off and caught her breath.

A chest-type freezer, not a stand, stood beneath the window. "Oh, my God."

Her eyes were riveted to the freezer as her stomach clenched. It was the same one that had been in the rental unit. The same one that held the body of River's former gardener, and the Melroses' sometimes handyman, Arty Mullins.

The room started to spin and warp and twist. Jax pressed a hand to the lump on her head and wondered if it was more serious than she'd thought. She hadn't been nauseated before, but she was now. And before she could analyze that further, she fell into what felt like a spiraling tunnel that took her into oblivion.

Dawn couldn't find them. They'd gotten too far ahead of her on the winding dirt roads, and even though she'd pushed the Jeep to greater speeds, she'd lost them. She sat at a crossroads, staring first in one direction, then another.

"Which way did they go?" she asked. She turned off the engine and got out. Then she stood there, turning and staring in each of the three directions she might take. None had a telltale dust cloud lingering in the air. She listened, but couldn't hear anything beyond the crows squawking, and a slight breeze whispering through the naked limbs of the towering trees.

Disheartened, she turned back toward her precious powder-blue Wrangler, half expecting to see the woman there— the ghost of Stephanie Corbett—pointing the way. She almost *hoped* to see her there. But there was no one.

Dawn looked skyward. "So what do you want me to do?" No answer.

Her father's curse was useless, maybe not even real. And instead of feeling relieved, she felt angry. Why couldn't it come when she needed it most? Jax was in trouble.

She stomped back to the Jeep, got in and slammed the door. "Screw it. I'll just pick a direction and go, fast as hell. If I don't

find a sign of them, I'll come back and pick another. I just hope Jax has that kind of time."

She jerked the stick shift into first gear, stomped on the gas and popped the clutch in her frustration, spitting gravel behind her as the vehicle lurched forward.

A woman stood dead in front of her, and Dawn shrieked and slammed her foot on the brake pedal, forgetting the clutch. Stalling the Jeep. The ass end of it had fishtailed around to one side, and she sat there, clutching the wheel, gasping and peering through the clouds of dust all around her.

But there was no one there. No one.

"Okay, okay. I get it. Not that way."

She managed to stop shaking just enough to back the Jeep up and turn it in another direction, the second possible route. This time she took the road to her right. She went slowly, though, didn't stomp it as she had before. Again, the woman appeared right in front of the car. Dawn met her eyes, saw the way she seemed to move them from side to side, as if to say no.

"All right," Dawn whispered. "Okay, third time's the charm. Besides, it's the last possible choice." She executed a three-point-turn, and drove in the opposite direction.

And this time, nothing showed up to block her path. So she kept on going, though she couldn't bring herself to drive fast, the way she had fully intended to do. The jolt of nearly hitting someone—even someone who was already dead—was too horrifying to experience more than once.

And maybe the ghost wanted her to drive slowly. Dawn rolled her eyes and shook her head. Her own thoughts sounded ludicrous. She didn't want this. Had never wanted it. Had been living in dread of it ever since she'd first begun to suspect... And now here she was, actually *using* it.

Was she insane? Was this the beginning of the end? Had she really seen what she thought she had seen on that street

in Burlington? Or had it all been part of the same delusion that had her talking to ghosts and driving over country roads with no clue where she was going?

She frowned, then, slowing the car to a stop in the road, because there were tire tracks in the snow along the side— tire tracks veering over a barely discernable path, narrow and seldom traveled, she figured. Beyond them she saw a gate. It was closed and had a heavy chain looped through it, and a large padlock dangled from one side. But the car tracks moved beyond that point. Someone had opened the gate, driven through it and then locked it again.

Clearly, she wasn't going to get in there by car—not even by Jeep. But she had a feeling that was where she had to go. What other car would have been driving over these roads recently enough to leave fresh tracks in the snow?

Sighing, she knew what she had to do. So she drove her car farther along the road until she found a spot where she could pull off to the side and park it. Then she got out, and paused, looking in at the front seat. At the items on it.

Swallowing her fear, she reached back into the car, taking both her cell phone and Jax's. She checked the panels, but neither had a signal. So she set the ringers to vibrate, just in case, and tucked them into her coat pocket.

She reached in again, this time closing her hand around the cool grips of Jax's handgun. A shiver went up Dawn's arm as she held the gun in her hand. She didn't know how to work the thing, wasn't sure if she squeezed the trigger whether or not it would fire. She wasn't sure if she'd have to do something else first. She looked for a safety button, found one, but couldn't tell if it was on or off.

She hoped to God she wouldn't need to find out.

River had Cassandra's car pulled off on a side road when six screaming police vehicles sped by, and as far as he could

tell, not one cop noticed him there. Granted, he was blocked by some sentinel pines, but he wasn't invisible. Cassandra's car was red, for crying out loud.

Not only were the police missing him, they were missing the correct route. There was only one place he could think of where Ethan might have taken Cassandra. And since the Mercedes's last known location was within a few miles of there, River was pretty sure his instinct was on target.

He put the cops out of his mind and refocused on his reason for pulling over in the first place. A crossroads. And before he went any farther, he wanted to make absolutely sure he was heading to the right locale.

He opened the door and got out, then held the door open. "Come on, boy."

Rex clambered out, as well. River held the balled up T-shirt he'd found in the back seat to the dog's face, and let him sniff. He knew it smelled like Cassandra. Even he could detect her scent clinging to the fabric. What he couldn't do was find its match on the air.

Rex could—and it was amazing he could track her, even though she'd been taken away inside a car. River knew of other dogs who could do it, but only bloodhounds. He'd always thought Rex had the best nose of any shepherd alive, but there was nothing official about it—it was only his opinion. "Find her, boy," he told Rex. "Find Cassandra."

Rex barked once, then got to work, sniffing the air and the ground, pacing one way, then another. Eventually, he settled on one spot, getting excited and then barking twice and moving up the road.

"Good dog, good boy." There was no doubt in River's mind now where Jax had been taken. To the hunting cabin he and Ethan had bought together so long ago. They'd retreated there every spring for fishing and every fall for duck hunting. Even though Ethan had never bagged a bird due to his lousy

aim. It was on the same road Rex had chosen. No way was that a coincidence.

It was Ethan. Dammit, it was Ethan.

River called Rex off, guiding him back to the car. Then he jumped in and drove, taking the shortcut he and Ethan had always used to save time.

Dawn walked beyond the gate, using the trees along the barely discernable track for cover. But she only went far enough to spot the silver Mercedes. It was backed into a spot amid a stand of thick pines. If she'd been in the Jeep, she probably would have driven right by and not seen it, and she figured that was probably exactly what its driver wanted.

She looked ahead and saw a small cabin. That must be where the car's owner had taken Jax. Dawn looked at the gun she carried, licked her lips and started forward again. But there was a man blocking her path.

She jerked the gun up reflexively before her mind acknowledged him for who he was. Her father.

She wanted to tell him to go away. To leave her alone. But the words wouldn't come. He met her eyes, shook his head slowly from side to side, then lifted his arm and pointed back the way she had come.

"I have to help her."

He bent his arm slightly and pointed again, jabbing his finger aggressively.

He didn't want her to go on. And she wondered if that was because he was still as evil as ever, still bent on inflicting pain and horror on everyone he could. But then, that had never been his intent. Not truly. He'd always *believed* he was doing what was right. Even when it couldn't have been more wrong.

She stared at his face, really looked at him for once. Every other time he had appeared to her, she'd made a point not to. He looked sad. There were tears in his eyes.

"I'll get help," she said. "And then I'm coming back."

He nodded three times, slowly, but strongly enough to be sure she understood. He didn't want her to abandon Jax to her fate. He wanted her to get help.

"Okay, then."

She could not believe she was doing what he wanted her to. God, she could not *believe* it. And yet, she sensed it was right. So she made her way back to the Jeep and marked the spot in her mind. Then she drove back toward the highway, holding her cell phone in one hand and shifting her gaze constantly between the road and the bars on the tiny screen. She didn't like having to go so far.

Ten miles, give or take, later, she had two bars on the panel. Good enough. She pulled the car off to the side of the road and dialed Bryan's cell.

He picked up on the first ring. "Dawn?"

"Yeah, it's me."

"Where the hell are you? God, I've been so worried."

"I'm okay. Got out of cell phone range, but I found them. Some crazy person has Jax, Bryan. They're in a cabin in the middle of the freakin' woods, fifteen miles south of Burlington."

"Is that where you are now? Dawn, did they see you?"

"No. No one saw me. I didn't have a signal up there, had to drive ten miles to get one so I could call you."

"Wait for me."

"But Bry—"

"You came back ten miles, you said. That puts you five miles south of me. I'm on my way. I'll be there in five minutes. Less. Dad and Beth are ahead of me—they followed the police. I'll call them and tell them to get back here. *Wait for me*, Dawn."

"Okay." She nodded. "Okay, Bry. I..." She bit her lip and closed her eyes. She had things she wanted to tell him, things— Hell, she wasn't even sure what they were at this point. "I'll talk to you when you get here."

"You sound—odd. Are you all right?"

She shook her head. "I'm in a rest area. Look for me."

He sighed, but rung off, probably so he could phone his dad, and focus on driving faster. Bryan would always come charging to the rescue when she needed him. Dawn would never doubt that, even if she wished he'd wise up and find someone more stable. Less dangerous.

She set the phone beside her on the seat, leaned her head back on the headrest and prayed Bryan would get there fast. Before it was too late.

In the distance, Jax heard someone calling her name. Not Dad. Dad called her Cassie. Not another cop—most of them called her Jax. Except the rookies; to them she was Lieutenant Jackson. No, this voice called her Cassandra, just the way River did.

River.

It was River's voice.

She lifted her head from the floor and tried to shout a warning—to tell him to be careful, before the killer got to him, too, but the only sound that emerged was a hoarse moan. She tried again, but this time it was even softer.

The cabin's door was suddenly flung open. She flinched, jerking a hand up to cover her face. And then he was leaning over her, gathering her into his arms, pushing her hair away from her face. "Cassandra. My God, are you all right?"

She tried to tell him what had happened, but was still having trouble staying conscious. "Car."

"I know, I know. It's all right. I'm here now."

She swallowed hard, tried to speak. "F-freezer."

"What?"

She nodded past him, toward the freezer that stood underneath one of the windows. River turned slowly, looking at it.

Then she heard a slam. A bang she felt right to her bones,

and it made her flinch. She saw River spin away from her at the sound, saw him looking toward the closed door.

He'd left it open when he'd come in.

Slowly, he rose to his feet. "Who's out there?" he called. He moved toward the door, sliding a gun from the back of his jeans, and reminding Jax that she had lost her own.

He moved closer, keeping to one side of the door, gun in one hand with its barrel pointing upward, as he gripped the doorknob with the other. "Ethan?" he called. "I know it's you. Give it up. It's over. I know everything."

River twisted the doorknob, but it didn't give. He frowned and tried again. "Dammit, Ethan, what the hell is this going to accomplish?"

Jax smelled something. She sniffed and felt her heart start to beat faster. "River."

He was back at her side almost before she finished saying his name. "It's all right. It's okay. I'll get us out of…"

His words trailed off. She could see the very moment when his expression changed, and she knew he smelled it, too. Gasoline. And following on its heels, smoke.

"River?"

He swore under his breath, looking around, as she was. She could hear it now. Crackling, snapping that seemed to come from many directions. Smoke rose, wafting through the air. Something exploded from beneath the floor, sending floorboards splintering and flying like shrapnel. River flung himself over her, trying to shield her, she knew, and when he eased aside to look, there were flames shooting up from the floor and licking at one wall. They leaped to life on the easy chairs, and gained energy from the fabric, surging toward the ceiling as smoke billowed into the small room.

"Hold on. I'll get us out, I swear." He grabbed a chair and smashed it into the shutters of one window, but the wooden barrier remained in place.

"They're blocked from the outside," she told him. "What about Rex? Where is he?"

"Left him in the car."

"God!"

She gripped the little table in clawed hands and dragged herself up into a sitting position. "River!"

He shot her a desperate, determined look, and lifted the wooden chair again, slammed it repeatedly against the shutters, but they didn't budge. And finally, exhausted, he sank to the floor, wrapped her in his arms, held her. "I'm sorry, Cassandra. I'm so freaking sorry."

"It's not your fault," she told him.

"It is. Jesus, everything I love, I destroy."

"No."

"Yes. God, I never wanted to hurt you...."

She didn't answer, because she couldn't. He was clasping her face in his hands and kissing her, and the desperation of the act scared her almost as much as the words that preceded it. She kissed him back, clinging just as desperately, but only for a moment. And then, despite her pain and her stupor, she twisted her face away from his mouth and breathlessly whispered, "Kiss me later, River. Right now, get us the hell out of here."

"I...Cassandra, I don't know if I can—"

"Get. Us. Out."

The smoke was choking them both by now, and smothering heat blanketed the place. River helped her to her feet and drew her to a corner, where he eased her to the floor again. "Stay down," he said. "The smoke's not as bad down low."

She nodded and crouched, but it hurt to bend her body that way, so she had to recline against the wall. River flipped the wooden table upside down, then hauled off and kicked one of the legs right off the piece. Picking up the solid post, he returned to the blocked window and used it like a battering ram.

And even then the shutters didn't give.

20

"How did you even find her?" Bryan asked.

He was driving. They'd left his dad's pickup on the roadside, and taken Dawn's Jeep, which was easier to maneuver in rough terrain. She hadn't spoken a word since they'd taken off, but now he was asking her a direct question and she thought it was high time she answered it. She owed him that much.

"A dead woman showed me. And my father helped, I think."

Bry blinked in shock, swinging his focus from the road to her and back again. "Your—?"

"I mean, I saw him. And I saw her. Stephanie Corbett, the woman who died in the fire out at Jax's house a couple of years ago, the one whose husband escaped from the mental hospital. I've been seeing her a lot lately. She was in my bedroom one night, and I saw her in the diner. She's a ghost, Bryan. I've been seeing a ghost."

Bry licked his lips, nodded slowly. "Okay. Okay, so you've been seeing dead people."

"You believe me?"

"Of course I believe you. You're not crazy, Dawn."

"I didn't say—"

"You didn't have to say it. I can read you like a book. This has been coming on for a while, hasn't it? It's why you pulled away from me."

She pursed her lips. "My father was poison. Every life he touched was tainted by that poison. Julie's. Beth's. Mine." She shook her head. "You don't want that kind of poison in your life, Bryan."

"You are not your father. *You're* not poison, Dawn, and even if you were, it wouldn't change the way I feel. And I think you know it."

Tears welled in her eyes and spilled over in spite of her effort to contain them. "Bryan, I'm afraid I'm going insane like he did."

Bry jerked the wheel and hit the brake, skidding the Jeep to a stop on the shoulder. Then he turned and pulled her into his arms. "You're not going insane. God, Dawn, how can you think that? Okay, okay, so maybe you inherited whatever it was that made your old man sort of—psychic or whatever. But that doesn't mean you inherited whatever it was that made him turn bad."

"But what if it's the same thing?"

"It's not." He held her to his chest, stroked her hair. "It's not, hon. It can't be. Hell, it led you to Jax, didn't it? When she needed your help? Our help, I mean."

She blinked her eyes and lifted her head. "We have to get to her."

"I know. But—"

"*Now,* Bry."

He nodded hard and got the Jeep going again. But he didn't stop talking, didn't stop rationalizing. "You've never hurt anyone. You're not getting urges to hurt anyone, are you?"

"Of course not."

"And when you do see these people—are they telling you to do harm?"

"I don't know what they're telling me. I can't even hear them, I can't understand…."

"You're okay, Dawn. You're fine. Is this the exit?"

"Yeah. This one." She guided him on, to the correct fork in the road. "I just hope you're right, Bry. Because I don't think I could—oh my God! Look!"

He looked. "Is that smoke?"

"Hurry, Bryan!"

He pressed the accelerator to the floor and the Jeep fishtailed, spat gravel and lurched faster.

"There, there's the gate," she said. "It was closed, padlocked with a chain, before." It stood wide-open now, though. And the Mercedes was gone. Bryan sped through it, and within seconds, they were skidding to a stop in front of a log cabin that was completely engulfed in flames. Dawn shrieked and jumped out of the Jeep, running forward until Bryan gripped her shoulders and stopped her.

"Jax is inside," she sobbed.

"You can't be sure—"

"Yes I can."

He looked at her, searching her face.

Sniffing and swallowing her tears, she pointed. "She's right there, that woman. Standing amid the flames. God, that's how she was killed. In a fire." She swung her face toward Bryan's, saw him staring at the cabin. "I don't suppose you can see her," Dawn whispered.

"I don't need to see her." He looked around, and the next thing she knew, he was racing toward a woodpile, yanking a rusted old ax free of a log and running toward the cabin, right at the window she'd pointed out. He lifted the ax and started swinging. And even amid the flames and smoke, Dawn knew that someone had nailed a two-by-four across the shutters, to keep them tight. The door was blocked, too, with a large board that had been dropped into brackets on the outside.

She ran toward him to try to help, but the heat drove her back. She tripped over a hand pump with a pail hanging from it, and scrambling to her feet, she quickly worked the handle

until water came gurgling out. She filled the pail and carried it to the window where Bryan worked, threw the water onto the flames and raced back for more. Five buckets later, she'd dampened the inferno down in that one spot, and Bryan had smashed open the shutters.

Even as he covered his face and tried to move closer, Dawn saw Jax filling the window opening, her body seeming to levitate. Bryan grabbed her and dragged her out through the hole, and quickly carried her back toward the Jeep. And then Dawn realized there was someone in there with her, even as the man, sooty-faced and damp with sweat, clambered out the window himself.

Dawn ran to his side to help him, pulling one of his arms around her shoulders, but before they reached the Jeep, he collapsed on the ground and took her with him. He lay there coughing as Dawn looked up.

The ghost woman stood there, staring at him, tears streaming down her face. And Dawn knew Mordecai was somewhere around. She *felt* him, lurking, and it made the hairs on her nape rise.

"Cassandra," the man rasped between bouts of coughing, struggling to sit up again. His eyes, watering and red, kept searching for her.

Dawn got up and helped him to his feet, even as she sought out Bryan. He had the Jeep's back open, was leaning inside.

"Bry? Is she…?"

"She's breathing," he said. "We've got to get her to a hospital."

They reached the vehicle, and Dawn looked at the man. He'd stopped still and was staring down at Jax. He looked stricken.

"We can't call for help from here," Dawn said. "We're going to have to take her ourselves."

The man reached down, as if to touch Jax's face, but Bryan

grabbed his wrist. "Just a minute. Who are you? What do you have to do with all this?"

The man looked at him like a deer looking at a bright light; clearly, he didn't know what the hell to say.

"I think this is Michael Corbett, Bry. The guy who escaped from the state hospital," she said. "I saw his picture in Dr. Melrose's office."

Bryan narrowed his eyes, which met hers, then slid right back to Corbett again. "The guy who killed his wife by burning his house down with her inside?"

"I didn't kill my wife," the stranger said in a hoarse, raspy voice.

"Funny then that I find you at the scene of another fire that almost killed another woman, isn't it?" Bryan asked.

"I don't think he did it, Bry."

Bry shot a look at Dawn. "Yeah, well, I'm not willing to risk it. You need to stay away from her, mister."

"The hell I will." The stranger shoved Bryan aside and leaned over Jax, one hand touching her face as he bent close and whispered something in her ear.

Dawn put a hand on his shoulder. "You should go," she said. "They're coming. Listen."

The man went still, and she knew he could hear the sirens wailing in the distance. He met Dawn's eyes, and his looked dead before he turned his gaze back to Jax again. "I'll come back for you," he told her, though Dawn didn't think she could hear. "I meant what I said. No more harm will come to you, Cassandra. It's time I put an end to this."

And then he leaned down, pressed his mouth to hers in a kiss so desperate it brought tears to Dawn's eyes. Jax didn't respond. Corbett lifted his head, turned and walked away. Dawn ran around to the front of the Jeep, yanked a cell phone off the seat and raced after him. "Wait."

He paused, turning slightly. He looked dangerous. She al-

most changed her mind, but something told her not to. "Here," she said, holding out the phone. "It's Jax's. I can let you know how she's doing."

He blinked, gazing down at the phone. "You'd do that?"

"I think she'd want me to."

"I think you're right." He took the phone from her, looked past her at Bryan. "Thanks for getting us out of there, kid."

Bryan only nodded, but he'd softened visibly toward the man, since that kiss.

"How did you get here?" Dawn asked. "Do you have a car or—"

"It's out by the road, a few yards down. Out of sight."

"Go then," she said. "I'll call you."

With a final nod, the man took off through the woods toward the dirt road.

Moments later, rescue vehicles pulled in, firefighters pouring out of them, paramedics racing toward the Jeep.

Dawn stepped backward, stunned and feeling shocky. It was suddenly as if she was hearing everything from a distance, and seeing it through a distorted lens at the end of a long tunnel.

It's like that day, isn't it?

Her father's voice rang in her ears. She squeezed her eyes tight.

That day at the inn. The day I died. I never did thank you for what you did that day, Sunny. For making them let me go.

Sunny. It was the name he'd given her when she'd been born, the name he'd always called her. "Please leave me alone."

I wish I could. And in the end, I guess I'll have to if that's what you truly want. But…I can't just yet.

"Why not? Why the hell not?"

She opened her eyes, half expecting to see Mordecai standing there. Instead she saw Bryan, standing by the Jeep, talking to the medics even while sending worried looks in her direction.

I did a lot of wrong, Sunny.

"Stop calling me that." She wanted to shout it, but she said it softly instead, all too aware of Bryan's concern, and the paramedics who were starting to glance her way now and then. She stood off by herself near the edge of the woods, carrying on an animated conversation with no one. She must look like a freaking lunatic.

I'm trying to help. It's what I'm here to do, to help.

"To help who?" she cried. "Because this sure as hell isn't helping me! I don't want this!"

I'm not sure it matters if you want it. It's who you are. You have a gift, Sunny—I'm sorry—Dawn. You received it for a reason—and you're going to make better use of it than I ever did. I can help you, if you'll let me. But even if you won't, you can't turn your back on the gift. I wasn't strong enough. It warped my mind. But you're stronger. You can handle it. And you will.

"I will not. I won't, do you hear me? I won't!"

"Dawn?" Bryan was coming toward her now.

She turned and ran into the woods, away from him, away from the voice of her dead father and the ghost of the woman who'd been haunting her. Away from all of it. She ran until she tripped and fell to the ground, sobbing. "I won't," she blurted. "I won't, I won't."

You already are, Dawn, Mordecai's voice whispered. *Stephanie couldn't get through to you—not alone. I had to help her. That's…what I do here. Help others get through. Channel them, much like I did before. Only now there's no mental illness polluting my mind. I help them.*

Dawn lifted her head and saw him, standing over her. Not touching her, just staring down, looking sad and so alone.

I helped Stephanie to contact you. Could have helped her speak to you if you would have let me. If you would have let yourself listen, the way you're letting yourself hear me now.

But even without hearing her, you listened to her, and you saved Lieutenant Jackson because of it.

"No," she whispered.

We're partners, Dawnie. You and me. You can't change that.

"*Nooo!*" The word emerged in the form of a shriek that split the forest's wintry air.

And then Bryan was there, gathering her up into his arms, holding her, his hands stroking her hair, her back and shoulders. "Easy, baby. Easy. It's okay, I'm here."

She couldn't speak. She could only sob and cling to him.

"They're taking Jax to the hospital," he told her, and then he slid one arm under her legs and picked her up. Started carrying her back toward the Jeep. "We've got cops waiting to talk to us—if you can handle that. And then we can head over there, too."

She nodded hard, not even arguing with him for carrying her, though it was totally over the line and she thought he knew it. She wasn't some helpless wilting flower. And yet, she didn't mind him overreacting this time.

He set her on the Jeep's tailgate. Jax was gone—Dawn saw the ambulance trundling away over the dirt road. The firefighters manned hoses, soaking the pathetic log cabin, where flames still leaped up now and then.

And cops were everywhere. They hadn't been there a few minutes ago. There were a lot of them. Dawn looked around for one she recognized and didn't see any. She glanced up at Bryan, told him with her eyes to follow her lead. Drawing a breath and lifting her chin, she got to her feet. She turned and closed the Jeep's tailgate, then moved to the driver's door.

A police officer put his hand on her shoulder. "Miss, if you don't mind, we need to get your statement."

"I know you do. There's not much to tell. I followed a car here. Left to call for help because there's no signal here, came back to find the place on fire. Bryan busted in and got them out."

"Them?"

She bit her lip, unsure whether to say more. "Her. I meant her. Listen, Jax is a good friend of my family's. I need to get to the hospital, call my parents. I'll be glad to give a more thorough statement—to Frankie Parker—at the hospital. Okay?"

The cop blinked. "You have something to hide, young lady?"

"Nothing. Can we please go now?"

"I think my daughter is being very reasonable," a woman said.

Dawn jerked her head up to see Beth and Joshua standing nearby. She didn't know when they had arrived, but God, she was glad to see them. She went into Beth's arms, and the warmth and love she felt there seemed to seep into her bones and make her stronger.

The policeman looked at another cop. Then someone called out, and he went to them. Dawn saw them kneeling down, examining some kind of tracks on the ground. Tire marks, maybe, or footprints. She didn't know. She didn't care.

"We have to go the hospital, Beth," Dawn whispered.

"I know. Go ahead, we'll be right behind you."

Nodding, Dawn got into the Jeep, started it up and shifted into gear. Bryan jumped into the passenger side just before it lurched forward and started down the road.

"Do we tell them about that guy? Corbett?" he asked.

"I don't know. That's what I hope we can find out before we have to talk to them. I have to see Jax—conscious. I have to ask her what she wants me to do."

River wanted nothing more than to follow the ambulance to the hospital, to stay with Cassandra, make sure she was all right. It was tearing him apart not to go. But he'd told her what he needed to tell her. He'd said what needed saying. And he'd taken care of her as best he could. His hovering over her on that stretcher wasn't going to make her any more likely to pull through. It would only ensure his capture and arrest. And

while he didn't give a damn about himself or his freedom at this point, there was one thing he was going to get done before he was put into another straitjacket.

One thing he probably should have done a long time ago.

Rex lay on the front seat, his head in River's lap. God, it was a good thing he'd listened to his gut and left the dog in the car. He hadn't thought it made a hell of a lot of sense at the time, but he wasn't sure if Rex would have survived the fire.

He stroked the dog's head as he drove Cassandra's car over the back roads, in the opposite direction from which he'd come, until he reached the main highway again. Then he headed back toward Burlington. He snatched up the cell phone the girl had given him. Dawn. She was sharp, smart. He punched in the cell phone number he'd committed to memory long ago, and hoped it was still the same.

It was.

"Dr. Melrose," Ethan said when he picked up.

River's throat was clogged with anger. "I suppose you're on your way back to the cabin to take a look at your handiwork."

"River? Jesus, River, is that you? Where are you?"

"Not in a morgue, or the back seat of a police car like you planned, pal. I'm still at large. Only now I'm *really* pissed."

"River, listen. I don't know what you think, but—"

"I don't think. I know, Ethan."

"You're wrong. I didn't—"

"I'm *wrong?* I was at the Harrington Inn today. I spoke to the housekeeper you always request by name. I showed her a picture of Stephanie. I know, Ethan. I know you were fucking my wife."

There was a long, strained silence. "There's still a lot...a lot you don't know."

"Yeah? Well, don't you think it's time you filled me in, old friend? Don't you think you owe me that much?"

Ethan sighed. It sounded tortured. River didn't give a damn. "Where are you, River?"

"Five miles from your place."

"You want to meet me there?"

"Will you have the cops waiting?"

"No. No, and Victoria's out. It'll just be the two of us, River. And I'll tell you—I'll tell you everything."

"You're damn right you will."

River flicked off the phone and pressed his foot harder on the accelerator.

"I can't believe River Corbett would do this," Frankie said softly, shaking her head. "I never, ever thought he was the one."

Jax tried to open her eyes and couldn't. She couldn't even feel them—it was as if they were no longer connected to her, as if no part of her body were connected to her. She tried to part her lips to speak, mostly just to ask for water, because her throat hurt—it hurt, and she knew it hurt, but it seemed to be disconnected, faraway. She couldn't convince her voice to work or her mouth to move, either. Her lips seemed stuck together, her throat gravelly and raw, off there in Neverland with the rest of her body parts.

Maybe it wasn't her body parts that were floating around in the distance. Maybe, she thought, it was her mind.

"Melrose's Mercedes was reported stolen this morning," said an unfamiliar male voice. "Clearly, Corbett took it, then used it to run her down."

No. Jax thought the word, but couldn't say it, though she tried.

"Then how is it he was spotted at the scene later in Jax's car?" Frankie asked.

"Simple. He ditched the Mercedes—witnesses had seen the hit-and-run, we were looking for that car. Not a red Ford. So he switched vehicles," the man said.

"Maybe, but tell me this—what's his motive?" Frankie demanded.

Good, Frankie. Don't believe it. Not so easily.

"Does he need one? Chief Parker, she's living in his house, taking care of his dog, and she winds up getting run down by his shrink's car. He takes her to his hunting cabin—"

"*His* cabin?" Frankie asked. She sounded surprised.

"Yeah, his cabin. He and Ethan Melrose own it together, bought it years ago."

"Hell."

"Take all that," the stranger said, "and then mix in the fact that the place was set on fire with her locked inside—the same way Corbett's house was torched with his wife inside—and you've got a pretty convincing case."

"But still no motive," Frankie insisted, though she sounded far less certain than she had before.

"Does he need one? Maybe he just had one of those brain lapses of his and didn't know what the hell he was doing."

Frankie sighed. "It's a bad way for a good cop to end up, Drummond. A damn bad way."

"I know that. I agree with you, but Frankie, the body count's piling up here. There's his wife, his unborn kid, that orderly from the loony bin—ex-con or not, he was still a human being. And now, one of your own officers."

"Jax isn't going to die."

"That's not the point, Frankie. The point is, we can't let Corbett keep on killing and trying to kill. Wounded hero ex-cop or not. We've got to take him down."

Frankie sighed deeply, but didn't disagree.

"Captain Drummond, Chief Parker?" a third voice called.

"What is it?"

"They've found something in the cabin. A body."

"Jesus, there was someone else inside?" Frankie asked, shocked.

"Yes, ma'am. But, uh—not alive. This body was stuffed inside an old freezer. You'd better come."

"One more to add to Corbett's tally," Captain Drummond said. "We have to end this."

Frankie cleared her throat. "He was last seen driving Lieutenant Jackson's car," she said, speaking slowly, carefully, and as if she didn't want to. "Red, oh-two Ford Taurus, NY plates SVG-135. Better put the word out." She sighed. "I guess it's time I phoned her parents."

Jax felt her fingers move just a little in response to her mind's endless commands. Her fingers curled, one by one, into a small, weak fist, and she managed to raise it up and drop it on the mattress. Not exactly the pounding motion she'd been going for, but at least she could move.

But not in time. The room was silent now. Empty.

Wait, footsteps.

"Hey, Jax. It's me, Dawn. And Beth's here, too." A soft hand moved through her hair, and she was surprised that she could feel it. Maybe her mind and body were somehow, finally, reuniting.

"The nurse said you should be coming around soon." Beth's voice was soft and quavery with worry. "So wake up already."

Jax tried again to open her eyes. She was shocked that they obeyed this time, but she had to close them fast due to the blinding light. Her hand rose of its own will to block it.

"Wait, I've got it." There was a click. "Get the curtains, Dawn." And Jax heard them closing.

Carefully, she tried again, and this time her eyes opened, and the dim room came into focus after several blinks. She tried to speak, but what emerged sounded like a bullfrog's croak.

Beth held a glass with a straw to her lips. Jax sipped, swallowed, sipped some more and nodded, and Beth moved the glass away.

"How you feeling?" she asked.

"R-River. They're...after...River."

"River?" Beth shot a look at Dawn.

Dawn nodded. "I think that's the guy who was trapped in the cabin with her. Michael Corbett. Right, Jax?"

Jax nodded, sighing in relief. "The police think...he set the fire."

"Are you sure he didn't?" Beth asked.

"He was in there with her, Beth," Dawn said quickly.

"But—but isn't that how his wife died? And didn't they say he did it during some kind of blackout? How do you know he didn't black out again, lock himself in there with her, and torch the place?"

"He didn't," Jax said. "I know him." She swallowed, cleared her throat. The words were coming more easily now. "He didn't, Beth. But the police know he's in my car. They're after him. I have to go—"

She sat up in spite of their protests, pushed back the covers, then stared at the thick layers of Ace bandages that were wrapped around her ankle, and the hospital gown she wore. Dizziness hit her hard and she sank back onto the pillows.

"Beth, close the door, will you?" Dawn asked.

Beth shot her a look, but did as she asked. When she came back to the bed, Dawn pulled a cell phone out of her handbag and hit the power button. "You can call him, Jax. I gave him your cell phone."

"How did you—"

"I found it on the road, after you were hit. This, too." She pulled out Jax's gun.

Beth gasped so loud Jax thought she would choke. Jax only nodded. "Good job, kid." She looked at Beth. "Help me sit up."

"Jax, you can't—"

"I can, and I have to. I just need to go slower. Help me up."

Beth hit the button that raised the upper part of the bed. Jax rolled her eyes. "That's not what I meant and you know it."

"It's enough, for now."

"I need my clothes."

"I had Beth bring fresh ones," Dawn said, moving to a locker on the far side of the room. "They're hers. Yours were a mess. Between the car hitting you and the fire…"

She handed a plastic bag to Jax, who sat up straighter, opening it and taking things out. "How did we get out? Last thing I remember it was looking pretty hopeless." She peeled the tape off her wrist and quickly, smoothly, slid the IV line from her arm, then pressed her thumb to the hole it left, fingers on the other side of her forearm, squeezing hard. "Anyone got a Band-Aid?"

"Dawnie and Bryan got you out," Beth said. "Jax, you really shouldn't be doing that."

Dawn was rummaging through her purse and emerged with a bandage. She peeled it open and deftly applied it to Jax's forearm.

"How did you find us, Dawn?"

The teen lifted her eyes, and Jax saw something in them. Something secretive and maybe afraid. "Long story."

"Dawn?" Beth asked.

"Not now. It's…I can't talk about it now."

Jax peeled off the hospital gown, tossed it to the floor. She picked up the bra and small T-shirt from the pile of clothes Beth had brought, and put them on without a hint of embarrassment or shyness. She managed to pull on the panties underneath the sheets, but the jeans were a little tougher. Dawn helped her.

Once dressed, Jax got to her feet, but her ankle gave and she sank back onto the bed again with a harsh wince and a jolt of pain. "Dammit."

"You have to stay off it," Beth said.

"No. I just need a crutch or something."

"Sorry," Dawn said. "If I'd known, I'd have had Beth bring one."

"It's okay. This is a hospital, they've got them everywhere. Go pilfer me a pair, would you, Dawnie?"

"You got it."

"Jax, you can't just leave."

"Watch me." Jax sighed, impatient now for those crutches. Beth excused herself, probably to go rat her out to the staff, Jax imagined. But she used the time to place a call on Dawn's cell phone to her own.

River picked up on the third ring. And the minute she heard his voice, something hit her dead center in the chest. It hit her so hard it knocked the wind right out of her. Something flashed in her mind: herself lying in the back of Dawn's Jeep. Him leaning over her, his lips moving near her ear, the words he'd said.

I am in love with you, Cassandra. You need to know that, because I don't know what's going to happen now. I know you told me not to let it happen, but I didn't have much of a choice in the matter. So there it is. I love you. And I'm going to make things right for you again.

"Cassandra?" he asked in her ear. "Cassandra? God, is it you?"

"Yeah." She shook off the memory and the emotional firestorm it set off inside her. This wasn't the time. There might never be a time. "It's me. I'm okay. Listen, the cops think it was you, River. They're looking for my car. You need to ditch it."

"Are you still in the hospital?" he asked.

"Yeah, but not for long."

"How badly are you hurt?"

He sounded so afraid for her. And it occurred to her that she didn't know how badly she was hurt. She hadn't even asked. She knew her ankle was sprained because of the wrappings, but beyond that...

"Cassandra?"

"I'm fine. Nothing big. A sprain, that's all. Where are you, River?"

"Don't worry. I'll be with you soon."

"I know. But where are you?"

She heard something in the background. The geese, the ones that wintered at the pond near Ethan's house.

"I'll be with you soon," he said again.

"River, don't do anything stupid."

"I have to go. Do you—do you remember…anything?"

"I remember *everything*. And if you meant what you said, River, you won't do what you're about to do."

"I meant it. Don't doubt that, whatever else happens. 'Bye for now, Cassandra. Be safe."

"River!" But he was gone; he'd disconnected.

Five people entered the room almost as one—Beth, Joshua, Bryan and two nurses—and a beat later, behind them all, Dawn with a rubber-tipped, rubber-gripped, metal cane. She tossed it over the crowd to Jax in the bed, and Jax caught it.

"Lieutenant Jackson, you can't just leave," a nurse said. "You've got broken ribs, a concussion, smoke inhalation, and we don't even know—"

"I know my rights. You can't keep me. I'm going."

"At least wait until we get the doctor in here to check you over," said nurse number two.

"You can't leave without signing yourself out," nurse number one insisted.

Jax pulled her gun from under the covers. Didn't point it at anyone, just pulled it out. Made a big show of checking it over, working the action. "Make no mistake about it, ladies. I *am* leaving. Now."

"I think she's leaving," Joshua said. He sent her a worried look. "And if I offer to go with you?"

"You're retired, pal. This is my collar, so back off." But she

knew he saw the gratitude in her eyes, despite the harshness of her tone. She got out of the bed, wobbled a little.

"Dammit, Jax," Beth muttered, gripping her upper arm—to steady her or to slow her down, Jax wasn't sure which. "What the hell are you thinking?"

"I need a car. You got a car?"

"Take my Jeep," Dawn said, and handed her the keys. "Down the hall to the right, out the double doors. It's left of center, not too far out in the parking lot."

"She shouldn't be driving, Dawn."

"I can drive her, then."

"No!" both women barked at once.

"No one's driving me," Jax said. "Dawn, you've done plenty already. Believe me. I'm fine. I promise. And I *have* to go. It's life or death."

"Yours?" Beth asked.

She shook her head. "His, I think."

Beth blinked, but seemed to understand. At least she stopped bitching.

Jax handed Dawn's cell phone to the girl, held her gun close to her waist with her other arm folded over it, so she wouldn't cause mass panic in the hospital, and limped, barefoot, out of her room. On her way down the main corridor she spotted a pair of disposable blue foam slippers on a shelf, yanked them off and took them with her.

Moments later they were on her feet, and she was shifting Dawnie's Jeep, groaning out loud in pain every time she had to use the clutch, and vowing not to wreck the vehicle on her way to Ethan Melrose's mansion.

21

River had driven past Ethan's house and looked carefully around the place as he did, but he'd seen no signs of other vehicles parked around it. Only Ethan's SUV sitting in the driveway. He'd gone a few hundred yards down the road and still saw no other vehicles. Satisfied, he'd turned around and pulled into Ethan's driveway. Maybe the cops would see the car there and come to arrest him. And maybe they wouldn't.

Whatever.

This was the end. It was ending right now. Before he got out of the car River buried his hands in Rex's fur, and the dog licked his face. River didn't say goodbye. Just left Rex in the car, whining as if he knew the shit was about to hit the fan.

River walked over the snow, which crunched under his shoes. The walk hadn't been shoveled this morning and a little more than an inch had fallen in the outskirts of Burlington overnight. His feet made tracks beside Ethan's own as he walked up to the door.

He didn't have to knock. Ethan opened the door before River even raised his fist. He met River's eyes, then his gaze wandered over his face. "You look like hell."

"Haven't had time to wash up since fighting my way out of our burning cabin. I'm supposed to look good?"

"There's blood on your neck."

River touched his neck. His hand, when he examined it, was brown with soot, and just a bit of blood colored his fingertip. Ethan reached out. "Let me take a look."

But River ducked his touch. "Don't. You put it there, Ethan, don't act as if you regret it now."

"River, I didn't do this to you. I don't know what else you think—"

"I don't think. I know. You were sleeping with Stephanie. Do you deny it?"

Ethan's eyes lowered instantly. "No. No, I don't deny it."

"Jesus."

Ethan turned and paced away from him, into the living room off the foyer. He stopped near a marble stand on which a bottle and a pair of glasses stood. "You've been off your meds, what—a week now?"

"Yeah, and amazingly, I'm fine."

He nodded, tipped the bottle and poured. "I...can't explain that, River."

He was lying. River knew it. "I can. You were overmedicating me. Keeping me comfortably insane enough so that I'd never be able to figure it out."

"You really think I'd do all that just to cover up an affair?" He handed River the glass. It held three fingers of whiskey.

"No, pal. To cover up a murder." River downed the drink.

Ethan only stared at him. "I didn't kill her, River. I adored Stephanie, I wouldn't—"

"Yeah, I'm well aware how much you *adored* her." He lifted his gaze and met his former friend's. "It wasn't even my baby, was it, Ethan? It was yours."

Ethan downed his own drink, turned and poured another. River moved closer, set his glass down, and Ethan splashed amber liquid into it, as well.

"She didn't love me. She loved you, River, and in the end, she was the one who ended it. She wanted to make things

work with you. She was determined to raise the baby with you, not me."

River closed his eyes. "And you knew you could never have any others. Not with Victoria. Is that why you killed her?"

"I didn't kill her."

"Then who did?"

His former friend met his eyes, held them. "You must have found out about us. The strain of it was too much. You killed her during one of your blackouts, River. You know that."

"I thought I did. But if that's the case, who killed Arty Mullins?"

"What?"

Ethan tried to look puzzled and River thought his friend was a better actor than he had ever realized. "His body was in a freezer, in the rental unit where all my worldly possessions were stashed, until it was firebombed. Then it was moved to the cabin. I imagine it's in a forensics lab by now. I figure he saw what really happened at the house that night. He saw who set the fire. He knew. So you had to kill him, too."

Ethan paced away slowly, shaking his head.

River slammed his glass onto a table, bringing Ethan around quickly. "Stop pretending you don't know what's going on here, Ethan. I know. I know it was you. You broke into the house the other night. You knew Cassandra was helping me. Jesus, it was your Mercedes that ran her down in the street. And who the hell else would take her to the cabin we bought together? It had to be you or me, pal, and I damn well know it wasn't me. I didn't black out. I can account for every minute of time I spent today. No gaps. So I know it wasn't me. The rest of the world might doubt it, but *I know.* And I know you know."

Ethan blinked slowly, and River could see his mind working, analyzing, running through every possible way out of this. "You saw the Mercedes hit Lieutenant Jackson?"

"No. But someone else did. More than one person, in fact."

"Could it have been a mistake?"

River shook his head. "No mistake. One witness even got the plate number. And Cassandra saw it, too."

"But...but the car was at your place—Jackson's place! I let her drive it home."

"And then you came and got it, early this morning. And I know you saw me. So you knew I was staying there, with Cassandra." River's anger was mounting. "Is that what this is about? Every time I find someone to love you have to kill them? Do you hate me that much, Ethan?"

Ethan blinked. "You...love her?"

"That's why I can't let this go on. I might go down for this— they might keep right on blaming me for everything *you've* done, Ethan. God knows I can't prove a fucking thing. But I'm not gonna leave you around to try to hurt her again. I can't."

"No. No, I don't suppose you can." He drew a breath and sighed, walking to the marble stand again, turning his back to River while he poured a final shot into his glass. "I never hated you, River. I mean that. We just need to get you back on your meds. Everything will be all right, after that."

He slugged back the drink and turned. When he did, River saw the gun in his hand, swore under his breath and then lunged forward even as Ethan raised the weapon. They grappled for it, until the firearm wound up skittering across the floor and slamming into the wall. River wrestled Ethan to the floor, straddled him and pounded him in the face. Ethan elbowed him hard in the rib cage, knocking him off. Then Ethan sprang to his feet and River did as well, and they leaped at each other—best friends fighting as if to the death.

When the woman burst into the room and began shrieking at them to stop, they barely took notice. River recognized the voice as Victoria's, and he felt damn bad for her—married to a murderer. Soon to be a killer's widow.

"Stop!" she shrieked. "Stop now or I'll shoot!"

That brought things to a grinding halt. River and Ethan stood, a couple of feet between them, sweating and bloodied, and turned their eyes slowly toward the woman. She stood ten feet away, near where the gun had wound up, and she clutched it in hands that shook so badly River was surprised she didn't drop it.

"Stop right now, River. I don't want to shoot you but I will! I swear I will. You leave him alone!"

River said nothing. Ethan held up a hand. "Don't. Victoria, don't. It's…it's over."

"No!" She pointed the gun at River, thumbed back the hammer and squeezed the trigger.

River felt as if it happened in slow motion, even though it was so fast he didn't have time to move. He heard the explosion—couldn't believe it. Couldn't believe Victoria would have it in her to shoot him. And even as that thought raced through his brain, he was vaguely aware of Ethan, shouting and diving toward him.

In front of him…

One arm thrown out, Ethan clotheslined him right across the throat so that he went down hard, gasping for air. He felt the stitches in his thigh tear free, felt the wound reopen and start to bleed.

It was all so damn fast.

The next thing River knew he was on his back, gasping like a fish, wondering if he was shot. And Ethan was on the floor beside him. And Cassandra was bursting through the door shouting at Victoria to drop the gun, and damn but she was in full cop mode. Down on one knee, gun drawn and steady on the armed woman, eyes scanning the entire scene, taking it all in even as Victoria let her weapon clatter to the floor and started sobbing.

Cassandra. She was incredible. Hair wild and all over the

place. Face as pale as a cloud. She wore hospital slippers on her feet, jeans and a little T-shirt he'd never seen before. He realized why she was down on one knee, when she got up. She barely put any weight on that leg, and Ace bandages bound her foot and ankle. A metal cane lay on the floor. He knew damn well she shouldn't be walking when she left the cane there, and limped over to Victoria. She grabbed up the fallen weapon, tucked it into the back of her jeans and quickly patted the woman down, in search of others.

"I was only defending my husband," Victoria said. "God, I came home to find an escaped mental patient attacking him. What was I supposed to do?"

"Save it for the judge, lady." Gripping Vicki's arm, Jax then turned toward the two of them. "Are you two all ri— Oh, shit."

And finally, River managed to take his eyes off her. He sat up, looking where she was—at Ethan, who'd probably just saved his life, in spite of everything.

Ethan lay in a pool of blood, eyes closed. He wasn't moving.

Victoria started to scream again and came racing forward, falling to her knees and wailing as she wrapped herself around her husband.

"He's got a pulse," Cassandra said, after managing to get in close enough to check the man. Victoria hadn't made it easy, until she collapsed and lay across his chest, sobbing.

River had the phone in his hand already. It was ringing, and eventually the 911 operator picked up.

"There's been a shooting," River began.

Jax managed to keep it together, to keep going, despite that she was dizzy and weak and that her leg was throbbing like a toothache and the broken ribs were like hot nails in her sides every time she moved.

River dragged a protesting, nearly incoherent Victoria off her husband and kept her occupied so that Jax could admin-

ister basic first aid. The bullet was in Ethan's head. No exit wound, which she figured was good or he'd be long dead. The gun was a little .25 caliber peashooter, not a cannon. And not the gun Ethan had used to shoot River in the leg. But damn, at such close range, even a small bullet was enough.

"Bitch intended it for River," she whispered, even as she used a white cloth napkin she found on the wet bar to put pressure on the entry wound and ease the bleeding. She glanced across the room at River. He'd moved Victoria all the way over to the sofa, where she was even now swallowing a handful of pills with the contents of a glass that had been a third full when Jax arrived. Whiskey, she thought.

"River, I need a blanket and a couple of those sofa pillows."

He nodded, sending a nervous glance toward Victoria as he got up.

"I've got her," Jax told him. She kept her eyes on the woman, confident she could pull a gun and drop her before she took three steps in any direction, if necessary. She was *good* and pissed.

River took what looked like an antique tapestry from the back of the sofa, snatched up two sofa pillows and hurried toward her.

"Put the pillows under his feet. Cover him with the blanket."

River did as she asked, his eyes focused only on her. "Are you okay? You look ready to drop."

"I *am* ready to drop. In fact I think I will as soon as we get some backup here." He held her eyes, worried, until she smiled. "He admitted it, didn't he?"

"No. Not yet."

Jax blinked. "Then you need to get out of here, River. You need to get out of here now, before the police…" She hadn't even finished the thought when the first sirens sounded. She shot him an urgent look.

"No way. I'm not leaving you, not again. Look what happened last time."

"Please," she whispered. "Please, River—"

Too late. Cops were swarming through the front door. She was relieved to spot Frankie Parker's face among them. Jax raised her hands above her head. "I've got two weapons tucked in the back of my pants," she said. "I'm gonna stand up slow, now, but I need someone to hold pressure on this man's gunshot wound or he'll bleed out."

A cop came forward, while another kept her covered. He took her weapons, even while a third officer spun River around and snapped a pair of handcuffs on him.

"Better cuff that one, too," Jax told them, nodding toward Victoria. "She's the one who shot him, and I know for a fact there's another gun in the house. At least."

Paramedics were rushing in by then. Jax was relieved. She turned to the cop who was leading River from the room, and said, "This is my collar, pal. I'm taking him in." And to another. "And I'll take my weapon back now that I've identified myself."

"She's one of mine," Frankie added. "Give her back her gun."

The cop did. And Frankie kept talking. "It's not your collar, Jax. Not this time. *I'm* taking him in."

Jax met her eyes, about to argue.

"You know damn well it's for the best."

"He's not safe in jail, Frankie."

"He'll be safe in mine. I've already cleared it with the state boys. And we can discuss it on the way. Come on."

"It's okay, Cassandra," River said. "It's time. Besides, Ethan's no threat to me now."

They watched as Ethan was carried to a waiting ambulance—he didn't look good. Victoria followed, climbing into the ambulance to ride with him. Just as well—Jax didn't think the woman was in any condition to drive.

No one arrested her. A cop went along with her, though. They'd probably sort all this out later and decide then how to

proceed. It was more humane that way, Jax supposed, though she'd have loved to see the bitch who'd tried to shoot River hauled away in handcuffs.

River let Frankie take him by one arm and lead him outside to her car. "Rex is in Cassandra's car," he said.

Frankie nodded and promised to have an officer drive it back to Blackberry as she opened the back door of her SUV.

He got in the back seat, and Cassandra slid in beside him, rather than taking the front seat beside Frankie. She didn't give a damn how it looked to every other cop on the scene. And as soon as Frankie pulled the car into motion, she thrust a hand over the seat, palm up. "Let me get the cuffs off him."

Frankie met her eyes in the rearview mirror.

"Come on, Frankie. There's no one watching to be sure we follow procedure now. It's just us. This man has saved my life more than once now. He's the same hero cop he was before. Not a killer."

"You sure of that?"

"I am. You will be, too, by the time we get to the station."

Sighing, Frankie snapped her key off her belt and dropped it into Jax's waiting hand. River leaned forward, and Jax removed the cuffs.

"Better?"

"Me? Hell, Cassandra, you should be in the hospital. Look at you."

She rolled her eyes and leaned back in the seat. "Frankie, Stephanie Corbett was having an affair with Ethan Melrose."

Frankie's head came up sharply, her eyes snapping to the mirror, narrow and inquisitive. "Can you prove that?"

Jax nodded. "Got a maid at the Harrington Inn who remembers them both. But I think we can do better with a little bloodwork. I'd lay odds the fetus was his."

"It was," River said. "I called him on it, back there. He didn't deny it."

Shaking her head slowly, Frankie sighed. "I'm sorry, River. This can't have been an easy thing to learn." Frankie turned her mirror so she could see him.

"It wasn't easy," he said. "Ethan claims she was trying to end their relationship. That she wanted to try to make our marriage work."

"So you think he killed her?"

"Yeah. I do. I think he intended to kill us both. But I was outside. So instead he set things up to make it look like it was me. Got me committed. And he's been drugging me into oblivion ever since."

"He probably even hired that goon of an orderly to kill River," Cassandra added. "He knew I was on to all of this— so he set me up. Lured me out to an empty street and ran me down. Hauled me to that cabin he and River own together, and waited for River to come after me. Then he locked us in and torched it. I was supposed to die in that fire. River was either supposed to die with me or be blamed for killing me, sealing his fate once and for all."

"It's a solid theory, Cassandra. But it's going to take evidence."

"River's lawyer has his medical records—they're being reviewed by experts in the field now. And we have Dawn and Bryan, who can testify that the door and shutters of that cabin were blocked from the outside. You can't put a two-by-four across the outside of a door and then somehow get inside the building."

"And there should be evidence on Ethan's Mercedes, as well," River said.

"Yeah, blood and hair, in addition to the dent I probably left in the front when he nailed me, the dirty bastard."

Frankie nodded slowly. "Phone your lawyer, River. Have him meet us at the station back in Blackberry. I'll do my best to see to it a judge meets us there, as well. All right?"

"Fair enough." He nodded at Cassandra. "Think we can drop this one off at the hospital on the way?"

"I'm not leaving you alone in a jail cell, River. Not until we're sure."

"Ethan's not going to come after me tonight, Cassandra."

"Suppose he's got some other thug out there waiting to take a crack, hmm? Suppose the newest criminal he hired to take you out doesn't know the game's over yet?"

He sighed, lowered his head. "Ever the optimist."

They pulled in at the station in Blackberry, where four cop cars pulled right in behind them. The state boys were not about to let a fish as big as this one get too far from their sight. Frankie admitted she'd done some fast talking to convince them to let her handle all of this from her own little PD. She'd reminded them of the orderly with the record, the possibility that someone was out to murder River, the still unanswered questions. She'd insisted River would be safer in a cell by himself in Blackberry than lost in the shuffle of a larger department. And they'd agreed.

Jax got out of the car, and River behind her. He was right beside her when she started into the office, and felt the ground start to spin. Or was that her head?

She was vaguely aware of Matthews and Campanelli coming out of the station to greet her, their worried looks, hands on her shoulders, the relief in their voices that she was all right. And then she started to sway.

"Dammit, I knew it." River scooped her up into his arms before she could hit the ground.

She rolled her eyes. "Put me down, I'm fine. And your leg—"

"You're not fine. You need to go home, go to bed."

Her eyes shot to his when he said it, but the crowd of interested spectators and fellow cops forming around them made the smart-ass comeback she had in mind a very bad idea.

Some of those fellow cops looked less than happy at the sight of River walking around without handcuffs, much less holding an officer in his arms. Even now she wondered if he was thinking about kissing her. He was close enough, and she wouldn't be able to do much about it, not while he was carrying her as if she were weightless. He looked at her lips, and his own curved just slightly. He was letting her know that he knew what she was thinking—that he was thinking it, too.

"We've got every cop in the county here, and my lawyer just pulled in, as well," he said. "I'll be fine. You need to go home."

"Who's gonna make me?"

His smile grew into a full-size one. "I'm calling your father."

"You wouldn't!"

"Frankie?" he asked.

"You can use my phone," Frankie said. "And if she manages to talk you out of it, I'll do it myself." She opened the door and held it.

"Bring her in here," Matthews said, leading the way. "Put her on the sofa. Jeez, Jax, you look like hell."

Campanelli said, "I'll bring you a phone."

River limped a little as he carried her through the station and lowered her onto the green fake-leather sofa in the reception area. Jax glared at him the entire time he was on the phone with her father. And when he hung up she knew her dad was on his way. "I really resent that, River."

"I can tell by the holes you're burning into my head with your eyes," he said. "But it's just as well I called. They've been worried sick."

She shrugged. "I don't like people telling me what to do. I don't like being pushed."

"It's part of the package, Cassandra."

"Part of what package?"

He didn't answer. Instead, he looked around at all the police, most of them standing there talking. Matthews was mak-

ing coffee. Campanelli turned a wastebasket upside down and set a pillow on top of it, then put it in front of her, so she could elevate her sprained ankle.

Frankie's nephew was hanging back, watching things, looking smug. The other cops—the imports—were sending River curious or down-right pissed off, looks.

"Don't you think someone ought to put me in the cage, now?" River asked softly. "These guys are looking suspicious as hell. I don't blame them. I'm not even cuffed and can't stop making eyes at the best-looking cop on the job."

"You're *not* going in the cage."

He lifted his brows. "I don't like people telling me what to do, either," he said. "But I understand why you're pushing so hard. Maybe *you* don't. But I do. That comes with the package, too." He shrugged. "But still, there's no point in screwing up your career over it."

"You make about as much sense now as you did when you were still on all the psychotropics, River."

"You wish." He got up and walked back to the cell. "Open it up, Frankie."

"No need for that," Frankie said, coming up behind him. "Judge Henry's on his way over here to see what we've got." She looked past him at the man just entering. "I take it that fellow in the overpriced suit is your lawyer?"

River looked, as well. "Yes."

"Perfect. Soon as the judge arrives we'll make a stab at sorting all this out. You, Jax, better take a load off and relax."

Her father walked in behind the lawyer, even as she was opening her mouth to reply. He looked across the room, not at her, but at River. And the two of them exchanged a silent message. Then her mother was pushing past everyone. "I couldn't believe it when we rushed all the way to the hospital only to be told you'd checked yourself out! What were you thinking, Cassie?" She sat on the edge of the sofa and hugged

Jax hard. Jax winced, because it was a little too hard, given the state of her rib cage.

"Actually, Mrs. Jackson, if she hadn't checked out of the hospital and shown up at Ethan Melrose's, I'd probably be dead right now," River said, moving forward.

Mariah looked up at him as he approached. He held out a hand and she closed hers around it without getting up. "I'm sorry we haven't met before now. I'm River Corbett."

As soon as he said his name, she jerked her hand from his and her eyes widened.

"He didn't do what they said he did, Mom," Jax said.

Her mother shot a look at her husband. "You knew about this, didn't you?"

Ben nodded. "Knew. Didn't like it. But you know your daughter when she gets something in her head."

"For what it's worth, Mariah," Frankie said, "it looks to me like she's been right about Corbett all along. We're going to be sorting all that out here, tonight. At least, making a start at it. But your girl there, she's got a few busted ribs and a bad ankle sprain. She needs to be in a bed. I'd prefer a hospital bed, but her own at home will do just as well, providing she gets into it soon."

"I am *not* leaving—"

River put a hand on her shoulder, stared into her eyes. "Go home, Cassandra. I can't focus if I'm sitting here worrying about how soon you're going to collapse. Go home. Let your mother pamper you for a couple of hours." He leaned closer and whispered, "And then, if all goes well, I'll be there to do it myself."

She was torn between melting into his arms, and turning and fleeing at those words. She hated being taken care of and he knew it. Why, then, was she looking forward to him keeping that promise like a kid looks forward to Christmas morning?

Hell, she knew why.

She got to her feet and paced a few steps away from him.

Her father moved closer and spoke to her, his voice low and for her ears alone. "Your mother can't be here with all this," he told her. "You know how hard this sort of thing is for her, the memories it stirs. Look at her. Already."

Jax glanced her mother's way and saw the lines of tension at the corners of her mouth, and how her eyes were darting around the station. God, this was no good for her.

"And she won't leave you. She can every be bit as stubborn as you."

"At least I come by it honestly." Jax sighed, turned back to River. "I need to see you in Frankie's office."

"Go ahead," Frankie said. "When you finish, stay there and I'll send your lawyer in, River. The judge will be another twenty minutes." She looked around the room. "I don't see much need for the rest of you to hang around. Go home."

"And leave you alone here with a fugitive?" one state cop asked.

"He hasn't been cleared yet, Chief Parker."

"She has her own men here," Kurt Parker said, stepping front and center. "Don't think for one minute we're gonna let him get away with anything."

Sighing, River took Jax by the arm and led her into Frankie's office. He closed the door behind them, and she turned to face him.

"Don't turn your back on Kurt Parker. He's a snake."

He nodded slowly. "But that's not what you brought me in here to tell me."

"No. This is." She twisted her arms around his neck, leaned up and kissed him. He was stiff—with surprise, not resistance—but only for the briefest flicker of a moment. And then he was wrapping his arms around her waist, holding her to him tenderly and kissing her deeply. One of his hands cupped the back of her head and he supported all her weight

in his arms. She felt herself wishing she would never have to leave his embrace again, and the thought scared her, yet she didn't break the kiss. Not for a long time.

Not until he lifted his head, maybe because he needed air. His eyes glittered with something unnamed and a kind of desperate wish, with hopelessness behind it. "I hope…"

"Shh. Just take care of this now. One thing at a time, River. The rest…we'll figure it out. Later."

He smiled just a little. "Are you sure there's anything to figure out?"

"Oh, yeah." She kissed him one last time. "Don't be long, okay?"

"No longer than I have to be."

Nodding, she limped out of the office, giving the lawyer a nod so he could proceed in behind her. As she moved toward her parents, who were waiting by the door, Kurt Parker leaned in close. "Don't think you'll still get that job, not after all of this. Heard he's been staying out at your place—course that's just gossip. That's aiding and abetting. There will be repercussions."

"Yeah, I know there will," she said. "I just don't happen to care very much right now. But you know one thing I *have* thought of?"

"What's that?" he asked, his voice dripping sarcasm.

"If I do get this job, my first order of business will be to send you packing." She reached up and gripped the collar of his shirt. "And if you put one finger on River Corbett, Kurt, I'll see to it you never work in law enforcement again. If I don't kill you instead."

She released him and he gaped at her, too shocked to reply.

As she limped out the door, the other two Blackberry police officers flanked her. Campanelli held the door open for her. Matthews caught her eye, gave her a nod. "Nice job, Jax. And don't worry about Parker. We'll keep our eye on things."

She stared from one to the other. "You don't even know I was right about this yet."

"Your word's all we need," Campanelli said softly. Then he leaned closer. "Besides, over time we've pretty much figured out that if Kurt's on one side of a fight, that *must* be the wrong side. Now you go home. Feel better."

She really liked these guys, she decided. And it seemed to be mutual. Yeah. Maybe things were going to be all right, after all.

22

Dawn paced. She hated this. *Hated* it!

"Dawn, will you relax?" Bryan sat on the edge of her bed, watching her. "You saved their lives. What more can you do?"

"I don't know. Something."

She looked around the room. There were others present. Bryan couldn't see them, of course. But she could. Stephanie Corbett was there, her face partly beautiful and partly black and disfigured from the fire that had killed her. In her arms she held the baby she'd never borne. Mordecai was there, looking as she imagined he must have when Beth had first known him—with his long sable hair pulled back in a ponytail, and his huge brown eyes intent and endlessly deep. He was silent now. They all were. There were others, others she'd never seen before. One man was dressed in a white getup, as if he worked in a hospital, and his face was smashed to hell and gone. He was the orderly River had been accused of murdering during his escape. Dawn didn't know how she knew that, but she did. And there was another man, grizzled and unclean. His name was Arty. She knew that, too. And there was a teenage girl who looked a lot like Jax. Her sister. Dawn hadn't even known she *had* a sister, and yet she knew that's who it was. Carrie. A teenage boy stood beside her, ligature marks on his neck. He'd killed her, but he was at peace now.

And there was an older man, who'd been accused of the crime and who had died because of it. He was there, too.

She didn't want to know all these things. These horrible things. But they were there in her mind, as if every one of those people were shouting their stories to her—shouting in silence. She didn't want to know, she didn't want to hear them.

They lurked, all of them, against the walls of her bedroom, watching her, just watching her. And waiting.

Waiting.

"How do you know you have to do something more?" Bryan got up and came to her, blocked her path so she had to stop pacing. "Look, my dad has been on the phone, pulling strings and asking questions ever since we got back from the hospital. He says Corbett and Jax, along with a judge and a pile of lawyers, are all over at the Blackberry PD with Frankie, working through all of this. He says it looks like Ethan Melrose is the real villain."

Dawn blinked as she looked at the roomful of spectral observers. "He does have a silver Mercedes," she said.

And then he was there. Ethan Melrose. She saw him, a hole in one side of his head and a ribbon of blood streaming down his face. He was very faint. For a moment she'd thought he was only some odd cloud of mist or vapor or something, but then she noticed his features taking shape. Weak, pale, translucent, and fading to invisible every few seconds. There was something different about him.

"But he was at his office, Bry. He had an SUV in the driveway. A Mercedes, M-Class, I think. I was there with him, and I freaked out and took off. And then I saw the Mercedes that had just hit Jax. He couldn't have done it."

"Maybe he had the car parked around a corner. Maybe he took a shortcut. Look, the police will figure it out. It's not your job. You've done enough."

She frowned and tried to see Ethan Melrose again, and then

she wondered why he was there. She said, "I think maybe Dr. Melrose is dead, Bry."

Bryan sucked in a breath, standing still. "What makes you think he's dead?"

She blinked, not taking her eyes off the spot where he'd been, even though he'd vanished again. "Shot in the head, I think."

"Dawn, where are you—" Bryan broke off, and looked around the room. But he saw nothing. She knew he couldn't. She wished she couldn't. "They're here, aren't they? The ghosts?"

"Yeah. A butt load of them."

He rubbed his arms. "I'll go check with Dad. He'll know. He's on top of this."

She nodded, and Bryan ran out of the room. Could he feel it? she wondered. The cold? The unearthly chill that permeated the place when they came? God, why did they have to come at all?

"I did what you wanted," she said, addressing Stephanie Corbett. "I saved them from the fire."

Stephanie just stared at her. Standing there, almost as real as if she were still alive.

"Why do you have to look like that?"

The woman tipped her head to one side, frowning as if trying to make out what she was saying, but unable to.

Dawn shot a look at Mordecai. He shook his head sadly, lowering it. And she knew, then. She knew he wasn't going to talk to her again unless she asked him to. Maybe it was some kind of rule.

She closed her eyes, so she wouldn't see them, but she could still feel them there, all around her. Death, closing in on her from all sides. And she wondered if maybe she *couldn't* run from it. If maybe, no matter where she went, they would find her.

Damn it, what did they want?

The bedroom door opened, and she jumped and spun to face it. But it was only Bryan coming back inside. Beth and Josh were close behind him, and man, did Beth look worried. So worried Dawn took a quick sideways glance at herself in the mirror, and almost gasped at what she saw.

She was pale and her hair was a wild mess that stuck up all over, probably from the countless times she'd pushed her hands through it. She had dark circles under her eyes, but there was more than that. Her eyes were wide and odd looking. She looked as if she'd seen a ghost, she thought, almost smiling at the phrase that popped into her head. She guessed she understood it now.

"Ethan Melrose was shot in the head an hour ago, at his house," Bryan said softly. "But he's not dead. He's in a coma in the hospital."

She nodded slowly. "That explains it."

"Explains what, Dawnie?" Beth asked, coming into the room. "Honey, you look terrible. Are you okay?"

"I don't know." She looked around at all the dead people, then closed her eyes. "Could you guys leave me alone for a minute?" she asked the living.

"I don't think—" Bryan began.

"Bry, let's give her minute," Josh said. He put a hand on his son's shoulder.

Bryan looked into her eyes. Dawn looked away, ignoring him. She didn't want him involved in this. It wasn't his nightmare.

When she heard the door close, she looked around her, at the dead, and finally, she faced her father. "I need you to talk to me. Tell me. What more am I supposed to do?"

Mordecai sighed as if in relief. "Ask Stephanie. She knows."

"I tried that. She can't hear me, and I can't hear her."

Mordecai moved closer, reaching out to her. "You can, if you let me help you."

"I don't want your help. Dammit, Mordecai, I don't want anything from you. Not your help, not your presence in my head and not your curse. Least of all that."

He nodded, and she'd never seen anyone look sadder. "I'm sorry."

She glanced toward the woman—Stephanie. She was speaking urgently now, gesturing with one hand while cradling her child in the other. She seemed desperate. Tears were flowing from her eyes.

Dawn looked at Mordecai again, lifted her hand. "All right," she said. "Help me."

He reached out, took her hand in his, and she felt it, but not like a physical touch. It was cold, clammy and not solid. Like holding a handful of icy cloud, only slightly more dense than that. It sent frigid shivers up her arm, and down her spine.

Mordecai looked at Stephanie, and Dawn did, too.

"She can hear you now," Mordecai said. "Talk to her."

Stephanie spoke, and Dawn heard her. And as she spoke, Ethan Melrose faded and didn't come back.

Moments later, Dawn opened her bedroom door to find Beth and Josh and Bryan standing outside it. They'd been talking. About her, no doubt. But the conversation stopped as soon as they saw her.

"I have to go to the hospital. I have to see Ethan Melrose. I don't know why, but I think it's pretty important."

"Your Honor." River's attorney, Derrick Brown, lowered his head as Frankie introduced him to Judge Henry. "I've never known a judge to go above and beyond like this. I'm grateful."

The judge grumbled some sort of reply. River recognized the man, remembered him from his hearing so long ago. He had skin like aging leather and hair the color of slate. His face was a transcript of every trial over which he'd ever presided; line by line, every one seemed etched there.

Then the judge was staring him in the eye. "Corbett, you look decidedly different from the last time I saw you."

River nodded. "I was under the influence of some pretty powerful drugs back then, Your Honor, prescribed by my psychiatrist at the time."

"Mmph. Dr. Melrose. I remember."

Frankie had arranged chairs around her tiny office. They all sat in them now. Her, the D.A., River and his lawyer, and Judge Henry. Frankie had filled the judge in on what had happened today before he'd even begun questioning River.

"This was my case," Judge Henry continued. "I don't much like being told I was wrong about a decision, but in this case, I believe the weight of the mistake falls squarely on your own shoulders, Mr. Corbett. Why did you plead guilty if you were innocent?"

"Your Honor, my client—"

River put a hand on the lawyer's shoulder. "How about I speak for myself here? It's my life that's on the line, after all."

Brown shot him a look, and nodded.

"Your Honor," River said, "I get these blackouts. I sort of zone out for a period of time and afterward I don't remember anything that happened. It's because of a bullet that's lodged in my brain, from a gunshot wound I received in the line of duty. At the time of my wife's death, I honestly didn't remember what had happened."

"And now you do?"

"No. I could tell you I did, but that would be a lie. I don't remember. But I have learned that the psychiatrist who convinced me I must have done it, was having an affair with my wife."

The judge looked up sharply, held up a hand when the D.A. started to argue. "Can you prove that, son?"

River nodded. "The maid at the Harrington Inn, where they used to meet, will testify to it. The manager, too, if pressed by the law. And I'm pretty sure that Ethan Melrose

fathered the baby my wife was carrying when she died. It's on the record that it wasn't my child—though no one told me back then."

The judge looked at the D.A. "Did you know about this?"

The man shook his head, flipping through papers. "The autopsy wasn't completed until after Corbett's plea has been entered and accepted. It was not brought to my attention."

"It's my belief, Your Honor," Derrick Brown said, "that Dr. Ethan Melrose had been keeping Mr. Corbett heavily and needlessly drugged during his time in the state hospital in a deliberate attempt to keep him from remembering what truly happened that night." He set a sheaf of papers on Frankie's desk. "These are his medical records, and a report from a top psychiatrist who's gone over them. In his opinion, none of the drugs Corbett was given were indicated by his symptoms."

The judge opened the folder, looking at the top sheet, then lifting his head. "Dr. Cameron. That's a very famous psychiatrist."

"I didn't want there to be any doubt about his credentials. I hired the best. I also have the sworn statement of a psychiatric nurse who worked with Mr. Corbett, who complained several times that he was showing signs of being over- and wrongly medicated, but her complaints were ignored." He handed another sheet to the judge.

The judge perused it, and nodded, glancing at the D.A. "You'll want your own expert to review all of this."

The D.A. nodded. "There's still the escape charge," he reminded the judge. "And let's not forget the orderly Corbett killed in order to get away."

"I didn't kill him to get away," River said. "I killed him to keep him from killing me. And it wasn't intentional, either. The man pulled a knife on me."

"A knife that has that so-called orderly's prints on it," the lawyer added. "And it turns out he was working there illegally,

using a false ID. He had a record, had taken money to do harm to people in the past. Did time for it."

The judge leaned back in his chair, blinking at the D.A. "Is that true?"

The D.A. sighed. "Yes."

"So you have here a man who was framed for the murder of his own wife, betrayed into a psych ward by his doctor, drugged into oblivion and then attacked by a felon with a knife, and you want to prosecute him?"

The D.A. lowered his head. "He hasn't *proven* anything yet."

"Your Honor," Derrick Brown said. "All I ask is that my client be allowed to keep his freedom while the evidence is reviewed and a decision made as to whether to prosecute him."

"He's a flight risk," the D.A. said. "He escaped the state hospital. Who's to say he won't vanish?"

"I escaped the hospital to save my life," River said. "I haven't left this town since. My only goal was to find the truth. I could have run a hundred times since my escape, but I didn't. And I won't."

The judge rubbed his chin. "Would he be in danger again, if he were put into custody?"

"He could be," Brown said. "We can't be sure until all of this is settled."

"Chances are I wouldn't, Your Honor," River stated. "Ethan Melrose was shot by his wife earlier tonight. She was aiming for me. He's in the hospital and in no condition to pose any real threat to me."

"I like your honesty, son." The judge nodded. "I hesitate to put a man behind bars who may have already done time in a mental ward for nothing. But I'd prefer to release him into the custody of a responsible person."

"He's been staying with Lieutenant Cassandra Jackson," Frankie said. "She's next in line for my job, came here to train for it, as a matter of fact. I trust her."

"Your Honor," the D.A. said, "that's the same woman who's been aiding and abetting him all along."

"Actually, she made the same decision I would have," Frankie interjected. "Had she turned him in, he could have been murdered while in custody. Had she turned him away, he could have been long gone, for all she knew. Keeping him secure while investigating his claims was a stroke of genius."

"It was also completely unprofessional and inappropriate, and I think you know it, Chief Parker," the judge declared. "That said, I don't doubt for one minute you'd have done the same." He looked around the room. "Where is this Jackson?"

"Home, nursing injuries she received in a hit-and-run earlier today."

"Ahh, that was her." Judge Henry nodded. "Then she's in no condition to guard a prisoner. I'll release him into your custody, Chief Parker. And you'd best keep him with you. I don't want any more screwups. I'll have my court clerk contact you two gentleman as soon as she's set up a formal hearing on all of this." He looked at the D.A. "How long do you need?"

"A month," the D.A. began.

The judge waved a hand. "A week is plenty. Just to be nice, I'll give you two." He turned again to River. "One thing I just can't get straight in my head, son. Why did you listen to this man? What would possess you to put so much stock in the opinion of one doctor?"

River lowered his head to hide the surge of emotion welling inside him at the question. "He was my best friend, Judge. Like a brother to me, since I was just a kid. I trusted him."

The judge shook his head slowly. "Makes it that much worse, doesn't it? Yeah. I know. Chief Parker, get him home, give him a good meal and a warm place to sleep. I intend to do the same for myself."

He got up, shook River's hand. "Son, although it's far from official, it's pretty clear to me what's happened here. You

have my sincere apology for what you've been through. I know it's not worth much, but—"

"It's worth a lot, sir. But you don't have anything to apologize for. I'm the one who entered the plea." He held the man's eyes. "Thank you for coming out here to listen to me, Your Honor."

The old man nodded, and left the police station. Within a few minutes, the others went as well. River promised his lawyer a lengthy meeting the next day. Then he turned to Frankie, when they were alone together in the station.

"Oh, no," she said. "Don't turn those big eyes on me, young man. I'm too old to fall for it."

"She's waiting for me, Frankie."

"You can call her from my house," she said. "I've stuck my neck out for you plenty—from here on in, son, this goes by the book."

He sighed, a deep yawning chasm opening up inside him. And he recognized it for what it was—the emptiness he would always feel without Cassandra by his side.

Dawn turned to look back into her bedroom before she closed the door. "I'm going to need you with me," she told Mordecai. It galled her to say it. She didn't want any part of her father—not even his ghost. But she needed to see this thing through to the end. She needed him in order to do that.

And after that—never again.

"Of course we're going with you," Beth said from the hallway.

Dawn looked at her, smiled and tried to avoid Bryan's knowing eyes. He was scared to death for her. And until she got this sorted out, figured out exactly what it all meant, he would keep right on being scared for her.

He deserved better than that.

He took her hand when she came out of the bedroom. She

let him hold it only until they reached the stairs, then pulled hers free as if she needed to hold the railing on the way down. She didn't. And she thought he knew it.

An hour later, they were clustered around the nurses' desk in the ICU, asking about Ethan Melrose. But before the nurse could even answer, there was a shriek from one of the rooms, then the door opened and a woman staggered out, supported by an older man Dawn didn't recognize.

She recognized the woman, though. It was Ethan Melrose's wife. She'd seen her in the photograph in the doctor's office. And from the way she was sobbing...

"I'm sorry, dear," the nurse at the desk said. "Dr. Melrose passed away a few moments ago. That's his wife over there. She needed some time with him."

Dawn nodded slowly, her eyes still on the woman, as the man—her father, Dawn realized, in the way she realized so many things—helped her down the hall. She was leaving, going home, getting out of here. They ought to sedate her, Dawn thought. Imagine shooting your own husband and having to live with that.

"Are you a family member?" the nurse asked.

Dawn looked back at her, ignoring the eyes on her. Bryan's, Beth's, Joshua's. Even her father's. Mordecai stood near the doorway to Ethan's room, staring intently at her. "I'm his niece," Dawn lied smoothly. "Would it be all right if I saw him? Just for a minute?"

The nurse blinked, then nodded slightly. "Sure. Go ahead."

Dawn thanked her, then turned toward the door.

"Dawn, you can't," Beth said. "There's no reason in world to put yourself through this—"

"I have to," Dawn told her, and she took a moment to look her birth mother in the eyes, to let her see into her own. "I *really* have to."

Beth frowned, and then her brows rose, and there was

something like horror in her eyes. "Oh, no," she whispered, as if it was finally hitting her what was happening to Dawn.

"I have to," Dawn said again, and she tugged her hands free and walked alone toward the dead man's room.

She went inside, her gaze focusing automatically on the body in the bed. It was pale, and very still, the head swathed in bandages, eyes closed. There was nothing all that horrible about it.

But the man who stood in the corner of the room was considerably creepier. He was staring at the body and looking horrified. And there was a hole in one side of his head, and blood on his face.

He wasn't fading in and out as he had before. He was solid, as solid as Mordecai or any of the other ghosts ever were, but terrified. His mouth was moving, but Dawn couldn't hear what he was saying.

She glanced at Mordecai. He nodded at her. So she reached out for his hand, and he took it.

"What…what happened?" Dr. Melrose asked. "I don't understand. What happened to me? How can I be here, and in that bed, and why was Victoria crying that way?"

"Dr. Melrose," Dawn said.

He didn't look at her, kept staring at the bed, babbling. "I remember—God, it was awful. It hurt, and then it didn't, and then I was here—but I wasn't. Not really. Hell, how can this be? What's going on? Why couldn't Vicki hear me? What's—"

"Dr. Melrose," Dawn said again. "Ethan." She said it firmly, loudly, and he looked at her that time. He frowned. "You can see me? Thank God. No one else seems to realize I'm here. What's going on?"

She blinked slowly, shooting a look at Mordecai. He nodded at her. "Tell him, Dawn."

Dawn took a breath and told herself she could do this. Some-

one had to. "You've died, Ethan," she said. "That's your body, there in the bed. You're not in it anymore. Do you understand?"

His eyes widened, and shot back to the body. He moved closer to it, reached out a hand to touch it, but his hand moved right through, and he jerked backward in surprise. "Oh, God. Oh, no. I can't be—"

"You are," Dawn said. "Do you remember what happened?"

"No. No. No, this isn't—it's a dream, that's what it is. It's all a dream."

"It's real, Ethan. I'm sorry. But your physical lifetime is over." She searched her mind for something to say that could comfort him. Even if he had done all the things she believed he had, he didn't deserve the stark terror she saw in his eyes. No one did. "There's a whole lot more to life than what you knew before, Ethan. Look at you. Your body's dead, but you're not. There's a whole new kind of existence for you. It's going to be all right."

He stared at her, shaking his head slowly. "I remember you," he said. "You came to my office. You knew things—"

"Stephanie told me things," she said. "She wanted me to help River prove he didn't kill her."

He nodded slowly. "River didn't kill her. He didn't. I tried to stop it—God, it was too late. When I got there, it was just too late."

"What do you mean?"

He was lowering his head, shaking it. "River came to me, demanding to know the truth. He thought it was me. He thought I was the one—and I let him."

"Are you saying you aren't the one who killed Stephanie Corbett?"

Lifting his head, he met her eyes. "You don't know?"

"That's why I'm here. Stephanie said I had to come here. To talk to you. I don't think she knows who killed her, either. But you do. Don't you, Dr. Melrose?"

Sighing, he nodded slowly. "I'll never tell. I won't. I have to protect her."

Dawn blinked. "Protect who?" And then she knew—it was his wife. Who else would he want so badly to protect? "It was Victoria," she said.

He met her eyes, closed his. "It wasn't her fault. She found out about my affair with Stephanie and it—it did something to her. The trauma. She couldn't handle it, her mind—"

"So you covered it up?"

He nodded. "The house was already burning when I got there. River was already outside, lost in one of his blackouts, and the gas can was right there. Right beside him. There was a little left in the bottom, so I doused his hands with it. I took Vicki home, after. I wasn't even sure she remembered the next day what had happened. We never...we never talked about it again." He shook his head slowly. "When I found Arty Mullins's body in that spare freezer in our garage—I had to cover it up. I couldn't let my wife go to prison. It was all my fault—if I hadn't had the affair—"

Dawn didn't know about these things. "Who is Arty Mullins?"

"A handyman. He must have seen...what happened that night. I think he may have been trying to blackmail Victoria. She'd given him money, bought him a bus ticket out of town, told me it was just to be nice to him—he'd helped us so much in the past. Everyone thought he'd moved away. But he hadn't. Victoria killed him and hid his body in the freezer. I didn't know what to do. I had some of River's things at my house—fishing poles, tackle boxes—so I asked his lawyer for the key to the storage unit he'd rented for River, so I could put them there. He didn't think anything of it at the time. I stored the freezer there, believing no one would ever find it. But then he did, so I burned the unit down—would have burned poor Arty, too, but the remains would have been found. And that

would have stirred up questions. So I moved the body to the cabin."

"Okay. Okay." She wasn't clear on that part of it, but she sensed the need to move on. "What about River?" she asked. "What about his mental illness?"

He closed his eyes. "Is there a hell? If there is, you know that's where I'll go—for what I did to him. Letting him believe he'd done it—killed Stephanie. And the baby." He closed his eyes. "My baby." He shook his head. "The drugs helped. I thought…he wouldn't remember the truth, and he wouldn't be in pain."

"So he wasn't really insane?"

"No."

"And the attempt on his life in the hospital?"

He looked up sharply. "I had nothing to do with that." Then his mouth contorted as if he were fighting back tears. "It must have been Victoria. I didn't want to believe it."

"What about the hit-and-run—trying to kill Lieutenant Jackson, putting her in that cabin and setting it on fire?"

"No," he said. "No, it wasn't me. When River said it was my car that hit her, I knew—oh, God, I knew. Vicki *did* remember. And it was happening all over again."

Dawn turned for the door, but her father still held her hand, and surprisingly, he wouldn't let go. "Don't," she snapped. "I have to go, I have to—"

"Help him, Sunny," Mordecai whispered. "Help him. Look inside yourself. You know what to do."

Frowning, she turned back to look at the tormented spirit. He seemed to be wilting. "Stephanie," she called. "Stephanie, come here. Bring the baby. And don't show up looking all toasted, either. Your body burned, not your soul. You can look any way you want to, now. So can the baby."

Instantly, Stephanie appeared. And she looked at herself, and at her baby, with amazement in her eyes. Maybe she

hadn't known. Hadn't realized. But they were both beautiful now. No more soot or burns or scars.

Stephanie's eyes met Ethan's, and she smiled gently.

"You don't belong here," Dawn told them both. "You have another life to live now, a different one. You need to let go of all of this."

Stephanie's look of peace vanished, and she whirled to face Dawn. "Not yet. It's not done, not yet. You have to stop her. You have to save Cassandra. My River—he needs her."

Her father's hand fell away from hers, and they were all gone. Just that fast.

Stunned, Dawn turned toward the door, where she saw Bryan standing, watching her. She drew a breath, lifted her chin.

"So what did Melrose have to say?" he asked.

She blinked at him, stunned that he would put the insane question so matter-of-factly. But there was no time to tell him how much that meant to her. Not now. "It was his wife all along," Dawn said. "And I think she's going after Jax."

23

Ben had left the house, yet again.

Jax was curled on the sofa, with a cup of hot cocoa, her mother sitting on the other end and a roaring fire in front of them. Rex sat close by, leaning against Mariah's legs, his head in her lap. He closed his eyes every time she stroked his head, and released an occasional sigh of pure ecstasy.

"Dad *has* figured out I'm a cop, hasn't he?" Jax asked. She set her cocoa mug down and snuggled her head into the pillows her mother had piled beneath her. "He does know I can take care of myself."

"He's lost one daughter. He's petrified of losing another," her mom said softly.

"I don't like him out there patrolling alone in the dark every half hour. He's sixty years old, for God's sake. What's he going to do if someone *does* try to get in? He wouldn't even take my gun."

"He hates guns. You know that."

Jax closed her eyes. "I know. I'm sorry, I probably shouldn't have offered it, given…" She let her voice trail off.

Mariah continued stroking the dog, her hand moving in a steady, hypnotic rhythm. "You know, I've been asking myself all day why you chose to help this—this Corbett fellow."

Jax opened her eyes and faced her mother. "My first night

here, I fell through the ice of that frozen pond across the street. He pulled me out. Saved my life." She shrugged. "I guess I figured I owed him the benefit of the doubt."

Her mother nodded slowly. "I think it was a little more than that. I think it's almost eerie, the way all this has played out."

Sitting up, Jax looped her arms around her blanket-covered knees and faced her mother. What was she getting at?

"The way he pleaded insanity—just the way the man tried for killing your sister did."

Jax frowned. "It's just a coincidence."

"No. No, I don't think it is. I think it's…some kind of… karma. Is that the word? You know what I mean, anyway. I think you're doing what…what your father and I can't do."

Jax felt her heart beat a little faster. "What are you talking about, Mom?"

Mariah met her eyes. "I think you know." She licked her lips. "Don't you, Cassie? You know that the man your father killed was innocent. Just like your River Corbett is innocent."

Jax went stiff, and when she could tear her gaze from her mother's, she shot it toward the door in case her father had heard. He was nowhere in sight.

"Does Dad know?" she asked, keeping her voice to a whisper.

Mariah sighed. "He doesn't talk about it. But he sends all his extra money to Jeffrey Allen Dunkirk's sister out in California—she's the only relative we know of. And he visits the grave, every time we're back in Central New York. I'm supposed to think he's golfing with his old friends. But no. He mows around the headstone, plants things in the summer, leaves flowers in the winter." She shook her head. "It's been eating at him, what he did. All this time. I honestly believe if he could change places with Dunkirk, he would. I don't know

if he knows the man was innocent or not. I'm not sure it even matters. Ben was a healer. And he took a life. In a way, I think he died, too, that day. He hasn't really been alive since."

"Oh, Mom." Jax felt like crying. "He—he hasn't talked to you about it, then?"

Mariah shook her head. "No. And I can't bring it up with him. I mean, I think he knows the truth. But what if he doesn't? I don't know what it would do to him…."

"I understand. I'll never tell him, Mom."

Her mother nodded. "How long have you known?"

"Since Jarred's suicide. His mother came to me."

Mariah sighed. "She told me, as well. I guess she needed to get it off her chest."

Jax frowned toward the door. Her father wasn't back yet, but she was glad she'd had a few minutes alone with her mom. "You're right, you know. Knowing the truth—how easily Dunkirk was believed guilty of a crime he didn't commit, and how easily he was convinced that an insanity plea was his only way out—it had a huge bearing on my decision to give River the benefit of the doubt."

"How could it not?" her mother asked.

"But only at the beginning." Jax sighed. "As soon as I started to get to know him, I knew…"

"There's something between you. I could see that at the police station." Her mother patted Cassandra's hands where they held her knees. "Do you love him, Cassie?"

Jax would have repeated the question in disbelief, if she could have forced the words out, but they stuck in her throat. "I don't know. I never thought I wanted that kind of thing," she said, and it sounded lame.

"What kind of thing? Love?"

She shrugged. "Giving another person that much control

over me. Being worried about, taken care of, told what to do."
She grimaced.

"Do you think that's what your father and I have done all
these years? Controlled each other? Told each other what to do?"

She looked at her mother slowly. "Sort of. I mean, not in
a bad way. It's more…it's different with you two."

"Love isn't about control, Cassie. It's about caring."

She supposed she had to concede that much. "So how do
you know? I mean, there's the attraction thing, of course. But
how do you know when it's real?"

"When you care more about another person than you do
about yourself. Oh, I don't mean you subjugate your needs to
theirs. It only works if they care more about you than they do
about themselves, as well. That way no one's got more power,
more control. It's all about giving and caring." She shrugged.
"You risked your career—even your life—to help this man.
To me, that says it all."

To Jax, that only said half of it. She rolled her eyes. "I must
have hit my head harder than I thought to even be discussing
the *L* word. Probably some brain damage the doctor missed."

"Probably," her mother agreed, but her smile said she
thought she knew better. Sighing, she got to her feet. Rex stood
up as soon as Mariah did. "You need some more cocoa, hon?"

"No, I'm fine, for now." Jax glanced again at the front
door. "Dad should be back by now."

"He'll be along—"

Mariah's words were cut short by the long, low growl that
came from the dog beside her.

"Rex?" Jax got off the sofa, ignored the metal cane,
snatched up her gun instead and limped to the door to peer
through the curtain.

Rex was at her side, and the fur along the center of his spine and haunches bristled in a way she'd rarely seen.

"Something's wrong," Jax said. She checked the gun's clip, worked the action. "Call Frankie, Mom."

Her mother hurried across the room as Jax opened the door, standing to one side, listening.

"There's no dial tone," her mother said. "Oh, God, Cassie, don't go out there."

Jax turned to see her mother on the edge of panic. This was not the kind of situation Mariah was used to. Imagining her only surviving daughter in danger every day of her life was bad enough. But witnessing it—she was living out a nightmare. "Mom, try the phone upstairs in the bedroom. Take Rex with you. Lock yourself in up there and call for help."

"Cassie…" Mariah put a hand on Jax's shoulder.

"Dad might be in trouble, Mom," she said softly. She covered her mother's hand with her own. "Please."

"All right." Mariah tore herself away and ran upstairs, and though he didn't want to go, Rex let her tug him along. Jax waited to hear the bedroom door close behind her mother, and then opened the door wider and stepped outside, onto the porch.

"Dad?"

No answer. Nothing but silence greeted her.

She could move faster without the bum ankle, she thought angrily, as she made her way onto the porch. She walked—limped—across the porch in her pajamas. She hadn't grabbed a coat and it was a cold night.

"Dad, where are you?"

She paused at the top of the porch steps, squinting at something on the ground in the distance. It looked like…

"Dad?"

Going down one step, as her heart leaped into her throat,

she realized that her father was lying motionless out there in the snow. But she got no farther.

Something heavy cracked down on the back of her skull, and the ground rose up to smash her in the face. She felt the blow, anticipated the pain of her landing, but was out cold before she ever touched down.

Joshua drove. Dawn sat in the back seat beside Bryan, and tried not to let her fears show in her eyes. So many fears.

She was afraid of the ghosts that had been plaguing her for days. But not in the same way she'd been afraid of them before. She was afraid, now, because they had left her, and she alternated between praying they would return and being terrified that they wouldn't. She was afraid she might be losing her mind, because she was so sure that she wasn't. This was real. She had to be nuts to believe that so strongly, didn't she? And more than anything else, she was afraid for Jax.

What was happening to her right now?

Fire.

Dawn blinked and looked around. "What did you say?" she asked. "Bry?"

"Me? I didn't say anything."

"No one did. Are you all right, hon?" Beth asked.

Fire!

"Oh, God, not again." She closed her eyes and nodded. "I need a cell phone. I left mine at the inn."

Joshua handed her one, his eyes full of worry. "What is it, hon?"

She dialed 911 and waited. And when the operator answered, she said, "There's a house on fire. One-ten Snowshoe Lane. It's pretty bad. Send ambulances. Police, too."

She hung up even as the operator was asking questions, and handed the phone back to Joshua.

Beth said, "Honey, what makes you think Jax's house is on fire?"

"I just know."

"But—"

"I know things, Beth. I know things the same way Mordecai knew things. I don't want to—but I do."

The look of horror on Beth's face, the way she shivered, told Dawn this hadn't been the right time. But she knew Beth had already been figuring it out. Beth looked at Josh, and the glance he sent her was full of worry, but tempered by love.

"Can you drive any faster, Joshua?" Dawn asked. "I don't think there's much time."

River waited only until Frankie ushered him into the guest room and closed the door. She'd offered him food, but he'd said no, that he was tired and just wanted to rest. She had to know he didn't plan to stay. But she pretended to believe him, told him good-night and left him alone.

He went to the bedroom window and opened it, climbed outside, closed it behind him, and went looking for transportation. Transportation that awaited him like a gift. An ATV was parked near the back porch, with the keys in the ignition. And he knew Frankie Parker was not stupid enough to have forgotten it was there. The softhearted police chief might as well have taped a bow to the handlebars.

He whispered a silent thanks as he pushed the machine around the house and down the road until he thought he was out of earshot. Might as well play along, give Frankie plausible deniability so she wouldn't have too many blemishes on her record when she retired a week from now.

He started up the four-wheeler and drove it over the narrow winding roads toward Cassandra's house. His house.

Hell, he barely knew how to think of the place anymore.

He didn't know how to think of *her.* So much had happened, there had been no time to sit down, to spend time just talking about their feelings and goals, and what they wanted in life. In a relationship.

There was so much to be said and done. And now, thanks to Cassandra, maybe he was going to have the chance to have a life again. It sure as hell looked that way.

He rode the little machine, enjoying the cold night air blowing in his face, and the bounce of the seat underneath him, and the thrill of high speeds and sharp curves. He felt alive—more alive than he had since…since before Steph had died. And maybe for a long time before that.

He gunned it a little harder, and deliberately drove over the bumpier spots in the road, smiling fully, every cell in his body singing with anticipation at seeing Cassandra again.

He loved her. God help him, he loved the woman.

His smile, and that feeling of elation, began to die at the first hint of the familiar scent that touched his nostrils. Hot, acrid, it was a smell he knew. It had been haunting his mind for more than a year now. It was the smell of smoke. And not the warm, almost comforting kind that came from a campfire or a wood stove. This was the distinct, menacing smell of smoke that came from a burning house.

He tried to tell himself he was jumping to conclusions, even as he gunned the ATV, pushing it to the top speeds he could without flipping it. And as he got closer, he saw the eerie yellow glow in the night sky. "God, no," he muttered, though the sound of his plea was swallowed by the roar of the machine. "Not again."

He came around a corner, and the nightmare became real. Like a blow to the chest, it hit him all at once. The house, his house—her house—was going up in flames.

"Cassandra!" He cried her name over and over, even as he brought the four-wheeler to a cockeyed stop on the lawn and

shut it off. He was off it and lunging toward the house when he nearly tripped over a body lying on the grass. He stopped himself and bent over it. "Dr. Jackson! Benjamin!"

He shook Cassandra's father, patting his face until the man opened his eyes and stared, blinking and apparently confused. "I know you didn't do it," he said. "I'm sorry."

"That doesn't matter now. Where's Cassandra? And…" River looked around as another thought assailed him. "And your wife? Where's Mariah?"

The man's face became a mask of horror, and he struggled up to his feet. "God, they must still be inside!" He started forward.

River gripped him. "Wait. Listen—"

Ben listened, and heard, River thought, what he did. The sound of a dog barking, barely audible beyond the crackling and roar of the flames. "This way," River said, racing around to the rear of the house, with the older man following close behind. From the back lawn, River stared up at the bedroom windows, and then he saw Rex—standing with his paws on the glass, barking furiously.

"Good boy. Good boy, I'm coming, Rex." He spun to Ben. "We need a phone. Someone needs to call for help."

"Yes. There's a phone in my car."

"Go for it. I can get up there. I know how." With that, River hurried to the house's back door, braced one foot on the railing beside the steps and clambered up onto its miniature roof, then stood, inching his way to the far edge.

From there, he could reach the bedroom window, the bottom of it. He made a fist, smashed the glass, curled his hand around the inside of the frame. He jumped, holding on for all he was worth, and managed to get a second handhold. And then he strained every muscle in his body to pull himself up,

over the windowsill, glass scratching and tearing his skin all the way. But he did it. He got inside.

Smoke was filling the bedroom by now. "Cassandra!" he shouted.

Rex barked, and River managed to see the dog, crouching on the floor over something. Moving closer, River dropped to his knees, then crawled the rest of the way.

Cassandra's mother lay on the floor, overcome by smoke. He wasted no time, but immediately slung her over his shoulder and carried her back to the window. And just as he was wondering how the hell he was going to get her out without risking them both, Benjamin appeared there, on the roof that covered the back steps. How the hell a sixty-year-old man had managed to climb up was beyond River.

"Give her to me," Ben shouted. "Give her to me and go find Cassie!"

"You'll never reach her from there."

"Lower her down, River. Lower her down, and swing her toward me. I can get her, I can!"

River nodded, seeing no choice but to try. Even if he had to drop Mariah to the ground from there, he didn't think she would be seriously injured. He lowered her to the floor, quickly dragged a blanket from the bed to drape over the windowsill. Then he picked her up again and eased her out through the opening, lowering her body, holding her by her wrists. Carefully he swung her toward her husband.

On the third try, Ben caught her, snapping his arms around her waist. He fell onto his knees on the porch roof, but somehow, didn't fall off.

"Can you get her down?" River called.

"Yes. Yes, I've got her. Go find Cassie!"

River left the older man to it, and turned back into the room. Rex was at the door, barking, though his bark was grow-

ing hoarse. River approached the door on hands and knees. He opened it, and crawled into the hallway with Rex at his side. "Find her, boy. Find Cassandra!"

The smoke was worse out here. The heat was suffocating, and River wasn't sure he could go on, but Rex had no such doubts. River took strength from the dog's fearlessness, and made his way down the smoke-filled hall.

His gut instinct was to search every room, but Rex made a beeline for the stairs and down them to the ground floor. River followed.

Walls of flame leaped up around them on the first floor, but the dog rushed on, picking his way through. River lost sight of Rex once, moving far slower on all fours than his dog was, but Rex quickly backtracked, licked River's face, barked twice and moved forward again.

Again, River followed. And then he found her. She was sprawled over a coffee table, face up, arched and splayed like a sacrificial offering. River wrapped his arms around her waist and tugged her to the floor. "Cassandra! Cassandra, wake up!" He smacked her cheeks, then turned and pulled her onto his back. Holding her wrists at his throat with one hand, and still kneeling, he began working his way toward a door, a window, anything.

Halfway there, he tripped over something—no, some*one*. Victoria.

She lifted her head, dragged herself up onto her knees and lashed out at him with a clawed hand, her nails raking his skin.

River jerked backward from the attack, letting Cassandra slide to the floor. "What the hell are you doing?"

Victoria was sooty, bruised, her hair in tangles—as if she'd been in a fight. Her face was a twisted grimace of insanity. "You're not taking her out of here."

"You set this fire, didn't you? And the last one, too? It wasn't Ethan at all."

She raised her arms in front of her, and River was startled to see a gun pointed at him.

"I blamed Ethan, and it was you," he said. "All the time, it was you." He put a hand to his mouth and coughed harshly. "We have to get out of here, Vicki. If we don't we'll both die."

"Ethan's dead," she whispered. "What do I have to live for?"

"If Ethan's dead, it's because of you, not me. And certainly not Cassandra."

"She was sleeping with him. Just like that whore you married. God, River, are you so blind you can't see it?"

River lowered his head. "You're right about Steph. She was sleeping with him. But not Cassandra. Never Cassandra."

"How can you be so sure?"

"I know. That's all. I just know." He looked beyond her. There was a clear path to the front door. He just needed to get past her.

Vicki looked up suddenly. "Did you hear that?"

He hadn't heard anything but the roaring fire. Then Rex lunged out of the smoke and hit her from one side with the full force of his body. He hadn't forgotten his training. He took her down hard, his jaws clamping on the wrist of her gun hand and not letting go, even when the gun went off. River lunged for the weapon, ignoring the shrieking madwoman. He got to his feet and scooped Cassandra up again. "Come on, Rex. Stand down and come!"

Rex released the woman, who cringed on the floor, sobbing and clutching her bleeding wrist. River stumbled, wheezing and choking, to the door. He got it open and staggered outside.

"There he is! He's got her!" someone yelled.

There were lights, emergency vehicles all around, and the

firefighters were pumping water onto the house. Ben Jackson surged forward, gathering Cassandra from River's arms, and handing her off to the paramedic who'd run up on his heels. Then Ben clasped River's shoulder. "Come on, son. Get away from the house, it's not safe."

Frankie shouted for Rex, and he ran to her, and to safety. "Check on my dog, Ben," River said. "I have to go back in. Victoria Melrose is still in there."

"River—don't—"

"I have to. I know right where she is, I can get her out."

And with that, River turned and ran back into the burning house.

24

Jax opened her eyes to chaos.

She was lying on the ground outside the burning house, with men bending over her, one of them holding an oxygen mask to her face. But she struggled to sit up, in spite of them, only to see River racing back into what looked like the jaws of hell.

She ripped the mask from her face, gripping the shoulder of a nearby firefighter to pull herself to her feet.

"Stay down, Lieuten—"

"Let go of me!" She jerked free of the restraining hands and managed two steps forward before she found her path blocked. Her mother stood on wobbly legs, a blanket around her shoulders. Her father was beside her, holding Mariah upright. Beth was there, and Joshua, looking torn. He'd be the last guy to stop her from going after River. He understood. Dawn was there, too, but she wasn't looking at Jax. She was staring back toward the house, where firefighters pumped torrents onto the front of the place, trying to give River a way back out. Trying to get inside, to go after him.

"Why did he go back in there?" Jax cried. "God, why?"

"He said Victoria was inside," Benjamin said, speaking slowly, turning his gaze back toward the house. "Said he knew right where she was. He ran back in there before I could stop him."

Dawn turned from the fire to face Jax. "Victoria's already dead."

Frowning at the girl, Jax asked, "How can you know that?"

"I just do."

She turned to the house again. They all did. And moments dragged like hours. "He's not coming back out," Jax whispered. "Dad, he's not coming back out."

"I think he's still alive, though," Dawn said.

"This isn't going to happen," Ben Jackson said slowly. "Not again. Not this time." He turned and started toward the house.

Jax lurched forward and grabbed him. "What are you—"

"I'm just going around back. Maybe he got out that way. Wait here, hon. Take care of your mother."

And then he ran off like a man half his age. He spoke to firefighters as he moved around the house. Jax heard them telling him to stay a safe distance back, heard him telling the men the same thing he'd told her. And it was only when he was out of sight that it hit her what he had meant by what he'd said.

This isn't going to happen. Not again.

He was talking about Dunkirk. He was talking about an innocent man paying the ultimate price for something he didn't do. The way River might, if he were to die in that fire.

"He's going in after him," she whispered.

"What?" Beth asked.

"He's going inside. He's going—Dad, wait!" Jax ran around the burning house, as the heat seared her skin. She followed the path her father had taken, knowing the others were on her heels. "Dad! Dad, don't do this!"

But when she reached the back door, it stood open, flames licking around the frame, and her father was nowhere in sight.

She lurched toward the door, and her mother gripped her hard. "Let him be, Cassie."

"Mom, don't—"

"Don't you understand? He has to—"

Before she even finished, Benjamin appeared in the back doorway, River at his side, their arms locked around one another's shoulders, their feet dragging. They stumbled down the back steps, landing on the ground. Josh and Bryan raced to them, each gripping one man and helping him to his feet, supporting them as they walked away from the smoke and heat.

When they were a safe distance from the fire, the men stopped. Jax ran to River, wrapped her arms around him. "You're all right."

He hugged her hard. "I wouldn't have been, if not for your dad." River turned toward Ben. Jax did, too, just in time to see him clutching his chest and sinking to his knees.

Jax dropped to the ground beside him, turning to shout, "Bryan, run around front. Get some paramedics out here."

"On it," he said, racing out of sight.

"Dad?" Jax asked, clutching her father. "Dad, tell me what you're feeling."

"Redeemed," he whispered.

"What?"

"I love you, Cassie. But I need you to back off now, give me a minute with your mother."

She didn't like his color. Didn't like the short, shallow way he was breathing. But from the look on his face, he wasn't panicking, so maybe it wasn't as bad as she feared. Maybe this was just minor. A little angina or the effects of the smoke, or something.

River put his arm around her shoulders and drew her back a few steps, and Mariah sank to the ground beside Ben. She held him in her arms, his head resting against her neck, and they spoke in whispers. Beth and Josh stood a few feet away, arm in arm.

Dawn sat on the ground near a pine tree, tears streaming down her face.

Within a minute, Bryan came racing back, paramedics keeping pace beside him with their heavy boxes of medical gear.

"Ma'am," one said to Mariah. "Ma'am, please, we need you to move aside so we can help him."

Mariah looked up from where she sat on the ground, and she smiled weakly through tears. Gently, she eased Ben backward, until he was lying down. And Jax caught her breath when she saw that her father's eyes were closed.

"He's gone," Mariah whispered, as she got to her feet. Her knees buckled, and River quickly caught her in the solid embrace of his arms, held her upright, helped her walk a few steps away to give the medics room to work.

One of the medics said he wasn't getting a pulse. They started CPR.

Jax took a trembling step backward, alone, her eyes wide and fixed on the scene in front of her, and then a warm hand closed around hers. She looked up, expecting to see River, except that he was still holding her mother, speaking softly to her, and this hand was small and tender.

Dawn.

"It's okay," Dawn said softly. "He's okay."

"He's not, Dawn. Look at him, he's not okay."

Dawn stepped in front of her, blocking her view of her father's body on the ground, jerking with the frantic efforts of the paramedics. "I *am* looking at him," Dawn said. "He's not there, where you're looking. He's right here, standing next to you. And your sister's with him. Carrie. God, she's so pretty."

Jax felt her eyes widen. "Dawnie, what are you—"

"I can see them," she said. "I could see Stephanie Corbett. She led me to you and River in the cabin. And she told me your house was on fire before I ever got here." Dawn shrugged. "I can't explain it all now, Jax. I don't know if I even understand it myself. But when my father died, just before he passed, he took my hand. And I *felt* it. Whatever it was he had, he—he gave it to me."

"Dawn?"

"God, this is all like some kind of nightmare flashback," Dawn said softly. "Remember? When it was *my* father lying there on the ground? Remember, Jax?"

"I remember."

Dawn nodded, lifted her other hand, as if to take someone else's—but there was no one there. "Your father says he took a life a long time ago. He says that he's been in hell ever since, knowing he could never make it right. But tonight, he thinks maybe he did. He saved an innocent life. Restored the balance. He's more at peace than he's been since that day in the courtroom when he shot Jeffrey Allen Dunkirk."

The medics were electrocuting her father now. Jax moved slightly to the side so she could keep watch. Dawn wasn't making any sense—but she was saying things she couldn't possibly know about. Beth hadn't known. No one besides Jax and her own mother had known about her father's past.

"He's with Carrie," Dawn said. "She says she loves you. And your father says River is a good man—a keeper, he says."

The medics were getting no response. They were still trying, but her father wasn't reacting. And then an ambulance trundled over the lawn, and they were loading him into it.

"I want to ride along," Mariah said.

Jax turned to see River help her mother into the ambulance, as attentive and gentle with her as she'd ever seen him be with anyone. He watched it drive out of sight, then joined Jax where she stood holding Dawn's hand.

"I'm so sorry," he whispered, sliding his arm around Jax, holding her close to his side.

"It wasn't your fault," Dawn said. "You were part of a bigger plan. All this happened for a reason. And Dr. Jackson is okay now. He really is, I wish you could see how he looks.

Like a thousand pounds has been lifted from his shoulders. He's okay." She met Jax's eyes. "They all are."

Three days later, Beth and Josh had gone to Dr. Benjamin Jackson's funeral. The inn was empty of everyone, except for Bryan. And the dead. And Dawn desperately needed for them to go, too. All of them.

Bryan wasn't touching her. Normally at a time like this he would have pulled her into his arms, but he knew that things had changed between them. He knew it—he just didn't understand why. He couldn't possibly understand.

"Everything's going to be okay, you know," he told her. They stood near the front door. They were supposed to be heading over to join Beth and Josh at the cemetery soon. But Dawn wasn't going.

She wanted to ask Bryan how everything was supposed to be okay when *she* was no longer okay. But she knew he couldn't answer that. No one could.

"Could you…just go on without me, Bry? I'm not feeling so great. I think I'll lie down for a while."

"I'll stay then."

She turned away from him, unable to meet his eyes and lie to him. "To be honest, everyone's been hovering lately— since the fire—and it's starting to get to me. I need some time to myself."

He gripped her shoulders and spun her around to face him. "Dawn, will you talk to me? You've locked yourself away behind a freaking brick wall and I don't know how to knock it down."

"You *can't* knock it down." Trembling, she lifted a hand, brushed it through his hair. "I've just…I've got some things I need to work through. That's all."

"I could help—if you'd only let me."

Smiling softly, she leaned closer, brushed her lips over his.

When he closed his arms around her and kissed her passionately, she didn't stop him. She even kissed him back. When he lifted his head, he said, "I love you, Dawn. You know that, don't you?"

"I know. I just...need some time."

He closed his eyes, lowered his head, sighed. "Okay. Whatever you need. Just...just come to me when you're ready. I'll always be there for you. Always."

She nodded, and held his eyes for so long she almost thought he understood just what a long wait that might be. And then he finally turned and left.

Dawn waited until she was sure he was gone. Then she hurried up the stairs to her room and grabbed the duffel bag and the backpack that held everything she needed. She paused for just a moment to stare at the ghosts, the silent ghosts hovering everywhere. Not the same ones she knew. This was a whole new batch, strangers to her, all of them reaching out to her, trying to speak to her.

And closer to her than any of them stood Mordecai. Her father.

She met his eyes, shook her head. "I don't want this anymore. I had to help Jax, but now it's over."

"It's your calling, Sunny. Dawn. You have to work to do."

"No. I'm through with it."

"You saved your friend's life."

"And now it's over."

"How can you refuse me? I'm a part of you. You can't run away from who you are," her father promised her.

"We'll see just how far I *can* run away," she said. She slammed her bedroom door on him, and hurried down the stairs. She tugged the envelopes from her bag. One had Beth's name on the front, the other, Bryan's. There was a third, addressed to her adoptive parents, Julie and Sean, but that would have to be mailed. She left the two envelopes on the coffee

table, and then she went outside to her Jeep. Tossing her bags
into the back, she got into the driver's seat, started the engine,
shifted into gear and drove away.

He's okay. They all are.

Jax thought of those words of Dawn's when she stood at
the graveside, in the prettiest cemetery she'd ever seen. Her
mother stood between Jax and River, clinging to them both,
leaning on them. Her heart was broken, and yet, incredibly,
she was at peace.

Jax wasn't surprised. She'd seen Dawn talking with her
mother several times since the fire. She didn't know if Dawn's
"gift" was for real or not. She only knew it had helped her get
through losing her father. It had helped her in a way not much
else could have, she thought. And she wasn't certain whether
Dawn had told anyone else what was going on or not.

Mariah released Jax's hand and moved forward. She placed
a rose on the coffin, then let her hand rest on the polished
wood for a long moment. Finally she turned, and walked over
to where Beth and Joshua stood with Bryan. She hugged the
nineteen-year-old, and said, "Dawn isn't here?"

"She wasn't feeling well," Bryan explained.

"Well, she's been through a lot. You tell her for me that
she's helped me. And I'll always be grateful." And then Mariah returned to Jax and River. "Frankie is going to drive me
back to the house now. Half the town will be coming by with
condolences and food. But you take your time, Cassie." She
glanced at River. "You'll take care of her, won't you?"

"You know I will."

"Yes, I do. Remind me, later, River. Benjamin left a vir-
tual tome of notes for you."

"He did?" River seemed perplexed.

"Mmm. Well, he never really lost his love of surgery.
Though he couldn't practice, he kept his finger on the pulse

of things. He'd been talking with a friend of his—Leonard Kreske."

"The brain surgeon?" River asked.

"Oh, you've heard of him, then. Well, it seems Dr. Kreske thinks he can help you with those blackouts. Ben was so pleased, he couldn't wait to tell you, but then everything happened, and…well, he wanted you to talk to Leonard. Remind me later, I'll give you the number and the notes."

River stood there, blinking in shock as he looked from Mariah to Jax and back again. Then he turned toward the coffin. "Thank you, Ben. I don't even… Thank you."

Mariah nodded. "See you two in a little while then."

"Bye, Mom." Jax hugged her mom, then watched her mother hug River just as warmly. In the past three days she'd been leaning on River almost as much as Jax had.

When her mother and everyone else had gone, Jax went up to the coffin to say her private goodbyes. River gave her the space she wanted, without being asked. But she didn't doubt he would know if she needed him, and would be there before she had time to blink.

When she finished, she moved back toward him, and he was there waiting. He put an arm around her. "Are you okay?" he asked.

She leaned her head on his shoulder. "Yeah. Amazingly, I am. I honestly believe my father really is at peace. And Mom seems to believe it, too."

"She does."

"River, before all this happened—I was asking my mother how…how I would recognize the real thing."

"The real thing?" He led her to a bench under a giant oak tree and brushed away the snow for her. She sat beside him.

"You're getting a bit too comfortable with all this 'taking care of the little woman' stuff."

"You let me know when you get tired of it and I'll cut it

out," he said. "But you're changing the subject. Are you chickening out on me?"

"When have you known me to chicken out of anything?"

"Never yet." He took her hand in his. "So this real thing you asked your mom about—did you mean love?"

"Yeah. That's what I meant."

She thought he tried not to tense up, or get nervous, but she felt him tense up and get nervous all the same. "And what did she say?" he asked.

"She said when I care more for someone else's well-being than my own, it would mean I loved them. And then she pointed out how much I risked by helping you."

His lifted his head, met her eyes. "So I guess you must love me, then."

"I guess I must. And since you damn near got yourself killed trying to get me out of that burning house, not to mention the frozen pond before that, I guess you must love me, too."

He made a fist and pretended to knock on her head. "Hello? I've been telling you that for a couple of days now, haven't I?"

"I wasn't sure I believed it."

"And now?"

She shrugged. "Before the D.A. decided this morning not to pursue any charges against you, I'd been trying to think about how my life would be without you, River. And I didn't much like it."

He leaned closer and kissed her softly. "I'll stay with you forever, if you'll have me."

"I think I'd like that a whole lot better."

He searched her eyes, as if not quite sure what she was saying. "The town is going to turn the insurance money over to me, and return the deed to my house. We could rebuild."

"We could," she said. "I'm going to need a new officer at the Blackberry PD, once I send Kurt packing. Will you take the job?"

"I'll do anything you want me to, Cassandra."

"I don't want you take it because I want you to," she said. "I want you to take it because *you* want to."

He got to his feet, pushed a hand through his hair. "I don't think you get it yet, do you?" He paced a few steps away. "When I met you, I was half-dead, mostly out of my mind, a fugitive without any hope, half convinced I'd murdered my own wife and unborn child. My God, Cassandra, do you know what you've given me?" He paced back to her, dropped to one knee and clasped her hands in his. "You gave me back my life."

"Oh, I didn't give it back," she said. "I'm claiming it for my own."

"It's yours," he told her, lifting her hands to his lips. "It's one hundred percent yours."

She licked her own lips, tried to keep them from trembling. "It's scary, isn't it? This…this idea of committing long-term. That is what we're talking about, isn't it, River?"

"It's exactly what we're talking about. And it won't be scary if we do it together."

"That's the only way I want to do anything from now on."

"I never thought I'd hear you say that, Cassandra. Free spirit. The girl who can't be tied down."

"It's you," she told him. "It's you, River. No one else ever could have… But you—you're what's been missing. I never wanted to need anyone. But I need you and I'm not afraid of needing you, because I trust you, too." She held his gaze steadily. "I never trusted anyone the way I trust you. No one— other than my dad, anyway."

"I won't let you down, Cassandra. Not ever."

"I know. I won't let you down, either."

"So…does that mean…" He closed his eyes briefly, opened them again and met her eyes. "Will you marry me?"

She smiled through a rush of hot tears. "God, it's enough to make me queasy, the way I'm feeling. All hearts and flow-

ers and romantic bullshit. Yeah, River. I'll marry you. White dress, tossing the bouquet, the whole sappy nine yards. And I'll love every minute of it."

He gathered her close and kissed her, slowly and deeply. And she knew her days of being a solitary woman were long gone.

MAGGIE SHAYNE

21503 BLUE TWILIGHT	___ $6.99 U.S.	___	$8.50 CAN.
32247 TWILIGHT BEGINS	___$12.95 U.S.	___	$15.95 CAN.
66737 THICKER THAN WATER	___ $6.99 U.S.	___	$8.50 CAN.

(limited quantities available)

TOTAL AMOUNT	$_____
POSTAGE & HANDLING	$_____
($1.00 FOR 1 BOOK, 50¢ for each additional)	
APPLICABLE TAXES*	$_____
TOTAL PAYABLE	$_____

(check or money order—please do not send cash)

To order, complete this form and send it, along with a check or money order for the total above, payable to MIRA Books, to: **In the U.S.:** 3010 Walden Avenue, P.O. Box 9077, Buffalo, NY 14269-9077; **In Canada:** P.O. Box 636, Fort Erie, Ontario, L2A 5X3.

Name: _____
Address: _____ City: _____
State/Prov.: _____ Zip/Postal Code: _____
Account Number (if applicable): _____
075 CSAS

*New York residents remit applicable sales taxes.
*Canadian residents remit applicable GST and provincial taxes.

MIRA®

www.MIRABooks.com

MMS1105BL

Also by MAGGIE SHAYNE

THICKER THAN WATER
COLDER THAN ICE

Wings in the Night series

TWILIGHT PHANTASIES
TWILIGHT MEMORIES
TWILIGHT ILLUSIONS
BEYOND TWILIGHT (novella)
BORN IN TWILIGHT
TWILIGHT VOWS (novella)
TWILIGHT HUNGER
RUN FROM TWILIGHT (novella)
EMBRACE THE TWILIGHT
EDGE OF TWILIGHT
BLUE TWILIGHT

*Watch for the next book in the
Wings in the Night series*

PRINCE OF TWILIGHT

*Coming March 2006
Only from MIRA Books*